Lord Worthing's Wallflower

Michelle Morrison

Kindle Direct Publishing

Printed in the United States of America

Contents

Chapter One

February 1816

"'Wherefore art thou, Juliette?' You mean like that?"

Miss Juliette Aston smiled tightly and heroically forbore from rolling her eyes at Lord Elphinstone, to whom she had just been introduced. She also forbore from pointing out that the correct line was "Wherefore art thou Romeo," as he was guffawing at his weak joke. Really, who could admire a man who guffawed, she thought as she executed a brief curtsy. As she straightened, she cast a sideways glance at her best friend, Lady Eleanor Chalcroft, who was smiling warmly at Lord Elphinstone.

"Just so, Lord Elphinstone," Lady Eleanor said, nodding. "You are so clever! Isn't he, Juliette?" this last said with a completely straight face.

Juliette pressed her lips together until her urge to laugh lessened. "Oh indeed! And to think, I have never heard a reference to Shakespeare in relation to my name."

"Shakespeare?" Eleanor asked, clearly confused. Juliette felt her eyes water with the strain of keeping her laughter in.

"From the Shakespeare play, *Romeo and Juliette*, Lady Eleanor," Lord Elphinstone said pompously.

"Is that who wrote it?" Eleanor asked sincerely.

"Indeed," Juliette said. A small snort of laughter escaped her. Lord Elphinstone glanced askance at her and promptly invited Lady Eleanor to dance.

Once the couple had made their way to the crowded parquet floor, Juliette took a restorative sip of her lemonade.

"Drat," she cursed under her breath as she felt a stray droplet splash onto the expanse of skin above her bodice. Glancing surreptitiously around, she made sure no one was watching and then dabbed at the offending drop with her gloved finger. Taking a more careful sip, she watched her friend glide gracefully about the dance floor in Lord Elphinstone's embrace. Eleanor and she had befriended one another when they first came out in society more than two years previously. Despite the fact that Eleanor had quickly been deemed a diamond of the first water, while Juliette was relegated to the ranks of wallflower, the two had remained steadfast friends.

Eleanor was everything London society deemed a lady should be: she was petite and small-framed, blessed with a pearlescent complexion that flushed delicately pink when overset by emotion, and endowed with a wealth of flaxen curls that never seemed to frizz or fall flat.

Juliette caught a glimpse of herself in a gilt mirror across the room. She, on the other, was of average height. Though her love of long walks in the country ensured she did not run to fat, she was certainly no will o' the wisp with long elegant neck and slender limbs. Sadly, she was also not of the round, deliciously curvaceous figure that while not en vogue for the high-waisted fashions of the time, nevertheless attracted much admiration. She was, however, quite fond of her hair; though it was not fashionably blond, it was dark and lustrous and if it refused to take a curl, well, at least it was long and thick enough that she never needed to resort to the false falls and curls so many other ladies employed. Shifting her weight, she concluded her assessment with the acknowledgement that her legs were quite shapely and trim, for all the good that did her, hidden as they ever were beneath skirts and petticoats. Still, she knew for a fact that her friend Eleanor bemoaned her rather thick ankles and dimpled knees.

Glancing down to make sure no other random drops of lemonade had escaped her cup, she waited patiently for Lord Elphinstone to return Eleanor to her side. She was unengaged for this dance and the next, though Eleanor of course had been claimed for them all. A brief glance at the chaperone's corner showed her that her father's elderly aunt was dozing, her chin quite comfortably ensconced on her rather impressive bosom. Aunt Constance had been widowed some thirty years previously, but still spoke of her departed husband as if she were still in her first year of mourning. She also was less concerned with watching Juliette's every move than she was with ensuring that she had a comfortable seat in which to take a nap as she chaperoned her great-niece. Juliette thought it unfortunate she wasn't one of the fast young ladies who were forever trying to sneak away from the watchful eyes of their chaperones to meet gentlemen in the garden or the library, or wherever it was such assignations took place. As it was, she would have appreciated having a chaperone she could at least sit with during the times she was not dancing.

She drained the last drops of punch and set her empty cup down. Glancing around for a distraction, Juliette saw a small excited crowd form around a newcomer. She rose up on tiptoes to try and see who could elicit such interest from the chronically bored members of London's *haute ton*, but there were too many heads in the way. Finally the crowds parted enough that she could see the dark-haired man in its midst.

He was tall, though not the tallest of his friends who she recognized as being members of that rarefied strata of wealthy, young, titled, and exceedingly sought after bachelors. Even from a distance, she could tell that his eyes were dark, deep set beneath two thick slashes of brows. His jaw was not square, but his chin certainly was. It was firm and, she decided after casting about for just the right word, yes, sculpted. He smiled at something one of the other men said and against her will, Juliette's heart skipped a beat. It had never skipped a beat before. Never. Ridiculous organ, she thought before quickly observing that the man's teeth were incredibly straight, framed as they were in a generous mouth that seemed permanently quirked in a humorous line.

Pulling her gaze from him, she chastised herself. He was clearly not the kind of man who would look twice at her. It was ridiculous to moon after him simply because he was incredibly handsome. Her traitorous gaze sought him out. Really, she told herself sternly, taken independently, there was nothing remarkable about any of his features. She saw his gaze sweep about the room, taking note of who was present. It briefly slid over her face and just as quickly returned to the people standing near him. Her heart did another little nervous jump and she pointedly turned her back on the spectacle of the society's elite bachelors holding court. Men such as they only ever danced with girls such as Eleanor. Girls who had been deemed "stunning," "exquisite," or "original." She glanced over her shoulder and saw the dark-haired man and his fellows surrounded by half a dozen girls who fit all three categories. All six of them were tittering at something one of the young men had said. Really, Juliette wondered, who decided that tittering was original?

She sighed and returned her attention to the dancers who were now leaving the floor. She wasn't bitter, she told herself, not really. Frustrated was a more apt description. This was her third and, in all likelihood, last, Season and she seemed no closer to finding a husband than she had at her first ball. Her father was older than most and did not enjoy attending London social events. Her father was not worried about her not finding a husband. He was quite content having her at home in Berkhamsted, serving as his housekeeper and secretary.

"What's wrong, Juliette? Good heavens, did you eat something off?" Eleanor's question interrupted her morose thoughts and she gave her friend a genuine smile.

"Not at all." She gestured with her chin to the group behind them. "Anne Parham has been laughing." A shrill sound rang out and Eleanor visibly shivered.

Stifling her own dainty giggle behind her gloved hand, she said, "Well that would account for your expression."

"And how was dancing with Lord Elphinstone?" Juliette

asked.

"Oh, he's a lovely dancer."

"Ahh," Juliette said in understanding. "A lovely dancer" was their code for "deuced boring." For Eleanor to use the expression meant one of two things: the man in question had lectured her on sheep farming, literature, or astronomy, all of which Eleanor found a waste of time; or, he really was dreadfully dull. Considering the pompous Elphinstone's Shakespearean reference, Juliette suspected the former.

Eleanor was craning her neck to study the group behind them. "I say," she declared in an excited whisper. "I believe that is Jacob Wilding."

"Who?"

"Baron Worthing. Heir to the Earl of Beverly. I met him just last week at my aunt's house. Well, I should say re-met him. I think I knew him as a child for we're something of neighbors in the country, though I only recall encountering him a few times while growing up." She shook her head to dispel it of that unnecessary knowledge. "Isn't he handsome?"

Juliette suspected she knew just whom Eleanor meant and she reluctantly turned.

"Do you see him? With the dark hair. Don't you find him remarkable?"

"Only if you might have another for working days," Juliette paraphrased. "He is too costly to wear every day."

Eleanor looked blankly at her. "But you don't work."

Juliette smiled and waved the statement aside. Her exchange with Lord Elphinstone notwithstanding, she loved Shakespeare and in particular his comedies. But Eleanor had no use for plays, playwrights, or riddles of any kind.

"He is one of the nicest gentlemen in London. Come, I shall introduce you," her friend said.

"Good heavens, why?" Juliette asked, truly discomfited.

"Because he is even more handsome up close."

"I don't think—" Juliette began, but Eleanor had already grabbed her wrist and was dragging her through the throng.

For all that she disdained scholarly knowledge of any kind, Eleanor was a masterful strategist when it came to navigating the perilous waters of London society. Rather than directly approach the group surrounding Lord Worthing, she allowed herself to be stopped by one of her many admirers just shy of her target. She laughed her delicate, tinkling laugh at something he said, which caught the attention of another young man on the edges of the group. In this manner, she smoothly worked her way to the very center, dragging a reluctant Juliette with her and making it appear as if she had been sought out, rather than the opposite.

"Why Lord Worthing!" Eleanor exclaimed. "I did not know you were to attend this evening."

The dark-haired man—he truly was even more attractive up close—bowed low over Eleanor's gloved hand and all but grinned at her once he stood. Juliette inwardly smirked. Even the loftiest gentlemen became clay in the hands of a master when in the presence of Eleanor's beauty, breathy voice, and blushing complexion.

"It is a delight to see you again, Lady Eleanor. May I enquire after your aunt? I heard she was ill."

"Thank you, she is much recovered, my lord. And your parents? I trust they are well?"

The man hesitated and Juliette thought he was going to deliver bad news, but he seemed to force a smile and said, "They are indeed. My father is buried up to his cravat in the business of Parliament and could not be happier."

The required social chatter continued and Juliette allowed her attention to wander. In a moment, they would discuss the weather and the decorations of tonight's ball. Across the ballroom, she saw a portly gentleman back into a servant carrying a full tray of wineglasses. The footman valiantly tried to balance the teetering glasses and finally managed to keep them all upright, only to turn and have the glasses wiped off his tray by the arm of a wildly gesticulating matron. Juliette smiled in sympathy with the footman. She was considering that such a scene would play well in the theater when a tap on her wrist and Eleanor's rising voice calling her name made her realize her friend had dispensed with the conversational niceties.

"I'm sorry," she murmured, and turned her attention to Lord Worthing.

"May I present my dear friend, Miss Juliette Aston. Juliette, this is Jacob, Lord Worthing. I met him last week at my aunt's house, though of course we've been friends for *ages*."

Eleanor had already told her this but Juliette pretended to be amazed and curtseyed politely. She glanced up to see him bow correctly, cast his gaze quickly from her hair down to her toes and then return to Eleanor's face. Juliette smiled tightly. Honestly, you'd think she'd be used to such quick dismissals, especially when in Eleanor's company, but was there not one member of this species—species in this case being the cream of the bachelor crop—who could simply look her in the eye, smile genuinely and perhaps even compliment her well-fitting dress before returning his devout attention to her friend? Heaving a not-entirely-silent sigh, Juliette decided the answer was decidedly "No."

"Juliette's name comes from Shakespeare, you know, Lord Worthing," Eleanor said, casting a worried glance at her friend. Perhaps the sigh had been a little too loud.

Juliette's gaze shot to her friend, but Eleanor was smiling benignly at the handsome Worthing, who was still, of course, looking at Eleanor.

"Indeed," Lord Worthing replied and Juliette could not help herself.

"Actually, the Shakespearean reference was mere coincidence. I am in fact named for a great-great-grandmother. She died. Of the plague, I believe. But I do love Shakespeare's works."

Eleanor and Lord Worthing seemed rather shocked by her statement. Eleanor flushed delicately as if the mere mention of illness upset her delicate constitution, though Juliette knew the notion of anyone loving literature was equally unsettling to her friend.

Lord Worthing boldly stepped into the awkward silence. "So, in this case, a rose by another name would not smell as sweet?"

"Undoubtedly not," Juliette answered wryly.

"But Juliette does smell sweet!" Eleanor protested, clearly not understanding the reference. "She has worn a new perfume this evening that is simply ravishing. Here," she said, rather forcefully for a young woman renowned for her lyrically soft voice and gentle manners. "You must judge for yourself." Pushing Juliette closer to Lord Worthing, Eleanor pointed just below her ear. Juliette stared in shock at her friend and even Lord Worthing looked somewhat taken aback. It was not at all the thing for a gentleman to *sniff* a lady. Her perfume might delicately waft toward him whilst dancing, or he might keep a scented handkerchief of hers as a favor, but to lean forward and deliberately smell her? Juliette froze as she saw Lord Worthing do just that. He leaned his head just inches from her own. Anyone looking would simply think he was leaning in to speak directly to her, the volume in the ballroom often making simple conversation difficult. She heard him inhale deeply and expected him to immediately straighten, his duty to Eleanor's whim fulfilled. Instead he remained absolutely still and carefully exhaled before he took another breath. She felt the warmth of his exhalation stir the wisps of hair which had escaped her coiffure, felt a shiver run down her spine. She took a quick breath and smelled his own expensive cologne: spicy and citrusy and something distinctly...masculine, which she suspected was not cologne at all.

The infinitesimal moment concluded and he stood abruptly. He stared directly at Juliette—right in her eyes—for another moment before returning his attention to Eleanor.

"Very lovely," he said.

Eleanor bestowed a dazzling smile on him and nodded. "Juliette is my very dearest friend."

This non sequitur surprised a short laugh out of Lord Worthing, but he quickly recovered with a smooth, "How very fortunate for the both of you."

Eleanor went on to tell him just how they had met three years before. Juliette had to give the man credit. The story was not that interesting—they'd merely fallen in together when they were both unsure debutantes at their first ball—and Eleanor had a way of veering off the course of her story to include tidbits about her favorite dress that first season and a dog she owned when she was a girl. Nonetheless, Lord Worthing managed to keep a polite smile on his face and tossed out a, "You don't say," or "How very interesting," at appropriate moments. Of course, most men were thrilled at the chance to be able to stare at the ravishing Eleanor for long uninterrupted minutes.

Finally, Eleanor wrapped up her monologue with, "And we have been friends ever since."

"Fascinating," Lord Worthing commented and Juliette started to roll her eyes. Fortunately, she noticed Lord Worthing's gaze shift to hers and she was able to pretend she simply wished to study the crystal chandelier overhead. When she glanced back at the man, his attention had returned to Eleanor and within moments he had requested a dance. Eleanor cast a small frown in her direction. Juliette knew all of Eleanor's dances had been spoken for within the first quarter hour of their arrival, but she also knew Eleanor's status was such that she could throw over a dance partner and leave the man feeling lucky to have even been considered. So her friend's small frown worried her. Perhaps she did not like the baron? Or felt ill.

Though Lord Worthing's hand was outstretched to escort Eleanor to the dance floor, Juliette laid her hand on her friend's arm. "Didn't you say you wished to take a break from the dancing, dear? To rest the ankle you twisted yesterday."

Out of the corner of her eye, she saw Lord Worthing scowl at her. Most likely the man had never been turned down in his life and was quite put out as to how to respond. Oh well, the experience will do him good.

"Well," Eleanor said slowly. She was not the best of liars. "I did say that...but it's not so very sore."

Juliette was perplexed. Did her friend want to dance with the man or not? She raised her eyebrows at Eleanor but before either girl could think what to say, Lord Worthing bowed low and said, "Perhaps another time." He straightened and immediately allowed his attention to be recalled by the group of gentleman standing behind him and to whom he'd been talking before Eleanor had "bumped" into him.

"I'm sorry," Juliette said quietly. "You looked like you didn't wish to dance with him. Did I ruin something?"

Eleanor flushed—Juliette wondered distractedly if she could do that on demand—and said, "Oh, no. It's not that. I had hoped he would—"

She was interrupted by a strong waft of perfume followed closely by the arrival of three girls, one of whom was flanked by the other two as if they were an honor guard. More like toady guard, Juliette decided. Cassandra de Courtney, one of the few rivals for Eleanor's status as this Season's "diamond," was even more petite and more blonde than Eleanor, Cassandra's features might have been considered finer if she had any of Eleanor's innate sweetness. As it was, Juliette found Cassandra's beauty to be a bit hard, as if she were an exquisitely made filigreed knife whose edge was sharp enough to slice your finger with just a glance.

"Well good evening, Eleanor. Sitting out the dancing this evening? Or are you not able to find a dance partner."

Beside her, Juliette felt Eleanor tense up. For all her ability to deal with the male half of the ton, her friend had never mastered how to deal with the likes of Cassandra de Courtney, and as a result, Cassandra sought her out at every opportunity and taunted her mercilessly.

When it appeared Eleanor was going to be unable to speak, Juliette jumped gamely into the fray. Laughing as if Cassandra had made the wittiest joke, Juliette said, "Oh that's a good one, Cassandra! Did you hear that, Eleanor? 'Sitting out.' "

"Actually," Juliette dropped all pretense of laughter. "Poor Lady Eleanor is in bit of a conundrum. She has overbooked all her dances. She is so very popular with the gentlemen, you know, and yet she is very kind." Grasping Eleanor's wrist with its delicate dance card dangling on a silver ribbon, she said, "You should see the earls, marquis, and even dukes who have begged for a spot on her card!"

Cassandra's expression soured as if she smelled something rotten. Pointedly ignoring Juliette, she said, "Perhaps Eleanor, since you are so very kind, you could send one of your admirers to dance with your poor duenna. It seems that is the only way she'll see the dance floor this evening. Perhaps if she were wearing a conundrum, she would have better luck."

Juliette and Eleanor both stared open-mouthed at the hateful girl, though Juliette's silence stemmed from trying to figure out what on earth Cassandra thought a conundrum was. Seeing her scrutinize Eleanor's elaborate gown, Juliette could not help but laugh. Really, did no young women read beyond their basic primers anymore?

"Yes," she agreed, trying to contain her mirth. "I shall have to order a conundrum from my modiste right away."

With a sniff, Cassandra tossed her head and led her silent minions away.

"Best beware my sting," Juliette said with a glare at their departing backs.

"Mercy!" Eleanor exclaimed. "I don't know why that girl hates us so much. And I don't know how you are able to stand up to her as you do, but I thank you, Juliette," Eleanor finished with a little sniffle. She dabbed delicately at her nose with a lacy handkerchief and Juliette wondered why her friend's eyes never grew red and puffy when she cried. Instead, her tears merely seemed to make her eyes sparkle more.

Giving her friend a brief hug, she nudged her toward the gentleman coming to claim Eleanor for his dance. "She's just jealous because you're everything she could never be. Plus, she knows you're going to make the match of the Season and she'll no doubt be stuck another year with the rest of us trying to land a husband."

"But I'm sure you're—"

Eleanor was interrupted by the arrival of her dance partner and Juliette was relieved to have a moment of relative quiet to gather her wits. She disliked having to deal with people like Cassandra de Courtney, but she was fundamentally unable to allow the girl to hurt her best friend's feelings. She was rather averse to being insulted herself.

A duenna! Indeed.

"Hmm… 'Much Ado About Nothing?"

Startled, Juliette looked up to see Lord Worthing had turned from his friends yet again. "I beg your pardon?"

"'Best beware my sting,' you said. It's from 'Much Ado About Nothing,' is it not?"

Juliette opened her mouth to correct him and then read the sparkle in his eye. The man bloody well knew the quote, she would wager. She pressed her lips together, refusing to answer. He raised his eyebrows expectantly. She gritted her teeth and ground out, "Taming of the Shrew, actually."

"Indeed," Lord Worthing said. Glancing at him, Juliette saw a grin tugging at the corner of his mouth. "Is that a confession?"

"More of an accolade, really. 'Shrew' is just man's title for a woman who speaks her mind."

The grin he had tried to suppress triumphed and Juliette felt her heart rate accelerate as a result. Glancing away as if she were through with the conversation, she willed herself to focus on something other than that dazzling, slightly naughty smile.

"Tell me, Miss Aston. Are you a follower of the late Mary Wollstonecraft?"

"You say her name with the same distaste the reverend back home says 'Catholic.'"

"Not at all," Lord Worthing argued. "I simply ask if you subscribe to the beliefs that Mrs. Wollstonecraft professed."

Juliette could not tell if the man was in earnest or teasing her. Certainly men of his ilk scorned the notion that men and women were of equal intelligence. And yet if he were teasing her...well, that implied at least some level of interest in furthering their conversation. And men of his ilk certainly never did that with her. Discomfited by this last thought, she pretended to see someone across the room.

"If you'll forgive me, Lord Worthing. It seems my next dance partner is looking for me."

Still smirking, Lord Worthing nodded and bid her good evening.

Juliette turned and made a good show of plowing through the crush of people to her fictional dance partner.

Chapter Two

Jacob Wilding considered himself to be a good son, attentive to his parents' wishes and guidance. And why should he not be, he reflected, as he sank into a comfortably broken-in leather chair at his London club, a glass of whiskey in hand. His parents were both exceptional and they had instilled in him a love of family, duty, and tradition. His father, the Earl of Beverly, had spent an inordinate amount of time with him when he was a boy. Disdaining the notion of simply handing over his son's education to a tutor, he had taken young Jacob on long walks about their properties, explained life as he saw it to his son, and answered, to the best of his abilities, young Jacob's endless questions. Jacob's beautiful mother was one of the wittiest people he'd ever met. She was forever delivering sly witticisms and delighted in playing jokes both on and with her only son.

Unlike most men his age, Jacob had not attended that many London Seasons since reaching his majority. He'd missed that first year serving in the military fighting Napoleon, then skipped a couple while he travelled abroad, searching for those places not destroyed by the emperor. Then there was the year his mother had very nearly died. He and his father had not left their home in Hertford for nearly six months that year. Those absences considered, one would think he should have been somewhat excited to be enjoying the festivities the Season had to offer. Even *he* thought he should be excited, or at least interested, or at the very least amused. Oh all right, he confessed to himself with a half-smile. He was amused. Somewhat.

"Bloody good whiskey or a bloody good joke, I say," predicted Lord Hugh Stalwood, flinging himself into the chair opposite Jacob.

"What's that?"

"Your grin. I credit it to the drink in your hand or a jest in that knob you call a head."

"I was not grinning," Jacob protested.

"If you say so," Hugh said skeptically. He made a show of trimming a thin cheroot before he lit it and leaned back in his chair, feet crossed at the ankles. Jacob knew Hugh loved to position himself to best display his manly charms, whether it was lounging indolently at the club or leaning against a column at a ball, arms crossed negligently as he pretended to critically survey the dancers (in truth, Hugh was terribly nearsighted and could only make out blobs of what he assumed to be dancers). It was an affectation to be sure, but Hugh was a good chap and had been a steadfast friend through university and war, so Jacob forbore from teasing him.

"I was merely reflecting on my good fortune at having very decent parents."

"Here, here," Hugh said, lifting his own glass. "I daresay you had the best fortune in that regard of all our mates. I wager they don't even nag you to marry and carry on the family line." Hugh affected a shudder and Jacob smiled at his friend's overacting.

"Well, as to that..."

Hugh let loose a bark of laughter and sat forward, all thoughts of manly lounging apparently forgotten. "You don't say! So now you're part of the Beleaguered Bachelors."

"I beg your pardon?"

"Beleaguered Bachelors. I came up with it. Clever, ain't it? Made up of we eligible unattached men who are plagued by the unmarried young misses and set upon by one or more of our family members to sacrifice ourselves upon the altar of –"

"You should have taken to the stage, Hugh. You're completely wasted on the likes of us."

"I quite agree. Pity I am doomed to stay wealthy. I quite

fancy myself a modern Marlow or Shakespeare."

The mention of Shakespeare made Jacob remember the ball he had attended earlier in the evening. Now why would he think—ah yes, Miss Juliette...Something-or-other. Odd little chit, he reflected. Rather sharp of tongue...but clever, for all that. And undoubtedly a good friend. Why she'd nearly drawn Cassandra de Courtney's blood with the edge of her tongue in defense of Lady Eleanor. Certainly not unattractive—the Shakespeare girl. God knew Lady Eleanor was exquisite, with that golden head of hair and those little bow-shaped lips that just cried out to—

"Oi! Worthing!" Hugh was waving his hand wildly as if trying to get Jacob's attention from across the room instead of across the low table between them.

"Yes?" Jacob asked politely.

"What's this about you joining the BBs? Don't say your mother is wanting grandchildren."

Jacob paused. Not many knew the extent of his father's illness. "Er, no. My father actually. He's decided he can see the end of his life and wants to go to his great reward confident that he has left all in order here in the mortal world."

"Gads, the man is fitter than I am!" Hugh exclaimed, self-consciously patting his midsection.

Jacob smiled and tried not to think of his father's mortality. "I suppose his work here will not be complete until he sees me leg-shackled."

In all truth, the old earl, Miles Wilding, had never been one to nag, harangue, or even lecture his son on his duties as the Beverly heir. But a few weeks back, his father said something cryptic.

"Life can turn in a heartbeat. There's nothing to say any of us will be here next month or even next week. You're not a green lad. You've seen war and are well prepared to take over when I die. It is past time you took life's next step."

Even now, a fortnight later, Jacob felt slightly chastised, as if he had let his father down somehow.

Jacob shook himself from his reverie and grimaced at the glee in Hugh's face.

"Oh come now," Jacob said. "Surely misery does not love company *that* much."

"Ho ho, you have no idea, old boy. Why once I let my sisters and mother know you are on the market, I may escape a week without their constant pestering! Perhaps a whole fortnight," this said with a wistful sigh.

Jacob pinched the bridge of his nose and said, "So help me God, Stalwood, if you make me regret confiding in you, I'll...make you regret it."

Hugh gave him a "do tell" quirk to his eyebrows.

With a lowering of his own brows, Jacob said, "I'll tell your sisters that you confessed to me that you are deeply infatuated with Millicent Scrubbs."

Hugh sat up straight. "You wouldn't."

"I would," Jacob assured him with a complacent smile.

"Hitting below the belt that is, mate."

"As is sacrificing me to escape your own family's...attentions."

Hugh shrugged and drew deeply on his cheroot. "Can't blame a bloke for trying." After a few minutes of contemplative silence, he asked, "So who do you have in mind?"

Jacob tossed back the last swallow of his drink before answering. "I've no idea."

Hugh laughed. "You always have an idea about everything. Come now, you're over thirty years old. Even without your father urging you to choose, you knew you'd have to marry sooner or later. So knowing you as I do, I know you have a nice neat mental list of who you would marry if you simply had to."

Jacob decided there were excellent reasons for not having a life-long friend, the first being that they tended to know you better than you knew yourself.

"Perhaps," he admitted.

"'Perhaps,'" Hugh mocked. "Perhaps who?"

Jacob sighed and mumbled, "Lady Audrey Blackburn, Miss Chloe Brooke, Miss Rosamund True. Oh, and Lady Eleanor Chalcroft." His father had specifically recommended Lady Eleanor.

"Exemplary young misses, all," Hugh said approvingly. "Have you spoken to any of them?"

"Well of course."

Hugh narrowed his eyes. "I mean *talked* to them, Worthing. Not just discussed the weather. Any of them have a brain?"

Jacob laughed. "Since when are you concerned with a lady's brain? Aren't you the one who said a gel's skull was only to provide a resting spot for a pretty bonnet?"

"Did I? Don't recall that. Deuced clever observation, that. But as I'm not the one getting married, I needn't worry about intellect. You're the one I can't imagine married to a hen wit. Especially considering who raised you."

At Jacob's raised eye, Hugh elaborated. "The Countess, your mother, is quite the smartest woman I've ever known. She makes me feel like a blooming idiot half the time just because I can't keep up with her. Can't imagine you'd want less in your own marriage."

"Rather intuitive of you, Stalwood."

Hugh grinned and leaned back in his chair, pleased with himself. "Ain't it?"

"It is. But I fear it will be asking a bit much to require intellectual abilities in a wife."

Hugh was in mid-sip of a brandy and he nearly snorted the liquid through his nose. "That impressed with the current crop of young misses, are you?"

Jacob shrugged philosophically. "They're simply that—young. All they can possibly be interested in right now is clothing and who's engaged to whom. Remember when we were fresh out of school and all we thought about was ballet dancers?"

A dreamy look crossed Hugh's face and he sighed. "I remember Daniella."

"Precisely. But now we've matured—"

"She had legs as long as—"

"Or I should say *I've* matured. At any rate, I want to ensure whoever I choose will one day be capable of intelligent conversation and possibly even develop a sense of humor."

"And if she remains a hen wit?"

Jacob grimaced. "Well, I'll always have you around for a laugh."

"Right you are! Right you are," Hugh said with a chortle. He signaled for another drink and leaned forward in his chair. "So how will you decide who will be the next Countess of Beverly?"

Before Jacob could answer, Hugh sat up straight. "Say! I know! You could devise a series of questions. Like a test to determine the most likely to develop a brain."

"Really, Hugh, they all have a brain. I'm just not convinced they've chosen to employ it yet."

Hugh waved this aside. "You know what I mean. Surely we—or rather, you—are clever enough to devise a method of questioning that will give you an idea of who will develop into your perfect wife."

Jacob smiled and shook his head. "You've a craven mind, Stalwood. I needn't anything so complicated as a test. A ride in the park should prove sufficient to determine if I can bear to converse with her at the breakfast table for the next twenty years."

"Oh is that all?" Hugh laughed and called for another drink.

Chapter Three

Despite being one of the less-pursued young ladies of the ton, Juliette had received flowers on the morning after a ball before. Three times, to be precise. Her two previous bouquets had come last Season from a young man who'd claimed himself to be completely infatuated with her. His infatuation had lasted precisely a fortnight, the end of which saw him eloping with another young lady to Gretna Green. Her first bouquet had been delivered after the last ball of her first Season. It had come from a very nice young man, with young being the operative word. Juliette was a bit older than the usual debutante, but she nonetheless wished to marry a man at least her own age.

Still, it was a pleasant surprise when she went downstairs the next morning to find a substantial bouquet of stock, carnations, and spray roses awaiting her in the front hall. Even as she felt her cheeks pinken in delight, she frowned, for she had no notion who might have sent the blooms. She'd not danced with any man more than once last night, had scarcely had conversation with any of them, unless it was as an adjunct to Eleanor. She pressed her cool hands to her warm cheeks, and then calmly opened the card attached to the bouquet.

"Mr. Theodore Pickering," she read aloud. Who in the world—ah, she remembered one waltz (her only waltz of the evening) with Mr. Pickering. A pleasant enough young man. Average height, nice smile...well, if she couldn't pick him out of a crowd, it was surely because they had only just met the once. Still, he indicated on his card that he should like to call on her this afternoon. Certainly that boded well. Juliette felt a mild queasiness in her stomach. What on earth would they talk about? She was abysmal at small talk, but she needed to rally to the occasion. This was her last Season, her last chance to find a husband. Juliette took the flowers and card with her to the small, sunny breakfast room where she had the footman fetch a vase.

In all honesty, Juliette's wish to marry did not stem from a desire to acquire a husband, per se—she'd not found any man who moved her heart enough to warrant more than mild affection—but she desperately wanted a family. She had lost her own mother at the age of twelve and as an only child, she'd always longed for siblings, raucous family gatherings, noisy Christmas dinners. If she'd had a brother or sister with children, she could handle being an old maid for she could be a part of their family events. However, she must marry, and this Season.

Her father, gentle and understanding though he may be, simply disliked London. He'd told her from her debut that he had three Season's worth of patience for the huge city so she must find a suitable husband within that time. Before she'd come to London that first year, she'd been sure she would find a good mate by the end of the Season. She was intelligent, had a good sense of humor, and was reasonably attractive, perhaps even pretty on occasion. Once she'd had Eleanor helping her, she'd met many nice gentlemen, but nothing ever developed beyond acquaintance. She'd had little help from Aunt Constance, whose house they stayed in while in London, while navigating the social intricacies.

And so it had gone for her second, and now the start of her third Season. Apparently intelligence and a sense of humor was not enough to guarantee that one "took." If only polite discourse was not confined to the weather, the wellness of one's relatives, or who one saw at the last musicale. Juliette frowned at her marmalade and wished her mother were still alive to guide her in this. Aunt Constance would only relay stories of her courtship with the late Mr. Smithsonly when asked for advice. Her only real guidance came from Eleanor who insisted a lady should not bore a man with talk over books or history. It seemed to work for Eleanor, but then men were content to simply sit and gaze at her perfect features.

"Eleanor!" Juliette exclaimed, startling the footman who was returning with a vase.

Why hadn't she thought of it before? She would invite Eleanor to be here when Mr. Pickering arrived, and her friend would ensure that the conversation did not grow stilted or awkward. Perhaps, given the chance to become more familiar with Mr. Pickering, Juliette felt certain she could find *some* topic for discussion.

Quickly finishing her toast and with a hasty kiss on the cheek for her father who was just entering the breakfast room, Juliette dashed out to send her friend a note.

Eleanor arrived—early no less, a feat that convinced Juliette her friend was worried she might make hash out of the visit. Eleanor was rarely on time, much less early to any event.

"Is that what you're wearing?" Eleanor asked, handing her pelisse to the footman.

"Er...it was. What's wrong with it?"

Eleanor said nothing, but circled Juliette slowly, taking in every aspect of her attire. Juliette glanced down at her dress. It was white cotton batiste with white embroidered flowers. A stiffened white satin ribbon just beneath her bust and small puffed sleeves made her feel very feminine. She self-consciously touched her hair, but it felt in place.

"Hmmm," Eleanor said, finishing her circumnavigation.

"Good heavens, as bad as that?" Juliette asked, not entirely in jest.

Eleanor squinted as she gave one last perusal from the tips of Juliette's white satin slippers to her bosom. Without warning, she reached forward and snatched the fichu from the neckline of Juliette's dress. "There. You look perfect."

"What?" Juliette gasped. "Give that back! The modiste

cut the gown too low," she exclaimed, her hand self-consciously covering the swell of the tops of her breasts.

"Nonsense. She cut it exactly right."

"For an evening gown, perhaps," Juliette countered, for while it was acceptable for even an unmarried young woman to wear a low cut gown at night, day dresses required a strict adherence to modesty. Juliette made to grab the scrap of lace back from her friend. Eleanor quickly crumpled it up and shoved it in her reticule.

Glancing about the hall, Eleanor asked, "Where is Mrs. Smithsonly?"

"Having a nap. She told me to wake her before Mr. Pinkerton arrives."

"Nonsense. I shall serve as chaperone."

Juliette gasped. While the only requirement for a chaperone was that she be married, even if she were younger than the girl she was chaperoning, for two unwed ladies to meet with an unmarried gentleman...well, it just wasn't done. Before she could utter a response, Eleanor had moved on to another topic.

"Now, what room shall you receive him in?"

Still slightly dazed at her friend's peremptory adjustment of her gown and dismissal of social etiquette rule number one, Juliette simply gaped.

"Not your formal sitting room," Eleanor decided, sounding a bit like Juliette imagined a general issuing battle plans would.

"Why not?"

"The lighting is not as flattering as it could be. It's too dark by half."

"Should we sit in the garden? The weather is lovely, I could have refreshments—"

Eleanor shook her head. "No, the light would be too strong outside. And with you wearing white, you might blind the man. I have it!" she snapped her fingers in a terribly unladylike manner that made Juliette grin.

"That small room you use as a solar. Nice and sunny, but the light is soft. Very becoming to one's complexion."

"But it's so informal."

"Nonsense, he'll be too busy looking at you to notice his surroundings."

Juliette laughed aloud at that as she followed Eleanor to the back of the house where the small room overlooking the garden was situated. It was a lovely room, painted in bright yellow and full of flowering plants and comfortable furniture.

They had just seated themselves when the doorknocker sounded.

"Do you have some embroidery?" Eleanor asked.

"Well, yes, but—"

"Grab it!" Eleanor ordered.

Juliette snatched the length of cloth she was working on from the basket on the table and pretended to be studying it as she heard the footman leading their guest back to the solar. Just as Mr. Pickering entered the room, Eleanor announced, "And that is why he decided you were the most lovely female he had ever met! Oh!" she exclaimed, affecting to have just noticed the new arrival.

Juliette found herself stifling a laugh at Eleanor's machinations as she rose to greet her visitor.

"Mr. Pickering," she said with a curtsy. "How very nice to see you. Won't you come join us?"

She made the proper introductions and tried not to laugh at the sharply speculative manner in which Eleanor was appraising the poor man.

Mr. Pickering bowed politely and took the chair directly next to Juliette.

"And may I thank you for the bouquet of flowers. They are quite lovely."

Mr. Pickering flushed slightly and glanced uncertainly at Eleanor. "Were they yellow? The flowers, I mean? I specifically instructed the florist to make sure they were yellow."

Uncertain, Juliette replied, "Why, I believe the stock was

a lovely shade of yellow. May ask why you chose that color?"

Seemingly interested in a snag in the fabric covering his knee, Mr. Pickering said, "You were wearing yellow last night. When we danced."

"Oh," Juliette exclaimed, rather delighted that he had even noticed. "That's...that's lovely. Thank you."

He smiled sheepishly and then took a deep breath, looking about the room. "My mother said you would like them." Another silence stretched out before Juliette glanced at Eleanor to see her pantomiming drinking tea.

"Oh!" she said again. "May I offer you some refreshments? Cook has made a fresh batch of shortbread."

"Can't say I'm much for shortbread, but perhaps lemonade if you have it."

Not much for shortbread? Juliette thought as she stepped out into the hall and sent the footman for a tray. What decent human didn't adore shortbread? Butter, sugar, eggs. Perhaps a dollop of jam in the center. Returning to the room, she fixed a bright smile on her face.

Eleanor was in the midst of telling Mr. Pickering all the people she talked to at the previous night's ball and once they found a common acquaintance, she launched into a detailed background of everything she knew of the person and his family.

Juliette resumed her seat and tried to feign interest in the conversation, but allowed her eyes to wander to Mr. Pickering. He was of moderate height, light brown hair and pale eyes —blue or grey, she could not discern as he was politely looking at Eleanor. A rather weak chin, she supposed, but he did have a nice smile. He was dressed well, with polished boots of good quality and a finely tailored jacket. His cravat was perhaps a bit too effusive for Juliette's tastes, but overall, he presented a distinguished picture.

Eleanor seamlessly pulled Juliette into the conversation with talk of Juliette's home in Berkhamsted. From there they spent only a minute or two on the weather before Eleanor asked Mr. Pickering about *his* country home which led him to his desire to breed hunting hounds. Before Juliette realized it, the clock was chiming the hour and the requisite thirty-minute visit was at an end.

Mr. Pickering stood and paused a bit awkwardly, his hat in hand. Juliette glanced to Eleanor for assistance. Eleanor quickly stood and excused herself from the room, bidding a fond farewell to Mr. Pickering.

Perplexed at her friend's departure, Juliette also stood to bid him goodbye.

Mr. Pickering cleared his throat and Juliette tried to look encouraging. The poor man seemed utterly at a loss.

"Miss Aston," he began.

"Yes, Mr. Pickering?"

"I was wondering, that is to say I would like, er..."

Juliette smiled, wondering that she should be so intimidating that he could not simply ask whatever it was he wanted. "Yes?"

"May I have permission to call upon your father?"

Juliette frowned in confusion. "My father?"

"Well, yes. To gain his permission. To court you, you know."

"Oh," Juliette said. And just like that, Juliette realized her life was set. With nothing more than one waltz and an afternoon visit, it seemed fate had decided her future. For formal permission to court a young lady was tantamount to a declaration of intention. Of course courting couples did not always marry, but Juliette knew—with a certainty not unlike the knowledge that heavy grey-green clouds mean a terrible storm is imminent—that Mr. Pickering intended to offer for her eventually. And since this was likely her last chance at a family, she would be obliged to accept.

"That would be...acceptable, Mr. Pickering."

Relief washed over his face and he shifted his weight from foot to foot. "Very good, Miss Aston, very good. Shall I... that is, is he in now?"

"Er, I believe so. I shall have the footman take you to him."

Mr. Pickering seemed again at a loss as to what to do. Juliette herself was unsure—never having been alone with a gentleman before, especially one who had all but declared his intention to wed her. Finally, to save them both further awkwardness, she gave him her hand. He bent over it and placed a quick, though rather wet kiss to the back of it.

Wishing she had thought to wear gloves—not general practice when receiving guests at home—Juliette surreptitiously wiped the back of her hand on her skirts as she called the footman back. She wondered where Eleanor had disappeared. With precise timing, her friend appeared not moments after Mr. Pickering had been escorted to her father's study.

"Well?" she asked expectantly.

Juliette couldn't help herself. "Well what?" she asked innocently.

Eleanor's eyes narrowed most unbecomingly.

"Oh very well," Juliette capitulated. "He is asking my father for permission to court me."

Eleanor clapped her hands together and the gleam in her eyes once again reminded Juliette of a battle-seasoned general. "I knew it! Now we must decide if you want him."

A surprised laugh escaped Juliette. As if she had so many options available to her. "I suppose I do, Eleanor. He's the only gentleman who's expressed even this much interest in me."

Eleanor waved this fact aside as if it were inconsequential. "He is the only son that I'm aware of to Sir Pickering, so nothing to sneeze at there. I'm not certain what his yearly income is—don't worry, I'll know by tomorrow at the latest—but if his attire is any indication, I suspect you shall not want for gowns and the like." Eleanor tapped her finger against her upper lip. "Unless he is in debt and only seeking to make a good impression with clothing he cannot afford to get his hands on your dowry." She pressed her lips together in thought but quickly shook her head. "Well, we shall know soon enough. I shall also inquire about his family. You wouldn't want a domineering mother-in-law or mad cousin about."

Juliette smiled fondly at her friend. Whether Eleanor truly believed she had a wealth of suitors and simply needed to pick the best of the bunch or she was being purposefully dense, she knew her friend had only her best interests at heart.

That evening, as Juliette, her father, and Aunt Constance ate dinner, Sir Lewis informed her of his visit with Mr. Pickering, apparently unaware Juliette had entertained him without his Aunt's supervision.

"Seems you've caught the eye of a young dandy, my dear."

Juliette nearly choked on her peas. "Surely not a dandy, father."

"Hhmph," Sir Lewis replied. "Had quite a bit of...froth, here," he said, waving in the general direction of his own simply tied cravat.

"I thought the cut of his coat quite tasteful," Aunt Constance replied and Juliette wondered if her great aunt were thinking of last night's ball attire.

"Well, I certainly did not intend to insult the pup. Young men today will wear what they wear."

"Very astute of you, father," Juliette said fondly.

Sir Lewis's florid face reddened. "Well, be that as it may, what do you think of Mr. Pickering, daughter? I daresay he's made his intentions known toward you."

Juliette studied the food on her plate. "We only met last night, father. I scarcely know him. He certainly seems pleasant enough."

Sir Lewis frowned. "Only last night and he's indicating his intention to court you? Perhaps I was too hasty in giving my permission. Why I knew your beloved mother for three years before I even asked her to dance."

Juliette smiled, remembering her mother telling her that she'd had to all but force Sir Lewis to ask her to dance, because he was so shy as a young man.

"Nonsense, Lewis. Not all men take so bloody long to decide what or whom they want in life. My own Mr. Smithsonly proposed marriage to me not two days after we met. We were wed three weeks later and a happier match I cannot imagine. Don't fault him for being a decisive young man."

"I'm not, I'm not!" Sir Lewis exclaimed defensively. "I'm certain young Juliette here knows her own mind, don't you my dear?"

All Juliette knew was that Mr. Pickering was likely her last shot at a family of her own. "Indeed, father. You have raised me, after all."

Sir Lewis was pleased at her compliment. "Seeing as how you have things in hand here, I shall be returning to the country for three weeks. Send word if I'm needed to meet with your young man before then."

Juliette smiled weakly, "Of course."

Chapter Four

Jacob had spent a disgruntled morning—or was it a disgruntling morning? he wondered. Either way, he was feeling out of sorts. He had attended meetings at Westminster on behalf of his father but had quickly grown tired of the constant rehashing of the same problems with no clear decision on how to solve them. As he strode out of the Parliamentary offices into the pervasive mist of a London morning, he fervently prayed his father would never die that he might never have to take his place in the House of Lords. He stopped abruptly, causing the man behind him to complain at his blocking the path. His father must be ill to ask Jacob to fill in for him today. The earl loved arguing his point, convincing others to back his bills, and verbally battling his opponents.

He was not prepared to lose his father, and not just because he didn't want to serve in Parliament. He darted across a street, dodging hired coaches. His father had been the center of his world since he was a child, always offering support and encouragement. Jacob had heard too many stories from his friends at school not to appreciate that his father's approach to parenting was the exception, not the rule. He knew his father could not live forever, but surely he had a few more years?

By the end of the first block, Jacob realized it was not a day for walking outdoors. Loathe to go inside where he would drive himself mad with worry over his father, he hailed a hackney and gave his direction: Burlington Arcade. The covered shopping pavilion had recently opened and allowed customers to peruse the goods of more than seventy vendors without the inconvenience of London's frequent downpours.

Once there, he let his feet take him where they would and let his mind wander to a dilemma he really would rather not face: that of choosing a bride. His blithe conversation with Lord Stalwood over brandy the week before had lulled him into a comfortable complacency. He had been sure that his short list of suitable brides would allow an easy and quick decision.

The trouble had started the night after his conversation with Hugh. He had made his way to a large dinner party where he'd been pleasantly surprised to find himself partnered with one of the ladies on his list: Lady Audrey Blackburn. Thinking this a fateful sign, he set about being his most charming self. He smiled, he gazed intently at her when she spoke, he laughed huskily, and he acted as though no one else were in the room. For his troubles, he had discovered that Lady Audrey was partial to giggling. Frequently. No, he corrected himself as his boots rapped sharply on the bricks paths of the arcade, she giggled incessantly. It had been all right when he'd made light joking remarks about his dislike of shellfish. He'd thought she was perhaps a bit nervous but encouraging with her titter. But when he asked her if she was enjoying her London Season, she giggled again. When he asked her about her cousin, with whom he'd served in the war, she giggled—perhaps it was a titter, he didn't know. Really, they all blurred together into one long dinner of simpering, high pitched squeaks.

Jacob paused, finding himself already at the end of the first row of shops. He must have been walking quicker than usual. Turning, he marched up the other side of the lane.

Clearly, he'd had to scratch Lady Audrey from his mental list of prospective brides.

Three days later, he danced the allowed two dances with Miss Chloe Brooks. They'd managed to laugh (not giggle) about her last name and how it was the same as his club but how she was not in the least related to the proprietor. She had danced very well and flushed prettily when he complimented her. He'd invited her to go for a ride in his curricle the next day, weather permitting. The weather had permitted, but Jacob rather wished it hadn't. Miss Brooks had spent the entire hour of their drive talking about her doll collection. When Jacob had asked her how old she was (granted, not a polite question under any circumstance), she had grown mightily offended and informed him that many of her dolls were antiques and worth more money than he could imagine (he doubted this—he could imagine quite a lot of money).

"Furthermore," she had informed him. "Dolls offer historical insights into the cultures they represented. Besides which, they are delightful toys!" They had spent the return ride to her home in awkward silence and she had been rather cold to him as she bid her farewell. Jacob had not been overly disappointed. Well, perhaps he had been disappointed that what started out as a promising acquaintance had so quickly deteriorated. However, he had been greatly relieved to learn about the doll collection early on. Dolls positively unnerved him. Something about those unblinking glass eyes...

At any rate, he had gone on to sit next to Miss Rosamund True at a musicale. She had been easy to talk to, certainly easy to look at, and easy to talk into taking a walk in the moonlit patio. She was amenable to his every request and they agreed to walk in Hyde Park the next day if the weather was agreeable. The weather had been agreeable and so had Miss True. In fact, she'd almost been too agreeable. She had concurred with every statement he made, whether it was regarding Sir Aubrey's new mount which they saw along their walk, or the precise color of the blue of the rare sunny sky.

"I would describe it as a few shades darker than skimmed milk. Truly, a London sky cannot compare to the fresh-scrubbed azure of an English country sky," Jacob said.

"That is just the description I was thinking of!" Miss True said.

"Skim milk?"

"Indeed! We are of a like mind on all things, my lord."

At some point, Jacob had been tempted to voice a shockingly outrageous claim simply to see if Miss True was even paying attention. He settled for, "I daresay men won't be wearing cravats at all next Season. They've gone quite out of fashion on the continent, you know."

Miss True had blinked at that—so she was at least paying attention—and stammered. "Why, I'm sure they must be uncomfortable to wear."

Because he was a gentleman, Jacob had restrained his heavy sigh and they resumed their walk. Certainly, there was nothing objectionable about Miss True, from her strawberry-blonde hair to her bow-shaped lips to the generous curves of her figure. They would no doubt have beautiful children and would probably never have an argument. But Jacob suspected he slowly go insane if his wife didn't have some pluck, some opinion of her own. He'd never considered it before, but a rousing argument was rather invigorating, assuming it was simply a difference of opinion and not a sign of vastly different characters. Yes, Jacob decided, he preferred spice to blandness. He had thanked Miss True for the lovely walk, was thanked in return, and then he escaped to his club, where he could be assured Lord Hugh Stalwood would argue with him simply for the sake of being contrary and that they could then enjoy a good laugh of it over a drink.

Jacob reached the entrance to Burlington Arcade and realized he'd again been completely oblivious to the shops he'd strode past. Seeing that the weather was still dithering between a heavy mist and out-and-out rain, he turned back into the arcade and slowed his steps. He might as well see what shops were about. His mother would ask if the arcade was worth visiting if she found out he'd been here and he rather enjoyed his mother thinking he knew everything.

Although, he reflected as he strolled more slowly down the rows of shops, to his eyes, one apparel boutique looked very much like the next. His mother would no doubt want to know which milliners had located to Burlington as well as the number of hosiers and whether a decent florist was to be found there. Love his mother though he may, there was no way he was going to fill his head with such information.

Thoughts of his mother fled his mind as he spied across the way the lovely features of the last lady on his prospective-bride list and his father's choice, Lady Eleanor Chalcroft. He knew from their meeting at the ball last week that she was a lively conversationalist as long as one didn't tread too deeply into intellectual waters. She was certainly this Season's reigning beauty and he was fairly confident she did not have a doll collection. His mood vastly improved, he made his way through the crush of pedestrians to approach her.

"Lady Eleanor! How lucky I am to meet you." This said with his most charming grin.

"Why Lord Worthing, are you shopping today?"

"To be honest, I was simply taking advantage of being able to take a walk out of the rain. But I thought to see what shops were here as well." Ladies loved shopping and if he need stretch the truth a bit to impress her, well, that's what courting was all about, wasn't it?

"Oh there are ever so many lovely shops here. I declare I've sent the footman to the carriage three times with armloads of packages and we've only been here an hour!"

"Four times, actually."

Jacob looked to Eleanor's left and discovered Eleanor's friend from the ball a few weeks past. He sought frantically for a name...something poetic? Shakespeare! Beatrice?

His flagging memory was spared by Lady Eleanor. "Surely you remember my dear friend, Miss Juliette Aston?"

"Certainly. We were introduced at the Sutherland ball, were we not?"

Miss Aston dipped her head in a brief nod. Terse little thing, he thought.

Turning back to Lady Eleanor, he said, "May I offer to escort you?"

"That would be lovely, wouldn't it Juliette?"

"Lovely," parroted her friend.

Wondering if Miss Aston were a complete antidote or

simply disgruntled that he was stealing her friend's attention, he flashed her the charming grin. It usually worked to get him out of all manner of scrapes and uncomfortable situations. Miss Aston looked rather startled—not the customary response, but at least she was no longer scowling.

Gallantly offering an arm to each lady, he allowed Lady Eleanor to direct them to the second row of shops. As they walked, she talked animatedly about the purchases she had made. Jacob recognized immediately that his full attention was neither wanted nor needed. He had a sister, after all, and he knew well that on certain occasions—such as when a lady was discussing clothing, hair styling, or floral arrangements—she simply wished to speak her thoughts aloud with no interruption from the man to whom they were ostensibly speaking, save for the occasional, "I quite agree," or "Just as you say!"

Such an arrangement would normally suit him quite well as he could let his thoughts roam to more interesting topics while still earning the favor of the lady in question. Today, however, he felt compelled to pay stricter attention to discover if Lady Eleanor (his very last candidate, after all) would make an acceptable bride. To that end, he would need to engage her in conversation above and beyond that of the lovely new yellow bonnet she'd acquired at the shop down the row. He needed to discover, for instance, if she had the spine to stand up to him if she disagreed about something. He'd also like to verify she had a tolerable sense of humor, for after his encounters with Lady Audrey and the Misses Brooks and True, he had added wit to his otherwise short list of requirements in a wife. He could have stood Miss Brooks' doll collection if she'd been able to make a little joke about it instead of taking immediate offense.

How to judge such a quality in a short time? He was not under a deadline, but if knowing Jacob was betrothed gave his father comfort, perhaps even the strength to recover, it was well worth rushing the courtship.

As they strolled down the covered lane, Jacob cast about

for something to talk about. Seeing a small gallery ahead, he drew the ladies to a stop in front of its window. There were several nice landscapes on display as well as a rather good watercolor portrait of a gentleman. Lady Eleanor cooed over one of the landscapes, which was complete with a passel of gamboling puppies in the foreground. Jacob's eye was drawn to another portrait, of two women, obviously blood-related from their similar features. While the overall effect of the painting was well executed, something about it felt off to him.

"What do you think of this painting, Lady Eleanor?" He indicated the portrait.

"Lovely, just lovely."

"I quite agree. But what do you think of the composition? Do you care for the dark background when the subjects are so fair?"

Lady Eleanor looked a bit perplexed, but gamely studied the picture again. After several moments, her brow cleared. "Well, one thing I'm sure of is that I should not be caught dead wearing a shawl that color of green with a blue gown."

Jacob smiled. He wasn't disappointed, per se, in Lady Eleanor's response. In fact, he wasn't sure what he'd been hoping for when he asked her opinion, just that he thought—

"Her head is crooked," Miss Aston blurted out.

Turning to her in surprise, Jacob raised his brows questioningly.

Miss Aston's cheeks pinkened and she refused to meet his eyes, focusing instead on the painting. "Look at her neck—the lady on the right. There is no way a woman can hold her neck at that angle and yet tilt her head as the artist has shown."

Both Jacob and Lady Eleanor leaned forward to inspect the painting closer. She was right, Jacob decided.

"And the other lady's hand. Why, she's wearing a glove on the fore hand, but look at the one on her sister's shoulder. It is bare! What artist forgets that he's put a glove on one hand and leaves the other bare?"

"Perhaps she was caught in the act of removing her

gloves," Jacob said, though he was in truth a little surprised he hadn't noticed that fact.

The gaze Miss Aston shot him was withering. "And paused to pose for a portrait?"

Something about Miss Aston's rather superior attitude got under his skin. Returning his gaze to the painting, he couldn't help but comment, "The artist has done a marvelous job on the ladies' form." Out of the corner of his eyes, he saw Miss Aston look at him and knew that she could tell just where he was looking. The lady on the right—she of the crooked head—was wearing a white gown of the current high-waisted style. But whereas her sister's gown had a modest neckline, the crooked-headed lady's gown was rather shockingly low. It's straight line appeared to be edged with flat lace which, were it an actual dress, would have barely covered the lady's nipples. A full third of her breasts was evident above the neckline.

Miss Aston made a sound that might have been a "harrumph," were it louder. Jacob glanced back at her and found his gaze drawn to her own bosom. Though she was covered from neck to knee with a burgundy pelisse, the coat was well-fitted and displayed Miss Aston's not inconsiderable curves. The pelisse was so well fitted, in fact, that he could tell when she took a deep breath. Glancing up to her face, he realized that the inhale was rather a gulp of shock, or perhaps anger at his unquestionably rude perusal. Her brows drew together and her mouth nearly disappeared as she compressed her lips together. A bright flush of color stained her cheeks. Rather embarrassed to be caught behaving so ungentlemanly, he offered a half-smile of apology. She did not seem appeased.

Transferring his gaze back to Lady Eleanor, he found her looking rather bored. Feeling his gaze upon her, she immediately brightened, casting him a pleasant smile.

"Shall we continue on?" he asked.

"Oh, let's," Lady Eleanor said. "Although I find myself a bit parched."

No gentleman worth his salt allowed a lady to utter

such a statement without immediately seeking to rectify the situation and Jacob quickly established that there was an ice shop just down the way. Seating the ladies at a table by the front window, he ordered a variety of flavors. Some were quite good, like the lemon—one could hardly go wrong with a lemon ice, after all. Others were not as appealing. The fig flavor rather reminded Jacob of the syrup his nurse used to dose him with as a child when she'd decided he'd eaten something that would interfere with his digestion.

To his surprise, Lady Eleanor would only taste the lemon and strawberry ices. She declared herself quite content with the usual flavors of ice and saw no need to sample the lavender or bergamot. She absolutely wouldn't consider the cardamom ice.

"Oh give it here," Miss Aston said shortly, after he had tried half a dozen times to get Lady Eleanor to experiment. He noticed she had sampled each ice, though had not offered an opinion on any of them.

She took the small silver spoon and the beautifully painted dish of cardamom ice. Jacob found himself watching avidly as she spooned a dollop into her mouth, drawing the spoon slowly from between her lips, which, he was discomfited to note, were rather pink from eating the cold ices.

She unobtrusively licked the corner of her mouth—an action that caused a feeling not unlike a static shock somewhere at the base of his belly.

"Well?" he asked when she remained silent.

She simply lifted her eyebrows at him. "Well what?"

"Is it good?"

Miss Aston paused to consider. "I would describe it as pungent."

Lady Eleanor laughed, a delicate tinkling sound. "Is that a good thing?"

Miss Aston tilted her head to the side and said nothing.

Intrigued, Jacob caught up the spoon and took a healthy bite. He immediately wished he had not. Perhaps the confectioner had mistaken the recipe this morning. Perhaps the cardamom was rancid. Perhaps cardamom ice should never have been invented. Either way, Jacob manfully struggled to swallow the spoonful. He then glared rather pointedly at Miss Aston while thrusting the full cup at a passing waiter.

"Pungent is all you can think of to describe that?"

"But what does it mean?" Lady Eleanor asked.

Miss Aston turned blithely from Jacob's glare and said to her friend, "Overpowering. Too strong. Rather caustic, in my opinion."

"Rather," Jacob said sourly.

"And that is why I stick to lemon and strawberry ices," Lady Eleanor said smugly. "They are never pungent."

"Ah, but what if it had been wonderful?" Miss Aston asked and Jacob was startled to hear a note of longing in her voice. "It might have just as easily been the perfect flavor for ice and you would have never known."

"But it wasn't, was it?" Lady Eleanor protested with a laugh.

"No," Miss Aston agreed with a sigh. "But it might have been."

Two things struck Jacob: one, Lady Eleanor would make a perfectly safe wife. She had none of the annoying quirks the other ladies on his list possessed. She was perfectly beautiful, perfectly bred, and perfectly predictable. Second, Miss Aston had spoken of more than just ice when she spoke of trying new things and finding them wonderful. How he knew that, he had no idea, but something in her tone of voice, or perhaps the way she sighed told him that she was looking for something...special. What that meant, he had even less of an idea.

At that moment, Miss Aston glanced at him and caught him staring, mouth agape, no doubt. Jacob sat back and turned his attention to Lady Eleanor, asking her if she were attending Lord and Lady Price's annual musicale the next evening.

"Is it time for that already?" Lady Eleanor asked. "I vow it seems to come earlier and earlier each year."

"Well, fear not, Lady Eleanor, next year it will seem later."

"Oh?" she asked with an adorable little crinkle to her forehead. Miss Aston, he noticed, was thriftily polishing off the bergamot ice.

"Indeed. It is the leap year, you see. So you'll have a whole extra day to wait for the Price musicale."

"Leap year? Oh yes! An extra day is added to—which month is it that has twenty-eight days?" This was directed to Miss Aston.

Looking up from the last spoonful of her ice, Miss Aston smiled sweetly and said, "They all do, dear." Jacob had to choke down his laughter, not just at Miss Aston's deadpan delivery, but also at Lady Eleanor's complete befuddlement.

"But I take your point. You are thinking of February. Every fourth year, it has a twenty-ninth day."

"How utterly ridiculous. Why should it do that? Isn't it difficult enough to remember that it is a short month—it is the short month isn't it?"

"It is," Miss Aston replied patiently and before Jacob could explain the reason for the extra day, the brusque young lady went on to instruct her friend on the rotation of the earth and what would happen if the calendar were not corrected every so often. It was enough to make a man feel positively superfluous.

When Miss Aston had concluded her lecture, Lady Eleanor blinked several times and said, "I had no idea!"

Determined to regain control of the conversation, Jacob said, "If you find that interesting, you may be interested in a lecture the Royal Astronomical Society is presenting next week. I understand they will have a model of the solar system and will be demonstrating just how the planets orbit. I should be happy to escort you, if you like."

Lady Eleanor laughed her delightful tinkling laugh and laid her fingertips gently on his forearm. "Good heavens, Lord Worthing. I dare say such a lecture would be lost on me. I scarcely understood one word in ten that Juliette just said and she knows how to explain things to me! But I'm sure she should simply love a Royal Astronomical lecture."

Jacob felt a bit poleaxed. "I shall of course escort Miss Aston if she cares to attend." He heard the reluctance in his voice and inwardly cringed. He hadn't meant to make the offer in such an ungentlemanly fashion, but the point had been to spend time with Lady Eleanor, not her dour friend. Valiantly trying to recover from his faux pas, he smiled in what he hoped was an encouraging manner at Miss Aston.

The animation, which had made her face so vivid as she described the Julian calendar to Lady Eleanor, had been wiped from her expression like the chalk listings of today's ice flavors from the chalkboard. Though she appeared to be looking at him, he suspected she was staring at a point just past his shoulder as she said flatly, "No, thank you."

No, thank you? He didn't know why he was perturbed. He should be delighted to be off the hook. Instead, he was incensed that she should so cavalierly refuse him. If his offer had been made in a less-than-gentlemanly manner, her refusal was even more unladylike!

Swallowing down his ire—he still found it inconceivable that this woman had the power to elicit anything as strong as ire—he turned back to Lady Eleanor and asked if she wished to visit any other shops today.

"I should very much like to visit all of the shops today, but I did promise Mama that I would be home in time for tea. She is hosting Lady Liverpool. I suspect we just have time to finish our ices before we must leave."

Jacob managed to ignore the irritating Miss Aston for the rest of their repast, and in fact, said very little to her beyond the basic niceties throughout their walk to the entryway of the arcade where the ladies were gathered by Lady Eleanor's coach.

He bowed over Lady Eleanor's hand, assured her he would see her the next night at the Price musicale, and nodded curtly to Miss Aston before stepping back and allowing the footman to close the coach door.

"Every month has twenty-eight days, indeed," he muttered as he watched the coach depart.

Chapter Five

The first half of the Price musicale was a lively affair. Eight musicians—several of them professional—took turns singing and playing singly and in small groups. There were Irish airs, country dance songs, a piece by Haydn, and several other songs Juliette had never heard before. When the musicians paused to take refreshments and allow the audience to move about a bit, Juliette sighed happily.

"Wasn't it lovely?" She asked Eleanor. "I wish I could play as well as they."

"Nonsense," Eleanor replied, fanning herself with the new silk fan she'd acquired the day before. "For if you played as well as these musicians, you'd forever be asked to play at various parties and then you'd never get to dance. It is far better to dance than not."

Juliette laughed. "Eleanor, I cannot recall a single formal ball or simple house party in which you did not dance every dance. You have no basis for comparison."

"I didn't need to try cardamom-flavored ice to know I wouldn't like it, either," Eleanor retorted cheerfully. "I know what I like and I know what I know. And I know that dancing with a handsome young man is better than sitting and playing dance music with a nearsighted old man."

"Spoken like one who has had nothing but handsome young men to dance with. Not all of us are so lucky," Juliette said archly.

Eleanor made a shooing gesture with her gloved hand. "They have simply not discovered you yet. When they do, you will have nothing but handsome young men filling your dance card."

Juliette smiled at her friend's serious tone. This was her third year in Society and if the men of the ton had not discovered her by now, chances were likely that they never would. She loved that Eleanor was convinced it was all simply a misunderstanding, her lack of popularity, that is. She liked to think it was because Eleanor saw the true Juliette and found her character beautiful while the rest of society simply judged her on her external qualities. She'd tried to explain to Eleanor that handsome young men simply did not see her, but her friend refused to believe it. She'd also tried to explain that she couldn't possibly care for a man who had previously dismissed her out of hand without coming to know her and therefore, it didn't matter if the men of the ton suddenly woke up one day. This bit of reasoning, however, was completely lost on Eleanor.

"Ah, there he is," Eleanor said under her breath. She poked Juliette in the ribs. "Sit up straight."

"I was," Juliette hissed back, but she pulled her shoulders back and lifted her chin defensively. "Who's here?" she asked, expecting Eleanor to announce Mr. Pickering.

Mr. Pickering may have asked for permission to court her after one short meeting when they hardly knew each other, but he was now making up for this deficit by seeking her out at every opportunity. Juliette knew she should be glad of it; if she were to determine that they were ill suited, she would need to get to know him better. He was a nice man. He was, she reminded herself. They just generally ran out of things to talk about after ten or fifteen minutes. Pasting a smile on her face, she turned to welcome her suitor.

"Oh!" she exclaimed, finding herself looking at a trim waistcoat. Mr. Pickering's waistcoat, well tailored though it was, contained a slight paunch. Raising her gaze, she found herself the recipient of an amused smile.

"Lady Eleanor, Miss Aston," Lord Worthing said, executing a gentlemanly bow. "You were expecting someone else?"

Juliette opened her mouth to answer in the affirmative

but Eleanor uncharacteristically cut her off. "Not at all, my lord. We are delighted to see you. Won't you join us for the second act? There are chairs aplenty," she said, gesturing at the empty row next to Juliette.

"I thank you."

Juliette felt incredibly awkward, positioned as she was between Eleanor and Lord Worthing. She tried to sit back in her chair so as not to block their conversation. They spoke of their chance meeting the day before and Lord Worthing dutifully complimented Eleanor's new fan. She asked him if he'd recovered from his trial of cardamom ice. Juliette felt as if she were watching a tennis match as the conversation was batted back and forth. She should participate, she knew she should. But she'd always been awful at finding new ways to talk about things that had already been discussed. Perhaps that was why she and Mr. Pickering ran out of dialogue so quickly.

"Don't you agree Juliette?"

Juliette jerked in her seat, startled. She hadn't realized she'd been staring aimlessly.

"I—I'm not sure."

Eleanor laughed that perfect little tinkling laugh that made men's heads turn, made them want to stand beside her and say anything to make her laugh again.

"Were you woolgathering, dear?"

"Perhaps our discussion is not stimulating enough to keep your attention," Lord Worthing said. Juliette looked at him sharply. Though his tone had been neutral, she could see the challenge in his eyes, the annoying man.

Unable to stop herself, she said, "On the contrary, I find whatever Lady Eleanor has to say very interesting."

A slight twitch of his left eyebrow was the only sign he took her pointed meaning.

"If you will excuse me," Eleanor said, standing. "I will return momentarily. I have a taste for one of Lady Price's shortbread biscuits."

Lord Worthing, who had stood immediately, said, "You

must allow me to fetch you a plate, Lady Eleanor."

"Oh! No. That is, I have another stop to make first." She blushed delicately.

"In that case, shall I go with you?" Juliette asked, starting to gather her wrap.

"Good heavens, no! You should save our seats. Someone may claim them and they are the best seats in the house." With that, she scooted down the row and hastened out the room.

Juliette frowned after her friend. Ladies never went to the retiring room alone. It was an unwritten cardinal rule. Juliette was fairly certain she couldn't find it if she weren't in the company of one of her friends. Beside her, Lord Worthing sat back down. An uncomfortable silence settled between them. Forcing herself to make conversation if for no other reason than that Eleanor seemed to like the man, she took a deep breath.

"Did you only just arrive or did you see the first set?"

"I saw some of the first set."

Juliette unclenched her jaw. "And did you enjoy it?"

"It was tolerable."

"Tolerable? Surely it warranted rosier acclaim than tolerable."

"That was simply my opinion. Surely a man is still allowed his own opinion on an amateur musical event." His tone was positively smug.

Juliette frowned. "They're not all amateurs. And besides, could you do better?"

"At what?"

She gestured at the silent instruments in the cleared stage area. "At any of it?"

"Are you asking if I perform? Not since I was twelve."

"Then perhaps you should not be so quick to judge."

Lord Worthing frowned at her. "I was not judging."

"You were! You said the playing was tolerable."

He laughed shortly. "Yes tolerable; fairly good, acceptable."

Juliette shrugged one shoulder. It was terribly unladylike but if there was a man she had no interest in impressing, she decided it would be Lord Worthing.

"So you're saying," he said incredulously. "That since I could do no better, I should rave about a performance that, while fairly good, was certainly not the best I've heard."

"Well, not—"

"By which logic I should, since I've no idea how to cook, be happy with runny eggs and burnt biscuits from my cook?"

"Of course—"

"Or since I cannot sew, I should accept an ill-fitting coat from my tailor?"

Juliette dropped her gaze to her tightly clenched hands.

"No?" Lord Worthing said.

"Please forget I said anything," Juliette tightly, feeling horribly foolish. "I did not mean to argue with you. I...I'm not feeling myself tonight." That was certainly true, she reflected, though it had nothing to do with feeling ill. This dratted man was too handsome by half and the fact that she knew he would never pass two words with her unless Eleanor had all but demanded it was like a burr in her slipper that she could do nothing about. It did not reflect well on her, however, that she let her own insecurities cause her to treat him so ill. She tried to be better than that.

Forcing herself to meet his gaze, she saw surprise on his face. "Of course, Miss Aston. I am so sorry you are ill. Shall I fetch your chaperone?"

She shook her head. "Not at all. Perhaps we could simply change the topic."

He dipped his head slightly. "Certainly. Tell me Miss Aston, how do you like cardamom ice?"

A surprised laugh escaped her and she quickly covered her mouth with a gloved hand. "I find it rather pungent, my lord, but otherwise quite refreshing."

"Indeed. I shall forever use that word as a euphemism for something detestable."

Juliette could not keep the smile from her lips. "It is a rather good word."

"Because it makes whatever you're describing sound interesting when it truth it is anything but?"

"Nonplussed is a similar word."

Lord Worthing frowned. "I don't take your meaning."

"Well it sounds like it should mean unconcerned or nonchalant, don't you think? When if fact it means something like perplexed, doesn't it?"

Lord Worthing gave her a sideways glance. "Do you do this often, Miss Aston?"

Instantly wary, Juliette asked, "Do what?"

"Sit around analyzing words and then looking for opportunities to toss them out, leaving your audience...er...nonplussed?"

She felt her cheeks warm. He no doubt thought her a bluestocking—one more reason in his book she was a wallflower. "I enjoy reading," she admitted woodenly.

"Tell me, do you routinely flummox Lady Eleanor?"

"What do you mean?" Juliette thought if her back straightened any more, she might pop a stitch in her gown or at the very least, a corset string.

"I gather Lady Eleanor does not use words such as 'pungent,' and 'nonplussed.'"

"Lady Eleanor is very intelligent. You abuse her to think otherwise."

"I do no such thing," Lord Worthing said haughtily. "I find Lady Eleanor to be the very model of gentility and decorum. In fact, I find her to be the perfect lady, and I assure you, I have judged her fellow debutantes thoroughly this Season."

Did the man mean to imply he was in love with Eleanor? Oh, but he was an ass! Let Eleanor marry well, but let him not be an ass! Juliette knew she should remain silent. She knew the man was no doubt passing the time by baiting her while he waited for Eleanor to return. And where was Eleanor? Surely she should have returned by now. She craned her neck but found no sight of her friend. Turning back to Lord Worthing, she found his smug expression entirely untenable.

"Do you mean to imply, Lord Worthing, that you care for Lady Eleanor? That you, perhaps intend to...offer for her?"

Worthing's eyes narrowed. "She would make an admirable countess," he said carefully.

"But do you love her?"

"Why aren't you a silly chit? Lady Eleanor and I have much in common. Love is not some Byronesque poem, Miss Aston. It develops out of a solid foundation of friendship. I am sure as Lady Eleanor matures, she and I could cultivate a true affinity for one another. Should I make her an offer of marriage," he finished precisely.

Juliette could not believe Worthing's gall. Was a man's arrogance in direct proportion to his handsomeness? It could be the only answer, for the dratted man made her heart flutter ridiculously even as she wanted to scratch his eyes out. Taking a deep breath, she willed herself to calm.

"Lady Eleanor deserves a man who loves her as she is, for she is perfect as she is. She deserves a man who will continue to love her as she grows and changes, whatever direction it takes her. He should not expect her to grow—good heavens! Like a topiary—into the shape he wishes to mold her."

"You are quite the champion of Lady Eleanor," Worthing said quietly.

"She is my very dearest friend and I like her just the way she is." She was spared having to say more by the lady in question's arrival.

"Look who found me at the refreshments table!" she exclaimed.

Juliette turned to encounter Mr. Pickering's rounded waistcoat and beaming countenance.

"Why Juliette," Eleanor said. "You're flushed. Has Lord Worthing been flirting with you?"

"No!" Juliette and Worthing burst out in unison.

"That is," Juliette continued in a calmer tone of voice.

"It's simply a bit warm in here, don't you agree?"

"Well actually, I was feeling chilled," Eleanor remarked, tugging her silk shawl more closely around her delicate shoulders.

"I've brought punch!" Mr. Pickering declared happily, offering it with a slight flourish that spilled a few drops over the rim. Juliette took the cup, grateful for the distraction.

"Why don't you sit here, Eleanor," she said, starting to rise from her chair next to Lord Worthing.

"Oh no, you're already comfortable. I shall sit right here with Mr. Pickering between us."

Juliette cast a glance at Lord Worthing, but his expression was inscrutable. She rather hoped he was brokenhearted, but she also hoped he didn't much care where Eleanor sat. If he decided to pursue her friend, Juliette had no doubt he would be successful. If such a man pursued *her*—Juliette shook her head slightly to dislodge the thought. A man like Worthing would never, *never*, pursue a woman like her. Now that she knew a little about him, she felt she could honestly say she was glad. Truthfully. Mostly truthfully. Desperate to turn her attention from the man on her right, she angled her body to the left and asked Mr. Pickering if he was enjoying the evening.

"Oh splendid! Splendid. The musicians are positively wonderful, wouldn't you agree?"

Juliette was acutely conscious of Lord Worthing's presence and she knew without a shadow of a doubt that he was listening to her conversation. She wanted to agree as effusively as Mr. Pickering had, she really did. But some perverse twist of her character would only allow her to say, "I found them rather good."

"Rather good? Oh my dear, they are better than good. Why I would hazard that tonight is the finest musicale I've attended."

Juliette could practically feel Lord Worthing's amusement. Hastily changing the subject, she asked after his mother, who she had met for the first time a few days before.

Mr. Pickering happily began recounting his mother's every thought on their visit as well as what she thought about politicians, this year's crop of debutantes, and the lack of taste in today's fashions. Mrs. Pickering, Juliette determined, was an opinionated harridan, though her son seemed to hold her in the highest esteem.

Finally the musicians resumed their places and the second portion of the concert began. Juliette resolutely refused to let Lord Worthing's earlier remarks cloud her enjoyment of the music, but she felt a sense of dissatisfaction as she sat. Surely the musicians were talented and the music was delightful. Why should she not be enjoying this act as much as the first? The answer came to her quite suddenly: Lord Worthing's presence.

She felt his coat sleeve brush her elbow as he moved. She was sure she could smell the clean citrus scent of his shaving soap, which was distinct from Mr. Pickering's much stronger perfumed scent. Beyond that, however, was a simple awareness of him that quite distracted her from giving her full attention to the concert.

She all but jumped in her seat when she felt him lean closer and he whispered in her ear, "I take it back. They are very good."

She turned to face him and found he had not leaned back in his chair. As a result, his face was mere inches from her own. She could see the dark brown of his irises distinct from the inky black of his pupils. She could make out faint laugh lines at the corners of his eyes. And there were three—no, four —gray hairs at his left temple.

She quickly turned back to the musicians, but she could scarcely hear them over the pounding of her heart in her ears. Concentrate! she sternly told herself. After several moments, her heart rate calmed and she resolutely kept her eyes forward and her attention on the music.

What an annoyingly perplexing man he was, she thought. Why, she wouldn't be surprised if he'd made that comment about the musicians earlier just to needle her, though why he would care about her opinion one way or the other was a complete mystery. No doubt, he was so perversely accustomed to every woman fawning over his every word that when he encountered someone with the backbone to say what she thought, he felt the need to attack.

The musicians *were* quite good, she decided.

At the conclusion of the entertainment, Juliette clapped as loudly as her gloved hands would allow. She pointedly turned to Mr. Pickering to ask his opinion of the second set but found him bent over in his chair.

"Mr. Pickering, are you alright?"

"What, what? Oh yes, just dropped a biscuit on the floor," he said, straightening. His face was flushed and his hair mussed as he presented the errant biscuit as if it were a trophy.

"Waste not, want not, my nanny always said," he said and popped the tidbit in his mouth.

Juliette felt her gorge rise and quickly averted her head. Surely the man was not so thrifty that he felt the need to eat a biscuit off a floor that had been trampled by at least eighty people this very night? To her right, Lord Worthing caught her gaze and she saw he was manfully trying to smother a laugh. She scowled at him and pointedly turned back to Mr. Pickering.

"Mrs. Smithsonly has awoken," Eleanor said, leaning forward so Juliette could hear her.

Juliette looked across the room to the farthest aisle of chairs. True to form, her Aunt Constance had chosen a seat in the dimmest, quietest corner of the room.

"So she has. I suppose we will be making our departure," Juliette replied and stood to leave.

Mr. Pickering and Lord Worthing quickly rose to their feet. Before Mr. Pickering could say a word, Lord Worthing captured her attention.

"Now that is a perfect chaperone," he murmured in a voice that required she lean slightly toward him to hear.

"I beg your pardon?"

"A chaperone that falls asleep at every event, allowing her charge free reign to…explore."

"She doesn't fall asleep at every event," Juliette hissed, though she'd had the same thought before, followed by the realization that such a chaperone was rather wasted on her.

"No?" She couldn't help but notice that the right corner of his mouth quirked up in conjunction with his lifted eyebrows. For some reason, she felt an answering smile tug at her lips.

"Not *every* event. She certainly manages to stay awake when there's a banquet."

"And a goodly supply of sherry, no doubt."

Juliette turned her surprised laugh into a cough. The man was incorrigible.

"Yes, well, sadly for you, Lady Eleanor's mother is much more wakeful and vigilant. You shall have to be on your best behavior to impress her of your worth for her daughter."

"And the devoted best friend, too, I would hazard." He dipped his head to her.

"I fear you've already lost my favor for your suit," Juliette said acerbically.

"Oh dear, that won't do." Worthing's voice was a low rumble. "I shall have to work to regain your approval."

"A challenge, to be sure, as you never had it to begin with."

"Say it is not so!" he exclaimed mockingly. "How did I begin in the red? Surely my manners were adequate, my grooming impeccable when first we met? Tell me, had someone poisoned you to me beforehand?"

It was all Juliette could do not to inform him that his immediate dismissal of her when Eleanor had introduced them had only confirmed her suspicion that he was an overindulged young nobleman; spoiled by the abundance of beautiful debutants who would hang on his every word, who would never challenge him, and who would never require he talk to them about anything deeper than a hand of whist.

But to admit as much would be tantamount to admitting time spent on her analysis of the men of the ton and her own shortfalls and *that* she would not do.

Instead, she lifted one shoulder delicately. "I fear I took your reading within moments of our first meeting."

"And found me..." His voice dropped even lower. She could not tell if he were offended or amused.

She scrambled for a way to tell him just what she thought without revealing her own insecurities. "I deemed you to be just like most men of your stature: interested in a lady solely for her beauty, her wealth, and her bloodlines and with no regard to what makes her truly valuable."

His voice was tight when he asked, "And what makes a lady valuable?"

Juliette licked her lips nervously. She wished she'd not begun this conversation. "Why, what's in her heart, in her mind."

"And you 'deemed' this about my character in what, two minutes of inane ballroom chat?" There was no doubt about it. He was angry.

Juliette lifted her chin, though she found she couldn't look him directly in the eye. "We have met many men in the past three seasons, my lord."

"Oh and I'm to be judged by their failings, am I?"

A charged silence fell and Juliette could hear Eleanor laugh at something Mr. Pickering said. She wondered what on earth they'd found to discuss, much less what delighted her friend to laugh aloud.

"Tell me, my lord. What is it about Lady Eleanor that you admire most?"

"Well she's—" he stopped abruptly and Juliette knew a moment of vindication.

"Yes, yes, it's well established that Lady Eleanor is beautiful. But what makes you consider her for the truly honorable position as the future Countess of Beverly?"

Worthing's mouth was a flat line as he looked down his

nose at her. Were her own blood not so fired up, she had no doubt she'd feel quite intimidated.

"I find her to be truly kind. She has a gentle spirit which is evident even in our brief acquaintance."

Juliette opened her mouth to argue—what she was going to say, she wasn't sure—but he interrupted her.

"And she must have the patience of a saint if she's friends with you, Miss Aston. All in all, three admirable qualities in a wife."

Juliette knew her mouth was hanging open idiotically, but she was so...so humiliated and embarrassed that she simply didn't care anymore.

Turning to Mr. Pickering, she lightly touched his forearm. "Mr. Pickering, would you be so kind as to see me to my aunt? I fear it is well past time I returned her home."

Mr. Pickering volubly agreed and Juliette was spared further conversation with Lord Worthing as they made their way through the departing crowd to Aunt Constance.

Chapter Six

Four days later when the invitation arrived from the Countess of Beverly for Juliette and Aunt Constance to attend a house party at Beverly Castle in Kent, she was tempted to toss it in the fire before her father or great aunt saw it. To be sure, it was the coveted house party of the season. Juliette had no doubt the only reason she'd been invited was because of Eleanor. In fact, she wouldn't have put it past her friend to have requested Juliette's family be included in the invitation. But the last thing Juliette wanted to do was see Lord Worthing anywhere, much less in his home environment. Beverly Castle, for heaven's sake! It was bad enough she'd replayed their last conversation over and over in her head—embellishing so she came out the victor in their battle of wits and he was left the one embarrassed. But to have to see him in his own environment where everyone already catered to him? Never!

"What have you there, Juliette?"

Startled by her great aunt's entrance into the morning room, she dropped the invitation. Drat, she'd missed her chance to burn it. A glance at the cold fireplace further squelched the possibility.

"Oh, just an invitation. I think we'll decline. We've already accepted Lady Craythorne's card party."

"Phllyddia Craythorne? She waters her sherry," Aunt Constance said dismissively as she took a seat on the settee. "Who is the invitation from?"

Juliette considered lying. For the space of five seconds, she actually considered lying to her dear Aunt Constance who'd been so kind to her since Juliette's mother had died over eight years ago. Taking a deep breath, she crossed the sun-filled room and handed the embossed card over.

Aunt Constance frowned at her niece's reluctance and took the invitation. She scanned its contents with a low, "Mmm." Looking up, she asked, "Why on earth should you wish to attend Phllyddia Craythorne's dull card party when the Countess of Beverly has invited us to a house party?"

Juliette scarcely resisted the urge to shrug and drag her toe over the carpet like a small child caught stealing cookies.

"Juliette?" Her aunt had the most imperious voice when she chose to employ it.

Juliette lifted her chin defiantly. "I don't care for Lord Worthing. Since his mother is hosting, I'm sure he'll be in attendance and I should rather not have to endure his company. Besides," she forced herself to add. "I'm sure Mr. Pickering will not be invited."

"Mr. Pickering." Aunt Constance flicked her fingers dismissively. "I wasn't aware you'd even been introduced to Jacob Wilding. How can you already dislike him?"

"I met him a fortnight past and then Lady Eleanor and I ran into him at Burlington Arcade." She paused but felt she must be truthful. "And he was at he musicale last night. He sat with Eleanor and Mr. Pickering and me for the second set."

Aunt Constance's thin white eyebrows rose astoundingly high. "Indeed? I am surprised I did not notice so many meetings."

Juliette could not keep her lips straight at that remark, but she did manage to make her smile as innocuous as possible.

Nonetheless, she saw her aunt's brows rise even closer to her hairline. "I must have been otherwise occupied. Nonetheless, this event will introduce you to the very cream of England's bachelors."

"But Aunt Constance, I've met England's bachelors." She forbore from mentioning that they had—with the exception of Mr. Pickering—largely ignored her.

"I know I need not remind you that your father has threatened this to be your last Season. If we do not find you a husband this year, you may be reduced to marrying the local vicar or Squire Ponsonby's eldest boy."

Again, Juliette bit her lip and did not remind her aunt that the vicar back home was already married and Squire Ponsonby's eldest boy was only sixteen years old. She realized her aunt was only making a point. Still, it wasn't as if she hadn't tried to attract a nice gentleman.

"There is Mr. Pickering, Aunt. He seems—"

"Theodore Pickering is a nincompoop," Aunt Constance proclaimed firmly.

"That is not fair! He is very nice." Even to her own ears, Juliette's protest sounded weak.

"Nice and a nincompoop. Do you wish to be bored to tears by the end of your honeymoon? I would wager that you and he run out of interesting conversation ten minutes after you start talking."

Juliette felt her cheeks redden. It was a thought that had occurred to her several times over the last few weeks. She had simply reassured herself that as they grew to know each other better, they would discover more things to discuss.

"Perhaps we can have a new gown made in time." Constance cast a critical eye at Juliette's white muslin—a gown the aunt herself had chosen last year. "And for the rest we can lower the necklines a bit—" She waved aside Juliette's shocked gasp.

"Desperate times call for desperate measures. I would not feel I had served your mother's memory well if I allowed you to settle for the likes of Theodore Pickering. You must stand out, Juliette. No more blending in. You've hidden for the last two seasons. It's time to blossom, my dear."

Juliette knew her mouth was open unbecomingly, so she turned to peer out the window into the small garden below, unsure if she was more shocked by her aunt's sudden interest or what she'd said. Had she truly hidden? Was that why she'd not attracted more notice? Surely not, she decided with a small shake of her head. The men of the ton were obsessed with beauty—at least their idea of beauty. The only way Juliette could have attracted the kind of notice Eleanor did was if she'd been a fabulously wealthy heiress. For if there was one quality that carried more weight in society's eye than a lady's beauty, it was the size of her dowry. While Sir Lewis had provided her with a generous settlement, it was certainly not of the size to compensate for her average looks. Juliette frowned at the flowers in the garden. And why after two seasons of dozing in the corners of ballrooms was her aunt now deciding to take bold action?

"You still have not told me why you dislike Jacob Wilding."

Turning away from the window, Juliette sorted haphazardly through the rest of the day's post. "I find him impertinent. He has all but admitted he intends to offer for Eleanor, but he will not even admit to mild affection for her. Eleanor deserves to be loved and I fear Lord Worthing is simply interested in acquiring her because she is the reigning beauty."

She felt her aunt's shrewd gaze on her, but refused to meet her eye.

"Though Eleanor Chalcroft is fond of appearing the simple henwit, I suspect she is actually very astute when it comes to men. I doubt she will allow herself to be coerced into marriage by a man who does not meet her every expectation. If ever there was a girl whose wishes were coddled to by her parents, it's that one. Are you sure you are not simply jealous?"

Juliette gasped and dropped the pile of letters. "Aunt! How could you? The man is rude and condescending! I would not be interested in him were he the last bachelor in all of England and Scotland. Why—"

"Yes, yes, I gather you don't care for him. Nonetheless, I must insist we accept this invitation. Perhaps Lord Worthing will improve upon closer inspection. I've known his mother, Eudora Wilding since she was a girl. It would surprise me greatly to find she'd raised a rude and condescending son. And if not, there are bound to be at least a dozen other bachelors in attendance."

Realizing Aunt Constance would not be swayed, Juliette took the invitation to respond with their acceptance. Her aunt pushed herself to her feet and paused a moment to surreptitiously unkink her spine. "Besides," Constance said, "Eudora does not water her sherry." And with that, the imperious woman swept out of the room.

After luncheon, Juliette sent word to Eleanor that she would be attending the Wilding party as well and asking if she would care to accompany her and Aunt Constance to order a new gown. She smiled to herself as she sealed the note, for there was not a day of the year Eleanor could not be talked into shopping. She had just sent it off with a footman when the butler announced the arrival of Mr. Pickering.

Squelching the vague feeling of resignation in the pit of her stomach, she asked that Aunt Constance be informed so she might serve as chaperone.

"Mrs. Smithsonly is already with Mr. Pickering in the front sitting room," Mr. Branson informed her.

"Ah. Well in that case, perhaps you would be so good as to arrange for—"

"Refreshments are on the way, miss."

Juliette smiled tightly. Did Branson need to be quite so efficient? It made it rather difficult to delay when the servants offered no valid excuse. Realizing the absurdity of avoiding her one suitor, Juliette made her way to the sitting room, pausing—understandably so—in the hall only once to check her hair. And straighten the stems of a few crooked flowers in the atrium arrangement.

Entering the room at a properly sedate pace, she discovered Mr. Pickering speaking quite animatedly with Aunt Constance, who, herself, wore a bit of a stunned expression.

"Juliette, dear!" her aunt exclaimed. "We were just ready

to send out a search party for you."

"Were you?" she replied innocently.

Aunt Constance's tone was quelling. "Indeed. Mr. Pickering has just been telling me all about his mother's renovations to their home in Chelsea."

"How lovely." Juliette took a seat across from Mr. Pickering.

"Mother is simply a genius at renovating homes. Why she completely redid the vicarage while the vicar was on holiday with his new bride last summer."

"I'm sure they found it a lovely gift to return to a refurbished home." Juliette hoped Mrs. Pickering had good taste.

"Well, they were a bit put out that Mother didn't ask their opinion, but that's Mother for you! She knows best!" A hearty guffaw followed this pronouncement and Juliette felt Aunt Constance's gaze on her.

Glancing at the older woman, Juliette could perfectly read her aunt's meaning: *"Do you truly mean to wed a man so firmly tied to his mother's apron strings?"*

"Of course," Mr. Pickering continued blithely. "We may be selling the house in Chelsea and moving closer in."

"Indeed?" Aunt Constance queried. "And why is that?" She still had not taken her gimlet gaze from Juliette.

"Mother says the area has taken a decided turn for the worse." He leaned forward and lowered his voice. "*Artists* have started moving in," he declared in a stage whisper.

"Oh good heavens," Aunt Constance said in a dramatic tone as she pressed a hand to her bosom. "Anything but that!" Although Juliette knew her aunt held artists in regard just a step above street sweepers, she also knew the older woman was mocking Mr. Pickering. As Juliette was quickly learning, Constance Smithsonly's penchant for sleeping through balls, parties, and musicales aside, she employed a devilish wit and she could no sooner ignore poking a pretentious person than she could keep herself awake at the theater. Juliette liked to think she'd inherited some measure of her aunt's wit. Certainly her father, though the very best man in the world, did not exhibit the same sense of humor as his female relations.

Mr. Pickering nodded enthusiastically. "We quite agree, Mrs. Smithsonly. Although our street has thus far escaped the incursion."

To stop herself from rolling her eyes, Juliette asked, "What is so dreadful about the artists moving into Chelsea? I should think their presence would add quite a lively feel to the area."

Mr. Pickering smiled in a thoroughly patronizing manner. "Oh my dear Miss Aston, I can assure you, 'lively' is the last word that comes to mind when I consider some of the reprobates who spend their hours lounging about the coffeehouses, pretending to be tormented souls."

Juliette and her aunt exchanged a brief glance.

"And are you so sure they're not?" Aunt Constance asked, leaning forward.

"Not what?" Mr. Pickering asked, pausing in his chewing of a lemon bar. The powdery sugar topping exhaled a soft cloud of white when he enunciated his W and Juliette couldn't help but wonder just how many of the sweet-tart treats he'd already eaten. They were quite her favorite and she'd hoped to have some left to enjoy with her breakfast the next day. She was pulled from her thoughts of desserts by Aunt Constance.

"Are you quite certain they are not tormented souls? I mean, why else would a young man engage in the pursuit or poetry or, good heavens, painting? Surely the mind must lament when it is called to such endeavors."

Mr. Pickering blinked several times. "I can't see as how I've considered the matter in that way. I shall ask dear Mama and see if she concurs."

"Haven't you your own thoughts on the subject, Mr. Pickering?" Truly, it was not fair that both she and Aunt Constance gang up on him, but the man's constant mentions of his mother and her strong opinions were beginning to worry her.

"Well, now that you mention it, I can't say as I do!" He

laughed quite heartily at his meager joke and Juliette smiled weakly.

Juliette pointedly ignored Aunt Constance's gaze and instead asked Mr. Pickering how he found the weather.

Twenty minutes later, Mr. Pickering made his correct farewells and departed.

"No," Aunt Constance said firmly once the door closed behind him.

"No, what?" Juliette searched for crumbs of lemon bars on the tray.

"I've allowed you to languish in relative obscurity these last two Seasons because I was convinced you simply needed time to find yourself and I was certain *some* decent man would recognize your worth and offer for you."

Juliette felt her face redden with embarrassment. She'd always thought Aunt Constance was rather oblivious to her social failings.

"But now I see that I shall have to step into the breach if I'm to see you suitably wed before your father takes you back to rusticate in the country for good. I cannot sit back and allow that nincompoop to wait for his mother to tell him to offer for you!" She stood and strode toward the door with the gait of a woman ten years her junior.

"Come, Juliette." Aunt Constance's imperious tone allowed no argument. "It is time to visit the modiste. One must be suitably armed when preparing for battle and no captain of mine will be outgunned."

Chapter Seven

Jacob Wilding sprinted up the back stairs of Beverly Castle, tugging on his cravat as he climbed to his room on the third floor. He was late—very late—to join his mother in greeting guests to the house party, but the day was so fine, he'd found himself loath to cut short his morning ride. His horse was full of barely restrained energy; the weather was spectacular with only a few brilliant white clouds to break the endless deep blue of the sky. The sun shone hotly on his bare head and the air was redolent with the sweet smell of fresh cut grass and rich, fecund soil.

Now he was going to owe his mother an apology for he'd assured her he would be back in time to join her in welcoming the arriving guests. She would forgive him easily, of course, she always did, but he did hate to break his word, especially toward his mother.

After a hasty wash and change, he bolted for the stairs again, smoothing his still damp hair into place, ignoring the pleas from his valet that his boots needed a final buffing. He leapt several stairs at a time until he reached the huge main staircase that led down into Beverly Castle's great entrance hall. Assuming a sedate pose, he continued down the stairs, pausing when he saw his mother warmly welcoming Juliette Aston. With a mental groan, he ducked behind a huge fern in a marble urn that sat atop the banister of the first landing. He immediately cursed himself for acting like a fool. The chit was harmless enough. Hell, she was even rather amusing. After their last conversation at the musicale, he'd found himself paying attention to particularly interesting words like "perambulate," and "erinaceous." But she was also rather annoying. She seemed to suspect him of pursuing Lady Eleanor on a whim or at least with no regard for anything deeper than the lady's beauty and popularity. Jacob was self-aware enough to recognize that this last was at least partly true and that he had no desire to admit as much to Miss Aston. He had no doubt she would scorch his ears with her insistence that Lady Eleanor deserved a paragon of a man who would worship her unconditionally and in advance of marriage.

A footman rushed by him carrying a portmanteau and Jacob affected an interest in his left boot, as if he wasn't satisfied with the fit of it, until the footman made his way up to the next level. Very well, if he was a bloody coward for not wanting to run into Miss Aston and her rapier sharp tongue, so be it. He was sure she'd cut her teeth on worthier men than he. And he was sure he'd have to spend at least some time in her company this week, considering the many social events his mother had scheduled.

Peering between the airy fronds of the fern, he saw that Miss Aston and her companion—oh, it was Lady Eleanor—were being ushered onto the back veranda to partake of refreshments while their chaperones began to make their way toward the stairs, no doubt to rest.

Refusing to be caught hiding behind a fern by the two older women, Jacob made his way down the stairs, meeting the ladies at the last step.

"Lady Chalcroft, welcome to Beverly Castle." He executed a respectful bow to his potential mother-in-law.

"Lord Worthing." Lady Chalcroft's voice was pleasant, her expression neutral. If she had any suspicion on why her family had been invited to the house party, she hid it with the expertise of a veteran card player. "Allow me to present Mrs. Smithsonly. She is the aunt of Sir Lewis Aston."

Jacob promptly bowed over Mrs. Smithsonly's hand, aware that she was Miss Aston's perennially napping chaperone, and apparently, great-aunt. He straightened to find Mrs. Smithsonly evaluating him with a keen speculative glance. The thought occurred to him that if he were to liken Lady Chalcroft to a seasoned card player, he would account Mrs. Smithsonly a hardened battle general surveying a field to be taken. He felt a bit as if someone had taken sight of him down the barrel of a rifle.

"We were on our way to rest in our rooms." Mrs. Smithsonly shot him a pointed glance. "But the young ladies await you on the back veranda."

He had his marching orders, he thought with a wry smile.

Crossing the wide foyer, he joined his mother near the front door, which stood wide open allowing guests and the warm balmy air to enter.

"Were you feeling ill, dear?" Lady Eudora Wilding asked. She glanced sideways at him and Jacob couldn't contain his smile. She'd used the same gentle remonstrance when he'd been a rather wild boy, returning home late for supper and covered in mud.

"Er, yes," he said, just to test her.

"Hmm." She squinted against the bright sunlight streaming in through the open front doors. "Spring fever, no doubt. And did the ride help?"

He coughed to cover his laugh. "Quite."

"Good, good. Since you're recovered, perhaps you'd be so good as to see to the younger guests on the back veranda."

"I thought you'd wanted me to greet the guests with you."

"Yes, but since this group should mark our last arrivals today, you may take over the hosting duties out back."

"Of course, mother." He bowed and turned to go but his mother's voice stopped him.

"Oh and Jacob, I met Miss Aston. Lovely girl. So fresh and genuine. I quite approve."

Jacob froze and cast a frown at his mother. "I beg your

pardon?"

"That's why you asked me to include her in the invitation, is it not? So that I might meet her?"

Clearing his throat, he waited while another footman rushed past to unload the new arrival's luggage.

"Well actually, I asked you to include her to make Lady Eleanor more comfortable. They are quite close, you see."

"Lady Eleanor? Chalcroft, you mean?"

Jacob inclined his head in acknowledgement.

"Oh," was his mother's only reply. Jacob was surprised his father hadn't told her.

She studied him for a long moment and Jacob couldn't help the feeling that she was disappointed. But Miss Aston? What on earth did his mother see in her to approve of? Especially with Lady Eleanor right next to her for comparison?

"Well, they are both on the back veranda. Please make sure everyone is mingling and not breaking off into little cliques right away."

Jacob bowed again, but his mother had already turned to greet her late-arriving guests.

Outside, he paused to allow his eyes to adjust to the brightness. Once he could make out the faces of the guests, he realized he was too late to fulfill his mother's request. The matrons had already decamped to the shaded tables, the married men seemed to be making their way to the stables, and the debutants were in several small groups, surrounded by young bachelors. Jacob scanned the small groups and found Lady Eleanor surrounded by the largest group of gentlemen. No surprise there, he rationalized, as she was clearly this Season's beauty. He circulated through the other groups, welcoming his guests and making small talk. As he made his way closer to Lady Eleanor's group, he couldn't help but notice Miss Aston stood a bit apart from her friend, as if Lady Eleanor's eager admirers had slowly pushed her out of the way. Finding himself in the company of a pair of matrons who required no conversational input from him besides an encouraging smile, he studied Miss Aston, noting that, while she rarely participated in the lively conversation surrounding her friend, she frequently lifted her eyebrows or bit back a laugh at one of the no doubt outrageous remarks made to impress the gorgeous Lady Eleanor.

He watched a startled expression overtake Lady Eleanor and saw her glance anxiously about. Miss Aston made a point of making herself visible to her friend and Lady Eleanor's face visibly relaxed, a winning smile replacing the worry as she turned back to her admirers. Jacob frowned as he contemplated the scene. Was Lady Eleanor worried her friend would be excluded from the conversation? The two girls were clearly very close. But no, the look on Lady Eleanor's face had been one more of fear rather than concern.

He bowed to the two matrons who scarcely acknowledged his goodbye as they chatted animatedly. Working his way behind Lady Eleanor's group, he saw Miss Aston turn her attention to the vista before her.

"On a clear day like today, you can see for miles," he said, stopping just to her right.

She didn't turn to look at him. "It's the most beautiful place I've ever seen." Her voice held a note of awe that surprised Jacob. He was so used to hearing her speak only in acerbic tones to him. Following her gaze, he couldn't help agreeing with her. Beverly Castle was situated at the top of a large, sloping hill. Shallow steps led from the veranda down into the formal gardens with their manicured flowers and precisely groomed paths. From his vantage, however, Jacob could see where the formal gardens blended into the less cultivated nature paths his great-grandfather had designed. Even beyond that, the rich, rolling countryside and wooded forests were visible. It had always given Jacob the impression that Beverly Castle had grown from the land, pushing its way up out of the wilderness.

"It's like the house is the center of civilization and the further you get from it, the more it melds into its wild origins."

Startled that Miss Aston had the same interpretation—if the opposite way of looking at it—he turned to her with a smile.

"I'm glad you like it," he said sincerely. She didn't turn away from the view, just nodded her head absently. He paused. "Your journey was tolerable, I trust?"

"Hmm?" Miss Aston finally faced him, a small frown marring her forehead. "Oh yes, of course."

"No trouble with the roads? We had a rather wetter than usual spring. There were some days the road between High Halden and Leigh Green were impassable."

Jacob wasn't sure, but it rather looked like a glazed expression crossed Miss Aston's face. It could simply have been a squint at the brightness of the sun, but something made him suspect otherwise.

"No," she replied evenly. "The roads were lovely. The weather is lovely, too, is it not?" she asked, just when he'd about to make the same remark.

"Er, yes. Yes it is."

They fell silent, the hum of conversation behind them reminiscent of bees working over a field of wildflowers.

"I suppose I should ask after your mother's health," Miss Aston finally said.

An abbreviated laugh escaped him. "Didn't you just meet her?"

Miss Aston nodded solemnly. "I did. But it seems the polite thing to do. Ask after a parent's wellness."

Jacob felt a crooked smile pull at his mouth. Miss Aston was certainly...unusual. "Well, having left her moments after you did, I can assure you she is the picture of good health and amiable humor. But what of your chaperone? Your aunt I believe you identified her as?"

"Mrs. Constance Smithsonly. She is my father's aunt." She paused and he knew—he didn't know how, but he knew—she was loath to say her next words. "She is resting upstairs."

His crooked smile evened out into a full grin. "You don't

say."

As if seeking to squelch his humor, Miss Aston hurried to assure him that Lady Eleanor's mother was also resting after the hours spent in the carriage.

"And you, Miss Aston? Do you not feel the need to rest after an arduous journey?"

She looked askance at him. "Good heavens, no. After so many hours confined to sitting I should like nothing more than to stretch my legs with a good long walk."

Jacob gestured to the gardens below. "There are nothing but good long walks at Beverly." And then, after a moment's taut silence, he rather surprised himself by saying, "I should be happy to escort you."

He must have surprised Miss Aston as well for her brows lifted and her mouth formed a soft "O."

Seeking to remind himself—and her—that he was merely being polite, he nodded toward Lady Eleanor, still surrounded by young men. "Lady Eleanor seems to be otherwise occupied, or I should invite her as well."

Miss Aston nodded slightly and then seeming to come to herself, shook her head in negation and looked to her friend. "Thank you, my lord, but Eleanor may have need of me."

Jacob bit back a smile at the ridiculous excuse. It wasn't as if he were dying to take her for a walk. She'd no doubt spend the entire time telling him how wrong he was about, well, everything. "I would hazard a guess that Lady Eleanor's needs would be met by no less than eight men. You might even find yourself knocked aside in their fervor to fetch her some lemonade or her parasol."

He was about to tease her about acting like a spinster chaperone when he saw Lady Eleanor again freeze with a worried look on her face. She glanced frantically about until her gaze landed on Miss Aston, who, Jacob noted, smiled reassuringly and nodded slightly. Quickly turning back to Lady Eleanor, he saw her features relax and she smiled prettily, first at Miss Aston, and then back to her bevy of admirers.

Jacob frowned. There was something decidedly odd about the nonverbal exchange between the young women.

"What was that about?" he asked, his voice low.

Miss Aston started and turned to him with a suspiciously smooth countenance. "I beg your pardon, my lord?"

"Lady Eleanor seemed quite distraught for a moment before she looked to you."

"Did she? I didn't notice."

"Of course you did. You smiled at her and she seemed relieved." He was studying Miss Aston's face—which, he was disconcerted to notice, was caught in the golden warmth of the setting sun. In the slanting hazy streak of sunlight, he could not discern her eye color, only that they were light and rather heavily fringed with dark lashes that matched the rich mahogany of her hair. Her softly rounded cheeks took on the color of ripe peaches, though from the sun's rays or his rather too-long scrutiny of her, he did not know. In her white gown and softly rumpled hair, she reminded him of a Greek goddess. Realizing that he had been staring, he jerked his gaze away.

"If she appeared relieved, it was no doubt to find me engaged in conversation rather than standing alone. She is a very dear friend and my wallflower status bothers her."

"You're not a wallflower," Jacob said automatically.

Miss Aston smiled. "It's quite alright, you know. There is no shame in it. Or, should I say, I take no shame in it."

Still slightly unnerved by the way he'd been caught off guard by her sunset beauty, Jacob sought to distance himself from further conversation. "I should urge everyone inside to prepare for this evening's festivities. My mother has a light supper planned to be followed by a small dance."

Miss Aston nodded. "Of course, my lord."

Without a backward glance, he bowed shortly and began moving from group to group to inform them of the schedule.

Jacob entered the small private family sitting room at the center of his parent's suite. His mother had sent for him to meet before the supper bell rang. He braced himself for a myriad of instructions. While these usually constituted her imploring him to pay attention to a certain shy young miss or assist in keeping a gentleman away from the gaming tables, he was very much afraid that this meeting would include an inquisition on his plans to take a bride. This suspicion was further supported by the presences of his father for the pre-party meeting. The earl was dressed for dinner which surprised Jacob.

"Good evening, father. Are you sure you should be out of bed?"

"I am quite well." His sire tugged at his cravat as though his valet had snugged it too tightly about his neck and there was a hectic flush to his complexion.

"Did you read the packet I delivered? Did old Hearnshaw finally say he'd lend his vote on your bill?"

Miles Wilding gave up on trying to adjust his necktie. "Bring me a drink, son." When Jacob handed him a crystal goblet, his father took a long sip before replying. "Old fool wouldn't listen to reason. Says the time is not right to reevaluate the Corn Laws. I'll need you to approach Lords Dabney and Curtis. You're of an age to them and more likely to be able to win them to our side than I am."

"Of course," Jacob agreed. "They are both present this weekend, are they not?"

His father nodded. "Yes, I expect they will arrive tomorrow."

"Consider it done." Though Jacob hoped he had years until he would need to assume his father's seat in the House of Lords, Miles Wilding had included him in his legislative duties since Jacob came of age, assigning his son tasks each session to ensure that once his son became the Earl of Beverly, there would be no dereliction of duty. Jacob knew he would not be the statesman his father was—his own interests lay more in the estate management and the incredible new engineering marvels that were sweeping the country. But he dutifully did his research and kept up on his social obligations so that he would not let his father down.

"Excellent." His father took another drink and closed his eyes. Jacob's heart contracted painfully at how frail his normally vibrant father suddenly seemed. Before he could say anything, the earl opened his eyes and smiled. "And speaking of excellent, I understand you've taken our conversation about seeking a wife to heart. Your mother informs me you've even settled on a potential bride."

Jacob had a terrifying, sudden vision of his father announcing a betrothal and having him wed as soon as the banns could be read. "Well, I have certainly made myself open to the idea, but as to settling on one young lady—"

"Beverly, I told you no such thing!" His mother swept into the room in a rustle of satin and a soft cloud of rose oil. "I merely said Jacob had added a few names to the guest list."

"Yes, but those names were young ladies, were they not?" The earl raised his bushy grey eyebrows knowingly.

Trying to distance himself from making a commitment —good God, he'd only been considering the idea for a few weeks—Jacob said, "Well, simply to get to know them—her—better."

"Who is she?"

"Lady Eleanor Chalcroft."

"And Miss Juliette Aston," his mother added.

"I only asked that she be invited because Lady Eleanor would not come otherwise." Why did his mother insist on bringing her up?

"Lady Eleanor? I was hoping you would settle on her."

Jacob and his mother both spoke at the same time.

"I didn't say I'd settled on her."

"Let's not rush this, Beverly."

The earl rubbed his brow and Jacob stood quickly to assist him. His father shook his head, then turned his attention to his wife. "He's no longer a boy, Eudora." Pointing at Jacob, he said, "You're not a young man, you know. I was married and awaiting your arrival by the time I was your age."

Lady Chalcroft crossed the room and took the glass from her husband. "You're not supposed to be drinking spirits!" She set the glass down out of the earl's reach. "Love is not something one can rush."

While Jacob was relieved she was trying to rein his father in, the thought of falling in love was as preposterous as marrying immediately. He'd felt nothing more than a mild interest in Lady Eleanor, and she was one of the most beautiful young woman he could ever remember meeting.

"Preposterous! Pick a beautiful young woman who is well trained in the arts of being a lady and love will follow quite naturally. Why you'll be mooning over her by the wedding."

Jacob was about to interject when his mother cut in with a tone of voice that was no less cutting for its softness. "Oh really, Miles. Is that the way it works?"

Pressing his lips together to keep from laughing, Jacob looked to his. His normally equanimous sire had flushed a deep shade of maroon and seemed to have taken a great interest in adjusting his crested cufflinks.

The silence stretched on interminably and Jacob almost felt sorry for his father. Finally, the earl cleared his throat and addressed his son directly. "Let us discuss Lady Eleanor Chalcroft after we've grown to know her better, what what?"

Jacob bowed respectfully. "Certainly, my lord," he murmured, and made his quick departure.

Chapter Eight

Dinner had been a pleasantly quiet affair as many of the guests had elected to eat in their rooms while still recovering from their journey to Kent. Lady Eleanor's mother was one of the still-recovering guests and Jacob suspected Lady Eleanor would have been required to remain upstairs with her if Miss Aston's aunt, Mrs. Smithsonly, had not seen fit to join the meal and serve as chaperone.

Jacob bit back a smile as he watched the indomitable lady dine. Though she might take herself off to a corner for a nap at a musicale or ball, when excellent food was presented to her, the matron was quite animated, scarcely pausing in her consumption of the delicacies laid before her to converse with her neighbors. No, that wasn't right, he thought. Mrs. Smithsonly deftly managed to talk non-stop while eating enough to feed a grown man in his prime. Hiding a chuckle behind a wine glass, Jacob realized that lady in question ate and talked with unabashed relish. Glancing around for her charges, he saw Lady Eleanor seated across the table and several seats down from him. She was exquisite, as always. Her soft golden hair was gathered in silken ringlets at the top of her head and across her brow. Her flawless skin glowed in the soft embrace of candlelight. Her lips were pink and bowed, almost as if they awaited the chaste kiss of a respectful suitor. Soft round shoulders peeped out above the lace at her neckline almost as if they awaited a not-so-chaste kiss of a more impassioned suitor. The froth of lace at the top of her gown hid any other physical attributes Jacob might wish to peruse, but he seemed to recall that every other bit of Lady Eleanor was equally feminine and perfectly proportioned. She smiled demurely at something her dining partner said and dabbed delicately at the corner of her mouth after each bite. She was a perfect lady and would make an admirable countess. If he felt nothing but mild interest in her, it was surely more than many marriages of his society began with.

Jacob returned his attention to his plate and ate uninterrupted for several minutes as the neighbor to his right was the nearly deaf vicar. The partner to his left was Lady Thea Badcock who'd not forgiven him for foiling her attempts to thrust him into a compromising position with her eldest daughter several years back. At every attempt he'd made to engage in polite conversation, she'd presented him with her ample shoulder.

As the diners waited for the second course to be removed and the third repast laid before them, Jacob found his gaze wandering again. He noticed his mother was in her element, holding up a lively conversation at her end of the table and laughingly fending off outrageously flirtatious comments made by several of the men who sat near her.

Half a dozen other lovely young ladies were present tonight, each perfect models of grace and decorum, though none quite so beautiful as Lady Eleanor. Still, the reason for their presence was obvious. While the countess had made sure to invite many eligible bachelors, they were simply to even out the numbers. Jacob knew his mother wanted him to have his pick of ladies—make that ladies he might fall in love with—so that he might finally settle down.

He leaned back to allow a footman to place a clean plate in front of him, and caught sight of Miss Aston. She was listening raptly to whatever story the elderly Viscount Sandeford was telling. Jacob noticed she rarely got a word in, but whatever she said only encouraged the old man to tell her yet another tale. She smiled encouragingly and never let on that she was bored out of her mind, though Jacob himself had felt his mind grow numb when cornered for too long by the viscount. Her dress was much plainer than Lady Eleanor's, though in truth, the style suited her. Her gown was of a pale sage green, its low scooped neckline revealing just the barest hint of décolletage. Her dark hair was piled high and threaded through with a matching velvet ribbon. A renegade strand had escaped her coiffure and draped down her neck, tickling her collarbone. Her color was high and she smiled widely, as if unaware that convention stated young ladies should moderate their emotions.

He was reminded of her earlier comment about being a wallflower and wondered at it. There was no reason she should not be invited to dance and included in the general attention of society's young bucks. She was very nice looking and, when the mood struck her, easy to converse with. Perhaps he would introduce a few of his friends to her. Surely once they saw past her shyness or awkwardness, they would flock to her side. And if the results made her think more favorably of him and relay that favorability to Lady Eleanor, so much the better. It did not escape Jacob's well-honed sense of irony that he was on one hand making sure his parents did not push him too quickly into marriage while on the other, doing whatever was necessary to ensure that if he did end up in the parson's noose, it would be with a lady of his choosing.

Sitting back, Jacob pushed all troublesome thoughts of young ladies and betrothals from his mind and dug into his soufflé with relish.

***

He should have known when his mother said a small, informal dance to kick of the festivities, she meant an event just short of a full-blown ball. An orchestra had been fetched from London, the Beverly greenhouses and gardens plundered for every pink flower in bloom, and his mother was bedecked in a fashionable new gown—French, he had no doubt—that quite belied her age.

A quick glance around the room showed him that Lady Eleanor was in the midst of a group of men and young ladies.

Her delicate laughter drew the eyes and then company of still more partygoers until she was practically holding court in the ballroom. Deciding he didn't wish to be one of a crowd of admirers, he made a mental note to seek her out later during the dancing. He looked about the large room to determine where best his presence as host was needed. His gaze slid over and then snapped back to Miss Aston, who was once again standing on the periphery of Lady Eleanor's contingent. She was sipping a cup of punch and staring intently at the chandelier overhead, which boasted several hundred lit candles. Against his own inclination, he found himself making his way to her. He told himself it was his duty to make sure all his mother's guests were enjoying themselves and felt welcome and included. He carefully ignored the half dozen young ladies who lined the opposite side of the dance floor.

"Have you found any unlit candles, Miss Aston? Shall I sack the footman responsible?"

Miss Aston started and then grimaced to see she'd sloshed punch over the edge of her cup. A stray droplet had landed near the hem of her gown, while the majority had formed a small puddle on the gleaming parquet floor. Jacob looked up to find Miss Aston's eyes closed—in mortification, he was sure. When she opened them he pretended not to have noticed her accident.

Though her cheeks were flaming, she managed to answer with equanimity. "Only one candle is unlit, but before you dismiss anyone, I should investigate the wick. The problem may not be the footman, but the candle maker." This she delivered with a completely straight face.

"Ah, shortchanged in the wax department," he said with a laugh. She smiled in return and unobtrusively stepped back from the splatter of punch on the floor.

Jacob saw that Lady Eleanor's group of admirers had grown by half a dozen and Miss Aston was being pushed even further from her friend. Wondering if this bothered her, he tried to think of a tactful way to ask.

"I believe you said you and Lady Eleanor met during your first Season?"

"Indeed. We were both terrified of making a mistake and clung to one another for support. I think my Aunt Constance knew her mother and so they introduced us. That slim connection was like a lifeline to us and we grabbed onto it at that first terrifying ball. Fortunately, we found that we get on very well and our friendship has blossomed ever since."

"Shall I return you to her side? These young men can be a bit oblivious to their surroundings," he added as Miss Aston was jostled yet again, nearly spilling more punch.

Wisely handing the cup to a passing servant, she shook her head. "Thank you, no. I am not at all whom they've come to see and Eleanor knows I don't care for the crowd. In a while they'll leave and she'll tell me all the gossip I've missed."

Jacob lifted his eyebrows at her. "I never would have taken you for an indolent young miss."

Visible startled, Miss Aston blinked. "I beg your pardon?"

"I never would have guessed that you were content to let others do the work while you sit back and reap the benefits."

He could tell by the hectic color in her cheeks that she was growing angry. "I'm not sure what you are implying, Lord Worthing, but—"

"To force your friend to stand for hours questioning and prying so that you might be entertained with this week's scandals."

She drew a deep breath and he was certain she was about to deliver a scathing retort. He could discern the exact moment when she realized he was teasing her. Her breath left her in a whoosh, though her cheeks remained flushed.

"Yes, well, I was ever one for taking the easy way out," she said with a smirk.

"Is that what Mr. Pickering is? The easy way out?" He didn't know why he said it. He didn't even know where the thought came from. Perhaps because he'd seen that his mother had added the insipid man to the guest list just this evening as his father wished to discuss a business venture with Mr. Pickering. He had no idea why he remembered that Mr. Pickering had attended Miss Aston at the musicale and several other events, but he was fairly certain his comment was the most ungentlemanly thing he could have said to Miss Aston.

Her cheeks, which only a moment before had been flushed with anger and then merriment, grew pale. Her mouth compressed into a thin line and, though he suddenly could not bring himself to look her directly in the eye, he could tell they showed the wound he had inflicted with his careless words.

"Mr. Pickering is a very decent man."

"Of course he is. I didn't mean—"

"He has treated me with nothing but respect and kindness." Her tone was positively icy. "I do not understand what you mean to imply by such a statement."

Damned if he didn't feel like he was twelve years old, wriggling in embarrassment at being caught acting like a boy half his age. "Please forgive my impetuous words. I simply have found your conversation to be quite sharp-witted and provoking. While, for all Mr. Pickering's decency and kindness, his is...not. I would think you would encourage the suit of someone with an...intellect more like your own."

If possible, her complexion grew paler. "What makes you qualified to determine whom I should encourage, sir?" Before he could answer, she continued, her voice low and fierce. "I should prefer Mr. Pickering were he completely dim witted for his kindness against those—" She cast a scathing glance at the horde of young men surrounding her friend—"who deem me a waste of their good manners simply because I am not beautiful, excessively rich, and lack that certain appeal that determines if a girl is a success by the *ton's* standards."

"Miss Aston, you must allow me to—"

"If you will excuse me, Lord Worthing. I believe I hear my aunt calling me. And I'm sure you have many other guests to make feel...welcome."

And on that note, she turned and strode across the

room, completely passing her dozing aunt. Jacob watched her leave the ballroom and silently cursed himself for being an idiot. He was not normally so maladept at talking to young ladies. Still, Pickering was an odd bird for her to have attracted. Perhaps she was not the most popular girl of the season, but surely someone else must have noticed that she had a devilish wit and smelled rather divine. He would make sure to introduce her to several men this weekend who would appreciate a little depth in a companion. Of course, if she loved Pickering, he'd made hash out of his attempts to win her good will and hence, an endorsement to Lady Eleanor. Deciding he'd waited long enough for said lady, he smoothly cut through the group of would-be suitors and took her hand.

"I believe you promised to open the ball with me, Lady Eleanor."

Eleanor blushed a delicate pink and looked at him demurely from beneath her lashes. "I would be honored, my lord," she said, nodding to her cadre of admirers.

Lady Eleanor danced divinely, following his lead with the merest pressure from his hand at her back. She chatted pleasantly about the dinner and ball decorations and smiled prettily when he complimented her pink satin gown. When their dance ended, he told himself that Lady Eleanor would make a splendid future countess. He resolutely avoided looking for Miss Aston's return and set out to make himself a most agreeable host, chatting with the older men, jesting with the younger, dancing with the ladies and even bringing punch to one of the wallflowers (while telling himself he was *not* doing so because of Miss Aston's comment about arrogant young lordlings).

He danced a second dance with Lady Eleanor during which he found her laugh to be both delightful and infectious and discovered they had a mutual admiration for strawberries.

By the time he retired well after midnight, he had a throbbing headache and nagging ache between his shoulder blades that he refused to attribute to a guilty conscience.

Chapter Nine

Juliette awoke to the unpleasant sensation of someone leaping upon her bed. A knee or elbow or some such bony protuberance landed in her stomach.

"Ooof!" she exclaimed, sitting up abruptly, prepared to do battle with her assailant.

"Goodness you're a slugabed!" Eleanor laughed "I never knew you to sleep so late."

Juliette flopped back onto her pillow. "I didn't sleep well."

"Were you ill? I noticed you left the ball early and did not return." Eleanor placed a soft hand against her friend's forehead.

Sick at heart, Juliette mused. "Yes, a terrible headache. No doubt from so many hours spent in the carriage."

"Shall I fetch the housekeeper? Have her bring her box of simples?"

Juliette propped herself up with more pillows and smiled at her friend's concern. "No, I'm feeling better. Just... weary."

"Well perhaps a pot of chocolate will perk you up." Eleanor hopped off the bed and crossing to pull the bell cord. "It always works wonders for me."

Juliette smiled. Eleanor had a ferocious sweet tooth, though, truth be told, so did she. It was one of the things they had laughed about that first Season.

The bell was quickly answered, the chocolate—for two —fetched, and within the hour, Juliette was fed, bathed, and dressed. They laughed over the crush of young men who had swarmed Eleanor the night before and Eleanor confessed sadly that no good gossip was to be had by the lot of them.

"And how did you find the dancing?" Juliette asked. She absolutely would not be the one to bring up Lord Worthing's name, but she knew without a doubt that Eleanor would have danced with him. Why she felt compelled to torture herself with thoughts of the vile man, she couldn't fathom, but she supposed it was rather like when she was a child and had a loose tooth. Though it would hurt to wiggle it, she simply couldn't stop herself from moving it with tongue, finger, and utensil.

"You know I have a tin ear when it comes to judging music—"

"I do."

"So I cannot vouch for the quality of the orchestra—"

"They were quite good."

Eleanor sighed at the interruption and took a restorative swallow of chocolate. "But the dancing was divine. I daresay the men are handsomer here at Beverly Castle than they are in London. Why do you suppose that is?"

"Perhaps the quality of the candlelight? Perhaps the Countess has a superior standard of beeswax." The mention of candles in the ballroom brought to mind her nonsensical conversation with Lord Worthing. She firmed her lips and resolutely dismissed the memory. Vile man.

Eleanor's thoughtful expression told Juliette her friend was seriously considering the possibility of better candlelight.

"I'm teasing, dear. I suppose it was just one of those magical nights where you get to dance each song with an endless supply of handsome partners." Though Juliette had never herself experienced such an evening, she knew Eleanor had enjoyed many such enchanted evenings.

"I suppose you're right, but I still believe I shall ask Lady Wilding where she procures her candles."

Juliette laughed and tossed a roll at her friend. "Now tell me about the gentlemen. Did any of these extra-handsome lords catch your eye?"

"Not more than ten or twelve," Eleanor sighed with mock disappointment, then grinned. "Truly, Jules, I wish you'd not left so early. There were ever so many nice men. You would have been the talk of the ball. House parties are much more personal, you know, and the men are more inclined to get to know you, and to know you is to love you."

Juliette smiled at her friend's steadfast loyalty. "I'm not altogether sure I would wish a man who only found favor with me because he was trapped into getting to know me."

Eleanor tossed the roll—now half-eaten—back at her. "That's not what I meant and you know it. You're just rather... well, shy is not the right word, but there is some quality that I'm sure quite intimidates the men."

"Yes, it's called plainness. Men's eyes are physically incapable of seeing me."

"Good heavens, Jules, that's ridiculous. You are certainly not plain. You're quite lovely, in fact. I think half of your problem is that you greatly underestimate yourself."

Juliette shrugged, a bit uncomfortable with the idea that her friend might be right.

"But we weren't talking about me. You were going to describe your dance partners. Begin with the first and don't you dare leave a gentleman out."

"Well if I'm to start at the beginning, I should tell you that Lord Worthing asked me to open the dance with him!"

"Truly, Eleanor? That is quite the honor."

"Is it not? I've never been asked to lead a dance. It was rather nerve wracking, though. I was terrified I would misstep and everyone would see me stumble."

Juliette laughed. "You have never missed a dance step in your life."

"Which is why I'm sure I'm overdue to do so! But Lord Worthing is an excellent dance partner. I scarcely had to think of my feet at all."

Somehow, Juliette was not surprised to hear Jacob Wilding was a graceful dance partner. She almost hated him more for it. "That sounds like quite a declaration on Lord Worthing's part. Do you fancy him in return?"

Eleanor lifted one plump white shoulder haphazardly as she popped the last biscuit from the breakfast tray into her mouth. "Now why did I eat that? I already had breakfast downstairs."

"Because it was delicious. Now about Lord Worthing."

"Oh, yes he's very nice and quite the dancer, as I said, but he's rather tall. I find Lord Curtis to be the perfect height for me. And such a nice head of hair he has."

Juliette wracked her brain to put a face to the name and came up blank. "But Lord Worthing will one day be an earl."

"Oh I know. And I know that if he offered for me, both Mama and Papa would strongly encourage me to marry him."

"But other than his height, do you care for him?"

"I suppose so. I daresay not many gentlemen find it amusing to visit three milliners with two young ladies and Lord Worthing was quite tolerant of our excessive shopping that day at Burlington Arcade."

"As I recall, you were the one who went home with more than a dozen packages, but your point is taken."

"I suppose we shall both get to know him better this weekend. That is, in large part, the point of a house party, is it not?"

"Both of us? I would wager my Kashmir shawl that my getting to know her son was not the reason Lady Beverly issued me an invitation."

Eleanor rolled her eyes. "Good heavens, Jules! Will you stop that? You are perfectly lovely and certainly much more intelligent than I am. Why, I never get any jest the men make! Don't you always have to explain them to me? Any man would be lucky to have you for a wife."

Juliette smiled. "Don't mind me. I must not be fully recovered from the headache last night. Tell me, what activities are planned for today?"

As Eleanor expounded on the lavish picnic and outdoor games planned, Juliette let her mind wander to the dreadful Lord Worthing. If he had settled his sights on Eleanor, Juliette knew without a doubt she would be attending her friend's wedding by the end of the Season. The thought gave her a dull pang below her breastbone. Certainly she had no expectations of attracting Worthing, but aside from his insulting remarks about her settling for Mr. Pickering, she'd rather enjoyed bantering with him the few times they'd met. There was something rather appealing about a man who could tease and be teased with good humor.

Perhaps last night's comment about Mr. Pickering had been a failed attempt at humor. She herself had made jests that had sounded perfectly amusing in her head, but came out dreadfully. Of course, she'd only ever done such a thing to her close friends who would immediately groan, frown, or say in a scandalized hiss, "Juliette!"

Juliette paused in the process of brushing crumbs off her lap. Perhaps Lord Worthing considered her a friend. Certainly they hadn't known each other that long, but their few interactions had the flavor of amusing antagonism. Suddenly Juliette wondered if she'd been too quick to take offense at his remarks about her "settling."

Her musings were interrupted by a knock at the door. The maid who'd been collecting breakfast dishes answered it and returned with an armful of flowers. Juliette looked to Eleanor, sure they were for her, but the maid held them out to her.

"Me? Are you certain?"

"Yes, miss. The footman said so."

Juliette felt a flush of pleasure warm her cheeks. She gasped as she took the flowers and realized there were not one but two bouquets. The larger one was a profligate display of daisies, candytuft, foxglove, and several other flowers she did not recognize. It was a riotous combination of color, clearly intended to garner attention and Juliette smiled in bemusement as she opened the sheet of paper tucked into it.

"I have been invited to join the house party at the EARL's—" this not only written in capital letters, but quite heavily drawn as well—*"request to discuss a matter of great importance. I, of course, look forward to the occasion to further our acquaintance. Yours respectfully, Theodore Pickering."*

"Who are they from?" Eleanor asked eagerly and Juliette looked at her friend with a warm smile. Eleanor received half a dozen bouquets a day, but she was most delighted when Juliette herself received one.

"Mr. Pickering. It appears he is a last-minute addition to the house party and looks forward to furthering our acquaintance."

"Mmph," Eleanor said.

Juliette set the bundle of wildflowers aside and looked at the second bouquet. It was much smaller, a delicate collection of columbine, wood violets, and grape hyacinths. It was tied with a dark purple ribbon, to which a small cream-colored card was attached. Juliette paused to take a deep breath of the fragrant blossoms before opening the card.

"Miss Aston--I regret my ill-considered words of last night and humbly beg your forgiveness. I am certainly in no position to offer judgments of my fellow man and was grossly out of line. I hope you will accept my apology and know that I wish you nothing but the best. Sincerely, Worthing."

"And those? Who are they from? They are so elegant!"

Juliette paused, staring at the bold pen strokes. If she told Eleanor that Lord Worthing had sent them, her friend would assume his lordship was interested in her. She could not bring herself to share the reason for his apology, as the idea that she was "settling" for the only man who'd ever expressed an interest in marrying her was still a sore spot in her heart. She very much feared—oh, drat it, she knew he was right but she longed to have a family and this was quite possibly her last chance to gain that. She looked up at Eleanor's expectant face and said, "They are from Mr. Pickering also. He said these flowers reminded him of me and since he'd already selected the others, he decided to send them both."

"Oh," Eleanor said, slightly crestfallen. "That's...that's terribly romantic."

Juliette nodded and carefully slipped the note from Lord Worthing into her pocket. She knew not if Worthing would make a good husband for Eleanor, but if there were a chance her friend cared for him, she would ensure nothing stood in Eleanor's way.

Juliette asked the maid to put Mr. Pickering's flowers in water, but elected to wear the smaller nosegay to the picnic. The pale purples in the bouquet contrasted nicely with her butter yellow gown. "Shall we go downstairs? I fancy a walk through those beautiful gardens."

A worried frown crossed Eleanor's face. "Perhaps we should join the ladies in the large drawing room."

"Come along, dear. You need some fresh air and it will be far easier for you to attend the picnic later today if you've explored the grounds and feel more comfortable with it."

Eleanor chewed her lower lip and Juliette's heart went out to her friend. As a child, Eleanor had been lost in the woods near her house and hadn't been found until the following day. Ever since, she'd had an overpowering fear of the outdoors. While she was a beautifully self-assured young woman in the crowded confines of a ballroom, once outside, her confidence evaporated. Their first Season out, Juliette discovered Eleanor crouched behind a rose bush at a luncheon party, pale and sweating. Juliette had helped her sneak into the house and talked soothingly until Eleanor was coherent. The shaken young woman had tearfully explained her predicament and ever since, they'd worked out a plan where Juliette never left Eleanor's side when outside. Even when, as had happened the day before, a crowd of people separated them, Juliette always made sure Eleanor could see her. Over the past three Seasons, they'd discovered that Eleanor's fearful attacks were significantly reduced if she was able to walk around the area prior to an event.

"You're right, of course." Eleanor took a deep, fortifying breath. "Very well. Let me fetch my shawl."

Juliette gave her friend a brief hug. "I'll go with you."

Arm in arm the girls went downstairs, chatting about the day's festivities and hoping the weather did not spoil them. Eleanor was waxing rhapsodic over one of the new bonnets she had brought and planned to wear. Feeling a gaze upon her, Juliette glanced down at the entry hall and discovered Lord Worthing staring at her. He was surrounded by several older men but paused in his conversation to offer a hesitant smile and a brief bow. Juliette realized he was waiting for her response to his note.

She offered a return smile and nod of her own and saw him return to his conversation. Well, she thought, I suppose that settles that. Juliette wondered briefly if his apology was due to sincere regret over his words or simply the result of a host ensuring his event proceeds smoothly. She decided that to even consider the latter option was churlish of her and she descended the remaining stairs with a spring in her step.

As they reached the grand entry hall of Beverly Castle, a cluster of young men and women immediately surrounded Eleanor. Juliette stood patiently by, content to listen to the excited voices proclaim over Eleanor's bonnet, her gown, her gloves, her complexion. While she was largely ignored by the men seeking Eleanor's favor, several of the young women were friends of Juliette's and they fell into easy conversation.

A hearty guffaw interrupted her discussion with a fellow young lady and Juliette turned at a touch to her elbow.

"Why Mr. Pickering. How very nice to see you here," she said with a smile that she was certain appeared genuine. Really, Lord Worthing had been wrong in his assessment of her relationship with Mr. Pickering and he'd even apologized for it. She needed to put her own uncertainties aside.

"A bit of a surprise, I've no doubt. An event like this is usually a bit rich for my blood, if you know what I mean." He laughed heartily again, and puffed his chest out. "Still, the old earl specifically requested I join the party. Seems he's considering investing in a venture I am facilitating."

Though it was considered quite crass for a gentleman to discuss anything as base as money at such an event, Juliette could tell Mr. Pickering was quite proud of having something that an earl such as Lord Beverly would require. She smiled gently. "I am sure you will prove invaluable to his lordship."

Clearly pleased with her comment, Mr. Pickering asked, "Did you receive my flowers?"

"I did and must thank you not only for the thought but for the selection. They are quite, er, colorful."

"Some chap at the stables told me some of them were weeds, but I thought, a weed in bloom is as pretty as any hothouse flower and a dem sight easier to get!" He laughed at his wit and Juliette smiled weakly. Truly, she reminded herself sternly, it was the thought that counted, not the expense or exertion required. Still, she couldn't help but touch the small nosegay of delicate purple flowers pinned at her waist.

"Sit with you at the picnic, shall I?" Mr. Pickering asked when his humor abated.

"That would be pleasant," Juliette replied.

"Of course, if I'm late, its simply because the Earl has kept me, you know."

"I understand. You must help him as much as you can."

Mr. Pickering laid a finger along his nose and nodded sagely. "Doesn't hurt a gentleman to have an earl indebted to you, you know."

A footman approached and indicated Lord Wilding was ready to meet with Mr. Pickering.

"If you'll excuse me, Miss Aston," he said in an overly loud voice, "I must meet with the earl now."

Juliette closed her eyes briefly—really, it was only a long blink—and took a fortifying breath. She tried to ignore the rolled eyes and snickers behind her as the fashionable crowd surrounding Eleanor made their disdain for Mr. Pickering known.

Having born their condescension herself often enough, Juliette felt a moment of camaraderie with her suitor and smiled warmly at him, hoping he was as oblivious to their slights as he appeared.

Eleanor finally broke away from her admirers and the two young women made their way outside.

"I noticed Lord Worthing smiled at you," Eleanor said once they were in the gardens. Her face was a little pale and she gripped Juliette's arm a little too firmly, but otherwise, she seemed to be managing her fear.

"Me? Good heavens. When?"

"When we were coming down the stairs."

Juliette felt her stomach clench in a not-unpleasant sort of way. It felt a bit like anticipation. She quickly squelched the feeling and said casually. "If he was smiling at anyone, it was you, dear. You look especially fetching in that pale pink."

"I beg to differ. I am well aware when a gentleman is looking at me, and I know Lord Worthing was *not* smiling at me."

"You're a goose, Eleanor, a positive goose. Was that Lord Strong I saw chatting with you in the hall?"

A bee drifted lazily past Eleanor's ear, startling her and causing her to jump. She took several deep breaths and then sent Juliette a glance that told her she recognized her friend's attempts at misdirection.

"Indeed it was. I—oh!" Eleanor jumped as a moth flew brokenly into her face. She batted wildly, managing to knock it into the curls framing her face. Realizing her friend was about to grow panicked, Juliette quickly combed the errant moth out of Eleanor's hair and dragged her over to a stone bench beneath a large, blossom-bedecked tree.

"I declare, you attract simply everything, Eleanor," Juliette teased gently. "I can't remember the last time I was ambushed by a bee and a moth in a matter of seconds."

Eleanor shuddered delicately. "I am sure the wild creatures sense my fear. They must see me as easy prey." She cringed and swatted at her skirts, but it was just a stray blossom floating to the ground.

"Hardly. You may look as pretty as a flower, but I'm sure the insects can tell you've neither pollen nor nectar to entice them. Perhaps they're simply affected by the nervous energy you exude. Try taking some calming breaths and see if that makes you less attractive to them."

Eleanor dutifully inhaled and exhaled.

"There now, I see no errant bugs in your vicinity. Tell me, where did the countess say the picnic was to be held."

Temporarily distracted from her phobia, Eleanor looked out over the extensive grounds and then pointed. "I believe beneath those trees. Lady Wilding said there was a charming little brook which feeds into a pond surrounded by those trees."

"And shall we walk?"

Eleanor's eyes widened.

"Well, it isn't all that far," Juliette said, judging the distance to be not more than a fifteen- or twenty-minute walk.

"No, no. Lady Wilding specifically said she had arranged for several open carriages to convey us."

Juliette studied the intervening countryside, unconsciously picking out the path she would take were she at liberty. "Pity. It looks like a delightful walk." Returning to the task at hand, Juliette said, "You'll be fine in the open carriage won't you?"

Eleanor nodded. "I usually am."

"Just consider: those trees where the picnic will be seem quite tall. And it looks as if their branches are quite lush and thick."

Eleanor frowned and Juliette wondered how a girl could make a frown look appealing. "I'm not sure I follow your line of thought."

"Well, if you think on it, the trees make a roof and walls around the picnic area. With lovely carpets on the ground—and I'm sure Lady Wilding will have tables and chairs for those who don't wish to lounge—it will practically be just like being in a drawing room!"

Eleanor frowned a moment longer, studying the distant trees. Slowly her brow cleared and she smiled. "I do believe you're right! How clever of you to notice."

Juliette smiled at her friend. "I suspect you shan't feel a moment's panic during the entire picnic."

"I shall endeavor to think of it as a ballroom decorated out like a forest. Remember when Lady Chisolm hosted that ball last year and tried to make it look like an African jungle?"

Juliette smiled in memory. Lady Chisolm, never having been to Africa or even spoken with anyone who had, had decorated her ballroom with everything from silk vines to a stuffed bear, which Juliette knew for a fact had been brought from America by Lady Chisolm's father.

"I suspect the picnic's setting will be much more elegant," Juliette said.

Eleanor glanced around her. "Why, sitting under this tree is a bit like being indoors also. Perhaps in my dressing room with lovely lacy gowns instead of flowers."

Juliette laughed. "Very imaginative."

"Perhaps I shall seek out a large lovely tree to take cover under every time I must go outside!"

"It might not always be possible to find a tree, but I say if it makes you feel more comfortable, we shall locate every tree on the estate and plant a chair beneath it."

Eleanor smiled and squeezed Juliette's hand. "You are a very good friend."

"Not at all. But you quite crushed my hand last time you had one of your attacks. I don't fancy a bruised wrist again."

Eleanor laughed and poked Juliette in the ribs.

Chapter Ten

As it turned out, Juliette was able to walk to the picnic after all. One of the carriages acquired to carry the ladies to the picnic lost a wheel and the ladies in that conveyance squeezed into the remaining carriages. There was room for everyone except one. Juliette happily offered to be the one.

"Nonsense," said Lady Wilding. "Several of us shall wait with you and one of the carriages shall simply come back for us."

"Actually, my lady, I should love nothing so much as to walk. Your grounds are so lovely and Lady Eleanor showed me right where the picnic was to be held."

Lady Wilding frowned slightly. "Are you sure dear? Shall I have one of the ladies join you? Lady Eleanor? Or perhaps a gentleman?"

Juliette smiled. She didn't want the vigorous walk to overset Eleanor. She'd convinced her friend that the picnic setting would be practically indoors and a quarter mile walk in the open would fray the calm Eleanor was valiantly keeping. Neither did she fancy twenty minutes alone with Mr. Pickering—the only man she was sure the countess could convince to join her. She would no doubt have years during which she could talk to him; surely she needn't seek him out too soon.

"If you think it would be acceptable, I should very much like to walk alone, my lady. I do so cherish my nature walks when I'm at home in Hertford."

"I quite understand, dear. The social whirlwind can grow overwhelming. You shall be perfectly safe on the grounds, though you may wish to wear sturdier shoes than slippers."

"I shall change directly." Juliette gave her a grateful smile. She turned to go but was stopped by her aunt's imperious voice.

"Where on earth are you going, gel?"

Approaching the carriage carrying her Aunt Constance, Eleanor's mother, and several other ladies of chaperone age, Juliette said, "Lady Wilding thought I would find particular interest in the wildflowers on a different route to the picnic area. I shall meet you there directly."

"Hmmph," was Aunt Constance's reply. "See that you do. I don't fancy eating outdoors like cattle if you're not going to be there. There is a reason I've come all they way up here, you know, and it's not for my health." Her meaningful look said, "Get to the picnic and find a husband." Unspoken by word or look was the addendum, "Someone other than that Pickering fellow."

Juliette grinned at her aunt. "I shall endeavor to beat you there."

Another "hmmph" was followed with the admonition not to "go and get you gown all soiled in your rush."

Juliette ran upstairs, changed her shoes, and was making her way through the back gardens before the last carriage was underway. Delighted to have a few moments alone, she took several deep breaths, paused to sniff a flower, watch a butterfly, and follow a bee to its hive. Ten minutes later, she paused and looked around, trying to get her bearings. She'd followed what she was sure was the correct path but the trees Eleanor had pointed out this morning were now far to her left. Backtracking a bit, Juliette took a different trail and set out confidently. After another quarter of an hour, she let out a frustrated huff. The paths were much more indirect than they had appeared when she'd inspected them from the high vantage point of the upper gardens this morning. Retracing her steps, she ended up at her original path. Her hair was slipping out of its pins, she was quite certain her nose was growing sunburned despite her bonnet, and an uncomfortable trickle of perspiration was making its way down her spine.

"Are you avoiding anyone in particular or the picnic in general?" Juliette jumped at the deep voice behind her. Turning, she discovered Lord Worthing looking as cool and composed as if he'd just stepped out of the drawing room instead of snuck up on her in the middle of nowhere in the warmth and humidity of an English May day.

"Your paths are not very well laid out." Juliette could not quell her peevish tone. She knew her remark was unfair, but she was frustrated and unkempt and was suffering no small worry over Eleanor's state of mind. Her friend had seemed enthralled with the idea of thinking of the picnic area as an indoor grotto, but suppose she had one of her attacks and Juliette was not there to help her?

Seemingly bemused, Lord Worthing only smiled. "I do apologize. I shall have the gardener mow new ones direct to wherever it is you wish to walk. Where *do* you wish to go?"

Juliette bit her tongue to keep from issuing a tart reply. Instead she forced a tight smile and said, "I should very much like to reach the picnic."

"Ah, of course. Fortunately, we only need take this path here and spare the gardener extra work. The poor man is in his seventh decade, you know."

She looked to where he gestured behind him and saw a narrow path overgrown with wildflowers and dogwoods. She must have passed the turnoff twice, she thought in irritation.

"Shall we?" he asked politely—too politely. She cast a quick glance at him and saw he was smiling broadly, no doubt delighted to find her at a disadvantage after having to apologize for his earlier rudeness. Though Juliette had no brothers, she did have male cousins enough to know that their species loathed being beholden to a female for their behavior and positively thrived when said female was beholden to them. Bracing herself for an endless stream of comments about her inability to navigate the countryside, Juliette brushed past Lord Worthing, obliging him to follow.

When he remained silent for several minutes, she reconsidered her assumption. Perhaps he simply was being polite. He was the host, after all. Embarrassed at her churlishness, she said, “What prompted you to search for me? Did your mother mention I might be, er, having difficulty?”

“My mother did tell me which path she thought you'd taken, but it was Lady Eleanor who asked me to come to your resc—assistance.”

Juliette frowned, wondering if Eleanor was becoming anxious. Wanting to inquire after her friend's state of mind without revealing Eleanor's secret, she carefully asked, “And is Lady Eleanor enjoying herself?”

Lord Worthing nodded his head slowly one time. “She is not growing anxious if that is what you mean.”

“What? No, I—why should she—“ Juliette froze, unsure of what to say.

Reaching to hold a branch out of her way, Lord Worthing allowed Juliette to precede him through a narrow part of the path. Pulling even with her as it widened, he said, “Lady Eleanor has confessed her...aversion to being in wide open spaces.”

“She did?” Juliette was amazed. She didn't think Eleanor had confessed her fear to anyone other than herself. Eleanor's feelings for Lord Worthing must be significant if she trusted him so.

“She did. I believe she wished to come find you herself but was unsure if she would prove to be a help or a hindrance.”

“Eleanor is never a hindrance,” Juliette said firmly.

“Of course not. But I believe she was concerned her discomfort out here—“ he gestured to the wide stretch of land through which they were walking—“might prevent her from being able to find you.”

Juliette had no response to this. Of course Eleanor would not be able to maintain her calmness out here. She was actually surprised their plan to help Eleanor feel comfortable at the picnic was still working.

"Eleanor is a very brave young woman," Juliette finally said. If her friend had feelings for Lord Worthing, she, Juliette, would make sure he held her in equally high regard.

"Indeed," Lord Worthing said, glancing sideways at her, a mild questioning look in his gaze.

"Not many people are able to confront their fears as she has. Lady Eleanor may look fragile, but she has the courage of...of...of a lioness," she finished, feeling slightly embarrassed at her metaphor.

"She is an admirable young woman," Lord Worthing agreed.

They walked down a slight hill. Juliette could see the grove of trees sheltering the diners ahead.

Lord Worthing started to speak and then paused. She glanced at him in question.

"And what are you afraid of?"

Juliette looked ahead, startled by the rather personal question. Affecting a light tone of voice, she replied, "Why, spiders, of course."

Lord Worthing huffed a short laugh. "That, I am given to believe, goes of all young ladies. But surely there is something you dread."

Juliette didn't know why he should ask such a question. It was not at all the type of topic mere acquaintances discussed. Seeking to turn the tables on him, she said, "Well, what is it that you fear?"

He paused just a moment before answering, "Losing my family."

"Oh," Juliette replied, as surprised by his answer as she was by the fact that he had confessed it.

"My mother nearly died several years ago. It was...a devastating time and made me realize just how important she, my father, and my sister were to me. How very much I love them. And now, my father—his heart." Jacob touched his jacket above his heart but said no more.

It was a surprisingly intimate revelation. English gentlemen were supposed to be masters of self-control and dispassion. Hearing Lord Worthing profess an emotion as strong as love—and for his family, no less—was rather startling. It made her pause and engage in a bit of self-reflection. What was she most afraid of? She had already lost her mother and while she loved her father, theirs was a more remote relationship. She studied the tips of her walking half boots as they peeped out from beneath her skirts with every step.

"I suppose," she began, and then paused. It was really rather difficult to admit one's weaknesses. "I suppose the thing that rattles me most is the fear of losing myself."

From the corner of her eye, she saw Lord Worthing smile. "As you did just a while ago?"

Juliette laughed. "Not literally. More…symbolically." She paused and continued to study her toes.

"Please elaborate," he finally said.

Juliette glanced up. They were behind a clump of bushes and just over the top, she could see the grove of trees. It must be just around the bend.

"Ah, we have arrived," she said, relief evident in her voice. She started to stride forward.

Lord Worthing's hand caught her arm. "Not quite we haven't," he said quietly. "Please. I'd like to know what you mean. How could you lose yourself?"

Juliette licked her suddenly dry lips and avoided his gaze. His silence bore down on her until she reluctantly relented. "I…I suppose I mean that…Well, it's like this. I am not considered by London's society to be a 'diamond of the first water,' or an 'original,' or even a beauty of any note."

Lord Worthing started to speak, but Juliette held him off with an upraised hand. "I am not seeking compliments, my lord. I assure you, I am well aware that my meager appearance would be overlooked more easily if I were of a bubbly personality or had a pedigree dating back to William the Conqueror, or a dowry the size of a small country. I am quite content with who I am, and my circle of close friends is gratifyingly large. But the fact remains that since I am not seen as extraordinary, my value on the marriage mart is negligible. And once I do marry, my worth will be further depleted. So my greatest fear is that I start to believe the value our world places on me. To do that would be to lose my inner happiness, my sense of who I am, who I was born to be, and who I could become."

Juliette paused, slightly out of breath from her rather rushed monologue. She'd had the feeling that if she had paused —even to simply breathe—she might lose the courage to say everything that was in her heart. As it was, she was rather dazed with the idea she had confessed such a private fear to this man, especially as she'd never really verbalized the thought to herself before.

Hazarding a glance at Lord Worthing, she was surprised to find he had stopped in his tracks. His brow was wrinkled as if he were deep in thought as he stared at some point on the ground. Finally, just when Juliette felt her face begin to flame with embarrassment, he glanced up and said quietly, "I pray that you never lose yourself either. It would be this world's greatest loss should you do so."

Juliette was amazed at his words, and as a rather sheepish expression crossed his face, she imagined he was feeling a similar amazement. After another moment of silence, a not quite uncomfortable one, but certainly not a relaxed one, she pasted a bright smile on her face.

"Well, so much soul-searching has left me famished. Shall we continue to the picnic?"

Lord Worthing nodded solemnly and then smiled back. "Indeed. I hope we are not too late for the cold chicken salad. It is one of Cook's summertime specialties."

"It sounds delicious," Juliette responded and their conversation for the remaining minutes of their walk continued along equally benign topics.

Chapter Eleven

Jacob adjusted a fold of his cravat, staring blindly in the mirror of his mother's sitting room. Instead of his reflection, he saw instead Miss Aston, flushed with embarrassment yet impassioned as she confessed her fear—a fear that would have never crossed his mind, so confident was he in his own worth. It was rather disconcerting, for Jacob had long considered himself to be rather forward thinking in regards to women and had even gone so far as to read a bit of Mary Wollstonecraft's treatise on the status of women. But hearing Miss Aston describe her situation—without an iota of self-pity —made him realize he'd very much taken his vaunted position for granted for...well, for his entire life. It was an uncomfortable realization.

His thoughts were interrupted by the arrival of his father's valet who asked indicated his father would see him.

"Your mother informs me that Lady Eleanor is a true English rose." His father was propped up against several pillows and his lips were tinged blue as if he were cold, despite the warmth of the room.

Jacob quirked a brow in confusion. "By which she means...?"

The earl paused, apparently startled by Jacob's question. "Why, I suppose she means that Lady Eleanor is beautiful and a model of comportment."

For some reason, the description struck Jacob as terribly bland. Forcing the thought from his mind, he smiled and simply said, "I am glad she likes her."

"Yes, yes. I could not be happier that you have chosen so

well."

"I—I haven't settled on her, father," Jacob protested.

"What, what? Nonsense. Why look further when the perfect specimen is before you? No reason we can't announce a betrothal by the end of the Season!"

Jacob felt his stomach clench uncomfortably. "Father, forgive me, but I don't understand the rush. Why now when you've always told me to take my time and find the right woman, as you did when you married mother?"

"I have time, my boy. I must see you wed before I die."

"But the doctors—"

Lord Wilding shrugged. "They know nothing. They've given me bottles and bottles of tincture to take, told me to avoid spirits and rich food, but I can't say any of it has helped."

Jacob walked woodenly to one of the stuffed chairs in front of the cold fireplace and sat down heavily. Unbidden, the memory of his discussion with Miss Aston returned, only this time, he remembered his own confession: his fear of losing his family. He started to speak, found he could not, and coughed to clear his throat.

"Do they know how much…"

"How much time I have left?" His father set down the watch he'd been idly fingering and looked about the room, anywhere but at his son. "Some say I could go for years."

"And the others?"

At this, Lord Wilding finally did look at his son. "Most say I could go at anytime."

Jacob felt as though someone had punched him very hard in the stomach. He scrubbed a hand through his hair and stared at his father. He could not remember a time when Miles Wilding had been anything other than hale and hearty. An avid sportsman, a hands-on steward of his vast lands, he'd always been active, never sick. The weakest he'd ever seen his father was during the months of his mother's illness. Refusing to leave her side for a moment, his father had lost a great deal of weight, not a little bit of hair, and his skin had taken on a pale, sickroom pallor. With the return of his wife's health, however, he had returned to his old self, or so Jacob thought. Now he was left wondering how he could possibly fill his father's shoes. He'd been so sure he had at least several more years to amass the knowledge necessary to take over as the Earl of Beverly.

"But that was not my intent in asking for you. I want to hear more about your feelings for Lady Eleanor."

Jacob's head swam from the abrupt change of subject and he had to force his mind to even dredge up a memory of who Lady Eleanor was.

"I, er..."

"I know I always told you to wait until you found the woman who was right for you, but I'm wondering if perhaps you're dragging your heels. Why by your age, I'd known your mother for three years and we'd been married a year and we were anticipating your arrival."

"Yes, I know," Jacob said through gritted teeth. His father had told him this very thing at least four times in recent weeks. "I just...I suppose I've not been *actively* looking. I just assumed when I met the right woman, I would know it and marrying her would be the next natural step."

"Well, I've no doubt your mother and I have indulged you a bit too freely on that count. But it would do me a world of good to know that when I leave this world, you will be happily settled, as your sister is. Lady Eleanor seems delightful. I merely ask that you get to know her better. Sometimes love blooms slowly, between two people who share similar backgrounds and interests. But suddenly you realize it has flowered and it quite takes your breath away. I suspect if you gave it a chance, you would find this could happen with Lady Eleanor."

For Jacob, still feeling rather poleaxed by his father's announcement, this was enough to settle the matter. If his father felt she was the best choice for him, he would pursue her avidly and offer for her as soon as was seemly.

"I will spend time with her this evening, father."

"That's all I ask," the earl said with a smile before departing.

Jacob stood and absently adjusted the knot in his cravat. And yet…for some reason, he was brought to mind of his walk with Miss Aston this morning. He frowned at his reflection in the mirror. What on earth would have made him think of her at this moment?

***

The house party was in full swing. The initial hesitancy natural at the start of any gathering of people had given way to familiarity and joviality. Ladies and gentlemen, young and old alike were enjoying the excellent food, libations, and flawless service presented by the Earl and Countess of Beverly.

As Jacob walked into the large drawing room where everyone had gathered prior to dinner, he purposefully sought out Lady Eleanor. She was surrounded by several lovestruck swains, her delicate laughter ringing out at their no-doubt outrageous compliments. Without quite realizing it, he also looked for Miss Aston and found her just outside the ring of men surrounding her friend. He would have expected to see jealously, perhaps resentment, or at least annoyance at her wallflower status next to her friend, but Miss Aston seemed quite content to simply sit and watch Lady Eleanor charm and be charmed. In fact a small, bemused smile curved her lips. Did Miss Aston not wish for suitors herself? It seemed the entire reason a young lady would have a Season. He knew of no lady who had willingly retired from the ranks of debutante without a husband.

Smoothly inserting himself into the crowd surrounding Lady Eleanor, he adeptly maneuvered himself to her elbow and began wooing her in earnest. He told one humorous story after another until Lady Eleanor's signature tinkling laughter turned into genuine giggles. She was a sweet young lady and certainly very beautiful. Perhaps his father was right. Perhaps he'd simply not been looking for love. Perhaps now it would simply come. Amidst that thought, Jacob glanced up and saw

Miss Aston. She was not laughing aloud, but her bemused smile had blossomed into a grin of genuine amusement and he realized she must have overheard his last story. He wondered what it would take to make *her* giggle.

"And then what did you do, Lord Worthing?" Lady Eleanor asked.

Jacob jerked his mind back to his companion and struggled to remember what he'd been saying. "Why offered to buy the sheep, of course."

Lady Eleanor and the other gentlemen burst out laughing. For some reason, however, Jacob found his gaze returning to Miss Aston. He saw that her smile had deepened, but her eyes were cast down to her hands. He supposed she would be considered rather odd if she were to burst out laughing when she was essentially sitting alone. Suddenly it seemed the greatest travesty that her own cadre of admirers did not surround her.

Before he could pursue that wayward thought, the dinner bell rang and he obligingly escorted Lady Eleanor to the dining room.

He was not surprised to discover that Lady Eleanor had been seated to his right. What did surprise him was that Miss Aston had been seated directly across from him, instead of a good distance down the table as would have befitted her rank. Glancing at his mother, he saw her smoothly directing servants and conversing with her dinner partners. No doubt feeling his gaze, she smiled absently before returning to her conversation, though he was sure she was behind the unusual seating arrangement. Surely his mother did not...surely she too wished to fulfill his father's dying wish, which was to see him wed to Lady Eleanor. And yet she had placed Miss Aston where he could not help but stare at her all evening.

With a shake of his head, he dismissed the ridiculous idea from his mind. For all he knew, his mother simply wished for Lady Eleanor to be close to her dear friend.

Putting on his best sparkling conversationalist smile,

Jacob turned to Lady Eleanor.

Lady Eleanor, as he'd known she would be, was charming, polite, and easily amused as her infectious, delightful laugh proved time and again. She didn't seem to care to stray into terribly deep topics—or indeed, anything beyond the shallow niceties—but then, he had only just begun to court her. Jacob held high hopes that once she became more familiar with him, she would share her thoughts on the world. Oh, very well, he acknowledged, perhaps "high hopes" was an exaggeration. He hoped to hell she would prove to have interest in topics more intellectual than the cut of a gentleman's jacket or the latest scandal from London. Having been raised by a rather strong-willed mother, and often bullied by his equally strong-willed older sister, Jacob rather thought that if he married a lady who was unable to stand up and give him a good what-for, well, life would be rather...boring.

A delighted laugh from across the table caught his attention. As Lady Eleanor was engaged in selecting a slice of roast from the platter being offered by the footman, Jacob turned to study Miss Aston, who was apparently greatly enjoying herself. Her dinner partner on one side was an elderly viscount and on the other, a not-much-younger lord from Yorkshire. Miss Aston seemed quite oblivious to the fact that neither man was in search of a wife and engaged them in animated conversation as if they were the most fascinating guests at the house party. Her animated expression positively sparkled in the golden glow of candlelight and she bestowed wide smiles to each of her companions as they good-naturedly argued about the merits of some play—Shakespeare was it? As she turned to utter a retort to the viscount, she spotted Jacob staring at her from across the table. Her smile did not fade, though she was no longer laughing and he felt its effect like a jolt through his body. After a moment—he could not say how long—the viscount tapped her wrist and she offered a shrug and a wry expression before turning back to her conversation.

Next to him, Lady Eleanor said, "Juliette is quite the

smartest girl I know. There is little she cannot converse about. She says it's because she reads so much, but really, she just seems interested in everything. Can you imagine?"

Jacob turned his attention guiltily to the lady he was supposed to be courting. He wondered if she'd meant her comment as an oblique criticism, but no, Lady Eleanor's face showed nothing but admiration as she gazed at her friend.

Pushing his perplexing reaction to Miss Aston to the back of his mind, Jacob spent the rest of the meal determinedly discussing bonnets.

Chapter Twelve

What she needs is a few introductions, Jacob decided after supper as he watched Miss Aston study a large watercolor landscape on the drawing room wall while Lady Eleanor held court with her usual crowd of admirers. The musicians were taking a break and the guests milled about, fanning themselves from their exertions in the country dances. He had not noticed Miss Aston dancing more than three times, and one of those was with Lord Mowbly, her elderly dinner partner. Surely there were men her own age who could appreciate Miss Aston's intelligence and sense of humor. And beauty, he decided several minutes later as he partnered with her for a quadrille. He remembered likening her to a Greek goddess in a wildly beautiful way, but she truly was lovely. Her smooth cheeks were flush with delicate color, her eyes were an intriguing shade that was not quite grey, but not quite green. Her dark hair was pinned high on her head in thick, glossy curls. Inside his gloves, Jacob's fingers positively itched to pull the pins from those curls—

Surely such attractions must be evident to other eligible young men—or at least they would be once he introduced her to the right men. Yes, it would be rewarding to match her with a man who would appreciate her many qualities and such a service would certainly endear him to her very good friend, Lady Eleanor.

"My lord, if I may be so bold, you appear to have much on your mind."

Miss Aston's tone was respectful, but also...gently mocking? "Indeed, Miss Aston, I find it takes all my concentration to keep the count in my head so that I don't step on your toes."

He saw the delight spark in her eyes at his self-deprecating humor. "Perhaps if you didn't over think it, your feet would move more naturally."

They parted as the steps of the dance took them to other partners. When she was returned to him, he said with as affronted a tone of voice as he could muster, "Are you implying, Miss Aston, that I do not move naturally?"

She quickly glanced at his face to ascertain if she had truly offended him. He held his mouth tightly but she must have seen the glint of humor in his eyes for she smothered a smile and said with false contrition, "Certainly not, my lord. I simply think you might enjoy the dance more if you were not counting your sixes."

"Sixes? I'll have you know I was counting to four and no more."

"Ah? Well perhaps that is your problem." Once again they parted ways and Jacob watched her travel around their circle on another man's arm.

He knew it was rude, but he found himself unable to turn his attention to his temporary partner and once he and Miss Aston were promenading together, he demanded, "What is my problem?"

"Counting in fours. This particular song is in 6/8 time. Can you hear it? One, two three, four, five, six."

He hazily recalled a dancing instructor marking the timing of the dance as such, but he normally didn't have a problem following the rhythm, and in fact had only latched onto the excuse as a way to avoid blurting out that he suddenly found her rather attractive. For some ridiculous reason, the realization gave him a rather panicky feeling, as if he was poised on the edge of a cliff. In a strong wind. With no shoes. Blindfolded.

Feeling a bit like a fifteen-year-old lad, he responded to the emotion by mocking the truth. "Yes I hear it. Perhaps I'm just so overcome by your beauty, I'm not able to concentrate."

He said it with just the right amount of irony—that practiced sarcasm that so often passed for humor in Society. He expected—and dreaded—her blush and embarrassment. Instead she laughed aloud.

Quickly recovering—for one did not generally express amusement during a dignified quadrille—she smoothed her face into a semblance of serenity. Her eyes, and the crinkles around them, gave truth to her hilarity.

"Oh very good, my lord. Yes, that is exactly what must have caused your clumsiness."

Now Jacob was feeling nettled. In truth, he hadn't been clumsy at all, simply distracted.

"Overcome by my beauty, indeed," she continued as they entered the final processional of the dance.

"I gather you do not consider that a possibility," he said.

She executed a very pretty curtsy as the music closed, but her smile when she straightened was anything but demure. "Let's just say you would be the only man thusly struck, and I suspect you are far too discriminating to see appeal in my meager charms."

Jacob's emotions, normally so even as to make people wonder if he had any, veered crazily in another direction: umbrage on her behalf.

"Perhaps I am so discriminating that I see beauty where others are too foolish to do so," he said quietly.

Miss Aston froze, her grey-green eyes wide, her mouth dropping open. She took a breath as if to speak when suddenly they were jostled by an inebriated guest who crashed into them. She was propelled against him and he instinctively grasped her elbows and held her steady against his chest. The commotion caused by the accident focused on the young drunkard and the not-so-young lady he'd dragged down with him. As a result, Jacob and Miss Aston were insulated in their own quiet bubble as people rushed to assist the fallen guests.

Jacob noticed this only peripherally, however. His primary thought centered on another startling realization about Miss Aston: she was not only quite beautiful, but her body appeared made for his. Her breasts were pressed against his chest and only the briefest glance at this fortuitous angle was required to determine that they were lushly rounded and filled out her bodice without the aid of padding or ruffles that many women used. He caught her by the waist, nipped in by a light corset, but which flared out into gently rounded hips; a fact he could ascertain because as they were jostled again by servants struggling to right the prone lady, his hand inadvertently grazed said curves.

His gaze returned to her face and he saw shock? surprise? awareness? cross her features. He realized that the thin silk of her evening gown probably provided little insulation against his body's evidence that he found her attractive.

Jacob knew he should pull back and set her gently away from him. He knew that it was ungentlemanly in the extreme to keep her pulled tight against his body—in the middle of his mother's drawing room, no less! But for some reason, he waited, savoring these few brief seconds until at last the fallen guests were righted and the atmosphere returned to normal. Even then, however, it was Miss Aston herself who pulled away, smoothing her gloved hands down her skirts.

"I should...I should join my aunt," she said, her voice shaky.

Jacob took a deep breath and felt rational thought and gentlemanly manners take over. "Of course. I shall escort you to her."

"No! That is, no thank you, my lord. That is not necessary. She is just over there, you see."

Jacob glanced in the direction she nodded and spotted the woman he recognized as her chaperone, cozily ensconced in a velvet chair, fast asleep.

He turned back to Miss Aston, only to find her gone.

***

"Worthing!" a voice called out to him some time later.

"Stalwood," Jacob said, shaking his friend's hand. "You're late."

"Nonsense, the party is just getting started, am I right? Besides, my horse went lame right outside of London. Took me forever to get him to a coaching station."

Jacob shook his head in mock reproach. "You're sure you're not just avoiding your duties as a Beleaguered Bachelor?"

"Gads, no. I believe I have no female relations at this event so I think I am safe from their haranguing. That only leaves the Matchmaking Mamas."

"Fond of alliteration, are you?"

"What's that? Oh never mind. If I didn't remember it from school, I ain't likely to do so now."

"What are the Matchmaking Mamas?" Jacob asked.

"All these ladies with a single daughter on the market. I daresay they're more determined than my own mother at seeing me leg shackled."

"And what of the young ladies in question?"

"Oh they're alright. A fellow can't dance by himself, can he?"

Across the room, Jacob spotted Miss Aston and Lady Eleanor. He felt his body tighten at the memory of Miss Aston pressed against him and promptly squelched it. Lady Eleanor was due for a waltz with him...and Jacob suddenly remembered his idea to introduce Miss Aston to some eligible men.

"So you're not adverse to meeting them?"

"What, the young ladies? Certainly not. I'm no fool; I know I'll have to settle eventually. Best to meet as many as I can so I can pick the best of the bunch when that time comes."

"You're an incurable romantic, Hugh."

Stalwood laughed and shrugged. "I'm guessing you have someone you wish to introduce?"

"Lady Eleanor's friend," he said with a nod.

"So you've decided, then? On Lady Eleanor?"

For some reason, Jacob hesitated, but only for a moment

before he said, "I don't see why not. She's everything a man could want in a wife."

Stalwood cast a cryptic look at him but said only, "And if you distract her friend, you will have Lady Eleanor's undivided attention."

"Something like that," Jacob said.

"Very well then, old boy, lead on!"

Chapter Thirteen

"Oh drat," Eleanor said.

"What's wrong?" Juliette glanced across the room in the direction of Eleanor's gaze. She saw couples assembling for a waltz, but nothing untoward.

Shaking her head, Eleanor smiled. "Nothing, nothing. Just thought of something I forgot to do. Are you engaged for the next dance?"

Juliette smiled at her loyal friend. While it was true she had danced several times tonight, in general, Eleanor could safely assume the answer to that question was "no," but Eleanor was always certain that *this* time, Juliette's dance card would be full.

"No. I am free this dance, which is fortunate as the waltz is not my favorite." This was true if only for the reason that Juliette had only ever danced it with gentlemen who routinely trod upon their partners' toes.

"Perhaps I shall sit it out too, then. My feet are sore and I think I've worn a hole in my slipper."

Juliette had known her friend to dance until her silk slippers were in tatters, but she appreciated Eleanor's thoughtfulness.

"With whom are you engaged to dance?"

"Lady Eleanor, I have eagerly awaited this dance with you."

Juliette knew immediately who it was, and she was piqued to notice that he hadn't *eagerly awaited* his earlier dance with her. Then she was irritated at herself for being piqued. Nonetheless, her body reacted to his voice. Something about the timbre of it ran like a velvet-clad finger down her spine. Stifling the delicious shiver that accompanied the impression, she turned with a carefully polite smile to find Worthing smiling directly at her. She nearly started in surprise. "Miss Aston."

"Actually, my lord—" Eleanor began.

Juliette cut in. "Actually, Lady Eleanor was just saying how she was so looking forward to your waltz as well."

Both Worthing and Eleanor stared at her for a moment before Eleanor relented and said, "Why yes, this waltz is one of my favorites."

"While the orchestra tunes, may I introduce a friend of mine? Lord Hugh Stalwood, this is Lady Eleanor Chalcroft. She is the daughter of the Marquess of Charville, you know."

"Ah yes, I've had the pleasure of meeting your father just this Season," Lord Hugh said amiably.

"And her charming friend, Miss Juliette Aston." Hearing herself described as charming caused Juliette to stumble slightly in her curtsy.

"It is my very great honor and pleasure to meet you both," Lord Hugh said, ignoring her clumsiness.

Juliette and Eleanor murmured equally polite responses and an awkward moment of silence fell before Lord Hugh gamely stepped into the breach. "Miss Aston, I realize we have just met, but would you do me the honor of granting me this next dance? Assuming of course, you have not already bestowed it."

Juliette felt her jaw go slack. Never before had she been asked to dance in such a gallant manner. Giving herself a mental shake, she bowed her head and said, "I should very much enjoy that, my lord."

Lord Hugh smiled, cast a quick wink at Worthing—Juliette wondered at that—and graciously offered his arm.

Once on the dance floor, Juliette quickly realized why Eleanor enjoyed the waltz so much. Lord Hugh was unlike her previous waltz partners. He moved gracefully, his arms strong as he easily guided her through the steps. Juliette was content to simply enjoy the flow of the music and the cadence of their steps. Finally, she realized she should engage in some sort of repartee.

"From where do you hail, Lord Hugh?"

"Northampton. Have you been there?"

"No, but I understand it's quite lovely." Juliette could have kicked herself were she not swirling around the drawing room. Witty banter, indeed.

"And how do you know Lord Worthing?" she asked, desperate for a topic of conversation.

"Oh, how *don't* I know him would be the question," Lord Hugh said with a laugh. "We've been mates since Eton. We were two skinny lads who thought they could make up for their brawn with false bravado and bluster."

Juliette smiled at the thought of the well-formed Lord Worthing as a skinny boy. "Let me guess, you found yourself on the receiving end of some rather large fists."

"'Some' would be an understatement, I'm afraid."

"So you joined forces and learned how to fight back to back?"

Lord Hugh laughed. "Hardly. We actually couldn't stand the sight of each other."

"Ah," Juliette said, warming to the conversation. "Disdaining that which reminds you of yourself?"

He considered this a moment as he guided her through an intricate turn. Juliette felt delightfully dizzy as they came out of it. "Now that you mention it, you're probably right. It would never have occurred to me that that was the case, but there you have it. I was never the most analytical of characters."

"So what joined you as allies?"

"He saved me from getting kicked out of school."

"How did he manage that?" Juliette was intrigued.

Lord Hugh grinned as he shook his head, not an easy feat considering he was still gracefully leading her through the waltz. "I had pulled a terrible prank on one of the older boys who had been tormenting me daily. Long story short, the rotten boy ended up with a broken arm. He fingered me as the culprit and I was all but packing my bags when Worthing steps up and says it's his fault and convinces everyone the ruckus was an accident."

"Why did he do it?"

"No idea."

"What? You didn't ask him?"

Lord Hugh looked at her askance. "You've no brothers, have you, Miss Aston?"

"No. Why do you ask?"

"I've confessed to not having an analytical mind and this after seven years of England's finest public schooling. Thirteen-year-old boys are about as interested in emotional questions as a tree stump."

Juliette couldn't help herself. She laughed aloud and it was further testament to Lord Hugh's dancing abilities that he was able to keep her upright and moving as she did so.

After another several phrases of music, during which Juliette caught sight of Eleanor and Worthing as they sailed gracefully past them, Lord Hugh asked, "Why do you suppose he did it?"

Distracted by what a fine-looking pair Eleanor and Worthing made, and no less disturbed by a tightening of her throat at the notion, Juliette had quite lost track of their conversation. "Why do I suppose he did what?"

Lord Hugh looked slightly embarrassed. "Saved my skin, as it were."

"Oh." Juliette thought frantically. "I suppose it was because if you left, he'd receive the full share of hounding. Bit of self-preservation, I should say."

Her partner looked impressed. "I daresay you're right."

Juliette frowned. "That doesn't make you like him any less, does it?"

He laughed loudly as he swept her into a final grand spin. "Good heavens, no. Actually, I quite admire him for the forethought. It'd never occurred to me to hatch such a scheme."

"You understand that is only a guess," she said as they came to a stop. She paused to curtsy in response to his bow.

"Oh I'm quite sure you're on the money, Miss Aston. How long have you known Worthing?"

"A few weeks, perhaps. I've really spent very little time with him. I just—"

"Well you seem to know his character very well. Come, let us join Worthing and Lady Eleanor at the punch table."

Cup in hand, Juliette was about to quench her thirst with punch (who knew waltzing was such strenuous work?) when Lord Worthing brought her attention to two other gentlemen he wished to introduce her to.

Setting down her cup, she made the appropriate curtsies and was flabbergasted to find herself asked to dance again. Lord Buchannan was perhaps not as graceful in his steps as Lord Hugh, but he was certainly a far sight more adept than her usual dance partners. Sadly, he seemed to be lacking Lord Hugh's sense of humor for, when she tried to introduce a conversational topic as she had with her waltz partner, he simply smiled politely and continued to dance. Two more times she tried, even resorting to commentary on the weather and each time, Lord Buchannan quite ignored her.

Upon returning to Eleanor's side, she was immediately prevailed upon by Mr. Conrad Strong, the other man Lord Worthing had brought round. With him, at least, she need not search for conversational gambits. He talked incessantly through the complicated steps of their dance, mostly about himself and how he was becoming quite the favorite among Society's upper echelons. When she interrupted to ask him why he was gaining such favor, he waved off her question with a, "far too complicated for a woman," remark that instantly raised Juliette's hackles.

She caught sight of Lord Hugh dancing with another young lady and decided she would not allow her current dance partner to dim the delight she had found at waltzing with a true gentleman. Of course, she had also enjoyed the quadrille with Lord Worthing, but that had been a different experience than the waltz. She suspected she would never waltz with Eleanor's future fiancée, a realization that was strangely disappointing. Shaking her head to dispel it of such ridiculous notions, she demurred from allowing Mr. Strong to escort her anywhere and left him at the edge of the dance floor to seek out the ladies' withdrawing room.

Returning a short time later, she began to make her way across the room to where Eleanor was sitting, being waited upon by two gentlemen—neither of who was Worthing—when Mr. Pickering stopped her.

"Miss Aston! At last we meet."

Juliette raised her eyebrows.

"By which I mean to say, at last we meet up with one another. Tonight. Here." Mr. Pickering waved further explanation aside. "I'm sure you've been wondering what has kept me from your side and away from Lady Wilding's festivities."

"Ah..." in truth, Juliette had given so little thought to her one prospective fiancée that she now felt a tad guilty.

Fortunately, Mr. Pickering needed no confirmation of her neglect, for he leaned conspiratorially in and whispered in a carrying voice, "I've been meeting with *the Earl*."

"How...er...how very nice for you."

"Indeed," Mr. Pickering said with a sage nod. "We've been discussing business, you know."

Juliette wondered if he didn't remember telling her this already. As to the type of business involved, she had a hazy recollection of Mr. Pickering—or was it his mother?—preening about how he helped wealthy gentlemen invest their money in various business ventures. Beyond that...well, in truth, she felt a bit ashamed. She'd not taken the trouble to learn very much about the man she'd set herself to marry. Perhaps if she took a greater interest in him, she'd find they had *some* common ground.

"And was Lord Beverly interested in your venture?"

"Shh shh!" Mr. Pickering sprayed spittle in his zeal to silence her. "Mustn't let anyone overhear you. Very sensitive topic. Vast sums of cash, though of course, I'd never be so gauche as to admit that." He ended with an absurd little snort of laughter that Juliette supposed was meant to imply that he'd just made a clever joke. She smiled weakly, which seemed the only response he required, for he rambled on about how his services were most sought after by the highest peers of the realm.

"I shouldn't be at all surprised if one day I'm granted a baronet for my service to His Majesty's coffers. Fancy yourself a Lady, do you?"

It was the most outright declaration Mr. Pickering had made to his intentions and Juliette wondered if he would even bother to ask for her hand or if he would just continue under the assumption that she would marry him.

Resignation warred with annoyance and she was tempted to ask him exactly what he meant, just to force him to declare himself when from across the room, she saw Aunt Constance. Awake at last, the elderly woman was glaring...at her? Juliette raised a hand and pointed at herself, silently asking her aunt what she'd done wrong, but Constance didn't bat an eye, just continued staring from beneath lowered brows.

Beside Juliette, Mr. Pickering said something that he must have considered quite amusing, for he laughed uproariously. Aunt Constance wrinkled her nose in distaste and Juliette realized she was not the object of the vinegary woman's stare. She smiled, allowing Mr. Pickering to believe she found him amusing also. Whyever had Aunt Constance never voiced her opinions of Mr. Pickering when he'd first appeared? Truly, Juliette could have used a little more help navigating the London social season than her perpetually drowsy aunt had provided. Why, with the right guidance, perhaps she could have learned how to be one of those girls whom men found irresistible. Or at least appealing. Interesting. She would have settled for being thought interesting enough to warrant more than one suitor.

With a sigh, she turned her attention from Aunt Constance back to Mr. Pickering.

"...haven't made the most of it, I say. Why the modernizations that are available nowadays leave the place looking like time stopped a hundred years ago."

Confused, Juliette said. "What does?"

Mr. Pickering snorted. "Why this castle. Everyone knows manor houses are much more comfortable and, to be blunt, *fashionable*."

Juliette could not believe the man was so crass as to criticize his hosts' home. Giving him the benefit of the doubt, she sought to clarify. "You don't find Beverly Castle to be stately and grand?"

"Stately and grand like a woman too far past her prime," he chortled. "No, the manor house I shall build will make this place appear no more couth than a pile of rocks."

Besides finding the man horribly rude, Juliette could not disagree more with him. "I quite disagree, sir. I find Beverly Castle to be timeless. It need not worry about being considered *en vogue*, for its elegant lines and well-designed layout are ageless."

"Well, I don't know about—"

"Furthermore, I find the Wilding family to be incredibly gracious hosts. Why, they could host an event in a barn and their guests would depart feeling cherished and pampered."

"I certainly didn't mean to imply...that is of course the Wildings are—" Mr. Pickering's gaze focused just over Juliette's shoulder. His eyes widened and he swallowed visibly. "I believe I shall fetch some punch. I find my throat is rather dry." Turning, he quickly shouldered his way through the crowd.

Juliette closed her eyes and inhaled deeply. It was common courtesy for a man to offer to bring punch back to any woman in his immediate vicinity. Her expectations for marriage were low, but she thought common courtesy was not too much to ask for in a husband.

Turning, she realized the reason for Mr. Pickering's stammering departure. Standing just behind her was Jacob Worthing himself, a wry grin curving his mouth.

Chapter Fourteen

When Jacob spotted Miss Aston returning to the drawing room, he sought her out to inquire if she'd enjoyed her dances with the men he'd introduced to her. He was halfway to her when Mr. Pickering approached her. Jacob was aware that his father was interviewing the man as a prospective broker. He felt bad for criticizing Miss Aston's choice and but wondered again what would induce her to allow the man to court her.

He approached the couple from behind Miss Aston and arrived just in time to hear Mr. Pickering announce, "No, the manor house I shall build will make this place appear no more couth than a pile of rocks."

Jacob raised his eyebrows at Pickering's comment. He took a breath to inform the idiotic man that Beverly Castle was considered one of Britain's best preserved and well maintained historic sites when Miss Aston responded fiercely.

"I quite disagree, sir. I find Beverly Castle to be timeless. It need not worry about being considered *en vogue*, for it's elegant lines and well-designed layout are ageless."

Jacob smiled, pleased at her remarks. Miss Aston had very good taste, he decided.

"Well, I don't know about—" Mr. Pickering said.

"Furthermore, I find the Wilding family to be incredibly gracious hosts. Why, they could host an event in a barn and have their guests would depart feeling cherished and pampered."

"I certainly didn't mean to imply...that is of course the Wildings are—"

The fool man finally saw Jacob standing behind Miss Aston and Jacob almost felt sorry for him as a look of panic crossed his face. Pickering mumbled something about fetching punch and removed himself promptly.

Miss Aston exhaled gustily and turned around, visibly starting when she saw him.

"Miss Aston," Jacob said heartily. "You look to be in need of refreshments. May I escort you to the dessert table?"

"Oh...thank you. That would be lovely."

She laid her fingers lightly on his forearm and he guided her through the throngs of people to the decadent spread of sweets that was his mother's pride and joy.

"My mother has an incurable sweet tooth," he said, as Miss Aston appeared amazed by the variety and quantity of treats. "Hence, she assumes everyone else does as well."

"Lady Beverly? I find that hard to believe. She's so slim." Her cheeks flamed red with embarrassment at having made such a personal comment. He smiled to reassure her.

"It is only through sheer willpower, I assure you. She used to claim that once she became a grandmother she would allow herself to eat whatever she likes and grow as big as a house, for of course the best grandmothers are soft and comfy. Once my sister had her first, however, my mother decided she would simply knit silk baby blankets to fill in for soft and comfy."

Miss Aston laughed and, while it wasn't the delicate tinkling laugh of Lady Eleanor's fame, it was genuine and hearty. Jacob couldn't help but laugh with her.

Once she sobered, she said, "I fear my will power is not as strong as the countess'. I believe I shall try a slice of that cake."

"A wise choice. Be sure and sample the chocolates as well. Oh, and the marzipan is particularly good," he said, adding each to her plate.

Miss Aston laughed again and moved her plate away when Jacob would have heaped a few cookies on it as well. "My lord, I fear you wish to see me grow round as well!"

Something about the comment—something quite ridiculous—caused his overactive imagination to picture Miss Aston pregnant, her curves grown abundant, her belly full with a babe. The outrageous thought made his body react in a way it never had before when faced with an expectant mother: he grew ferociously aroused. Aroused! Clearly, the whiskey had been stronger than normal tonight. Or perhaps he'd drunk more than he realized. Maybe he was coming down with a cold.

Struggling to regain control of his traitorous body, he cast about for an innocuous topic of conversation.

"Thank you for your compliments to my home. And my family."

Miss Aston froze mid-bite, her eyes wide, her cheeks flushed again. She struggled to quickly swallow the bite of cake she'd ingested. "I'm sure Mr. Pickering didn't mean to sound... ungracious."

A spot of icing clung to the corner of her mouth. Jacob was overcome by the desire—another ridiculous desire, he told himself—to lick it off for her. She saved him from himself by dabbing daintily with an embroidered serviette.

Jacob struggled to remember what she'd said. "Oh, no, I'm sure he didn't. At least, not where I could hear it. I have no doubts as to the quality of his character."

This seemed to bother Miss Aston for she frowned at her dessert plate before setting it back on the table. "He is, I think, simply aware of what he himself lacks and so occasionally gives in to the temptation to...criticize others. To make himself feel better, you see."

Jacob had no idea why she felt the need to defend the pompous Pickering. He recalled that the last time he had questioned her about the man, she had also spoke in Pickering's favor. He sincerely hoped she did not entertain serious feelings for the man. Though he was loathe to examine the reason, the thought of Miss Aston actually enamored of Theodore Pickering made him slightly nauseous.

"Forgive me for criticizing him."

"There is nothing to forgive," She said quickly. She looked as if she were about to say more, but something behind him caught her attention. A look of relief crossed her expressive face and she said, "Please excuse me, Lord Worthing. I see my great aunt is beckoning me. I must attend her at once."

He bowed and murmured something polite, then watched her scurry across the room. She approached an older, turbaned lady who was dozing behind a plant and gently woke her. "Hhmph," Jacob grumbled. It had been a long time since a young lady had deliberately sought to escape his company. Spending time with Juliette Aston was dangerous. He should be relieved she was gone, but found the rest of the evening dull with her absence.

Chapter Fifteen

The weather had been too good to be true, so it was with no real surprise that the next day dawned overcast and rainy. The previous night's festivities had lasted well into the early hours, though Juliette had retired before the party had ended. As a result, she awoke before most of the other guests and found herself breakfasting alone. With no doubt several hours to kill until Eleanor made her way out of her room, Juliette wandered the huge halls of Beverly Castle, amazed to find room after room filled with beautiful furniture, exquisite artwork, richly woven rugs and tapestries.

Every room epitomized grace and nobility, but she wondered what the family quarters looked like. She hoped they were more modest in scale and cozier in appointment, for surely one could not completely relax when surrounded by such ornaments as crystal chandeliers and silk brocade-covered settees.

A staircase and several turns later, Juliette found herself in the library. The room itself was massive and faced the east with large mullioned windows that flooded the room with diffuse light. Ornately carved bookshelves not only lined the outer walls, but also were constructed at right angles to the walls, essentially creating three smaller rooms, each of which featured a cozy seating area with well-worn sofas, deep armchairs, plush rugs, and small fireplaces.

"Now this is more like it," Juliette murmured, strolling down the wide main aisle of the room, perusing the leather-bound books. She was not surprised to find virtually every topic covered, and sighed happily when she discovered an entire bookcase devoted to plays. Hastily running her finger along the spine, she stopped at a huge folio of Shakespeare's works. She tugged it off the shelf and, selecting the settee furthest from the door, made herself comfortable and opened the volume. It was not the First Folio, but was almost certainly one of the earliest printings.

"Ah ha!" Juliette cried in delight. "1664," she sighed, caressing the imprint date with a reverent touch. She spent the next hour pouring through the pages. When finally her eyes swam with the medieval typeface, she closed the folio and stood to stretch. A glance at the small clock on the mantle indicated it was not even close to luncheon and Juliette was certain most guests were still abed. She walked to the nearest window and watched the rain run in rivulets down the rippled glass—itself no doubt of medieval origins. She moved to put the folio back on its shelf when she spotted another book out of line on a lower shelf in her little seating area. Setting down the Shakespeare, she crouched down and withdrew the well-worn volume. She turned it over and read, *"Black Bess: or, the Knight of the Road."*

"Hmmm," Juliette mused with a smile. She sat down on the floor and opened the book. "I never would have guessed you to be a reader of penny dreadfuls, Lord Worthing." Of course, it was possible the books belonged to someone else—even a servant might be allowed to use the family library, but she preferred to believe these belonged to Jacob Wilding.

Looking back at the shelf, she discovered easily a dozen more such books.

"The Castle of Otranto," she read, pulling the book out. "Of course, no gothic collection is complete without that," she informed the settee. "*The Mysteries of Udolpho*. Yes, yes, Radcliffe is quite venerated. But where are the truly awful—aha," she said with satisfaction. *"Mad Melisande; or, The Lass with the Laconic Limp*. Laconic limp? Really?" Juliette set the novel aside—she'd not read that one—and proceeded to pull out *The Adventures of Captain Swing, 'Til Death We Do Reunite*, and *The*

Ironclad Case against Miss Nelson (or, Why Young Ladies Should Not Stray).

"Oh yes, that was a good one," Juliette happily informed the fireplace.

"What was a good one?" the fireplace answered.

Juliette gasped and dropped the book in her lap. She hastily picked it up and tried to decide if she was at a greater disadvantage sitting sprawled on the floor than she would be if she clumsily climbed to her feet. Realizing her left leg had gone to sleep while she perused gothic novels, she opted for remaining sprawled.

Lord Worthing bent over and plucked the book from her nerveless fingers. "It was not my favorite."

"These are yours?" she gasped. So she'd been right!

"Well...mine and my mother's"

Juliette felt her eyebrows rise, quite without her intention. "Lady Wilding reads..."

"Penny dreadfuls, penny horrids, gothic horrids. Yes, yes. Loves them, she assures me, though I'm not certain she's read them since—" He broke off mid-sentence, seemingly absorbed in studying the torrid illustration on the cover.

"Since when?" she asked.

Ignoring her query, Lord Worthing crouched down on his haunches and perused the books she'd pulled from the shelf. "Some seem to be missing. Perhaps my sister has them."

"You have a sister?" she asked, surprised. Though why she should be, she had no idea. It wasn't as if she and Jacob Wilding were close friends, or even anything beyond mere acquaintances. A confessional walk to a picnic notwithstanding, she had only the most cursory knowledge of him.

"Indeed. Lady Avis Lidgate. Married and raising children in the Lake District. Though she cannot be considered a true connoisseur of gothic literature as she mostly reads them in order to laugh uproariously."

Juliette laughed herself. "Well, some of the plots are a bit preposterous."

"Preposterous? Madame, how dare you!"

She laughed harder. "And those poor tortured heroes. How do they stand to live with themselves until they are reformed by their lady loves?"

Lord Worthing sniffed loudly. "Not all of the heroes are tortured. Most are merely just distracted by the mountainous travails facing them."

"Indeed," Juliette said, smothering her smile. Now she really wasn't sure if Lord Worthing were joking or if he had truly taken umbrage at her criticism of the books.

"Indeed. Now I'll grant you the descriptive passages grow a bit tedious. I don't need to know just how the darkening sky waxed from indigo to plum and I certainly don't need to be burdened with a lengthy recitation of the bows and baubles on a lady's dress."

Juliette gasped. "Those are quite my favorite parts!" she exclaimed.

"Truly?" he said, appearing shocked, though the crinkle about his eyes belied the expression. "Then perhaps we ought to stop disparaging one another's favorite bits and simply be glad we both enjoy the publications."

"Very well," she agreed, distracted. Good heavens but the man was attractive! She'd realized it before, of course, but when he had that devilish glint in his eye and just one corner of his mouth drew up in a rather rakish grin, why, Juliette felt a bit like the heroine of the book in his hand, with her heart palpitating and her senses quite overwhelmed.

Deciding it really was time to climb off the floor, she curled her legs beneath her as gracefully as one numbed limb would grant.

Clearly realizing what she sought to attempt, Lord Worthing set the book on the table and bent to assist her. "Allow me."

"Thank you," she said, embarrassed and ridiculously delighted all at once. She was a bit wobbly when fully upright and Worthing kept his hands on her elbows until she steadied. "I fear my leg did not enjoy the book either." Good Lord! Had she just uttered the word "leg" in front of a baron?

If he noticed the word as being taboo for mixed company, he politely ignored it, instead laughing, "Asleep is it?"

"Dreadfully," she admitted, surreptitiously stomping her foot to return circulation.

"Here. Sit. This is my favorite chair."

"Oh but I couldn't! You must—"

"I insist, Miss Aston."

Sure she was flushing beet red, she nodded and thanked him.

"Did you come seeking a book, my lord?"

"Hmm? Oh, I suppose I did. It seems everyone is still recovering from last night's festivities for I believe we are quite the only people up yet, aside from the servants, of course. I was wandering the halls and found my feet bringing me here."

Juliette licked her lips nervously. She was quite aware that they sat in a rather cozy corner of a room completely unsupervised. Clearly the thought had not occurred to Worthing, however, for he simply sorted through the books she'd pulled off the shelf, selected one—was it the *Languid Limp*?—and settled himself in the settee across from her chair. He propped his feet on the low table between them, opened the book to a random page and began reading.

She couldn't help it. She knew it was rude to interrupt his concentration, but she couldn't help it. "You don't begin your books at the first page?"

He glanced up and a sheepish smile crossed his face. She felt her heart accelerate and she willed it to slow.

"I..." he began. "I have read it numerous times. I know how it begins."

"Oh, of course," she said. She returned her attention to *Miss Nelson*.

"I read it to my mother," he paused as if debating whether to explain. Apparently he decided to, for he continued, "When she was ill."

"Oh," was all Juliette could think to say. She remembered him saying as they walked to the picnic that his mother had been very ill. "I'm sure she enjoyed it."

His face wiped clear of all expression, he said, "Likely she would have if she'd been conscious. As it was, I read this and several others to her as she lay insensate for several days."

Juliette gasped. "I had no idea her illness had been so serious."

Worthing shrugged. "Why would you?" He was silent a moment. "Not many people realized how close we came to losing her then. We all took turns sitting with her. My sister would spend mornings, my father afternoons, but I insisted on staying with her at night. I suppose it was restitution for all the nights she kept me company when I was a boy."

"Were you ill?"

He grinned. "No. Nightmares."

"I'm so sorry!"

"Oh don't be. It was my own fault. I played far too many gruesome battle games as a boy. Beheaded dragons and ogres by day, had bad dreams about them by night."

"Ogres?"

"Great wicked ones with horrible fangs."

"I fear I shall suffer nightmares tonight just thinking about it!" They both laughed and Juliette continued, "So you read to her every night?"

He nodded. "The books aren't that long, however." When she nodded, he said, "So I read each one over and over. I'm surprised they are not falling apart."

Juliette ran her fingers over the spine of the book. "They must be as resilient as your mother proved to be." She paused, her throat tightening, though it had been years since her mother had died. Taking a shaky breath, she said, "I wonder if it would have worked with my mother."

"Was she ill?" he asked.

She nodded but did not look up.

"I take it she..."

"I was so young. I doubt it would have occurred to me to read her books. Especially penny horrids. She preferred Bible readings, I think." She hated that she could remember so little of her mother, who had died of childbirth fever after delivering Juliette's stillborn brother. Trying to lighten the mood, she smiled and said, "Although I do have one book of hers my father gave me before I came out."

"What was it?"

She grimaced cast him a sideways glance. "*A Proper Lady's Guide to Perfectly Proper Manners*."

"Good heavens," he said, stifling a laugh. "Not exactly Miss Nelson, is it?"

She shook her head and smiled.

Sobering, he said, "I'm sorry about your mother."

"Thank you. I'm glad yours recovered."

"Me too."

"And I'm glad you appreciate her."

"I—" He cleared his throat. "Me too."

A maid entered the library with feather duster in hand. Upon seeing that it was occupied, she murmured an apology and left. Juliette realized that a guest might wander into the library at any time and find them cozily ensconced. Deciding she did not need a minor scandal to impugn her last shot at the marriage market, even if it was only Mr. Pickering in the running, she stood.

"May I borrow this?"

"Of course. Please help yourself to any book while you are here."

"Thank you," she said. She curtseyed, but paused before leaving. Their gazes locked and each seemed unwilling to part. Finally she turned and fled.

Chapter Sixteen

When the rest of the guests finally arose—good heavens, how could they sleep so late?—Jacob sought out Lady Eleanor. He was certain it was time to advance their courtship and decided upon a walk through the gardens. Perfectly proper (he smiled as he recalled Miss Aston's book) and yet romantic enough to get Lady Eleanor's thoughts moving in the right direction. Upon asking her to join him however, he was rebuffed.

"You will recall," she said in a low voice. "That I suffer distress when I am out of doors."

Jacob winced. He *should* have remembered, of course. "Forgive me. I—perhaps I might show you the portrait gallery?"

Lady Eleanor hesitated the merest moment. Good heavens, was she uninterested? Jacob was duly chagrined to note that the thought had never crossed his mind that the lady he had settled upon would not be receptive.

"I should enjoy that very much. Thank you," she said so sweetly that Jacob's fears were allayed.

They made their way upstairs and down a series of halls to the brightly lit gallery. As they walked along the rows of paintings, Jacob told her a bit about his family's history and in turn asked after hers. They had reached the middle of the long room before he realized he had not one recollection of what she had said. With a brief shake of his head, he forced his attention back to what she was saying.

"...Of course, I'm closest with dear Juliette, Miss Aston. It's from Shakespeare, you know."

"What is?" He must have missed more of their conversation than he realized.

"Her name. 'Wherefore art thou' and all that."

Jacob frowned, remembering. "Actually I believe that line referred to Romeo—"

"It's such a lovely romantic name, don't you think?" she said, apparently not hearing his reply.

"Well, I suppose. Except that Juliette dies at the end."

"What?" Lady Eleanor seemed truly shocked. "How terrible! How?"

"By her own hand. Knife, I believe. Plus she was only fifteen years old. Or was it fourteen?"

"Why, that is a perfectly horrible story! How can it be considered romantic?"

"Er...well, I believe that is why it is dubbed a tragedy."

"Hmmph," she replied with a frown. "Well *my* Juliette would never do such a thing and she is more than worthy of Shakespeare."

Unsure of how to respond, Jacob continued to stroll along the polished parquet floor of the gallery. He was aware that Lady Eleanor continued to ramble on about her friend, but he was trying to think of a topic of conversation they might share to further their interest in one another.

They reached the end of the room and stood before a floor-to-ceiling set of windows that looked out on the gardens. Sheer draperies softened the light and when he glanced at his companion, he saw that the light flattered her delicate complexion. Her golden hair was smooth and glossy, pulled back off her face to cascade in ringlets at her crown. Her delicate bow-shaped mouth was petal pink and practically begged for a kiss. He glanced up the gallery, checking that they were alone. If he kissed her now, it would all but ensure their eventual nuptials. Feeling unaccountably resigned, he leaned closer to her. Lady Eleanor's eyes widened and he thought she pulled back just a bit. It wasn't much, but it caused him to pause and in that instant, he realized he had no desire to kiss her at all.

Damn, he thought. What was he to do now?

"Is that the clock I hear? I'd best go change for supper."

Jacob realized the clock was indeed chiming four o'clock and wondered that Lady Eleanor would need two full hours to prepare for a meal. Stifling the urge to sigh mightily, he escorted her back to the hall that would lead to her room, then found his own chambers and poured himself a stiff drink.

***

After dinner, Jacob sought out Lord Hugh Stalwood. He'd noticed his mother sat his friend by Miss Aston and that the two had had an animated dinner conversation. Hoping his plan to provide Miss Aston with matrimonial options was paying off, he wanted to hear Hugh's thoughts.

There were no formal festivities planned for the evening. A group played cards at a table in the drawing room while several ladies exhibited their musical accomplishments. The next day would see the gentlemen pursue a hunt while the ladies did...whatever ladies did while gentlemen hunted. A final ball would close the house party and see guests home the following day. Jacob knew he should be seeking out Lady Eleanor's company, but wanted to nudge Hugh along as well.

"Worthing!" his friend exclaimed. "I was just looking for you. What say we grab a few of the fellows and sneak away to play some serious cards?"

"In a bit. My mother will kill me if I abandon the guests so soon."

Stalwood sighed. "Tied to her apron strings. You'll choke on them one of these days."

Jacob lifted his eyebrows. "Right. And my mother will tell your mother you led me down the path of ruin. What do you suppose your mother will do?"

"There's no need to become uncivil, Worthing," Hugh said with unfeigned nervousness. "I was only joking. Of course we'll keep the young ladies entertained for a while."

Jacob pressed his lips together to suppress a smile. "Speaking of young ladies, I noticed you and Miss Aston seemed quite engrossed in conversation at supper."

"Who? Oh yes, yes."

"So?" Jacob prodded.

"So what?"

"So what do you think of her?"

"Oh she's a good egg," Hugh said, nodding at a group of friends across the room.

"Is that all?"

"All? What do you mean?" Hugh looked at his friend and visibly started. "Good heavens, you don't mean…why, whatever gave you the notion I would be interested in her that way?"

"You said yourself you were open to meeting potential brides. And I've scarcely heard you describe anyone else as a 'good egg.'"

"Sure I have! My sister, for one. Aunt Dotty—I referred to her as such just the other week."

"Your sister? Aunt Dotty? But Miss Aston—"

"Is a very nice young lady. Clever, good-natured. Easy on the eyes."

"Then why—"

"No sparks, my man. No sparks."

"Sparks?" Jacob felt his stomach drop, though he refused to examine why.

"It's one thing to enjoy the company of a gel like your sister, but for a wife, I require at least some spark of attraction."

Ignoring the looming thought that Hugh's description perfectly described his feelings toward Lady Eleanor, he pushed on.

"But she is, as you say, clever and witty and good looking…"

Hugh turned and stared at Jacob. "Look, old boy. If you're so keen on her, why don't you pursue her?"

Jacob pulled back. "I can't. You know I am going to offer for Lady Eleanor."

Hugh shrugged. "If you're sure."

"Of course I'm sure," Jacob snapped. "She is who my—I find to be the best pairing for me."

Hugh stared at him for a long moment before saying, "Then why are you trying so hard to play matchmaker for Miss Aston?"

"She is Lady Eleanor's closest friend. It is all to gain Lady Eleanor's favor, I assure you."

Hugh's tawny brows twitched but he said nothing else.

Jacob glanced around the room and, spying an empty seat next to Eleanor, took his leave of his friend. He resolutely did not notice Miss Aston sitting on the other side of his intended.

His shoulder collided with Lord Buchanan's and he apologized profusely.

"No, no," the man protested, a cloud of brandy fumes wafting into Jacob's face. "'Smy fault. Or your father's, I should say."

"My father's?"

"Hish brandy. It kicks like a mule!"

Jacob chuckled and then realized that an inebriated Buchanan might be inclined to talk. "I've been meaning to ask you, Buchanan. How was your dance with Miss Aston the other night?"

"Whoseat?"

"Miss Aston. I introduced you to her the other night. You asked her to dance." At the blank look on the lord's face, Jacob sighed and said, "Oh for heaven's sake. The young woman sitting over there wearing yellow."

Buchanan squinted and even leaned forward as if that would assist his brandy-blurred vision. "Oh her."

"Yes. I found her to be quite amenable. Did you enjoy dancing with her?"

"She talks too much."

"What? What did she say?"

"Kept asking me questions, like, did I read books or see plays or have horses."

"And that's bad?" Jacob queried.

"I like a gel that's quiet. Leaves me to my thoughts."

"Which are, no doubt, as deep as a puddle," Jacob said under his breath.

"Whasshat?"

Jacob shook his head. "Nothing. Perhaps you'll want to sit down so you're not so wobbly on your feet."

Buchanan nodded and ambled off, no doubt in the direction of more spirits. Jacob returned to his objective only to discover the empty seat by Eleanor had been taken. Feeling as if he were engaged in an onerous task instead of courting a woman who would share his life, he stomped up to the small group and glared pointedly at the young man beside Eleanor until the chap grew uncomfortable and stood.

"Lady Eleanor," Jacob said a little too heartily. "I've been meaning to ask you what your favorite book is."

If Eleanor was surprised by his abrupt question, she gracefully did not show it. "Well, my lord, let me think." She sat in contemplation; tapping one finely gloved finger against her perfectly bowed lips. A tiny frown marred the perfect ivory of her brow.

"Do you know, Lord Worthing, I cannot think of a single book I've liked well enough to call my favorite."

Jacob felt his stomach clench but he kept a polite smile on his face. "No?"

Lady Eleanor shook her head slowly, her glossy ringlet curls bouncing on either side of her face. Suddenly her expression cleared and she smiled. "But I do so enjoy *La Belle Assemblee*."

"Indeed," Jacob murmured, suddenly daunted by the image of a future of solitary evenings spent in the library.

Miss Aston leaned in. Jacob studiously avoided glancing down her gown, the bodice of which gaped slightly displaying a shadow of soft cleavage.

"Eleanor, you remember you love the short stories in *La Belle Assemblee*. Remember? I read you one on the way here."

"Oh yes, but that's only because of how you read it," Eleanor said and turning to Jacob explained, "Juliette reads all the characters with a different voice and makes the stories so exciting."

Jacob raised a brow at Miss Aston. "We shall have to have you read for us."

Her eyes widened and she sat up straight, removing the temptation of ogling her. "Oh, no! I just do it for Eleanor." Then turning to her friend, Miss Aston said, "I'm sure you would enjoy a novel if you tried it."

Lady Eleanor shrugged. "I suppose, but I'd much rather you just tell me about them. I've just never been one for reading."

Jacob didn't realize he'd been studying Miss Aston until he saw her cast him an apologetic glance. He turned abruptly back to the beautiful countenance of Lady Eleanor. "Well, I'm sure you have many other interests."

"Indeed, but if you wish to discuss books, Juliette is ravenous for them."

Jacob's mouth went instantly dry. For some reason, the words "ravenous" and "Juliette" in the same sentence produced images in his mind he should *not* be entertaining. Images like her naked in his bed while he satisfied a ravenous appetite…

"I promised my mother I would keep the young gentlemen in line so they don't simply disappear into the card room. Please excuse me," he said, and beat a hasty retreat, studiously ignoring his own rudeness.

Chapter Seventeen

Jacob mounted his horse the next morning for the hunt, feeling bleary-eyed and ill-rested. He'd tossed and turned much of the night, and awoke disgruntled. It should have been a simple matter, this marriage business. He respected his father in all ways, trusted his judgment more than his own. It should follow that he found Lady Eleanor to be all that he sought in a wife. Why was he then feeling like a lad forced to eat boiled spinach for dinner? And why on earth would someone so clearly wrong for the position of his wife—namely Miss Juliette Aston—plague his thoughts so? She was like a burr in his side with her constant arguing. No, that wasn't right. They hadn't argued in quite some time. Instead they'd had conversations about books and life and hopes and fears.

He was most definitely not attracted to her. In comparison to Lady Eleanor's golden beauty? He tried to picture Eleanor's hair, but all he saw was lustrous dark hair. He tried to call to mind Eleanor's musical laugh, but he only heard Juliette's, genuine and precious for its rarity. As he guided his horse into an open field, the sun struck his eyes and he was reminded him that he'd been mesmerized by Juliette's sun-kissed face on the back verandah. And there'd been those moments last night, first when he'd inadvertently glanced down her bodice, seeing the soft valley between her breasts. The resulting fantasies had been damned uncomfortable thoughts to entertain about the best friend of the woman he was courting.

He guided his horse to the front of the assembly of gentlemen and led them off the manicured grounds and into the woods, riding mostly by rote over paths he had traveled thousands of times.

Lady Eleanor was everything a future earl's wife should be: she was beautiful, elegant, clearly well trained in hospitable arts. She was almost universally well liked amongst the *ton* and that would do him no harm once he assumed his seat in Parliament. As a gently bred lady, he was certain she'd been instructed on household management and could no doubt play the pianoforte or sing or something of that ilk. If she and he did not share a love of reading—and in fact, he had discovered very few deep interests they did share--well, he certainly could not expect to have the same type of marriage as his parents. No indeed, he and Eleanor were very different people from the Earl and Countess of Beverly. For example, he for one would never presume to choose his son's bride for him, especially when—Jacob stopped himself in the midst of that disloyal thought. His horse, responding to a tug on the reins he hadn't been aware of making, reared slightly and sidestepped. He quickly calmed the animal and drew it to the side, allowing the other riders to tear past him on the narrow trail, the dogs baying as they picked up a scent.

He refused to consider that he might feel any sort of antagonism over his father's seemingly out-of-the-blue decision that he should marry Lady Eleanor. He simply needed to liberate himself from his previous notion of what his marriage would be. His life-long notion.

"Tcha!" he spat, disgusted with himself. Good God, you'd think he was the first man to marry a woman he didn't love. Why it was practically an institution in and of itself amongst the aristocracy to marry someone who was perfect for you in all ways but matters of the heart.

"Lord Worthing!" A voice called from down the trail. Jacob looked up to see Mr. Strong nudge his horse to come up even with him.

Jacob recollected he had nudged Strong to dance with Miss Aston. "Strong. Glad you came along on the hunt. Your mount is acceptable?"

Strong pulled too strongly on the reins and his horse reared, nearly throwing the poor man to the ground. Jacob leaned forward and caught the horse's bridle, settling the animal.

"Quite spirited isn't he?" Strong asked nervously.

"She is," Jacob said, suppressing a smile.

"I must admit to being a bit out of practice on the hunt."

"No need to push yourself," Jacob assured the other man, though the notion was completely foreign to him. There was nothing he loved more than pushing himself and his mount to their physical and mental limits. The notions of being a good host had been bred into him, however, and he felt compelled to keep the other man company.

The men rode slowly down the trail, the other mounts long since gone.

After an awkward silence, Jacob said, "I believe you danced with Miss Aston the other night."

"Indeed I did, indeed I did," Strong said jovially.

"She is a lovely young woman, wouldn't you agree?"

"Lovely, lovely. I was happy to partner her. Happy, I say."

Jacob wondered why Strong was suddenly repeating himself. "Did you find her pleasant company?"

"Quite, quite. She is all that is amiable in a young miss. Perfectly mannered. Quite pretty too. Lovely blond hair."

Jacob frowned. "You do recall me introducing you to Miss Aston, don't you Strong. Her hair is dark."

"Of course, of course. A particular friend of yours, I believe. I was delighted to be of service to you."

"Service to me?" Jacob asked, surprised.

"Yes, yes. Anything at all, old man."

"I only introduced her to you so that you might—"

"And I will certainly ask her to dance again. Er...if you would be so kind as to point her out to me, that is."

"What? But you danced—"

"Speaking of favors among friends, have you given any more thought to selling me that mare I asked about last spring?"

"Mare?" Comprehension dawned and Jacob's mouth tightened with displeasure. "I introduced you to Miss Aston because I find her to be a most agreeable companion and I sought to do you a favor by making you known to her. I did not suggest you dance with her as a favor to *me*."

"Er...well, of course...?" Strong mumbled, clearly unsure of himself. "And I, er, was grateful, of course. Lovely gel."

"Lovely. Except you can't recall what she looks like."

Visibly uncomfortable, Mr. Strong jumped when he heard the dogs baying. "I say, we'd best catch up to the others, don't you think?" And without waiting for a response, he whirled his horse and took off after the hunt, barely keeping his seat.

"As if I'd trust a horse into your care," Jacob muttered as he nudged his own mount to a canter.

What the devil was wrong with the men at this house party—or in London for that matter? Miss Aston mightn't be considered a diamond of the first water, but the more he thought of it, the more he couldn't understand. She was easily as beautiful as any of the girls who had received two or three offers last Season. And she was a damn site more interesting than any of the young misses he'd ever met. The irony did not escape him that he found Miss Aston an ideal specimen for the marriage-minded...for everyone except himself.

Perhaps when he and Eleanor were wed, he'd be in a better position to assist Miss Aston. The memory of Hugh suggesting he himself marry Miss Aston popped in his head. Or was it his gut? There was a distinct clenching in his chest when he thought of her in any capacity other than his future wife's friend. He refused to analyze it beyond a natural compassion for a fellow—good God, he couldn't even convince himself of that. There was something there, something that evoked distinctly uncomfortable feelings. No, he could not afford to give the girl any more thought. He must devote his attention to Eleanor and his courtship of her. Surely if he put enough effort into it, he would discover some modicum of passion for her.

He spurred his mount on to catch up to the hunting group and threw himself into the day's activities with fervor.

He was one of the last to return late that afternoon, sweaty, disheveled, and thoroughly exhausted, but with a greater sense of equanimity than he had experienced earlier in the day. He made his way from the stables as the sun was nearing the horizon. It cast a heavy golden haze across the earth, gilding flowers, illuminating each leaf on the trees. The pale sandstone of the house took on a rosy hue, as if it were a flower in full bloom. The buzz of bees and occasional chirrup of a cricket were the only sounds in the lazy peacefulness of the early evening. He paused to inhale deeply, noting the sweetness of his mother's garden flowers, the rich loam of recently watered dirt, the tang of trimmed grass. Up on the veranda, a few guests sat at the tables scattered about. They were clearly moving indoors to begin dressing for dinner and Jacob recognized his mother's distinctive posture as she urged the guests inside. She sat at a table with someone, clearly enjoying her conversation as she laughed and chatted enthusiastically. As he climbed the wide shallow steps, the sun struck him full in the face and he shaded his eyes as he approached her.

"Jacob! Did you have a good ride?"

"I did," he said, blinking to recover from the sun's glare. When his eyes regained their sight, he looked to his mother's companion and was surprised—and truth be told, slightly dismayed—to discover it was Miss Aston.

He bowed slightly, "Miss Aston."

"Juliette has been regaling me with truly awful stories of her debut season," his mother said, chuckling.

Jacob studied Miss Aston. Her eyes were downcast and her lashes cast deep shadows on her cheeks—cheeks that were again dusted with gold from the waning sun. The sun also plucked coppery highlights out in her hair and, he suspected, would make the outline of her figure clearly transparent through her fine lawn day dress were she to stand and were he to look.

"Did you hear what I said, Jacob?"

Jacob started from his ridiculous reverie. "I beg your pardon?"

His mother lifted one eyebrow slightly—an expression he was well aware meant that she knew his mind had been wandering, having been the recipient of it hundreds, if not thousands, of times in his youth. He also knew it meant he would feel obligated to accede to whatever she was about to suggest.

"I asked if you would show Miss Aston to my herb garden —the ornamental one, not the kitchen one."

"Your herb garden."

"Yes," his mother stated firmly. "Specifically the new French lavender I recently planted. Miss Aston has a keen interest in collecting some to make a sachet."

"Truly, I've no wish to—"

His mother turned to Miss Aston with a determined smile. "Nonsense, my dear. This is the absolute best time to collect the lavender, after it's been warmed by the sun all day."

"I thought that would have been at midnight under a full moon," Jacob muttered to himself. His mother, of course, ignored him, but Miss Aston shot him a glance that was one part incredulity and one part hilarity. He couldn't help grinning like an unrepentant schoolboy.

"In addition, the oils, once released, will delicately permeate the clothes in which you tuck the sachet. One's chemises, for example."

It was Jacob's turn to raise an eyebrow. Had his mother, ever one for propriety, just mentioned Miss Aston's unmentionables? A quick glance at the young lady in question showed a complexion rather rosier than sitting in the fading sunlight should cause. Why on earth had his mother wanted him to think about Miss Aston's chemises? His earlier supposition that he would be able to see her body silhouetted through her dress transformed into an image of her in nothing but a nearly sheer chemise, standing in front of a candle. Or better yet, a fireplace.

A prickle of heat that had nothing to do with the wool of his riding jacket or the setting sun washed over him and he surreptitiously tugged at his loosened cravat. His mother continued to smile, and he knew that he was doomed to do as she requested.

"Truly, Lady Beverly, I should retire to change for dinner. All the other guests have already—" She began to rise and Jacob thought he would be spared, but his mother cut her off.

"Nonsense. Dinner will be rather late as I've forgotten a crucial menu change that will throw Cook into a tizzy. You've plenty of time and it's the least I can do to thank you for such an enjoyable afternoon."

Miss Aston looked rather perplexed but smiled gamely. Her smile turned apologetic as she looked to Jacob, who smoothed his features into careful neutrality and offered her his arm. She tentatively laid her fingers on it, and he turned to guide her down the wide stairs he had only recently climbed.

"You'll want this, Jacob," his mother called, holding out a basket and shears. As he took it, he shot her a glare, which she blithely ignored.

Chapter Eighteen

Jacob and Miss Aston made their way through the formal gardens in silence. He wondered again what the devil his mother was up to. She knew very well his father's feelings regarding Jacob's wife selection so surely she wasn't seeking to play matchmaker, was she? He scrutinized his companion as they wended through the narrowing paths of the outer gardens. Surely his mother did not consider the daughter of a baronet to be a better choice than Lady Eleanor?

Finally deciding the silence was growing awkward, he cleared his throat and said, "What stories were you telling my mother that amused her so?" He cringed inwardly to hear the accusatory tone in his voice. Miss Aston looked up sharply and then returned her gaze to the path.

"She was simply being kind. I'm sure none of my stories could be considered amusing," she replied woodenly.

Feeling like a cad, he tried again. "Come now, Miss Aston, my mother is regarded as a great wit—in her own mind, of course. Nonetheless, if she found your stories amusing, I am sure they must be."

She gasped at his irreverent comment about his mother, and he gave her his most rakish grin to let her know he was joking. She smiled and walked another few steps in silence before speaking.

"When Eleanor and I first met—our first Season—she was instantly popular, of course."

She seemed to require a response, so he murmured, "Of course."

"I was…well, Eleanor used to call me the Invisible Lady."

Jacob started, taken aback by the notion of Eleanor saying such a mean thing to her supposed best friend. "That's not very—" he began, but she cut him off.

"Oh no, we came up with the name together. It was amusing, truly."

"I don't see how, but go on."

"Well, I was rather timid that first Season. I'd no female relatives anywhere close to my own age to guide me through... anything, really. Eleanor and I struck up an unlikely friendship, but even still, I seemed to be, simply...invisible...to the rest of the ton. We took advantage of my invisibility rather too often for our own good."

Jacob felt that uncomfortable tightness at the base of his ribs again. He was unaccountably angry with his fellow peers for making Miss Aston—Juliette—feel worthless. He was struck with a ridiculous frustration that he'd been unable to spare her such hurt, for though she might speak lightly of it now, what must it have felt like to a young girl in her first Season?

She tugged on his sleeve and he realized he'd come to a halt. She smiled quizzically at him and he pushed the uncomfortable feelings aside and affected a humorous mien. "And what mischief did you enact to earn your sobriquet?"

"We stole people's desserts."

"I beg your pardon?"

She smiled rather sheepishly, but the look on his face must have been something, for she quickly burst out laughing. It was a glorious sound, he decided abstractly. It sounded rather like the late golden sun felt on his skin. Soothing and mesmerizing and...magical. Shaking his head to free it of his nonsensical notions—truly, he must be more exhausted than he thought—he said, "You stole people's desserts? How on earth did you do that?"

"It started out when we were at a rather large ball. The food was not near enough to satiate the crowd. The pastries were long gone by the time we made our way to the tables, but all around us people were exclaiming how good they were, how unfortunate it was that there were not more of them. I think they were something chocolatey, with some sort of crème filling."

Jacob felt his stomach rumble at the thought.

"Eleanor and I soon found ourselves attended by two of her admirers, both of whom had said pastries on their plates. Untouched, mind you. Eleanor mentioned how disappointed we were not to have been able to try them. Do you think either of those silly lordlings offered us—well, her at least—their plates?"

Jacob laughed shortly and shook his head. Gentlemen were trained from an early age that their duties at balls was to see to the comfort of the ladies, regardless of what was asked of them.

"What did you do?" he asked, though Lord help him, he suspected he knew.

"I simply snatched up a plate from a passing footman and helped myself to one of each of their pastries. Neither gentleman even noticed me doing it, despite my being right in front of them. They were too busy making calf eyes at Eleanor and trying to impress her with tales of horse races they'd won."

"The fools."

Juliette—when had he taken to thinking of her as such?—shrugged lightly and stepped around an overgrown rosemary hedge. They'd reached his mother's herb garden.

"It became a bit of a game after that," she said. "Eleanor would get the gentlemen talking and when they were each trying to outdo each other for her attention, I would swipe whatever was on their plates. Or in their hands. Wine glasses, books, tickets to the theater they were about to see. They were quite oblivious. If we'd had a mind to become criminals, we'd have made a fortune." She laughed at the idea and while Jacob smiled in return, it was more in honor of her ability to laugh than at the stupidity of his half of the human species.

"Then I needn't ask the housekeeper to count the silver?"

She smiled—no, grinned, really—and Jacob attributed the hitch in his breath to a bit of pollen or dust in the air.

"Your silver is safe. Your pastries..."

Jacob gave in to a hearty laugh. "No wonder my mother was enjoying herself," he said.

"Oh, she told many more amusing stories than I," she assured him.

He lifted his brows in surprise. "Do tell."

She glanced sideways at him, a small smile tugging at the corner of her mouth. She looked delightfully impish and Jacob felt an overwhelming urge to kiss her. Ridiculous notion, he told himself, but there it was. Her color was high, her eyes sparkled with amusement, and she walked with the unselfconscious sway of a country girl. A more kissable female he could not imagine.

"Well, they are your mother's stories. I would not presume to tell them."

"I'm sure I've heard them all," he assured her.

"Like the one where she invented an imaginary fiancée in France to make your father jealous?"

"What?" Jacob felt an incredulous smile curve his lips.

"Never heard that story? Tsk, tsk. Perhaps she didn't care for you to know it then," she teased. Teased! Jacob couldn't remember if a young miss had ever had the temerity to tease him. It was rather refreshing.

"I'm not certain I believe you," he said, trying to egg her on. It worked.

"Well it was not so much as to make your father jealous as to gain his attention in the first place. I gather your sire was a bit of a man-about-town and had grown rather accustomed to young ladies throwing themselves at his head. Lady Beverly said she needed to be different to gain his attention, and thus contrived a mysterious French nobleman who absorbed all her thoughts so she was quite unable to even bid Lord Beverly good day when they met at the park or a ball."

"You're quite serious," Jacob said, for some reason unable

to reconcile the thought of his genteel, refined mother doing anything so outrageous as inventing a suitor.

In response, Miss Aston simply raised her eyebrows at him.

"And what led you to a discussion on the outrageous habits of young debutantes?"

Her cheeks flushed red and while it could have been a reaction to their walk in the final heat of the day, he suspected she was suddenly uncomfortable. They walked in silence several more steps before he prodded her.

"Planning to conspire together were you?"

She lifted her chin and though she refused to look at him, affected an unconcerned air. "We were discussing the lengths to which a wallflower must go to find amusement."

"Wallflowers?"

He wasn't sure but he thought she actually ground her teeth before saying, "Wallflowers. Those unfortunate women overlooked at social events due to a lack of prestige, beauty, or wealth."

"Thank you for that edifying definition," he said wryly. "I believe we have already had this conversation. You're quite fixated on that label, aren't you?" He held up a hand when she opened her mouth to argue. "But how does a discussion of wallflowers lead to tales of your mutual foibles?"

She stared at her feet—they had stopped walking at some point and were in the middle of his mother's garden, surrounded by shades of green and the apothecary shop odors of dozens of different herbs.

"As I am a wallflower and your mother vows she was one as well before she married your father, it was a natural conversational progression."

Again, Jacob felt something like vertigo—he'd never pictured his mother as anything other than the Society grande dame that she was. Pulling his thoughts from that notion, he tipped Juliette's chin up with the tip of his gloved finger. He wished he'd removed the dammed thing to feel the warm softness of her skin.

She reluctantly looked up and Jacob realized he'd never noticed the color of her eyes before. They were an intriguing cross between blue and grey—slate one might even call them. He had the absurd notion that he could spend hours staring into them.

"You're not a wallflower," he said gently.

She looked around the garden as if searching for someone. Turning back to him, she laughed. "I'm sorry, were you talking to me? Because I can assure you, my lord, I am indeed a wallflower. I rarely dance, I never take walks on the veranda with gentlemen, and I doubt if one in ten men I've been introduced to at every event for the last two years could remember my name if his life depended upon it. If that's not wallflower status, I'm sure I don't know what is."

"You danced with several men here."

A wistful smile crossed her face and was as quickly gone. "I did, didn't I?" She shook her head. "It was an anomaly. For all I know, someone put them up to it—perhaps Eleanor. She's always trying to find me anyone other than—" she cut herself off and abruptly turned to begin clipping bits of lavender. Jacob had no idea if it were the one he was supposed to show her.

"Other than Mr. Pickering?"

She ignored him, instead hacking away at the lavender with a bit more aggression than was absolutely necessary. The aromatic scent of lavender permeated the warm air, the only sounds in the garden those of the clicking shears and the low buzz of bees. He watched her for a moment, unsure of what to do or say. He told himself he should drop the subject. He had no right to question her about her suitor, should avoid any interest in who she ended up married to. Unfortunately, the thought of her married—especially to the lamentable Mr. Pickering—left him feeling nauseous. Or perhaps it was anger? Certainly not jealousy!

She continued to snip at the hapless plant and in a fit of frustration, he grabbed for the shears. He'd clearly surprised her for she started, turned, and promptly dropped the shears.

"Ow!" she cried, dropping the basket and lifting a foot.

"Juliette!"

With visions of her impaled by the shears—and himself to blame—he quickly swooped her into his arms and carried her to a bench in the center of the garden.

"I'm so sorry."

"What are you--? I'm fine, my lord. I assure you. Please set me—"

Jacob set her on the bench and knelt to inspect her wound. With hands that were shaking, he gingerly lifted the hem of her skirts, prepared to see blood and a wretched wound. Instead he simply found a neatly turned ankle, encased in a kid slipper and white silk stocking. He ran his thumb over the top of her foot, eliciting a gasp of surprise from Miss Aston.

He looked up to see her surprised expression. "I thought you'd stabbed yourself," he explained hoarsely.

She shook her head slowly. "I think they must have landed handle-side down."

"You're not hurt?"

She looked at her foot, still in his hands. "The top is a bit bruised, but I shall live."

He ran the pad of his thumb more firmly over the curved top of her foot. "I'm sorry," he said when she hissed as he touched a tender spot. "I want to make sure you didn't break it."

She huffed a laugh. "I simply dropped the shears on it, not a cast iron kettle."

She was right, he knew, but he found himself unable to release her foot, instead turning it gently side to side, pretending not to notice her firm, trim calf beneath his hand. There was a small snag in her stocking just beneath the raised hem and it was all he could do not to smooth it, perhaps run his hand further up—

"I assure you, I am quite well," she said in a whisper.

Looking up he realized she knew exactly what he was staring at. She was flushed, her eyes heavy-lidded, her lips parted as if in anticipation. Jacob knew he had to break this sensuous spell that had wrapped itself around them. He set her foot down, dropped her skirts, and quickly stood. He took a step back and offered her his hand. She took it and stood, gasping in pain and tottering forward. Without thought, he caught her to him, supporting her against his chest, his right arm locked around her waist.

"Juliette—"

"I'm fine," she breathed, staring at his...mouth? "I think I just put weight on it too quickly. It's...it's better already."

She cast a surreptitious glance up and he saw her eyes were dark beneath her lashes. He was acutely aware of the press of her body along his, from the brush of her skirts against his riding trousers to the slope of her breasts against his chest and the gentle curve of her belly against his.

Her lower back beneath his hand was a firm arch. He was aware that her figure was not that of a willow sylph, nor was it an opulent, Rubenesque one. Regardless, it—she—felt right, as if their bodies had been designed to match. Other parts of his anatomy seemed to agree and he realized he was in danger of embarrassing himself or shocking her. Slowly setting her away from him, he held onto her arms while she tentatively put weight on her foot.

"Are you sure you can walk?"

She nodded and took a step away from him. He watched her face for any sign of pain, but she seemed in a bit of a daze, her focus still on his face as if she were seeing him for the first time, or perhaps memorizing it for the last time.

What a ridiculous notion, he firmly told himself. He was acting like a green lad alone with a lass for the first time.

"Have you enough lavender, Miss Aston?"

"I—yes, I'm sure it's plenty."

"Very good, he said briskly, striding over to retrieve the basket of cuttings as well as the errant shears. He returned to her but when she moved to take the basket, he refused to relinquish it.

"Why Pickering?" he demanded.

"Wh-what?"

"Why would a girl such as you settle for a man like Pickering?"

She frowned. "Partly because I'm hardly a girl, Lord Worthing. Besides, Mr. Pickering is very nice. He has treated me with respect and..."

"And?" he prodded.

"And he is very nice. I am sure we will get on smoothly."

"You'll be bored to tears."

"I beg your pardon?"

"Does Pickering know you read penny horrids?"

"I fail to see—"

"Has he shown any interest in things that interest you?" he demanded. A detached part of his brain was watching the scene with horror. Why was he demanding anything of Miss Aston? Why did he care who she married? For good or for ill, the rest of his brain ploughed ahead.

"I thought not. The man is an idiot."

"Now see here," Miss Aston said, beginning to sound irate. "In the first place, I fail to see how my...my attachments are any concern of yours. Secondly, Mr. Pickering is a busy man and we've scarce had any time to explore our mutual interests. And finally," at this, her voice was quite loud, "I don't see any other bloody men jumping up to court me! Not in my first year out, not in my second, and certainly not this one!"

"That can't be true," he said softly.

"Oh I assure you, it is," she snapped, refusing to meet his gaze.

"Then the men of London are fools, to a one."

She huffed a laugh and shrugged her shoulders. "No more so than I am."

"Why do you say that?" He studied her profile, noting the stubborn jut of her chin, the large freckle high on her cheekbone, placed like the beauty patches of old to draw the eye to the wearer's finest features. He could not at this moment decide which was her best feature. Her eyes were quite fine, that velvety earlobe practically begged him to nibble it, her lustrous dark hair made his fingers itch to drag it from its coiffure. When she finally spoke, he had to scramble to remember what she had just said.

"What sort of fool marries a man she knows has no interest in her as a person? Who does not look forward to her wedding with even a modicum of excitement? Who dreads the day her one and only suitor takes her in his arms and—" she clamped her mouth shut and continued to stare out over the herb garden.

"Then why will you marry him?"

The eyes she turned to him were flat and wiped of emotion. "Because my father has determined this is my last Season. I will marry this year or return to keep house for him in Hertford. Forever."

"But—"

"The options for a spinster are decidedly slim, my lord. I should count myself fortunate that my father would be able to keep me should I not marry. But as it is, I shall accept if Mr. Pickering lives up to his hints and implications and offers for me."

"Have you no dreams then for your future?"

"I dream of having children. Several of them, if possible, for I did not enjoy my existence as an only child. They shall be my family and I shall be their confidant and playmate as well as their mother. All that I cannot attain for myself, I shall work to make sure they have laid before them, son or daughter." Her voice shook with determination and Jacob could see, as if they were right in front of him, a cluster of children with dark curls and laughing faces. The image made his heart pound with unfamiliar emotion.

"But surely you wish to have such a family with a man you love. Perhaps you've just not been introduced to—"

She shook her head. "I've been introduced to everyone, Lord Worthing. I simply do not appeal to the men of the ton. I suppose it's partly because I'm unable to simper and pout and toss my curls coyly. I'm not beautiful and my wit requires more than a passing nod or dance to assert itself."

"But if you just exerted yourself a bit, the men of the ton would realize that you are in fact a beauty, and that your wit is well worth the time to draw it out. I can attest to that."

"And yet you are pursuing Eleanor, not me."

Jacob felt her words like a blow to the solar plexus. He had no response—what could he possibly say? She had a look of pity on her face and he frowned in return.

"It's alright. Eleanor is worth a hundred of me. I don't mind being in her shadow, not at all. I must simply do what I can to carve out a life for myself. And you will be quite the fortunate man should Eleanor accept you."

Jacob let the implication that there was a possibility he would be refused pass. He was still incensed at the notion of Juliette married to Mr. Pickering. And, truth be told, he felt a little panicky at the idea that he was pursuing Eleanor and not her. He never panicked! Not when he was down by a hundred pounds at cards nor when he'd fallen from a tree and broken his arm as a boy, not even when his mother had been ill. What on earth did such an emotion now imply?

With a sigh that sounded more than resigned, Juliette said, "We should return. I must change before dinner and I'm sure it has grown quite late."

Jacob pulled himself from his reverie and glanced around. The sun had just set and the garden was bathed in the pearly light of dusk. Without saying a word, he offered his arm to Juliette and guided her back to the house.

Chapter Nineteen

On the short walk back, Juliette cursed herself for being foolish. What had she been thinking to blurt out her feelings regarding Mr. Pickering, her complaints about not being more popular, or even that bit about having children? Her dreams, meager as they were, were her own as were her disappointments. Why Jacob Wilding was able to needle such personal confessions out of her was a mystery, but it was an incident that must not repeat itself. She only hoped he didn't share her wild assertions with Eleanor. Though they were dearest friends—indeed, Juliette did not count herself closer to anyone other than Eleanor—there were certain things she would not share with anyone. She cringed to remember that she had confessed to Lord Worthing that she dreaded being taken into Mr. Pickering's arms.

Beneath her fingers, she felt the firm ripple of Lord Worthing's arm as he guided her along the garden path and up the wide steps to the verandah to the French doors leading inside. She felt the sharp sting of tears behind her eyes and in the back of her throat for she wished for nothing more than to feel those arms around her, comforting her and assuring her she was indeed desired for just who she was. This attraction is ridiculous, she told herself firmly. A man such as Jacob Wilding was meant for none other than a diamond of the first water. She would be happy for Eleanor. She *was* happy for Eleanor. Her...unfortunate feelings for her friend's suitor would pass. She would ensure that they did.

At the top of the steps, Aunt Constance called out to her. "There you are, Juliette. I'd quite despaired of seeing you alive."

Beside her, she heard Lord Worthing laugh softly.

"I assure you, Aunt, I am quite alive. Did you fear I'd been eaten by wolves?"

She saw Constance narrow her eyes at Lord Worthing speculatively. "Stranger things have happened," was all the older woman said. "Now you'd best hurry. Dinner is about to be served and you've the look of a milkmaid about you. Did it even occur to you to wear a bonnet, miss? I declare, you'll be as freckled as an egg before we return to London."

Juliette cast one quick glance at Lord Worthing. He had a bemused expression on his face and when she saw him turn his head toward her, she jerked her gaze away and quickly followed her aunt into the house.

"Decided you won't settle for that dolt Pickering after all, eh?" Constance said with a dry chuckle. Truly, Juliette decided, it could only have been classified as a cackle.

"It's not what you think, Aunt. Lady Wilding simply asked him to guide me to her lavender. See?" She held up the basket of wilting herbs.

"Clever gel, to woo the mother first." Her aunt gave an approving nod.

"Aunt Constance!"

"What is it gel? Did he take liberties out in the garden?"

"I can assure you that Lord Worthing has absolutely no intentions toward me other than those of a host to his houseguest. He is courting Eleanor and I'm sure the two will be betrothed by month's end."

"Pity that. She'd bore him to tears," Constance mumbled.

"What did you say?" It was odd that it was such a similar comment to what Lord Worthing had made about she and Mr. Pickering.

But Aunt Constance only shooed her upstairs and went into the library, no doubt in search of the sherry before the dinner gong rang.

Juliette was just opening her door when she heard Eleanor say, "Oh there you are. I was wondering where you'd got to."

"I was just picking some lavender to make a sachet. Lady Wilding assures me it is a particularly sweet species of lavender."

"Yes well you'd better hurry. You know I'm always late and here I'm ready before you. Shall I keep you company while you change?"

"Certainly."

Once in Juliette's room she rang for a maid and then quickly undressed and washed while waiting for her.

"So were you in the garden alone?" Eleanor asked.

"No. Lady Wilding asked her son to show my where in the garden this particular plant was."

"Lord Worthing, you say?"

Juliette swallowed the lump of hurt in her throat. "Indeed. I believe he is quite enamored of you."

"Of me?" Eleanor asked.

Juliette looked at her friend in surprise. "Yes, of course you. Has he not been courting you these last weeks?"

"Oh I shouldn't describe it as courting. We are simply friends, is all."

The maid arrived and began assisting Juliette into a fresh corset and her evening dress. She grimaced at the rose pink of her gown. Red or dark green would suit her so much better, but when Aunt Constance had taken her shopping for a gown for the house party, she just hadn't felt bold enough to order the rich garnet or Kelly green she'd seen, much to her great aunt's disappointment. Well, that would be one consolation once she wed Mr. Pickering; she'd be free to choose whatever clothing colors she wished.

"He is very handsome, though, is he not?" Eleanor asked.

Juliette stifled a shudder at the thought of Mr. Pickering but realized that was not whom Eleanor meant.

"He is." It was all she could bring herself to say. She couldn't allow herself to think about the cut of his jaw or the straight, slightly long line of his nose. Or those lips--

"Pity his hair isn't fair, though. He'd be so much more attractive with golden hair."

Juliette frowned at her reflection in the mirror. Eleanor was mad if she thought Jacob Wilding's looks could be improved upon at all. "He is very handsome," she repeated woodenly.

"Are you sure you haven't developed a tendre for him?" Eleanor's tone was light.

Juliette knew if she confessed her wayward attraction for him, Eleanor would have nothing more to do with the man. She was that good of a friend. However, since Juliette also knew that Lord Worthing had absolutely no interest in her beyond the bounds of friendship, their encounter in the herb garden notwithstanding, she did not wish to rob her friend of the chance to make an excellent match.

"I assure you. My feelings toward Lord Worthing are completely platonic."

"Pla—what?"

Juliette bit back a smile. "Non-romantic in nature."

Was it her imagination or did Eleanor look a bit crestfallen. "If you say so."

"Your mother must be thrilled Lord Worthing has sought you out," Juliette said, desperately trying to keep her voice enthusiastic.

Eleanor sighed and plucked at the embroidery on the counterpane. "I suppose, she is. She has notions of me catching the eye of a duke or a foreign prince, but seeing as those are in short supply, she'll probably settle for a future earl. Lucky for her, there are three on the marriage mart this year. She is quite adamant I marry this year. Father seems equally determined I finally choose a husband."

Juliette watched her friend in the mirror as the maid finished arranging her hair. "Count yourself lucky then that you can simply snap your fingers and any of those men will come to heel."

Her friend laughed. "That makes them sound like dogs."

Tamping down the knot in her throat, Juliette returned her attention to her own visage in the mirror and said, "I am sure Lord Worthing will make you very happy." Conversation seemed to stop after that and Juliette's toilette was finished in silence.

In short order the two young women made their way downstairs, to the dining room. Tonight's dinner would be especially grand as it was the last official night of the house party. Most of the guests, Juliette and her aunt included, were leaving first thing in the morning.

"Ah, Miss Aston! How fortuitous that we are seated together for this final feast."

Juliette stopped midway to her seat, then forced herself to calmly finish her descent. "Mr. Pickering. How nice to..." Juliette could not bring herself to say more but Mr. Pickering didn't seem to notice.

Instead he laughed in a rather smug, self-satisfied manner. "Well, I must confess to having arranged things with the maids. The countess had me far down at the other end for some reason. An oversight, I'm certain," he finished, seating himself and draping his serviette across his belly with a flourish.

Juliette glanced across the table to see Lord Worthing assisting Eleanor into her seat. Eleanor gurgled her signature laugh and men throughout the dining room turned to look at her, admiring smiles on their faces. Juliette was rather surprised to see Lord Worthing appear unaffected by Eleanor's laugh. Instead he studiously pushed her chair in and took the seat next to her. He placed his own serviette in his lap and nodded at something his other dinner partner said to him. Not once did he look up, a fact which Juliette swore was best for all parties considered.

"I'm sorry, Mr. Pickering. What was that?" She'd been so caught up in watching Lord Worthing, she'd completely missed Mr. Pickering's comment.

"I myself am quite looking forward to returning to

town."

"Oh?" Juliette wished she could say the same, but she'd loved every moment here at Beverly Castle and wished she might never leave. The thought had not coalesced until Mr. Pickering's comment, but she realized it was completely true. She was suddenly awash in melancholy at the thought of her departure.

"Indeed. I am a busy man, you know. My time is in great demand by those of the highest echelon of society, you know."

"So you've mentioned."

Apparently oblivious to her tone, he continued. "My expertise is seeking out promising investments. The nobility is finding it harder and harder to assure their income simply as landowners, you know. They seek my advice in greater and greater numbers to put them in touch with those of the lower orders whose businesses need only initial capital to flourish. I daresay it won't be too long before I am able to afford a manor house at least as grand as this one."

Juliette was glad to realize that at least this time he did not seek to disparage the Wilding home as he had a few days previously. Perhaps the man simply needed some polish.

The first several courses were served to the accompaniment of boisterous conversation the length of the table. Mr. Pickering seemed too intent on enjoying the delicious food to join in, but Juliette found herself laughing at the increasingly outrageous tales the other young men at the table were telling.

As the ladies rose to leave the men to their port and cigars, Mr. Pickering laid a restraining hand on her forearm. "I shall be retiring early as I leave at daybreak." He smiled, again with a degree of self-satisfaction that made her stomach slightly queasy. "I shall be calling upon your father within the next week or so. No need to prolong the inevitable, what what?"

Juliette tried to swallow the lump in her throat, found she could not, and instead pulled her arm free, clutching it protectively to her chest. Feeling someone's gaze upon her, she glanced up to see Lord Worthing staring intently at her, concern etched on his brow. He appeared to be on the verge of saying something, but Juliette could not reply if her life depended upon it so she turned and fled the dining room. She ran down the marble hallway, past the drawing room where the other ladies were laughing and chatting, and didn't stop until she was in the gardens, surrounded by the chirrup of crickets and blanketed by a velvety night sky dotted with stars. She put a hand to the stitch in her side and tried to catch her breath. She felt one of her stays gouging her in the ribs and tried to rearrange it. Giving up, she found a stone bench and sank onto it gratefully.

It was what she had expected, she told herself. She'd planned on his offer, planned to accept it, as it was no doubt the only one she would ever receive. Why, then, did the reality of being married to Mr. Pickering suddenly fill her with such dread?

Perhaps if he had actually *asked* for her hand instead of acting like their union had all the romance of a brokered business deal. She snorted with laughter. Romance? Since when did she fancy herself entitled to romance? Mr. Pickering's "No need to prolong the inevitable," was not so very different from her father telling her earlier this year, "You're a sweet girl, Juliette, but you just don't seem to take with high society. I'll give you this one last Season, but then you'll stay in the country with me, aye? No need to keep gallivanting in that polluted London air. We'll continue on as we always have with no more bothersome distractions."

Tears burned the back of her eyes and she dropped her head back to stare at the stars. She would not cry. She wouldn't! Not over the silly notion that she deserved someone to sweep her off her feet. She should be thankful she had options. She knew of many well-born young women who, lacking family and money, found themselves even less popular than she herself was. They ended up as governesses or companions if they were lucky, in much less savory positions if they were not.

The stars blurred before her eyes. It appeared she would cry, after all, she thought with resignation. But she would not cry about marrying Mr. Pickering. She would allow tears to fall for her girlish dreams of handsome princes and love matches.

She heard the heavy tread of boots on the garden path and quickly dashed the back of her hand across her cheeks. It was one thing to act foolishly, another to do so in front of someone.

"Miss Aston?"

She felt her heart stutter. Lord Worthing. What was he doing out here?

"Juliette?" he called. He'd called her by her given name earlier. She wished he wouldn't. She wished he would keep things distant and impersonal so she wasn't tempted to dream again.

"Ah, I thought you'd come this way. Are you...are you alright?"

"As you can see, I'm quite well," she said, impressed that her voice was even, if a bit husky from her swallowed tears.

"Truth be told, I can't see much of anything. My eyes haven't yet adjusted to the dark." He approached slowly, as if afraid she might bolt like a wild animal. The thought almost made her smile. "May I?" he asked, gesturing to her bench.

In response, she scooted over, tucking in her skirts to make room for him.

After a full minute of listening to the gentle chatter of a summer night, he said, "I—I thought something may have disturbed you at dinner."

Juliette waited, gathering her composure. When she finally spoke, her voice was almost composed. "Not at all. Mr. Pickering informed me he was going to arrange things with my father when he returned to London."

"What do you mean 'arrange things?'"

She looked askance at him and if he could not see her look, he must have felt it, for he continued, "You don't mean arrange marriage."

"As I'm fairly certain he's not going to sell my father investments, yes, that would only leave...marriage for them to discuss."

"He proposed, then?" When she said nothing, he pressed, "Well did he?"

Affecting nonchalance, she shrugged one shoulder airily and said, "It really doesn't matter whether he did or not. We both knew what his intentions were from the first."

"But that doesn't mean he shouldn't ask you, shouldn't present you with some token of his regard."

"I don't want a token of his regard!" she said, suddenly angry. There was no regard, either on Mr. Pickering's or her side. But did this fool man have to rub that fact in?

"Why do you insist on interrogating me in this manner?" she asked, standing suddenly. He immediately rose too, his broad shoulders blocking the faint glow of candlelight from the distant castle.

"I'm not interrogating you," he snapped. "I'm merely asking."

"Well it's not your concern." She moved to brush past him. He refused to budge, however, and she lifted her hands to shove at his chest. It was like trying to push a mountain out of her way. She felt herself ricochet slightly back. His hands quickly rose to catch her upper arms. He wore no gloves and the touch of his bare hands on her upper arms was like being singed by a hot poker. But rather than pulling away from it, she found herself moving closer to him. In a flash, he hauled her up against his chest and lowered his head to catch her mouth in a kiss. At the touch of his lips against her, they both stilled, the wild anger disappearing, replaced by a hesitant curiosity as he slowly explored the curve of her mouth with lips that were warm and firm. She softened her own mouth, parting her lips to more thoroughly experience this, her first kiss. He immediately took it as encouragement, for his mouth pressed more firmly against her own, his lips working deliciously, his tongue darting out to sip at the overly sensitive skin of her inner lips.

She inhaled shakily, opened her eyes just a slit, and found her hands were knotted in the fine fabric of his coat.

As if weighted with lead, her lids dropped and she sank into the wealth of sensations evoked by this man's lips on her own. His kiss grew bolder, his arms tightened around her; one at her waist, one at her back, pulling her tightly to him. The kiss's effect spread beyond her lips—her body felt flushed, her limbs loosened, and she began to feel deliciously languid, as if she would find herself content to remain here, kissing him for the next century or so.

It finally sank into her befuddled brain that she was kissing Jacob Wilding, Lord Worthing. The man who professed to have his sights set on her best friend, Eleanor.

Though it took every ounce of strength she had, she turned her head, breaking their kiss. Jacob—how could she ever think of him by any title now?—dropped his forehead against hers, his breathing as ragged as her own.

A long, slow minute later, he slowly straightened. She carefully unclenched her hands, smoothing his crumpled jacket while he slid his hands back to her arms and gently set her away from him.

"I—" he began.

Suddenly, Juliette could not bear to hear an apology or an explanation, or whatever else he might say to dismiss one wild, impetuous kiss. It was likely the most delicious memory she would have to sustain her in the coming years when she was married to Pickering and Eleanor and Jacob were wed. Before he could say anything to destroy the recollection of their kiss, she brushed past him and ran to her room as if the very hounds of hell were on her heels.

Once in her room, she found she could not flip the lock, for her hands were shaking violently. She ran to the washstand and splashed water on her cheeks to cool them, then struggled out of her gown unaided. She could not face anyone right now. Climbing into bed, she pulled the covers up over her head and in the suffocating darkness, allowed herself to cry for what she would never have.

Chapter Twenty

Juliette awoke early the next morning. Her eyes felt puffy and her head felt as if it were stuffed with cotton, but nonetheless she felt a calm resolve about her life. Well, at least a calm resignation. As she washed her face, she put away her resentment at Mr. Pickering's unromantic offer, as well as her frustrated longing for Lord Worthing. She adamantly refused to allow herself to relive the kiss they had shared in the garden. It had been a mistake born of the summer evening, sympathy on his part, desperation on hers, and the familiarity that house parties invariably bred. Once they both returned to London, all would return to normal. Their interactions would be few and formal. He would continue to court Eleanor and she would go on to—she swallowed and forced herself to think it—marry Mr. Pickering. Once they were both wed, Juliette had no doubt they would never run into one another again. Despite Eleanor's unwavering friendship, the differences in their stations would be even greater once Eleanor was a future countess and she was the wife of a rather toadying bank broker.

She took some small pleasure in packing her trunk, making sure each chemise was perfectly folded, her gowns neatly cushioned in paper, her shoes wrapped in flannel, as if the orderliness of her possessions would somehow translate to emotional equanimity.

When the maid answered her ring, she quickly dressed. She hoped Aunt Constance was amenable to leaving post haste. If she had to face Lord Worthing today...

Running lightly down the stairs to the breakfast room, she paused to slow her breath, then peaked around the doorframe, crossing her fingers that neither Lord Worthing, nor Eleanor were present. At the end of the long morning table, sat three women, their heads together as if plotting a coup. When they simultaneously sat back and laughed, Juliette was stunned to see her Aunt Constance, Eleanor's mother Lady Chalcroft, and Lady Beverly. She'd never seen her aunt look so...young, she supposed. Despite easily being two or three decades older than the other two ladies, Aunt Constance was engaged in avid conversation with them both over something quite obviously intriguing for they all spoke in excited but hushed voices. Juliette doubted even the footmen standing at attention by the buffet could hear what they were saying.

Smoothing her features so it wouldn't be obvious she'd been spying on them, Juliette sauntered into the breakfast room. "Good morning Aunt. Lady Beverly, Lady Chalcroft," she said with a curtsy.

After salutations were exchanged, Juliette filled a plate and sat beside her aunt.

"Did you enjoy my garden?" Lady Beverly asked as Juliette lifted a forkful of eggs to her mouth. The eggs tumbled back to her plate and Juliette quickly lowered her fork to cover her clumsiness.

"Er..." she began.

"I hope the lavender was to your liking."

"Indeed, the lavender is the best I've ever smelled. Thank you for allowing me to cut some."

"You are welcome to come back anytime to gather more," she said graciously. "It is the rare young woman who appreciates the simpler things in life."

Juliette felt the ridiculous urge to cry overcome her. For a brief moment she wondered what it would be like to have such a maternal figure in her life. Aunt Constance had been an infrequent presence after Juliette's mother died and even these last two Seasons, she had only served as an unenthusiastic chaperone, her current interest notwithstanding.

"That is very kind of you," she murmured, focusing on

her plate.

"What happened to you last night, Juliette?" Aunt Constance asked. "You disappeared after supper."

"I—I didn't feel very well. I thought to lie down for a few minutes and then must have fallen asleep."

"Hmmm." Her aunt's skeptical response surprised Juliette.

"I wonder if it was the same ailment that affected my son," Lady Wilding said.

Juliette felt her stomach clench and she laid down her fork carefully. "Oh?"

"He too must have retired after supper for he did not join us in the drawing room."

Juliette felt Aunt Constance turn and look at her, but she refused to meet her eye. It was entirely possible that two people at a house party could be ill at the same time. Completely commonplace occurrence.

"I hope you didn't pass your ailment along to Eleanor," Lady Chalcroft said with lowered brows. While she'd never discouraged her daughter's friendship with Juliette—in truth, had made Juliette feel most welcome at her home on numerous occasions—Juliette always felt that Eleanor's mother was perplexed at how her popular daughter could be best friends with such an unpopular young lady.

Glancing up, she saw Lady Beverly looking at her with a rather strange expression. It was halfway between curiosity and...amusement? Surely not.

Thankfully the butler entered with the morning's post for Lady Beverly, distracting her. Lady Chalcroft excused herself to go check on Eleanor. Juliette turned to her aunt and asked how soon they might depart.

"Why are you in such a hurry if you were ailing last night? Perhaps we should stay at least until this afternoon. I'm sure Lady Beverly won't mind."

"I—I have an appointment with the modiste. I can't miss it."

Aunt Constance looked unconvinced. She cast a skeptical glance down at Juliette's pale green traveling gown. "Hmmph." The word seemed to be her favorite this morning. "Well I'll countenance such rush only if you choose a decent color this time. I still cannot believe how you resisted my advice last time."

Juliette swallowed a laugh. "Indeed. I was thinking of red. Dark red."

She'd half expected her aunt to snort her tea through her nose. Instead, Constance set her teacup down carefully, dabbed her pursed lips with her serviette and nodded sagely. "That would suit you excellently." When her aunt raised her eyes to Juliette, it was with an approving gleam.

She looked from her aunt back to Lady Beverly, wondering if the women had been indulging in spirits this morning for they both seemed to see things in her she wasn't sure were there.

Abandoning her breakfast half eaten, Juliette excused herself. "I'll see to having the carriage brought round and our luggage loaded." Feeling a bit like a sneak, she crept through the still-empty halls, straining her ears for Jacob Wilding's voice. Having sent a footman to order their carriage, she ran upstairs to hide in her room until she thought it safe to depart. She cracked her door open, decided it was clear, and then ran lightly down the hall to Eleanor's room where she was informed by the chambermaid that Eleanor was still sleeping.

Not wanting to take the time to search out pen and paper to leave her friend a farewell note, she decided to send one round once they were both in London. Eleanor would understand, or, if she didn't, wouldn't press for details if Juliette didn't offer them.

She made it back downstairs and out the grand front door undetected, feeling foolish the entire time. She scrambled into the carriage unaided and awaited her aunt.

"That was a rather furtive departure," Aunt Constance said, climbing up shortly after her. "I saw you sneaking about the halls like a rat. Are you sure you haven't made off with Lady Beverly's silver?"

Relieved that she'd escaped Beverly Castle without having to face Jacob Wilding one last time, Juliette laughed. "Indeed not. Only a bottle of sherry."

"Oh very good. Let's have it then," Constance said, digging in her voluminous reticule and withdrawing a small silver cup.

"Aunt Constance!" Juliette gasped. "I was jesting!"

"Bother," her aunt huffed, stashing her cup back in her bag. "I was just beginning to think you'd developed some spirit."

Juliette stared at her aunt as if seeing her for the first time. Why had Aunt Constance never shown this interest in her before?

"Oh don't give me that look. At my age, a bit of sherry is mostly medicinal."

"Mostly?"

"Mostly. At my age, I'm also entitled to a little enjoyment. Sitting at balls, watching you hold up the walls is not my idea of entertainment."

A horrified giggle escaped Juliette. "I'm terribly sorry to have burdened you, aunt."

Constance waved her apology away. "I'm thinking you've started to become interesting. Am I wrong?"

"I—"

"Course if you marry that oaf Pickering, I'll never speak to you again."

"Aunt Constance!"

"What? Oh all right, the man's decent enough. But he needs a girl with no backbone. One who will say 'Yes, Mr. Pickering,' 'As you think, Mr. Pickering.' If you're finding your spunk, you'll be a terrible wife for him. And he'll be an even worse husband for you."

Juliette felt the blood drain from her cheeks. She'd heard the phrase before, but only now did she know that it was a literal expression, a very definite feeling of the life leaching from one's countenance. Aunt Constance's declaration was exactly what Lord Worthing had said to her. Right before he kissed her.

Thankfully, Aunt Constance did not appear to be on the verge of indulging in a fit of physical affection.

"Well I'm not sure whom you think I should marry," she said, more harshly than she'd intended. "Perhaps you've noticed as you sat watching me hold up the walls at every event that I've had no other offers. I'm not exactly...popular."

"Pish posh. You're well liked. I've never heard an ill word spoken of you. But it is true, you have not dazzled the society. Do you know why?"

Juliette felt her ire rising. "Which reason would you like? Perhaps my lack of beauty? Or my mediocre lineage? Certainly the men of London do not find me to be a desirable dance partner. My dowry is generous enough, but apparently not sufficient to overlook my other failings." She'd felt the blood leave her cheeks before; she now felt it flood them, leaving them hot with embarrassment.

"No. Those reasons are not why."

"What?!"

"Calm yourself, girl. Pity you didn't swipe the sherry. We could both use a tot.

"No. The reason you've never been popular is because you hold yourself apart from everyone. You say with your posture, with your eyes that you do not wish attention to be paid to you. Perhaps you feel you don't deserve it. Perhaps some other nonsensical notion. Regardless, you make yourself virtually invisible to those who are wanting to be impressed."

Juliette frowned. She opened her mouth to speak, but could find no words.

"I blame your mother." At Juliette's gasp, Constance continued, "I do. I blame her for dying. And you should too."

"That's a terrible thing to say!"

Aunt Constance laughed wheezily, coughed into her lace-trimmed handkerchief, and waved away Juliette's protestations.

"Nonsense. Everyone knows when someone dies, you feel sad and then you feel angry. Then you feel better. You never got angry, did you?"

"Well, I—"

"Just as I thought. You were too good, never giving your parents a moment's grief." She sighed gustily. "When I was a girl, I was responsible for turning my mother's hair gray before she was thirty," she finished proudly.

Juliette swallowed a laugh. "That's quite an accomplishment."

"Indeed. If my two older brothers had not been able to do as much, clearly it required a force of some substance. Now you, as I recall, ate your porridge without complaint, never fussed when told no, and obeyed your parent's every edict."

"Not *every* edict," Juliette grumbled.

Constance waved her aside. "You had no real rebellion."

"I was a happy child," Juliette protested. "My parents were very good to me. I saw no need to rebel."

"Yes, yes, that's all very good. However, it clearly left you with the inability to get good and angry. Until you do that, you won't finish grieving and you'll find yourself settling in life. If you're not careful, you'll end up married to a man like Pickering."

Juliette sat back in shock. She'd never considered that what Aunt Constance said was true. She evaluated her first Season. She'd been so shy, so unsure of what to say or do. Her father had escorted her and Constance to events but when he'd remained by her side, his dour visage had no doubt discouraged any young men from approaching and even when he would disappear into the card room, she'd been too overwhelmed to know how to act. If it hadn't been for her friendship with Eleanor, she'd have been quite isolated. She'd never yearned for her mother more than she had that year. She wondered, not for the first time, how different things might have been had she had her mother's guidance.

Taking her aunt's admonition to heart, she decided she was a little angry that her mother had not been with her. It started as a slow burn in the pit of her stomach, but by the time they reached Aunt Constance's house in London, her throat was choked with grief and anger. She excused herself from supper and retired to her room where she spent a perfectly miserable night.

"Bother, Aunt Constance. All you've managed to do is give me a raging headache and a swollen nose," she said as she stared at herself in her dressing table mirror. She splashed cold water on her face and took herself off to bed.

The next morning Juliette gingerly made her way downstairs to the breakfast table with a throbbing head. She winced at the bright light spilling in through the windows and eased herself into a chair.

"Ah, you found the sherry after all," Aunt Constance commented. "Rather selfish of you not to share."

"I assure you, I did not indulge in spirits."

"Hmph," was the reply. "If I felt like you look, I'd at least have wanted the pleasure of being cobbed."

"Aunt Constance!" Juliette gasped. Truly, she felt as if she'd never met her aunt before today. What on earth had turned her from a disinterested, perpetually drowsy chaperone to this goading, slightly inappropriate advisor on life?

The indomitable lady simply shrugged and continued to thriftily polish off a stack of toast.

Juliette sipped tea, found her headache diminishing, and ate a good breakfast. As both ladies were finishing, Aunt Constance said, "What invitations have you for this week? We should determine your course of action."

"Course of action for what?"

"For stirring up the young bucks and bringing one to scratch. What about Worthing? I saw you two after your adventure in the garden. He'd be a man worth waking up next to."

"Lord Worthing? No, he—Eleanor—her mother is all but —" She shook her head and tried to slow her frantic heartbeat.

"Mr. Pickering—"

"Oh don't go on about that Pickering fellow. Do you truly want to be married to him?"

Juliette paused, her mouth open.

"I thought not. Where is the man, by the way?"

Juliette glanced at the letter she had read coming down the stairs. It was more of a note, really, delivered early this morning from Mr. Pickering, excitedly telling her he would be away from London for a fortnight while he met with a Very Important Client.

"He is away on business."

Aunt Constance smirked—smirked! "Very well, we shall proceed with my plan."

"You have a plan?"

"Oh indeed I do."

Juliette felt a strong sense of trepidation. "Er, Aunt... what kind of plan?"

"A plan to get you noticed and betrothed to someone else by the end of the Season. Are you quite certain Jacob Wilding is out of the question?"

Juliette closed her eyes so Aunt Constance wouldn't see her longing. She wanted more than anything to confess the riotous feelings the man had elicited.

"He is decided upon Eleanor."

"And is she decided on him?"

"She finds him very handsome. And she says he is a true gentleman. I've not heard her speak of anyone else so fondly."

"Hmmph. Be that as it may, I shall attend you when you visit the modiste today. You need gowns more suited to your coloring, though it's my opinion that no young lady benefits from a wardrobe of nothing but various shades of white. Now don't give me more arguments about what is appropriate for unmarried girls," she said when Juliette opened her mouth. "You mentioned a red dress yesterday. Very daring. I approve completely. We are seeking to break that mold, are we not?"

"Er—" Juliette had not intended to argue her aunt's

point, but the indomitable woman steamed on.

"We are," Constance declared firmly. "I shan't go overboard, but some rich colors will not come amiss just to spice things up. Oh what is it, girl?"

"The modiste?" Juliette asked.

"Yes. You told me yesterday you had to return early for you appointment."

Juliette felt her cheeks warm at the memory of the small lie. She'd been desperate to leave Beverly Castle without running into Lord Worthing.

Aunt Constance's heavy brows rose alarmingly. "Well if you didn't have an appointment, why did we leave so precipitously?" When Juliette prevaricated, she continued, "Were you trying to *avoid* someone?" A note of scandalized delight filled her voice.

"Of course not," Juliette said, but could not bring her gaze to meet her aunt's. Instead she toyed with her teaspoon and affected interest in what the tea leaves had to say in the bottom of her cup.

"Well what other excuse could you possibly have? Don't clam up on me. Speak girl!"

"No one!" Juliette blurted. "Please aunt. Let's just go shopping. I'll let you have full say in my selections."

"Hmmph," Constance said again. Juliette decided it must be her favorite expression. "Very well, but no opposition this time, do you hear? I've plans to fulfill."

Juliette was not entirely sure she was confident in Aunt Constance's sudden plan—the woman had dozed through two previous Seasons, after all—but she gamely went upstairs to fetch her pelisse.

As Juliette returned to her room that evening to deposit several hatboxes and various packages, she reflected that while the events of the day were decidedly unusual, it had been rather nice to shop with Aunt Constance.

During her first Season, her aunt had accompanied her

to the modistes and instructed them to outfit her as a respectable debutante. She had then commandeered the largest chair in the room and slept while Juliette, completely ignorant of fashion was left to the mercy of an indifferent seamstress. The resultant wardrobe had been...respectable, but little else.

Once she and Eleanor became friends, Lady Chalcroft had taken her under her wing and Juliette's wardrobe improved by cut and quality. The proper debutante colors of whites and pale pastels, however, did little to flatter Juliette as they did Eleanor's golden perfection.

Today had been a different story altogether. Aunt Constance—truly, Juliette scarcely recognized her, so energized was her personality—had taken her to an entirely new dressmaker. She then proceeded to order bolts of fabric to be brought out and held up against Juliette's face, judging the effect by both candlelight and natural. She scrutinized, pinched, poked, and prodded Juliette as the seamstress's apprentice fit her. She ordered cuts, changes, and fittings like a general ordered up fresh troops.

By the time she was finished, Juliette and the modiste were exhausted. Aunt Constance, however, appeared to be just getting started. They ordered half a dozen hats at the milliners and two new pairs of shoes. Aunt Constance ordered silk undergarments in abundance, though Juliette wondered what on earth she could possibly need *those* for?

"Trust me," was all Aunt Constance would say.

Now back home, all Juliette wanted was to order a hot bath and soak before stuffing herself with shortbread and falling into bed. Unfortunately, Aunt Constance had ordered her to wash, dress, and arrange her hair so that they might attend a dinner party. Juliette was a bit surprised, not just that Aunt Constance had the energy to go back out, but that she managed an invitation to the rather exclusive gathering.

"You don't think I was always wrinkled and gray, do you?" her aunt asked acerbically.

"Of course not, Aunt Constance," she'd said, and dutifully gone upstairs.

Now she was scrubbed and dressed—one of her older white dresses, but with a cunning deep purple velvet Spencer, the tight-fitting short jacket pushing her breasts up and forward better than any stays. Juliette's maid must have also received instruction from Aunt Constance, for the hairstyle she concocted was absent many of the tiny ringlets that were de rigeur for young ladies. Juliette admired the sleeker hairstyle before being shooed out of her own room to join her aunt downstairs.

"Come here gel. Let me have a look at you."

Juliette obediently followed her aunt's voice into the drawing room where the lady in question was fortifying herself for the evening with a rather full glass of—

"Is that port?" Juliette asked. Ladies might imbibe in a glass of watered down Madeira, but the stronger wines were generally only a gentleman's prerogative.

"Bordeaux," was Aunt Constance's succinct reply. She took a healthy swallow and gestured for Juliette to come closer. "Turn," she commanded.

Juliette obediently pirouetted and awaited her aunt's pronouncement.

"Pity the entire dress couldn't be that color. The jewel tones suit you. In my day, color was the thing, you know. None of this silly Greek—" she waved her hand to encompass Juliette's high-waisted white gown. "Nonsense. Boned stays, low necklines, and sheer fabrics—now that was the way to a man's heart, I tell you. Why Mr. Smithsonly loved to see me in—" she stopped mid-sentence and Juliette could have sworn she saw her aunt's parchment-colored cheeks pinken.

"Well, be that as it may." Constance polished off her wine, then held out a hand for Juliette's assistance. Once standing, she ushered them out to the front door. "Now then. It will be rather difficult for you to play the role of wallflower at a dinner party. But don't, for heaven's sake, simply sit there. You must be lively and entertaining. I understand there are some very eligible men invited this evening. Let's not waste the opportunity."

Juliette's stomach tightened. "I do talk to my dinner partners. At Lady Beverly's party I had several lovely conversations."

"Yes, I saw you talking to two old men long past the marriage market. What about those young men you danced with?"

"Aunt, I tried! They weren't interested in anything I had to say. What am I supposed to talk about, the weather?"

"Oh come now, you silly girl. That is only a starting point. Besides, how a man describes the weather tells you a great deal about what he wants to talk about." The butler indicated that their carriage had arrived and the ladies gathered their reticules and wraps and went outside.

"What do you mean?" Juliette asked as she waited for the footman to assist Constance into the carriage.

Once they were both ensconced, Aunt Constance explained. "Well, if a man complains of the rain, you know he is an outdoorsman. Ask him about his horses or hunting or the like. If he is grateful for the rain, you know his lands are foremost in his mind. Find out what crops his tenants grow. If a man is indifferent to the rain, God help you."

"Why is that?" Juliette asked with a frown.

"That, my dear, is an indication that he is a scholar. Spends his days with his nose in a book. He's not aware if it's sunny or snowing and likely couldn't care." Aunt Constance adjusted the rather tight bodice of her gown. "Either that or he's an idiot. Stay away from them at all costs."

Juliette smothered a laugh.

"But why must I exert all the interest in him? Shouldn't he wish to know if I enjoy the outdoors or would rather be reading a book too?"

Aunt Constance frowned. "Because it's a man's world. Don't you forget it, gel. Should have thought you'd learned that much by now, what with all that schooling your father provided you. You start him talking about himself that then bring the attention to yourself."

"You mean what I'm interested in?"

"Good heavens, no! Get him to look at your chest. Lean forward if you can. Dab at your lips. Pretend to check your necklace and let your fingers linger on your neck. *That's* the interest a man first has in you."

They rode in silence for several minutes, Juliette digesting her aunt's advice. "Was Mr. Smithsonly not interested in what you liked?"

At mention of her late husband, Constance's features softened. "Ah, he was a rare breed, Mr. Smithsonly was." She was silent so long Juliette thought the conversation was at an end. They were nearly to their destination when Constance spoke again.

"Never thought I'd marry."

"I beg your pardon?"

"I told you I gave my mother gray hairs. Imagine what the men of the *ton* thought of me. I was decidedly on the shelf. Proud of it, too. Wouldn't have suffered those fools." Juliette watched her aunt gaze out the window, lost in memory. "But then Smithsonly returned. He'd been traveling, you know. Had been gone for all the years I was on the marriage market. He took one look at me and decided he must have me. Pursued me as if he was in competition with a herd of other men."

Constance turned back to Juliette, who was floored to see tears in her normally peppery aunt's eyes. "And yes, he did ask after my interests. Made a fool of himself learning about crocheting so he'd have something to talk to me about."

Juliette frowned. "I've never seen you crochet a stitch."

"Course not! Can't stand anything that has to do with sitting still making useless items. I only said I crocheted to test him, you see. I didn't believe he was truly interested in me."

"But he was," Juliette whispered.

Constance swiped at her eyes as if surprised to feel moisture there. "He was."

They sat in silence the remaining minutes of the ride.

In spite of her vow not to think about Jacob Wilding, Aunt Constance's words brought him to mind. Juliette had ruthlessly suppressed any memories of her encounters with him—especially that last night. Now she could not help but remember spending an hour in the library with him debating the merits of penny horrid novels and their mothers. Even Eleanor had never asked about the death of Juliette's mother like Jacob had.

Feeling a ridiculous, uncontrollable urge to sob begin at the back of her throat, Juliette surreptitiously bit down on her knuckle, using the pain to distract her from the dreadful suspicion that she had fallen in love with Jacob Wilding, future fiancée to her very best friend. The self-inflicted pain did not distract her from the shattering realization, but it did help her calm herself enough that she was able to serenely exit the carriage at Lord and Lady Blackburn's house.

Chapter Twenty-one

Once inside, Juliette resolved to do Aunt Constance proud and impress the men of the dinner party. Who knows, she rationalized, perhaps I'll become so popular I won't even remember Lord Worthing.

It was, at first, painfully difficult to push herself to engage her dinner partners in conversation. She felt an absolute idiot when she said for the third time this night. "Hasn't the weather been absolutely splendid these past few days?"

When the gentleman to the left agreed and said he'd never had such wonderful riding weather, Juliette took her cue and asked about his horses. She kept an animated expression and encouraging smile on her face while her mind slowly numbed at the unending monologue concerning the merits of his Arabian stallion compared to his English hunter. When the gentleman in question paused to take a sip of wine (truly, he must have worked up a thirst talking as much as he did, Juliette reflected), she adjusted her necklace, pausing to stroke her neck. The man's gaze obligingly strayed but she suddenly found herself repulsed by his ogling. She quickly dropped her hand and turned to her right to ask the young lordling there if he had enjoyed excellent rides lately. When he admitted he rarely rode, she took a chance and asked him if instead he'd spent his time in the more pleasurable company of a book.

"Why yes I have," he said, growing more animated. Juliette felt some inner relief. If he was a book lover, perhaps they might share a real discussion.

"There is nothing I love more than to bury my nose in a book, good weather or foul," she said, trying to sound somewhat intelligent without appearing a bluestocking.

"I should not recommend you put your nose too closely to a book. It is detrimental to one's eyesight, you know."

"It was just a turn of speech—" She cut herself off, cleared her throat and began again. "Wise advice, my lord. I thank you. Won't you tell me what types of books you like to read? Novels perchance? Or poetry?"

"Good heavens, no," exclaimed the young man. "Just as detrimental to one's mind as reading too closely is for one's eyesight. I prefer books that enlighten the mind and, perchance, the soul."

Juliette sighed inwardly. Could one not simply read for *fun*?

"Philosophical works. That is my preferred subject of reading, though I will indulge myself with the occasional military history."

"Phil.... philosophy?"

He nodded sagely. "The classics of course; Plato and Aristotle. But of a more contemporary bent, I would recommend Descartes, Locke, perhaps Hume."

Juliette smiled weakly. She'd had some instruction on philosophical ideals, but too often she'd simply daydreamed through her tutor's lessons. She realized she must be daydreaming now, for the philosophical lord was apparently expounding on his interpretation on each philosopher's thesis.

She smiled weakly, silently cursing Aunt Constance. She could be enjoying her rather fine roast pork and stuffing instead of feigning interest in Lord....oh what was his name?

"Goodness, you sound as if you could compose your own treatise on the topic."

The young lord laughed delightedly and patted the back of her hand. Juliette could not decide if the move was proprietary or condescending. "I will confess to you, Miss Aston, that I am doing just that. How clever you are to find me out."

She smiled again, deciding to take his assertion as a compliment. "At what stage are you in your paper? Have you sought out a publisher?"

He patted her hand again. "Now don't get ahead of yourself, Miss Aston. That may be how novels are written, but truly great works require much more forethought."

Ah, she decided, that hand pat was definitely condescending. She withdrew her hands to her lap. "Indeed?" she said unenthusiastically.

"Yes. You see I employ rational thought and extreme concentration to formulate my thoughts."

"And you don't write them down?"

"No need, no need."

"But you will, won't you? Write them down? I mean eventually?"

He waved a hand dismissively. "Perhaps."

"But how else will you publish?"

He scoffed. "I am Lord Guy Stratford—" ah! That was his name! "Heir to the viscountancy of Stratford. It is not necessary that I publish."

"Of course," Juliette murmured. Really, what was the point in spending your life ruminating on philosophical arguments if you never intended to share them with the world beyond your poor trapped dinner partner?

Thankfully, Lady Blackburn signaled the ladies to withdraw, leaving the men to their port.

Aunt Constance took Juliette's elbow as they made their way to the large drawing room. "Good show, good show!"

Juliette knew she referred to her dinner conversations. Though she had a crick in her neck from turning to her dinner partner, feigning interest in his endless stories (though he'd shown none in return for her), she was glad her aunt approved.

"I cannot believe Worthing was absent," her aunt grumbled.

"Wor—Lord Worthing?" Juliette asked weakly. "Was he supposed to have attended?"

"Indeed he was."

"Aunt...you can't think I told you—"

Aunt Constance looked sideways at her through slitted lids. "Hmph. Of course not. I wished to ask after his mother. She wasn't feeling well when we departed."

Juliette frowned, remembering Lady Beverly at breakfast the morning she and her aunt left the house party. She'd seemed in perfect health at the time. Still suspicious of her aunt, she picked up her pace a bit, towing Constance along. "I'm sure Lady Beverly is fine. If you're concerned about her, why don't you send her a letter instead of hounding her son?"

"Well that would take days now, wouldn't it? And why are you hauling me down the hall? I am not a canine you can drag to the park!"

Juliette bit back a smile at the image of Aunt Constance on a lead and dutifully slowed her pace so that they entered the drawing room sedately.

The after-dinner conversation and games went much as dinner had. Juliette found herself in greater demand than she ever had at past events, but she also found it exhausting. It was not easy to constantly be thinking of ways to make men talk about themselves. How on earth did Eleanor do this day after day? Although, she reflected, once she got them started, she couldn't seem to shut them up. But initiating the conversation, determining where their interests lay, and asking the right questions was daunting work. After that first attempt, she quickly abandoned Aunt Constance's advice about drawing attention to her physical attributes. She had to draw the line somewhere. If she was obliged to feign fascination in a man's cufflinks, for heaven's sake, she bloody well wouldn't then offer herself up like a platter of sweets!

Now her cheeks hurt, sore from hours of smiling encouragingly. She wondered if this training was what she had missed by losing her mother at such an early age. Had Lady Chalcroft schooled Eleanor in the art of social conversation? Was that part of her appeal to the men of the ton? Juliette vowed to ask her the next time she saw her friend.

In the carriage on the way home that night, Juliette collapsed back against the squabs.

"Don't slouch, Juliette," her aunt remonstrated.

Juliette turned her head on the cushions to look at the woman who'd never corrected her before. "Why? No one is here to see."

"If you slouch when no one is looking, you'll forget and slouch when someone is."

Juliette pushed herself up and smoothed her skirts. "You've never worried before about my deportment."

Aunt Constance flicked her hand dismissively. "I told you already. That's because I thought you were destined for mediocrity. Now I hope for better."

Juliette started to smile, but frowned instead. "Truly aunt, I cannot see how marrying a man such as those I talked with tonight could be better."

"Nonsense, tonight's guests were some of the best London has to offer. What could you possibly have to complain about?"

"I just don't think I should have to spend my evening fawning over their most minor accomplishments when half the time, the men don't even bother to remember my name."

"We already discussed this. Now leave me alone. I wish to nap."

Juliette forbore from pointing out that they would be home in less than five minutes. Once her aunt's eyes were closed, slouched back against the cushions and pouted.

Chapter Twenty-two

Jacob normally considered himself a very fortunate man. He knew he'd be considered ridiculous were his gratitude widely known, for the entitled class was considered so by right of God and king. Nonetheless, Jacob had seen enough of the world to realize that most people lived in far less comfort than he himself did. He'd also spent enough holidays at various friends' homes to know that his family was rather singular in its devotion to one another. Such gratitude usually allowed him to travel through the ups and downs of life with a great degree of equanimity.

That composure had been conspicuously missing from his life for the past week and he only had himself to blame. Well, himself and Juliette Aston, but truly, if he was to be fair, her only crime was that she'd kissed him back with a passion that seemed to have scorched his very soul. How else to explain how he'd been unable to think of much else these past days but their few conversations and that one rather remarkable kiss?

He'd been unfocused when he'd met with the estate manager, had paid even less attention to Hugh Stalwood's rantings on his mother's current scheme to marry him off to a distant cousin. He'd even found his mind wandering while having tea with his mother shortly after his parents' return to London.

It was ridiculous how distracted he'd found himself. He and Miss Aston had shared, what, perhaps four conversations? Granted, they were rather unusual conversations, sharing deepest fears, memories of their childhood, even thoughts for the future, but all in all…Jacob's line of thought trailed off. Deepest fears? Thoughts for the future? He hadn't realized how intimate their discussions had grown. They'd been interspersed with good-natured teasing and laughter, certainly. Alone is his coach on the way back to London, he reviewed their walk to the picnic, their encounter in the library, and then those two times in the garden. It was amazing how thoughts of Juliette Aston could completely consume him when a fortnight before he'd scarce given her a thought. He couldn't even say for sure when he met her—oh that's right, Eleanor had introduced them at a ball. He remembered not a word she said but he did remember that Eleanor insisted he sniff her friend's perfume. And he remembered smelling much more than a pretty floral aroma. He remembered being briefly intoxicated by the warm scent of *woman*. The very smell of her had again captivated him in his mother's garden, when all he should have been able to smell was the overpowering bouquet of the lavender Juliette had been hacking to pieces.

Jacob scrubbed a hand over his face as if to dispel his memories. He stared unseeing out the carriage window, willing himself to remember Lady Eleanor Chalcroft's face. His father's hopes tolled in the back of his mind like an ominous knell. Perhaps if he talked to him, figured out why his father was set on having Eleanor as his daughter in law. Perhaps if his father met some of the other young women—oh, alright, met Juliette—he would not be so set on a young woman who, while very nice and quite lovely, simply did nothing for Jacob beyond elicit mild feelings of friendship.

He found his father still in a dressing robe while his valet stood over him with a packet of medicine.

"Bah," his father said upon finishing a glass of water. "A good medicinal whiskey would do me better than this."

"Not according to your doctor or mother," Jacob said firmly.

His father made a face not unlike those Jacob used to make when he was five and facing a distasteful bowl of porridge. The valet urged him to take another dose of medicine.

"The least you could do is distract me from this vile stuff," the earl complained.

"Forgive me, I forgot to bring the minstrels and opera dancers."

Finally, the packets emptied and the water drunk, the valet left, closing the door behind him.

"Speaking of women," his father said.

"Were we?"

"Well you mentioned opera dancers. And your mother."

Jacob raised an eyebrow. "Not sure she would appreciate being mentioned in the same breath with opera dancers."

"Of course she would. Though she'd probably take umbrage at being mentioned second. Be a good son and don't tell her, will you?"

"Only if you are a good patient and refrain from the whiskey."

His father narrowed his eyes. "Who taught you to negotiate? Me?"

"Mother, I dare say."

"Hmph. Well be that as it may, we were speaking of women."

"Ah yes."

"I noticed you spent a good bit of time with Lady Eleanor at your mother's house party."

Jacob frowned. Had he? He supposed he had, but honestly, he couldn't remember one remarkable moment.

"Such a beautiful young woman."

"She is," Jacob agreed.

"She sat with me that last evening you know. Spent quite a bit of time listening to me ramble about my golden youth. Didn't seem the least put out, even though everyone else was playing charades. Says a bit about a young woman's character when she treats her elders with such respect."

"It does indeed."

Jacob felt an invisible weight settle slowly onto his shoulders. Or perhaps it was around his chest. It was suddenly more difficult to draw a full breath. God help him, it didn't take much intelligence to catch his father's blatant hints.

"So?" his father prodded, looking less like an invalid and more like the scheming manipulator he was proving to be.

"So, what?" He didn't have to play right into his father's hand after all.

"So, how is your courtship progressing? Are you prepared to make an offer for her?"

"Not just yet."

"What? Why not? Have you found another young woman her equal?"

Jacob paused. Eleanor was the reigning *ton* beauty. Certainly no other woman could be considered her equal in that. And yet...

"And her lineage is impeccable. Such an asset to our family."

Jacob stared as his father who only last year had been hale and vibrant with life. The weight on his chest took the form of a steel band that was slowly tightening. He had nothing against Eleanor Chalcroft. Nothing at all. But there was a certain sense of inevitability in marrying her that made him vaguely resentful. As if he'd had the chance for something... different. But he'd be damned if he let his father down in this one simple request. After all, he and Eleanor were at least friends, of a sort. They would certainly not have an unbearable marriage. It would likely prove remarkably pleasant. Just not—

Breaking off that line of thought, Jacob walked to the window where he noticed the overcast clouds had started to divest themselves of their burden. He watched the raindrops roll down the windowpane for a long moment before finally saying, "I believe I am to attend another musicale later this week."

His father laughed. "I don't envy you that, my boy."

Jacob remained at the window, his back to his father. "I've been given to understand that Lady Eleanor will be in attendance. I shall...see if she is amenable to a proposal."

"Only a fool would not be. And Lady Eleanor strikes me as nobody's fool."

Jacob nodded to the rain and turned to leave. His father's voice stopped him at the door.

"You are happy with the choice, aren't you son?"

Jacob looked over his shoulder. His father looked every day his age and then some. Jacob realized that he could be gone any day.

"Of course father. She is a lovely young woman."

Jacob spent the next two days focusing on meetings with his father's man of business, replying to correspondence that really didn't require his attention, and riding until he was exhausted. Anything to keep his mind off of the upcoming musicale. He'd heard the works of Handel were to be featured and while the composer was not his favorite, it was not hearing his music that filled him with dread. Once he suggested the idea of marriage, he was as good as married to Eleanor, for a gentleman did not withdraw such an offer. Of course, a gentleman did not passionately kiss a lady in his mother's garden without then presenting an offer of marriage either, but Jacob was trying very hard not to dwell on Juliette Aston and what might have developed were his father not dying.

Chapter Twenty-three

The night of the musicale, he had his valet take special care with his wardrobe and grooming. He may not have chosen the path his life was about to take, but he'd be damned if his future wife had any inkling of his feelings. He would be the most attentive suitor and the most solicitous husband. He would regain his equanimity and live a satisfied life…as long as he didn't run into his wife's best friend too frequently. Perhaps once she was married—he paused to physically cringe at the thought of her with a man like Pickering—they would not see each other at all.

Tonight's event was hosted by Lord and Lady Pocock. Once there, Jacob allowed himself to be steered through the mingling guests by his hostess. She plied him with a glass of punch and seemed to take great pride in introducing him to all of the ladies in attendance. Ordinarily, he would never allow himself to be shown about like prize horseflesh. Usually when he attended musicales, he timed his arrival to just before the program began so he could simply take his seat at the last minute. But his overall resignation with the evening's festivities left him feeling a bit like a pawn on a chessboard so he dutifully bowed over matron's hands and complimented their daughters' appearance. He kept glancing toward the door for he knew that at any moment, Lady Eleanor would enter and his life would officially be over.

"God, I need a drink," he mumbled to himself. He was beginning to grow a little weary of his own self-indulgent pity bacchanal.

"I think you will find my husband's secret stash of spirits

behind that screen over there," Lady Pocock said with a nod to the corner of the room.

"I beg your pardon," Jacob said. Surely she didn't say—

"You heard me. Make sure none of the other gentlemen see you. Lord Pocock is rather stingy with his best whiskey."

Jacob bowed smartly to his hostess. "I thank you, my lady."

The decorative screen was hemmed in with large potted plants. Jacob affected an interest in their foliage before ducking behind them where he discovered a small cabinet stocked with glasses and three crystal decanters of sparkling liquid gold. "Thank God. And Lady Pocock," he said to himself as he poured and drank a healthy tot.

As he surreptitiously stepped out from the hidden alcove, he felt the warm burn of the whiskey buoy up his flagging spirits. Deciding he might need to invest in some hidden stashes like Lord Pocock, he began scanning the gathering for Lady Eleanor.

"Damn," he said under his breath. She was here. Just across the room, in fact, standing with her mother and surrounded by three young men who were clearly besotted with her golden tresses and dimpled smile.

He tugged on his cravat and strode purposefully across the room.

"Lady Chalcroft, Lady Eleanor," he said with a low bow.

"Lord Worthing," Eleanor's mother said with a nod. "How nice to see you here. Is your mother in attendance?"

"Ah...no, she is at home with my father."

"Please send her my regards when next you see her."

"I shall. Thank you. Lady Eleanor, may I say how lovely you look tonight." Jacob paused. Was that a look of irritation that crossed his intended's face? Surely not.

"Thank you, Lord Worthing." She seemed to be surreptitiously glancing around the room. Dear God, he hoped she wasn't looking for her friend. Or rather, he hoped she didn't find her friend. He'd already noted every dark-haired lady in the room and had been relieved—and disappointed, if he were to be completely truthful—to find Juliette absent.

"Are you looking forward to tonight's presentation? I understand the pianoforte player is quite exceptional."

Eleanor let escape a tiny sigh before dutifully—dutifully! —smiling at him.

"I fear I am not capable of judging an exceptional player from a mediocre one, Lord Worthing, but I am certain I will enjoy the performance. Juliette quite enjoys Handel."

Jacob felt his eyebrow twitch of its own accord. Perhaps he hadn't truly listened to Handel's music in a while. Shaking his head of that ridiculous thought, he said, "I believe we have a few minutes still before the music begins. May I fetch you a plate from the dessert table?"

Eleanor was still glancing about the room and Jacob felt a twinge of irritation. "Lady Eleanor?" he asked a bit more loudly than he'd originally intended.

She turned back to him immediately. "Please forgive me," she said, dimpling prettily. He was quite certain she'd used those dimples to be forgiven for sundry transgressions over the years. "That would be lovely. I am particular to lemon."

He bowed, said, "Of course," and took himself off to fight the crowds at the dessert table.

Jacob returned to Eleanor, plate in hand complete with every lemon-flavored desert available. The very large drawing room was growing crowded and it proved a challenge not to be jostled to the point of losing a tart or biscuit. As it was, he suffered several white specks of powdered sugar on the superfine of his evening jacket. His valet would no doubt think he'd spent the evening playing nanny to unruly children.

"I have returned victorious, Lady Eleanor," he said, presenting the dessert plate with a bit of a flourish. Eleanor seemed utterly unimpressed. In fact, she seemed to be trying to catch someone's attention across the room.

"Oh...fiddlesticks," she finally said, frustrated. Turning

her attention back to Jacob, she gave him a weak smile as she took the plate of goodies. As she daintily bit into a biscuit, Jacob hazarded a glance across the room to try to determine who had gained Eleanor's attention. Even with his superior height, all he could see was a sea of heads bobbing to one another. At the front of the room, Lady Pocock stepped up onto the musician's dais and began asking everyone to take their seats. Several servants were gesturing guests to the chairs and the crowd slowly coalesced into order as people filed into the rows of spindly gilt chairs.

Lady Eleanor deftly handed her plate to a passing servant and gestured to her mother who was commandeering a row, apparently for her daughter's many suitors. Jacob dutifully offered his arm and guided her forward. As he waited for her to arrange her skirts, Jacob glanced up. The standing crowd had dissipated considerably, and Jacob had a clear view to the back of the room where he saw Juliette standing with Lady Pocock's son. Jacob had attended university with the man, though Pocock was a few years younger than him. Regardless, the younger man seemed to be engrossed in conversation with Miss Aston, whose cheeks were growing redder by the second. Jacob frowned, wondering if young Pocock was making offensive statements. He was ready to stomp across the room and accost the man when he felt a tug at his sleeve.

"Aren't you going to sit, Lord Worthing?"

He glanced back up and saw Juliette smiling at her companion, no sign of distress evident on her animated face. Jacob forced himself to sit and concentrate on the performance, though he kept wondering why Juliette did not join her best friend before the music began. He should be grateful she did not, of course. They were going to have to come to some sort of reconciliation or understanding, but he sincerely hoped he would not be forced to account for it before he and Eleanor were good and safely betrothed. He recognized and abhorred his cowardice, but for some reason the thought of talking to Juliette Aston about their...embrace...was daunting. Though, he rationalized, it would be far more awkward to have to sit and talk with her and *not* refer to the incident.

A terrible thought occurred to him. What if Juliette confided in Lady Eleanor about that kiss? Jacob surreptitiously scrutinized Lady Eleanor's profile. She had shown no loathing of his presence tonight, which led Jacob to one of two conclusions: either the two women had not visited since returning from Beverly Castle, or Juliette had refrained from confiding in her friend. And if the latter were true, then she either thought so little of the kiss that had rocked him to the core, or she was remaining quiet so as not to upset his courtship of her friend. Since he'd already determined that she was a steadfastly loyal and devoted friend, he could only surmise that if she were remaining silent, it was because she believed her friend wished to proceed with their courtship.

And yet, if that were the case, why did Lady Eleanor seem rather annoyed at his presence tonight?

Jacob sighed and furtively rubbed the knot of tension at the base of his skull. Did all men suffer such agonies when it came to marrying? The whole notion had seemed so simple a few weeks ago when he'd decided to accede to his father's wishes to pick the best young miss and have over with the whole courtship thing. The musicians ended in a vibrant crescendo and Jacob realized he'd heard not one note the past hour. Around him, people leapt to their feet, applauding wildly. He ruefully laid another liability on the courtship altar.

He turned to ask Eleanor if she'd enjoyed the performance, only to find himself staring at the back of her head. She was turned in her seat, craning her neck to spot someone at the back of the room. He didn't need a crick in his neck to know she was looking for her best friend. Well, perhaps he was more flexible than that. He turned in his seat and looked to the corner of the room where he had earlier spotted Juliette in conversation with the Pocock heir. It took a moment to locate her as she was now seated, with her for-once alert chaperone beside her. Another young man was delivering a glass of lemonade to her and she bestowed a dazzling smile upon him. Her great aunt beamed at the couple's interaction. Some perverse intuition must have been at play, however, for the aunt turned and delivered an eagle-eyed stare right at Jacob. He felt himself start but forbore from pretending to look at something else. That was always so obvious. Instead he nodded his head politely. In turn, the old harridan raised a haughty eyebrow at him and pointedly turned her attention back to her ward, who was laughing at something her drink-bearer said. Jacob frowned. He was glad—delighted really—to see Juliette venturing beyond the realm of the wallflower, but both young Pocock and this lad, while no doubt closer to Juliette's age than he himself was, were simply too...green for her. They would not appreciate her rather dry wit and he would bet his last farthing that neither of them had read *The Ironclad Case against Miss Nelson*. And he was certain they would not be understanding of her utter loyalty to her friend, Lady Eleanor. Both these young men would wish all of her attention to be focused solely on them. Jacob couldn't blame them, but really, Miss Aston needed a more mature suitor, one who could appreciate her unique charm.

Forgetting that he had vowed to avoid her until he and Eleanor were betrothed, he cast about in his mind for a suitable gentleman he could send in her direction. At his mother's party, he'd tried to persuade Hugh Stalwood to spend time with her. He now saw that Hugh was all wrong for Miss Aston, of course. So who could he—

"Lord Worthing?" Eleanor said rather loudly, as if she'd been repeating his name for a while.

"I beg your pardon, Lady Eleanor. I was, er, thinking of how much I'd enjoyed the music."

"Yes, I can see that," she replied sardonically. He wasn't quite sure when the lovely Eleanor had added that tone to her repertoire.

"May I fetch you some lemonade, Lady Eleanor?" he said, remembering his objective tonight, though how acting like a footman was supposed to win a lady's hand, he wasn't sure. It was only one of a dozen ridiculous rules a gentleman must follow when courting a lady.

"No thank you, Lord Worthing. But I should very much like it if you would escort me over to my friend. I haven't seen Juliette since your mother's lovely party and even then she departed quite hastily. I wasn't even able to wish her a safe journey."

Jacob wondered if Juliette had been keen to avoid him after their kiss. If so, he wondered if she fled from fear or loathing?

"Of course," he said, rising and extending a hand to help her. He glanced up and found himself looking directly at Juliette whose eyes had widened and cheeks paled. His own mouth went suspiciously dry.

He tried to convey with his eyes that she should act as if nothing untoward had occurred. He stared his message at her until his eyes began to water.

As he guided Eleanor through the crowd, he tried to send reassurance through his gaze that there need not be any awkwardness between them, but Juliette's face only grew paler and her eyes wider.

A matron stopped them to inquire as to their opinion of the night's entertainment and to introduce them to her son. No doubt, Jacob reasoned, she wished to introduce Lady Eleanor to her son. There was no reason he could see to make the acquaintance of the pup. He patiently made the appropriate responses, hovered proprietarily over Eleanor's shoulder and sent the younger man a speaking glance. Young though the man might be, he clearly was no idiot for he nodded his reception of said message and promptly withdrew from the conversation, dragging his mother along with him.

"That was odd, don't you think?" Eleanor asked, glancing up at him with a frown of confusion on her normally placid, creamy brow.

"There's no accounting for young men's behavior these

days, I'm afraid. Shall I deliver you to your friend? Miss Aston, is it not?" He made sure to add just a touch of uncertainty to the phrase.

Lady Eleanor cast him a sharp glance, her overall demeanor suddenly focused like a sharpshooter.

"Yes, Miss Aston. Juliette. I'm sure you remember her from your mother's party. You did go and find her when she was lost, did you not? I believe you also danced with her and escorted her through your mother's herb garden."

Jacob realized he may have overplayed his hand just a bit. "Er, of course. I—I simply wanted to make sure that's who I was taking you to. Your other friend is just over there," he said with a gesture. Eleanor turned to look.

"No!" she exclaimed, a look of distaste now creasing her lovely features. She certainly had an expressive face. At least he would always be able to tell what was on her mind once they were married. "That is Cassandra de Courtney" she said, in much the same tone one might say "That is a plague-ridden corpse that has been sitting in the sun for too long." Jacob stifled a laugh at his morbid humor.

"She and I are *not* friends."

"Of course," he murmured. "Forgive me."

He steered them around another group of conversationalists and made their way to Juliette. Or rather, where Juliette *had* been standing. Neither she nor her aunt was anywhere to be seen. The young man who'd been talking to Juliette remained, however.

"I say, Balfour, isn't it?" he asked.

The man bowed smartly. "Indeed it is, Lord Worthing. So good of you to remember me. How are you this fine evening?"

"Very well, thank you. Lady Eleanor here was hopeful of speaking with her dear friend, Miss Aston, with whom we noticed you were conversing."

"As yes, Miss Aston. Such a pleasant chat we had. It turns out, we are very nearly neighbors for my family home is but a day's ride from her own in Hertford."

"Yes, yes," Jacob interjected when it appeared Lord Balfour was going to expound on the subject. "But do you know where she is now?"

Lord Balfour glanced about as if surprised Juliette was not standing right next to him. "Oh! I believe she was suffering a megrim. She was quite animated as I told her about the horse I'm looking to buy, but she excused herself rather suddenly and dragged her aunt off with her."

"I do hope she is alright," Eleanor said, worry evident in her tone and expression.

"I'm sure she is fine," While he could not rule out the possibility that Juliette had suddenly taken ill, he suspected the real reason she had left was to avoid him. The thought didn't please him, of course, but he couldn't help feeling relieved that he disturbed her peace of mind. God knows she'd plagued him the last few days.

"I believe I will leave now as well," Eleanor declared. "If you would be so good as to escort me to my mother, Lord Worthing."

"Hmm?" Jacob started. "Yes, of course."

It was with no small amount of relief that Jacob deposited his future wife with her mother and left the musicale, his original plan to broach the subject of marriage completely forgotten.

Chapter Twenty-four

"First the final ball at the Beverly house party and now this. I do hope you're not coming down with a cold. I should hate to catch it," said Aunt Constance, studying Juliette closely.

Juliette closed her eyes and groaned just a little. She feared Aunt Constance would sniff out the truth if she did not convincingly play her part. "It—" she lowered her voice. "It doesn't feel like a cold. Just a very bad headache."

"Mmph." Juliette heard the cushions creak as her aunt leaned forward—no doubt to scrutinize her condition. Willing herself to look pale and shaky (*could* one will the blood from their cheeks?), she kept her eyes firmly shut until she heard Aunt Constance settle back against the carriage's squabs. When she dared to open her eyelids just a crack, she discovered her aunt had shifted her gaze to the window where she looked positively thoughtful.

"Pity it struck you when it did. That Balfour chap seemed quite taken with you. He would make an excellent match. Bit more between the ears. His estate is so close to your father's home as well."

Juliette chewed her lower lip. She'd faked quite a few sudden illnesses lately. She was going to have to be careful lest her aunt find her out.

It was true, Lord Balfour was a more appealing match than Mr. Pickering. Tonight at her aunt's urging and instruction, she had forced herself to smile encouragingly and utter the most ridiculous phrases such as, "Do tell me more!" and "You don't say!" The results had been rather astounding. As she had experienced at the dinner party several nights before and again tonight, she'd actually had conversations with men who had previously only nodded politely before turning their rapt attention to Eleanor or fleeing her presence altogether.

Lord Balfour's rather one-sided conversation aside, he was a very nice gentleman. And it had been nice to reminisce about Hertford, even it was only about those places Balfour had visited personally.

But seeing Jacob Wilding there had disturbed her more than she could have ever anticipated it would. She'd known it was inevitable that they would run into one another eventually. For heaven's sake, he was poised to make an offer to her best friend. She simply wished she could have put off seeing him for at least...oh, another fortnight or so. Long enough to forget that one spectacular kiss. She and her aunt had been a little late arriving at tonight's musicale and as a result, they'd been obliged to sit in the back row. It was the preferred row for young bachelors forced to attend such events by their mothers or married sisters, but who had little or no interest in actually paying attention to the performance.

That was how she'd happened to meet Mr. Pocock, the hostess' son, and then Lord Balfour. All things considered, Juliette thought it might be the best seat in the house for a recovering wallflower. If only she hadn't glanced up after the performance to find Lord Worthing staring at her. His gaze had been quite intent. It was the gaze of a man who was about to do something drastic. She fancied she would have seen that very look in his eyes right before he kissed her. Of course it had been dark in the garden, but Juliette had replayed the event so many times in her head that she had enacted every possible expression. And daydreamed many alternate endings to the encounter.

Be that as it may, Lord Worthing's stare was one she'd visualized. She may have read other intentions into it except he was standing next to Eleanor, had clearly sat beside her the entire musicale, had certainly fetched her lemon biscuits and would no doubt beg for the honor of escorting her home.

As soon as he and Eleanor began making their way toward her, she knew precisely what message his gaze was sending: "Stay calm. Act as if nothing happened."

The thought of acting as if nothing had happened was more unbearable than seeing him at Eleanor's side. She knew he and Eleanor were meant to be together, she just didn't want to pretend that the most impetuous, delicious moment of her life had never occurred. Yet. Eventually, she was sure she would be able to forget the kiss had ever happened. Just not now. Tomorrow was not looking promising either.

Hence, the affected sudden illness. Worthing had been almost predatory in keeping his gaze on her while he and Eleanor navigated the throngs of milling guests. She had kept her expression neutral while she told her aunt of her "condition" and smiled politely at Lord Balfour while begging his forgiveness for leaving abruptly. Then when Eleanor and Worthing were stopped in conversation, Juliette had grabbed Constance's hand and all but dragged her out the door.

She realized Aunt Constance hadn't spoken in several minutes and she glanced at her, expecting to find her asleep. After all, Aunt Constance had remained steadfastly awake both tonight and at all of the events they'd attended since returning to London. Surely the older lady must be exhausted.

Which is why it was surprising and uncomfortable to find Aunt Constance staring at her as if deep in contemplation of the inner workings of her great niece's mind. Juliette wasn't sure what expression her face held, but she quickly smoothed it and smiled politely.

"What is on our schedule for tomorrow, Aunt?"

Constance started, "Hmm? Oh, a card party in the afternoon, I believe. Then the Ramsbury ball at night. It's not a large one, but I have it on the best authority it is the event to attend."

"Is there something special planned for it?"

"I've no idea. It's a ball, for pity's sake. What plan could make it special?"

Juliette frowned. "Then what—"

"It's *who* will be attending that makes it worthwhile."

Juliette's frown deepened. Did her aunt have someone in mind? She'd never made a preference for a certain gentleman known, only disparaged Mr. Pickering.

"And *who*, exactly, will be attending?" she asked as their carriage stopped in front of Constance's townhome.

Aunt Constance merely shrugged and allowed the footman to assist her down. As they entered the foyer and divested themselves of their wraps, Juliette asked her question again.

"Simply many eligible gentlemen, any one of whom would make you a far better husband than that dreadful Pickering."

Juliette said nothing beyond bidding her aunt good night. What was there to say? Though Aunt Constance seemed to have finally decided to take her role as Juliette's sole female relative seriously and offer guidance and wisdom regarding the marriage mart, it was too little too late. There was perhaps a month left of the season. Far too short a time, she was sure, to secure a new suitor, much less one who was marriage-minded. Juliette's father, while normally complacent, was intractable on this point. She had this last Season to marry or return to Hertford as her father's permanent housekeeper. A small and disloyal but noisy part of her brain wondered if perhaps her father was loathe to part with his comfortable life which was largely possible because of all she did to ensure the mundane obstructions of everyday life did not intrude on his study. She didn't think he intentionally wanted her to remain unmarried...he simply didn't want to face the thought of managing his life without her constant assistance.

As Juliette prepared for bed, her traitorous mind returned to thoughts of Jacob Wilding. For the thousandth time, she wondered what had led him to kiss her that night. She tossed and turned in bed, refusing to allow herself the bittersweet torture of replaying that kiss and instead forced herself to ruminate on his obvious courting of Eleanor. Some hours later, her exhausted mind finally gave up and she slept.

Chapter Twenty-five

The next day's card party was disappointing; both for its desultory play and for the lack of players anywhere near Juliette's age.

"That's the last time I believe Harriet Ashbrook," grumbled Aunt Constance as they made their way home to begin preparations for the Ramsbury ball. "'Young people, Constance,'" her aunt mimicked. "'There will be oodles of young people."

Juliette smiled at her aunt's ire. "Perhaps she meant younger than her."

"Oh I've no doubt!" Constance snapped. "She clearly believes herself to be a scandalous woman inviting a host of men in their fifties to her card party! As if we are *that* desperate."

Juliette choked back horrified laughter.

"Never you mind," her aunt continued, shooing her into her bedchamber to bathe and dress for the evening's ball. "Tonight is guaranteed to prove ripe for our mission."

At this, Juliette did laugh aloud.

"And what is so funny, miss?"

Juliette gave her aunt a brief hug. "It's just that for a moment, I imagined you as one of Wellington's generals, plotting your line of attack."

Constance made a noise that could only be described as a snort. "Wellington should have been so lucky." And with that, she pushed Juliette into her room and firmly shut the door.

Perhaps it was Aunt Constance's multiple references to the Ramsbury ball being something particularly special that did it, or perhaps there was something in the balmy air of the late spring night, but as Juliette stepped down from the carriage in front of the well-lit and elegant residence, she felt certain that something momentous was bound to happen this evening.

As she'd been preparing for tonight's festivities, Aunt Constance's butler had delivered a letter. Mr. Pickering had written to tell her of his activities. The letter was full of subtle and not-so-subtle allusions to the fabulous financial deals he was making in Bath. He implied that he was perhaps the smartest broker in all of London (Juliette's snort was not unlike Aunt Constance's). And he spoke of how many invitations he had received from the crème de la crème of Bath society, how the wealthy men of the city daily sought out his advice. He finished with the confident assertion that his mother was quite proud of him.

At no point did he inquire as to her well being. He made no reference to his declaration that he would speak with her father when he arrived in London. In fact, his letter could have been written to a cousin or sister.

A small niggle of hope unfurled in Juliette's breast. Perhaps her fate was not yet sealed. Perhaps Mr. Pickering had had second thoughts. Perhaps she would be able to find an alternative to marriage to him or caretaker for her father.

Aunt Constance and Juliette left their wraps and paused in the ladies' retiring room for Constance to take one last critical look at her niece's new jade silk gown. Juliette's hair was piled high atop her head and secured with a filigreed gold headband while several long soft ringlets caressed one side of her neck.

Aunt Constance nodded in approval, pinched her niece's cheeks to heighten their color, and said, "Let us go forth and conquer."

Thus it was that Juliette entered the ballroom with laughter on her lips. She didn't know if it was that kernel of hope, the new gown, or her genuine smile at her aunt's quip that started it, but the Ramsbury ball proved different for Juliette than any which preceded it. She was asked to dance within moments of entering the room and within an hour had a nearly full dance card.

As her present dance partner returned her to her aunt's side, she heard Eleanor call her name.

"I've been trying to catch your attention all evening," her friend chided.

Juliette smiled guiltily. She had seen Eleanor earlier, but was loathe to attach herself to her friend for fear of having to face Lord Worthing.

"I'm sorry. I've been...well, dancing!"

"I noticed!" Eleanor exclaimed delightedly.

Juliette impulsively hugged her friend. Despite the value the *ton* placed on her beauty, popularity, and position, Eleanor was a true friend, happier for Juliette's successes than she was concerned for her own.

"I was trying to make my way to you last night at the Pocock's musicale, but you disappeared before I could reach you."

"I apologize. I was feeling unwell." Juliette hated the lie, but could not under any circumstances tell Eleanor the truth. For the millionth time, she reminded herself that Lord Worthing was the type of husband Eleanor deserved and she would say or do nothing that would impede their brilliant match.

"Are you recovered?"

"I am, thank you."

"Good. Then spill it."

"What?" Juliette half gasped, half laughed. She had never heard Eleanor speak so...colloquially.

"You heard me. I want to know why all of a sudden you are dancing non-stop. And you spoke with *two* men last night. Don't try to deny it, I saw you."

Juliette laughed fully this time. "I thought you *wanted* me to converse and dance."

"I do," Eleanor affirmed. "I just want to know why all of

a sudden you're doing so when for the last three seasons you have resisted."

"I didn't resist. I just..."

Eleanor cocked her head to the side. "What?"

Juliette shrugged. "I don't know. I guess I just decided to give the marriage mart one more go."

"Before you settle for someone like Pickering, you mean?"

Juliette avoided her friend's gaze, studying instead a garland of flowers looped about a wall sconce.

"And then there's Aunt Constance."

"Aunt Constance? What has she to do with your decision to finally emerge from your cocoon?"

"She decided rather suddenly that I was—let's see, how did she put it? Oh yes—I was finally proving to be rather interesting and she's given me a list of directives to ensure that I behave in such a way as to make myself amenable to gentlemen."

Eleanor looked impressed.

Juliette frowned suddenly. "What do you mean by my 'decision to finally emerge from my cocoon'? And since when do you even know what a cocoon is?"

It was Eleanor's turn to shrug. Young ladies were not supposed to shrug, but sometimes nothing was more eloquent. "Nothing really. It's just that I've told you since we both debuted that you'd be ever so popular once people realized how lovely you truly are. If Aunt Constance's method forces you to mingle more with gentlemen, then they'll see how special you are and you will have your pick of the most eligible bachelors out there. Oh and I have quite a good memory. I remember you telling me all about your father studying butterflies our first season. They come out of cocoons."

Juliette clasped Eleanor's gloved hand. She was touched at her friend's unwavering loyalty and belief in qualities Juliette wasn't altogether sure she possessed. After a moment, she smiled wryly.

"There is one problem," she said.

"What is that?"

"The instructions Aunt Constance gave me require that I act a complete ninny. I'm to smile encouragingly, ask questions that encourage a gentleman to speak about himself and then appear completely mesmerized by his fascinating life."

Eleanor appeared nonplussed. "But everyone likes to talk about themselves. Your aunt is completely correct."

Juliette sighed. She saw her next dance partner making his way toward her so she rushed to explain herself. "But Eleanor, don't you wish for the gentleman to be interested in you in return?"

"Well he is interested in you, isn't he? If he's telling you about his fascinating life? I can't see a man telling such things to someone he finds uninteresting."

"Yes, but I mean interested in what makes you who you are. Your likes, dislikes, how you spend your days. Your dreams for the future. Shouldn't a gentleman—especially one you are considering marrying—shouldn't he want to know these things about you?"

Eleanor frowned, but quickly smoothed it into a smile as her dance partner approached as well. "Good heavens, Juliette. It's just small talk while you dine or dance. There will be plenty of time for likes and dislikes once you're wed."

At that, both ladies were claimed for the next dance by their respective partners. Juliette found herself unable to focus on her usual string of "do tell me more" and "fancy that" and as a result, the conversation between her and her partner, a Mr. Haddington, dwindled to awkwardness. Was Eleanor truly content to know everything about a suitor without him returning the interest? Was she serious that a gentleman would get to know his wife only once they were married? But what if he then found he didn't much care for her interests? Juliette knew with a certainty that a wife would be compelled to change her interests to suit her husband. It was so bloody unfair, she thought.

Rousing herself as she recognized the final strains of the

dance, she tried to offer a simpering smile to Mr. Haddington, who was looking as if he could not wait to be done with the set.

"Forgive me for not being a better conversationalist, sir. You are such an accomplished dancer, I fear I was lost in the movement."

Mr. Haddington's expression cleared instantly. He smiled as the dance came to its conclusion and bowed deeply over her hand. "I thank you, Miss Aston for your kind words. I have often been told I am exceptionally light on my feet."

Juliette bit her cheek—actually bit down on her inner cheek until it hurt—to not laugh out loud. He was clearly pleased by her compliment and proud of his dancing abilities. It was just the way he said it, it rather brought to mind a preening peacock she'd seen on the grounds of Hampton Court Palace the year before.

"If you'd like, I'll be happy to describe some of my techniques to you."

Juliette forced herself to smile gently. "That would be very kind of you. However, I fear I am committed for the next dance and see my partner looking for me."

Mr. Haddington murmured his regrets and bowed over her hand. Within moments, Juliette found herself claimed for the next dance. She tried with greater success to exert herself and learned that Sir Tobias Beauchamp raised greyhounds.

"To what purpose?" Juliette inquired. Since taking Aunt Constance's advice to heart, she'd learned breeding dogs was quite popular among the English nobility, though she'd yet to be lectured on the merits of greyhounds.

"Racing," was Sir Tobias' succinct reply.

"I beg your pardon?" Juliette tried to imagine someone riding a rather bony dog. Sir Tobias, while not fat, was a rather large man.

"Yes, yes. Several other gentlemen and I are trying to establish it as a sport."

"But...ah...how do you stay on the dog?"

Sir Tobias missed a turn as he laughed heartily.

"Miss Aston, you are quite witty. One does not ride them, of course. You simply race them against each other along a course."

"Oh." Juliette did not see how her now rather embarrassing question qualified as witty. "Do dogs like to race?" She'd had a collie as a child and while it had loved to run, it tended to zigzag about the fields near their home with a complete lack of destination.

"Well, greyhounds do love to run. They're built for it, you see. We have had difficulty getting them to stay the course, unfortunately. The beasts insist on jumping fences to chase after rabbits, you know."

"Poor rabbits," Juliette muttered under her breath.

The rest of the dance was spent with Juliette learning about greyhound diet and exercise regimens. Sir Tobias was so enamored with his subject (and Juliette's feigned curiosity) that he stayed by her side even after returning her to Aunt Constance's side. Eleanor soon joined them and Juliette sent her friend a look imploring rescue from the monologue.

Eleanor nodded discreetly and said, "Sir Tobias, have you had the acquaintance of Lord Worthing?"

Chapter Twenty-six

Juliette froze, and while her breath stopped, her heart seemed to race at a maddening pace. She'd not noticed Lord Worthing behind Eleanor. How on earth had she not noticed him?

She avoided eye contact with him while Eleanor introduced the two men, who, it turned out, had attended Eton together. She tried to pay attention to Eleanor's questions to both men about their school days, but found her every nerve was attuned to Lord Worthing's presence. He stood just to her right and every once in a while she caught a faint scent of him. It was ridiculous, really, that she should be able to identify his particular scent in a crowded ballroom already aromatic with beeswax candles, flowers, ladies' perfumes, and the exertions of a hundred dancers. And yet, Jacob Wilding had a very distinct scent that was part soap, part citrus and part...him. And the only reason she knew this was because of that dratted kiss.

"I trust you had a pleasant journey home from Beverly Castle?" Lord Worthing inquired.

Juliette started and forced herself to inhale slowly, ignoring that warm and rather spicy scent of his. Looking toward him but not directly at him, she said. "Yes. The weather was mild, and even once in the city, the traffic was not great." She was peripherally aware of Lord Worthing nodding politely.

Eleanor was talking animatedly with Sir Tobias and they and Aunt Constance seemed to have moved a step or two away. Juliette stared hard at her friend, willing her to look in her direction, but Eleanor only turned more away and drew another gentleman into their conversation.

"I should like to thank you and your family on our behalf for the invitation. It was a lovely party. Your mother is an exceptional hostess."

"She does love planning events," Jacob replied. "You should have seen her with my sister's wedding. She was enraptured with every detail. I fear the day I become engaged," he said with a low chuckle.

The laugh felt like a caress on the back of her neck, but his words made her throat tighten. She looked again to Eleanor whose back was fully turned to them by now. She and Lord Worthing were for all intents and purposes, alone.

"Have she and your father returned to London as well?"

"They have."

"I hope they are well," Juliette said sincerely. She'd had very little interaction with Jacob's father, the Earl of Beverly who had been ill during much of the house party, but she had greatly enjoyed conversing with his mother.

"They—" he hesitated and Juliette looked at him fully for the first time. He seemed to be conflicted about something. "My father suffered an attack shortly after returning. His heart, the physician says. He is still recovering."

Juliette unconsciously laid her hand on his arm. "I am so sorry, my lord. How dreadful for you. And your mother! What is the physician's long-term prognosis? Will he return to full health?"

Lord Worthing seemed to be staring rather intently at her. "It is what we hope for, but I fear no physician will issue us such a guarantee."

"I am so sorry," Juliette said again. She wished the pain of losing a parent on no one. They stood in mutual silence for a full minute. Finally, Juliette felt compelled to speak. "I am sure your mother has plenty of assistance...what I mean to say is... if you feel there is anything I can do to aid her or your family, I should be honored to do so."

Lord Worthing gave her another long stare but finally bowed shortly. "Thank you Miss Aston. There is one favor I would ask…" he trailed off.

"Of course," Juliette quickly replied, wondering what on earth she could possibly do for an earl's family.

"I should like your forgiveness."

She frowned and then felt her face warm as she realized to what he referred.

Though she wished he wouldn't, he continued. "I behaved most inappropriately upon our last meeting and… well…I simply wish you to know I am deeply sorry for it and hope that we might put my transgression behind us and resume what had become a pleasant friendship."

Juliette swallowed the lump in her throat and forced down the ridiculous disappointment she felt. "Of course, my lord," she murmured, carefully studying the mother of pearl buttons on his waistcoat. "Please think nothing of it." Her voice was raspy and when she hazarded a look at his face, she saw his brow furrowed, though whether in concern or confusion, she could not tell.

"Thank you, Miss Aston," he replied quietly.

Why must he be so polite? she asked herself. The ridiculous idea occurred to her that her heart was breaking. How could it possibly break when it had never been engaged—had it? Regardless, it would be much easier to bear if he ignored her or at least ignored the topic of *that kiss*. But to beg her forgiveness for his *transgression* and hope that they might resume their *friendship*…

"Of course, Lord Worthing. Nothing should make me happier."

Juliette cast another desperate glance at Eleanor who was still happily engrossed in conversation with Sir Tobias and half a dozen other young men and debutantes.

"Did you enjoy the musicale last night?"

Juliette snapped her gaze back to Lord Worthing. "I—it was lovely," she answered neutrally.

"I noticed you left immediately after the performance."

Juliette searched his expression for any indication that

there was a hidden meaning to his comment. She found none.

"I was not feeling myself, my lord."

"But you are better?"

Juliette raised her brows at him to say, "obviously."

"No need to gather the penny horrids, then?"

She was instantly reminded of their morning spent in the library, pouring over his mother's collection of overly dramatic but thoroughly gripping novels. The memory was bittersweet for it made her realize how enamored of him she had allowed herself to become. And yet, it was proof that their friendship was genuine, based on more than simple acquaintance or even their mutual relationship with Eleanor.

She smiled wanly and said, "Well as to that, perhaps a new one would not come amiss. Have you a recommendation?"

"As a matter of fact I do. A sequel to *An Ironclad Case Against Miss Nelson*."

"Apparently the case was not, indeed, ironclad."

"Apparently," he smiled. "I found it yesterday at a small bookseller on High Holborn."

"And how is it?" she asked.

"I've not started it yet."

"And yet you purchased it yesterday?" This with incredulity.

He raised an eyebrow at her.

"I should expect a true aficionado of the genre to have read at least half a dozen chapters by now."

"Yes well, there was the musicale. And since I did not leave early, I did not have sufficient time to read it last night. Besides, my mind was full of Handel."

"I do so enjoy Handel," Juliette sighed.

"I know," he said.

"You do? How?"

Juliette could have sworn Lord Worthing blushed. Well, perhaps not *blushed*. But his color certainly deepened and he looked distinctly uncomfortable.

"I'm sure you mentioned it. At the house party."

Juliette frowned. She was quite certain they had not discussed music.

"Well...perhaps Lady Eleanor mentioned it."

"I didn't realize Eleanor knew Handel was a composer. Oh!" Juliette inhaled sharply. "I didn't mean that to sound so—"

Lord Worthing laughed. "I understand what you meant. Lady Eleanor confessed to me that she was not a fan of music beyond that required for dancing. Or reading, apparently."

Quick to rise to her friend's defense, Juliette said, "Eleanor's greatest interest is in those she loves. Perhaps she is not well versed in literature or composers, but she knows what makes the people in her life happy. She is a steadfast friend, a devoted daughter, and will make her future husband the luckiest man in all of England."

She stared pointedly at Lord Worthing, willing him not to undervalue Eleanor. He might be witty and handsome and funny and incredibly appealing—to her, at any rate—but if he did not appreciate Eleanor for who she was, he was not the husband for her.

She expected Lord Worthing to shift his gaze to his intended and murmur reassurances that Eleanor was the epitome of everything a man could want. Instead, she found him studying her closely. His expression was impassive. She could not tell if he were aggrieved at her reprimand or chastened by it. She frowned, willing him to speak.

He finally did so. "You are quite an impassioned young woman."

She blinked. "I beg your pardon?"

"You are clearly as steadfast a friend to Lady Eleanor as she is to you. You should both consider yourself fortunate. Not everyone can claim to have such good friends."

"Do you?"

"I do. You met him, I believe. Hugh Stalwood."

"Yes, I met him."

Lord Worthing nodded. "He and I have been friends for

years. And," he said, but paused a moment and studiously avoided her gaze. "I consider you a good friend, Miss Aston."

Though the blow to her heart had already occurred, Juliette felt this announcement like the tolling of an ominous bell. Or perhaps the slamming of a door. No, a box. That was it. A box into which she had been put and neatly labeled "friend." Then put up high on a shelf to be forgotten except when the "love interest" box was otherwise engaged. It was a ridiculous notion, she knew, but there it was.

"I—thank you, Lord Worthing." He raised his brows slightly as if he were expecting her to return the sentiment and while she did like him—very much—she could not bring herself to mouth platitudes about their friendship when she was only just realizing how engaged her heart had become in such a short period of time.

"I see my next dance partner. I should join him as the musicians are starting up." And with that, she ducked around him and strode off through the crowd, even though her next dance had not been claimed. She made her way to the ladies' retiring room, which she was relieved and amazed to find empty. She threw herself onto a spindly chair and dropped her elbows onto the dressing table, burying her face in her hands. How had she not realized she had fallen in love with her best friend's suitor? She had certainly never intended to have any feelings for him whatsoever.

Juliette heard the door open and the sound of chattering women entering the room. She quickly lifted her head and pretended to be rearranging her hair, allowing her arms to block her face from the newcomers, who were so engrossed in talking about their dance partners, they never noticed her anyway.

Fine, she silently told her reflection in the mirror. You lost your heart as well as your head, but neither Eleanor nor Lord Worthing are aware of it so if you can just...calm yourself, you should be able to carry on. She took several fortifying deep breaths and willed her expression back to pleasantly neutral. She would maintain this façade for as long as it took for

Eleanor's sake and with luck, eventually her infatuation would fade away.

Perhaps, just perhaps, she would even meet a gentleman tonight, fall madly in love, and end the Season a happily married woman. She stood and smoothed the wrinkles from her skirts. And if not, there was Mr. Pickering.

Chapter Twenty-seven

Juliette awoke the next morning feeling as though she'd overindulged in brandy—or at least how she imagined she'd feel if she'd overindulged in brandy. Her head was throbbing, her throat parched, and her body was tired and sluggish. As she made her way gingerly downstairs, she reflected that if heartache was as debilitating as the aftereffects of alcoholic debauchery, no wonder the bachelors of the *ton* eschewed love. If that didn't quite make sense, Juliette ascribed it to her general malaise and plopped gracelessly into a chair at the breakfast table.

"Were you at my sherry again?" Aunt Constance snapped.

"What? Your sherry? No! Wait! Again? I've never—"

The elderly woman surprised Juliette by laughing uproariously. When she sobered, she gestured for the footman to bring Juliette a cup of coffee. Juliette reached for the milk and sugar.

"You'll want that plain," Constance said, nodding to the brew in the delicate teacup.

At Juliette's dubious look, her aunt said, "Trust me."

Juliette lifted the cup and took a tentative swallow. "Ugh!" she exclaimed. "It's bitter."

"More," her aunt commanded. "Drink it all."

She was unable to finish the cup, but Juliette did force herself to drink most of the coffee. Strangely, her head did seem a little clearer, though it may have been from aversion to the taste more than any true medicinal value in the brew.

"Now tell me what has caused this…melancholy."

There was no way Juliette was going to confess her broken heart to Aunt Constance. Though her aunt had proved to be more understanding and, dare she say it, sympathetic, since returning to London, Juliette feared her response to the admission that she had fallen in love with a man who was practically betrothed and therefore, unavailable.

"I...I'm sure I don't know. Perhaps I'm simply tired. We have been attending many more functions than we normally do. I've scarce gone to bed before two in the morning all week."

"That's because we're finally making headway."

Juliette did not need to ask what that meant. Her aunt generally tallied up the men Juliette had danced with or spoken to the previous night with the same compulsive attention to detail that her father did when classifying a new species of butterfly. In fact, she kept copious notes written in a hand so shaky she was the only one able to read them. Constance dipped her pen in the inkwell and made a note on a page.

"I noticed Mr. Haddington danced with you again last evening. I hope you furthered your acquaintance with him. I understand he has seven thousand a year, and that is just his portion from his dear departed mother. Imagine when his father dies?"

"Why are the departed always 'dear?'" Juliette asked. "Surely not everyone who dies is beloved by their survivors."

Aunt Constance glanced up over the rim of the spectacles she wore when doing close work. "What are you talking about, child? I say, your mother spoke such nonsense as often as you do. Why she and your father found themselves infatuated with one another, I'll never know."

Juliette was surprised and a bit delighted by the revelation that she was like her mother. There was so little she knew of her mother—just her own childish memories that were of little assistance when viewed through the eyes of an adult. She blinked and sat up straight as her aunt's last words sank in.

"My parents were infatuated with each other?"

"Hmmm?" Aunt Constance said, scratching off a name at the top of her list and writing something in the margin of the page.

"My parents," Juliette repeated. You said they were infatuated with each other."

Constance set her pen down and straightened her notes on London's bachelors. "Indeed. Once your mother finagled your father into a courtship, they were inseparable. It was mortifying to see how they took on. No sense of decorum. You'd have thought they were the only couple to have fallen in love." She sniffed haughtily and Juliette was reminded that her aunt still spoke most highly of her deceased husband.

"What was their marriage like?" she asked. "My parents'."

"Your father was considered a good catch for your mama, for all that she was quite lovely. But if you must know, he was the lucky one."

"Truly?"

Aunt Constance nodded distractedly as she picked up her pen and made another note next to a name. "Your father was just as distracted then as he is now. Your mother, though, she shook him out of his shell. He became quite enamored of her, introduced her to Society as if she were a diamond of the first water. Made quite a fool of himself, if you ask me. But for all that, they seemed happy together."

"I never knew that," Juliette said. She could not picture her withdrawn, preoccupied father behaving so...passionately.

"Well, just so long as you don't behave so precipitously. Finding a good husband is difficult enough work without the added disorder of violent emotions." Aunt Constance removed her spectacles and leaned forward earnestly.

"Now what about Lord Worthing?"

Juliette was in the midst of trying to choke down another swallow of coffee. She struggled valiantly not to snort it through her nose. She succeeded, but only just, and the back of her throat burned in protest.

"Lord Worthing is all but betrothed to Lady Eleanor Chalcroft, my best friend. Why would you ask after him?"

Aunt Constance narrowed her eyes shrewdly. "All but betrothed is still unattached, last time I checked. You spent an inordinate amount of time with him at the Countess' house party as I recall."

"I spoke to him a few times only!" Juliette protested. "And it was generally about Lady Eleanor." Well, she reasoned, Eleanor's name *had* come up several times. The wild hope that briefly flared to life in her breast was quickly extinguished as she recalled their conversation of last night. "We are friends, Aunt. That is all," she said definitively.

"Hmmph," was her aunt's only response.

Chapter Twenty-eight

Later that morning, Eleanor arrived and asked Juliette to walk with her in the park. "It's clear now, but Nurse says she can feel in her joints that rain is coming so we'd better enjoy the good weather while we can."

A little surprised that Eleanor was initiating an outdoor excursion considering her lifelong fear, Juliette laughed as she put her bonnet on. "Do you mean to tell me that you've never walked in the rain? I was certain you'd never lived anywhere but England."

Eleanor frowned prettily and tucked an errant curl of Juliette's back into her bonnet. "Well of course, but isn't it more enjoyable when the sun is shining?"

As there was no argument to that, Juliette pulled on her gloves and they soon departed for Hyde Park, Eleanor's maid in tow as chaperone.

Once amongst the flowers and trees in the park, Juliette took a deep breath and sighed happily. "London does have its attractions, but fresh air is not generally one of them. It is so nice to inhale and smell something other than coal dust."

"Mmm," Eleanor agreed, glancing behind them.

"Is anything amiss?" Juliette asked.

"Oh, no. Just seeing who was out and about today. It's a bit early for the fashionable hour to walk."

Juliette smiled at the idea of one hour being more fashionable than another. She was actually rather happy to find the park so empty. She and Eleanor had not had a good long chat since the before the Wilding's house party. The occasional group of children under a nurse's supervision and an old lady or two with her companion was all she saw about.

"So tell me everything," Eleanor said as the crested a gentle slope, the soles of their boots crunching the fine gravel of the path. "How is Aunt Constance's strategy proceeding?"

"Well enough, I suppose."

"Have any of the men you've been dancing and conversing with come to call?"

"A few," Juliette conceded.

"And?" Eleanor stopped and as her arm was linked with Juliette's, so did she.

"And what?"

"And do any of them seem suitable?"

Juliette knew what her friend was asking, but she was growing heartily sick of focusing every moment of her life on landing a husband. "Suitable for what?" she asked, deliberately coy.

Eleanor was not taken in for a moment. She leveled a withering glance at Juliette before tugging her in a new direction, across the closely trimmed lawn. "You know what I mean."

Juliette sighed—loudly as there was no one else within earshot. "Yes I know, and I suppose so. Although that's not really the point, is it?"

"What do you mean?"

"I mean, the point is whether or not the gentlemen in question find *me* suitable, is it not?"

Eleanor frowned. "I'm not entirely certain I agree with your aunt if that is her consensus. There are your feelings to take into—"

"Lady Eleanor!" a man's voice called.

Eleanor glanced over her shoulder but Juliette had no need to look to know who it was. She would recognize Jacob Wilding's voice anywhere, more's the pity.

"Lord Worthing! How nice to see you. Isn't it a lovely day for a walk in the park? Juliette and I were just commenting that the air here is so invigorating after the close atmosphere of the streets."

"It is lovely, as are you ladies."

Eleanor laughed and Juliette finally forced herself to meet Lord Worthing's gaze. It was perfectly cordial, perfectly impersonal.

"Miss Aston," he said, tipping his hat.

Juliette curtseyed. "Lord Worthing."

"May I join you ladies on your promenade?" he asked.

"We would be honored. Here, I shall take one arm and Juliette can take your other arm, if you are quite sure you're up to the challenge of escorting two ladies at once," Eleanor said flirtatiously.

"The honor is mine," he said, extending an arm for Eleanor to take. When he turned to Juliette, she shook her head slightly.

"I've no need of assistance. I thank you, however." She saw something flare in Lord Worthing's eyes. Irritation? A challenge? She studiously ignored it.

They continued walking over the lawn. Eleanor chatted happily, Lord Worthing made appropriate responses when required, and Juliette stewed in self-pity. Fortunately she soon wearied of that and forced herself to focus on the beauty around her. Good heavens, she chided herself. He was just a man. If he and she shared similar interests and friendship, surely there would be another man with whom she could feel so equally well matched. She had only to meet him. And hope that their mutual attraction would develop rather quickly. Preferably before both her father and Mr. Pickering returned to London. Juliette began to feel sorry for herself again.

"Oh!" Eleanor exclaimed. "There's Lady Falconbridge!"

"Who?" Juliette and Lord Worthing said at the same time.

"I've been meaning to talk to her for some time about a charitable project I've been thinking of. Won't you please excuse me? I'll be right back!"

"We can go with—" Juliette began but Eleanor was already tearing down the slope to a small cluster of women and children who were feeding the ducks on the Serpentine. "You," she finished lamely. Now what was she to do with Lord Worthing?

"Er...I had no idea Lady Eleanor was such a sprinter."

"Hmm?" Juliette asked, preoccupied with the idea of claiming to see someone she wished to speak to and deciding it was just too outlandish a scheme, even for her.

Lord Worthing repeated his comment.

"Oh!" Juliette laughed aloud. "I daresay that's the fastest she's ever moved. Young ladies should glide to their destinations, you know. It is unseemly to ever appear to be in a hurry," she said, her tone sardonic.

Lord Worthing smiled and lifted an eyebrow quizzically. "Even if they should find themselves in a house fire?"

"Especially then," she said loftily. "It would benefit no one to lose your composure. Besides, one must set an example for the servants, you know."

"The servants who are probably already safely out of the house?"

Juliette nodded regally, trying very hard not to smile and ruin her charade. "Of course. What should they think if you came tearing out of the house? All respect would be lost," she sighed dramatically.

"It's a good thing there are no servants about today then —oops!" He pretended to be startled at the sight of Eleanor's maid who was dawdling a few yards behind, looking dreadfully bored.

Juliette glanced over her shoulder, saw the maid, and burst out laughing.

"Eleanor will have to find a new maid, I fear. All deference is lost from this one."

Lord Worthing glanced back again. "I'm not sure that will be necessary. I don't think she saw anything; she appears to be asleep."

"What?" Juliette turned fully around, which startled the

maid. She straightened and affected a look of attention.

Juliette laughed again and swatted Lord Worthing's arm. She glanced up at him and saw a wide grin on his face.

"You have a beautiful smile," he said.

"Oh!" she exclaimed. "Ah...thank you."

She glanced down at the ground. When she lifted her gaze again, she saw that he was looking out across the river, a scowl marring his brow.

Several moments of awkwardness followed before Juliette cleared her throat. "How is the book?"

"I beg your pardon?" He turned back to her, his perfectly polite expression resumed.

"You said you had found a sequel to *Miss Nelson*. How is it?"

"I still haven't had a chance to begin."

"You purchased it two days ago, I believe you said?"

"I did."

"And you still haven't read even a chapter?"

"I was busy. I met with my father's solicitors, did some research on a bill he wishes to sponsor in Parliament. And settled funds on an old family retainer who is too infirm to work anymore."

"Of course," Juliette murmured. "And last night? After the ball?"

"I believe I returned home somewhere around four in the morning. It may have been five. I was too weary to focus on the clock in my rooms."

"I've never been too weary to read a new book," she muttered under her breath.

"I heard that!"

Juliette lifted one shoulder delicately. She hadn't actually intended for him to hear her, but she decided to brazen it out. "I'm sure you did. The point remains that a true book lover would not have let mere fatigue stop them. Urgent business, perhaps, but not fatigue."

"Oh really?" Lord Worthing drawled. "Stay up all night

reading often, do you?"

"Frequently."

"And do you—if urgent business does not distract you, of course—spend all day reading a new book?"

Juliette stared off over the Serpentine, seeing neither the river nor the children clustered at its edge. "Young ladies enjoying a Season rarely have urgent business, my lord. We are expected to sit for long hours, being very careful not to muss our gowns or disturb our curls so that we might be ready to entertain at a moment's notice." She heard the bitterness in her voice and strove to erase it. "As a result, I am fortunate that reading is considered a genteel way to spend many hours."

Lord Worthing was quiet for a long moment. She could feel his gaze on her but decided she did not wish to look at him just yet.

Finally, he spoke. "And what would you do if young ladies were not restricted to such sedate activities?"

Juliette burst out laughing. "Probably what I already do when I'm at home with my father: manage his estate, help him keep his research notes."

She glanced at Lord Worthing from the corner of her eye to judge his response. He seemed merely surprised and so she continued. "My father is an amateur entomologist. His studies consume most of his time and interest."

"What is an entomologist?"

"One who studies insects, if you must know."

"And you say he is an amateur entomologist? Does that imply that there are gentlemen who study bugs professionally?"

Juliette smiled. "I suppose I must say yes, though in truth, I believe they are grouped into the category of 'naturalist,' and instruct at university."

"Do you ever assist your father in his work—and what exactly does he do?"

Juliette made a face—an expression that would send Aunt Constance into apoplexy were she to see it. "He captures bugs, pins them to a card, sketches their likeness and records his observations. He does compel me to assist him from time to time."

"Go on," Lord Worthing urged when she said nothing else.

She sighed. "I have been required to hold a skewered spider so that my father could sketch the beast's underside. Countless times, his specimens have escaped before he could affix them to their card and I've been compelled to help him catch them." She shuddered as an imaginary insect skittered down her spine. "I would much prefer meeting with a solicitor or balancing a ledger full of numbers."

Lord Worthing laughed. "You are quite the intrepid young woman, Miss Aston. I had no idea."

"I warrant you have no idea about a great many things, my lord."

Lord Worthing drew back, looking slightly offended and Juliette rushed to clarify. "About me, I mean. We've known each other scarcely a month, after all."

His expression smoothed but he remained silent. They watched Lady Eleanor chatting animatedly with the Falconbridge children. Juliette had yet to discern which adult in the group qualified as Lady Falconbridge.

"I know that you smell like honey," Lord Worthing said quietly.

It was Juliette's turn to start. She turned, wide-eyed, to look at him. He appeared lost in thought, almost as if he were unaware he had spoken aloud. She moistened lips that had suddenly gone dry. Good heavens but such a statement made her feel...well, decidedly odd. Not unpleasant, by any stretch, just...as if she'd suddenly stepped in front of a roaring fire after not realizing she was chilled.

She could think of no response—she was quite sure she should not respond to such an...intimate comment. Instead she stared blindly at the grass beneath her feet, noting a small beetle making its laborious way over the blades. It was a fur beetle...or perhaps a larder beetle. She wasn't sure and she had no desire to inspect it more closely. She took a surreptitious step away from the insect, only realizing after she did so that she had edged closer to Lord Worthing. She heard him inhale deeply and from the corner of her eye, saw him turn his head sharply to look at her. She wondered if he was again thinking she smelled like honey—and that was a good smell, wasn't it?

Realizing that she was standing entirely too close to Lord Worthing for propriety's sake, she gestured to Eleanor who was crouched down beside a small girl, apparently helping her feed a duck.

"How goes your courtship, my lord?" She immediately wished she'd bitten off the end of her tongue instead, for she could feel his gaze turn incredulous. If standing too close to him was inappropriate, asking after a courtship with another young lady was quite beyond the pale. But Juliette had needed to ask, if for no other reason, than to remind her ridiculous heart that Lord Worthing was not for her.

The silence stretched uncomfortably and Juliette finally hazarded a glance in his direction. He was staring at Eleanor in a rather distracted manner—not at all like a man smitten. After a moment, he murmured, "My father is quite taken with her."

A short laugh escaped Juliette. "I can't imagine that Lord Beverly finds himself in need of another wife."

His gaze returned to hers and his expression was one of both amusement and embarrassment.

"No," he finally said. "But he seems to think he need guide my every move in choosing one. As if I am not capable of choosing my own." At this, his gaze roamed over her face, ending with an overlong glance at her mouth.

"Oh," she whispered through suddenly dry lips. When she licked them, she could have sworn she heard Lord Worthing draw in a quick breath. Her mind whirled with hidden meanings to both his words and his gaze, but before any could coalesce into an emotion or a question, she was distracted by movement across the park.

"Ah, here comes Eleanor," she said, trying to hide the disappointment in her voice.

"I can't thank you enough for waiting," Eleanor said breezily. "That was ever so important."

"Of course," Lord Worthing murmured.

They resumed their walk and Eleanor asked what they had discussed while she was with Lady Falconbridge.

Juliette felt her cheeks flame.

"Books," was Lord Worthing's prompt reply.

Ah yes, Juliette recalled. "Lord Worthing confessed he'd purchased a new book the day before yesterday and had yet to so much as open it. Can you imagine?"

The expression on Eleanor's face was rather what Juliette imagined she looked like when she helped her father with his insect work. Unable to contain herself, she burst out laughing. "I can see that you certainly can imagine such a thing. Very well, I shall own that I am the eccentric one in this trio."

"Oh I wouldn't call you eccentric, dear. That makes you sound so...old," Eleanor said emphatically. "You're simply... interested in books. Not," she said pointedly to Lord Worthing, "that she is a bluestocking!"

Juliette knew that Eleanor considered such a term to be tantamount to calling someone a termagant spinster.

"Juliette is the perfect combination of cleverness and ladylike reserve, Lord Worthing. Truly, I aspire to be more like her."

"Er...thank you Eleanor," Juliette said. While Eleanor was always first to cite Juliette's qualities, never before had she been quite so blatant about it.

"I am sure that she is," Lord Worthing said, a faint smile playing about his lips.

"Did you know that she is the most wonderful artist, too?"

Juliette looked askance at her friend. She was adequate with charcoal, as she'd needed to develop a skill to assist her father in his scientific sketches. But when she'd tried to parlay that talent into portraits...well, Eleanor had practically laughed her head off at the attempt.

"Indeed? And what are your talents, Lady Eleanor? Are you an accomplished watercolorist or perhaps you play an instrument?"

Eleanor shook her head, causing the feathers on her bonnet to bob playfully over her eyes.

"Oh no. Watercolors are quite messy, you know. And I fear reading music leaves me as cold as reading books. Juliette is the much more accomplished musician."

Again, Juliette stared at her friend. Eleanor's voice—like her laugh—had been likened to the sound of an angel. Not a dinner party went by that she was not asked to sing. Juliette had actually been surprised Lady Chalcroft had not yet hosted a musicale to highlight her daughter's talent.

Lord Worthing looked to her with raised eyebrows. His slightly ironic half smile remained. "Reading books *and* music. Impressive."

Juliette frowned and shook her head. "No, no. Eleanor is being entirely too modest—" The oddest thought suddenly hit Juliette. Was Eleanor trying to turn Lord Worthing's interest to *her*? Surely not! And yet...

"Lady Eleanor exaggerates," she said firmly. "Eleanor, we had best return. You said you must go for a fitting on your newest ballgown, didn't you?"

"I suppose you are right. Though how it will ever look as good on me as that one you recently ordered looks on you—"

"Good day, Lord Worthing," Juliette said and tugged her friend by the arm.

Jacob tipped his hat to them and purposefully strode in the opposite direction.

"Good heavens, Eleanor, what were you thinking?"

"About what?"

"Saying such nonsense about my 'talents'."

"It wasn't nonsense. You are witty and make lovely

sketches as well as play the pianoforte."

"Nothing on an exemplary level. Really, Eleanor."

Eleanor merely shrugged as she looped her arm through Juliette's. "You make it most difficult to compliment you when you do that, dear."

"Do what?"

"Contradict everything I say."

"I—I'm sorry. I just don't know why you were telling Lord Worthing such things."

"Because they are true and because I wanted him to know and admire you."

Juliette looked at her friend who gazed placidly ahead. "But why?"

"I have a suspicion that you two will be much in each other's company in the future."

When he's married to my best friend, Juliette thought. Eleanor wanted her and Lord Worthing to like each other since they would see each other often once Eleanor became Lady Worthing. A cold lump of ice settled in her stomach and the beautiful day suddenly dulled. There was no way she could spend the next years watching Eleanor and Lord Worthing's life unfold. In fact, it might be best if she did not attend her friend's wedding. How would she be able to bear watching Eleanor marry the man she herself loved.

Juliette stumbled. Dear heavens, had she just admitted that she had feelings for Jacob Wilding? Granted, it was just to herself, but the moment seemed monumental, nonetheless. She'd previously considered that she was falling in love with him, but thought she'd sufficiently squashed that notion. Clearly, her heart had proceeded to tumble regardless of her brain. How could such a thing have happened? Well, she knew of course how it had happened: Jacob Wilding was a handsome, intelligent, witty man who cared about his mother enough to read her torrid books and who had an unerring ability to draw from her confessions she had never told anyone. She suddenly realized that it really didn't matter one whit who she married. If it wasn't Jacob Wilding—which of course it wouldn't be—she wasn't going to love him. The thought was perhaps the bleakest of her life.

"Juliette?"

The concern in Eleanor's voice finally reached her. "Yes, yes, I'm so sorry. I…thought of something."

"What is it?"

Juliette shook her head. "Nothing! Just something I, er, must do when I return home."

Guilt suddenly flooded her. It was one thing to be attracted to the handsome suitor of her best friend, but to allow herself to fall in love with the man who would no doubt offer for Eleanor by the end of the Season? She was a horrible, horrible friend. Perhaps it would be best for all parties concerned if she withdrew herself from Eleanor's friendship. The idea brought sharp tears to her eyes.

"Why, Juliette! Whatever is wrong? You have me quite worried now!"

Juliette glanced at her friend and quickly away. Eleanor's face reflected nothing but concern.

"I—" Juliette began. What on earth could she say that her friend would believe? She scrambled for a half-truth. "I am simply worried that I shall end the Season a spinster and shall have to return home to serve as my father's…caretaker. Despite the best efforts of you and Aunt Constance, the other men of the ton don't seem to find me of marrying quality."

"But it's only been a few days that you've been heeding our advice. Surely it is too soon to despair. Give them time to see that you are charming and delightful. They will be competing for your affection."

Juliette's misery seemed to be growing. Who knew unrequited love would be quite so painful? "I fear I simply haven't the energy to keep this charade going."

"It is no charade," Eleanor protested. "You *are* charming and delightful. If one must…exert one's wiles, that is simply the cost of living in a civilized society."

Juliette smiled bleakly. “At least there is Mr. Pickering.”

Eleanor frowned. “Surely it hasn’t come to that?”

Realizing Eleanor was studying her with an uncharacteristic intensity, Juliette forced a smile. “I am simply being melancholy. I shall continue to act the featherbrain to convince a man that I am clever and desirable.” She swallowed the bitter taste of the words as they hurried home.

Chapter Twenty-nine

Jacob climbed inside his carriage and threw himself against the squabs. What a bloody mess he'd made of his courtship, he thought. The night before, Eleanor had coyly hinted she would be walking in the park today and he had gamely taken her hint to join her, convinced she was finally responding to him. He should have realized that no young lady goes for a walk in the park alone (chaperoning maids excluded, of course). It only made sense that Miss Aston would be with her. He should have been prepared, should have perhaps brought along Hugh Stalwood to even the numbers, provide a distraction. Oh who was he fooling? He could have brought an entire party of people and he still would have found himself drawn to Juliette. That Lady Eleanor had run off on her ridiculous errand only facilitated their interaction.

He was making a complete and utter hash of this courtship, something that was brought home to him at his morning visit to Beverly House. When he checked in on his father, he found him feeling better but still startlingly weak.

"I've been working on the wording for an announcement in the Times," his father had said when Jacob informed him he was on his way to walk with Eleanor.

Jacob had felt something akin to panic—an emotion he had not felt since his first battle when a bullet had snicked a lock of hair off his head. "Father, that is a bit premature. Besides, I suspect the…" he forced himself to say it, "bride's family will do the honors when the time comes."

"Yes, yes," his father relented, surreptitiously tucking the sheet of paper in his hand under his covers. "But Chalcroft is not the most eloquent chap. I'll want to advise him on phrasing."

Jacob squeezed his forehead in his hand, then combed his fingers roughly through his hair. "Nonetheless, it is too soon."

His father shrugged a frail-looking shoulder. "The Season is more than half over. If you wish to be wed before fall, you need to exert yourself."

The panicky feeling took on an edge of anger. "Surely there is no need for me to wed this year at all. A long betrothal —"

"I should like to see my only son wed before I pass."

Jacob ground his teeth. "You are not going to die, father."

The earl's gaze softened. "Of course I'm going to die. I may last until next year, perhaps only until next week. The doctors really have no idea. It's only a matter of time, son. I want to go on knowing you are settled. Knowing that our line will continue."

"You don't trust me to see to my duties on my own?" Jacob asked, anger beginning to win.

"Of course I trust you—"

"Then let me choose a wife on my own."

His father struggled to sit up from the mass of pillows supporting him. "Why? What is wrong with Eleanor Chalcroft? You assured me you found her appealing. She is the perfect choice for the Beverly line."

"Nothing," Jacob sighed. "There is nothing wrong with her. I just—"

"What?"

"I should go. She'll be at the park by now."

"Let me know how things progress," his father called as Jacob closed the door.

Now staring unseeing out the window, Jacob tried to come up with a plan to further his relationship with Eleanor.

Perhaps if he called upon more of his friends to accompany him to parties and such, one of them would find Juliette

—Miss Aston, he had to think of her only as Miss Aston—as intriguing as he did. He recalled that it has been his intention at the start of his mother's house party to assist Eleanor's friend in making a better match than that Pickering fellow. At the time of course, it had only been to win Eleanor's gratitude. He needed to redouble his efforts on that front. Then he could focus his undivided attention on Lady Eleanor and surely their courtship would progress.

Once in his study back home, he made a list of his unmarried friends. He cared enough about Ju—Miss Aston as a friend, of course, to want her to only meet the very best of eligible men.

Cambers was first on his list. "No," Jacob muttered. "He's an idiot. Miss Aston needs at least a modicum of intelligence. Not Elphinstone either," he said, crossing out the next name. "He's too pompous by half." The next three names Jacob scratched out just on principal. The last name was Lord Hugh. What had his friend said about Miss Aston? Oh, that she was a "good egg," but that there were no sparks. Sparks! Why the infuriating woman could start a forest fire just by opening her mouth. He recalled her taking him to task for not reading his new book right away. Ridiculous chit. She was also quick to chide him if she thought he was slighting Lady Eleanor's intelligence in anyway.

Then there were those sparks when he'd kissed her...

Jacob shoved himself away from his desk and went to look out the window.

Truth be told, he had no idea why Juliette Aston had not been snatched up her first Season out. She was so clever; he quite enjoyed their verbal sparring for it kept him on his toes. He actually had to think when he was around her instead of mouthing platitudes about the weather or her gown. She made him laugh, and somehow coaxed him into revealing bits of himself that he'd shared with no one else. He still couldn't believe he'd told her of his addiction to penny horrids or confessed that his greatest fear was losing a member of his family.

Did no other man in London appreciate a woman he could actually talk to?

She had said she was not considered a great beauty, but this perplexed him as well. Perhaps the problem was that when she stood in Eleanor's shadow, no other man bothered to take the time to truly look at her. Jacob dispassionately recognized Eleanor's golden beauty and creamy skin was considered English perfection. Juliette's charms were more subtle. Her glossy dark hair was not ephemeral like Eleanor's blond curls, but heavy and lush. It was the kind of hair that promised a silken waterfall if released from its pins, the kind of hair that would look best spread across a pillow...or his chest. Her eyes were very fine—a grayish blue that reflected impish delight when she was teasing him or softened to mistiness when she expressed concern for his father. The curve of her mouth was lush and full, made for kissing. He should know. The memory still haunted his dreams.

Furthermore, she should have received half a dozen offers based on the quality of her bosom alone. Hers was not the overly plump variety that sat on display in the high-waisted gowns that were the current fashion. But neither was she lacking in lush curves. Jacob well remembered his inadvertent glance at the smooth shallow valley that was visible above her neckline when she'd bent to snip lavender in his mother's garden. God, he'd wanted to run his tongue along that intriguing curve.

The rest of her curves were equally intriguing. His hands itched at the memory of her firm buttocks—clearly she was a girl who liked to walk a lot.

Strangely, however, he found himself just as mesmerized by less...overt displays of her femininity. The wispy curl at the base of her neck that never seemed to get swept up into her coiffure begged for a kiss to be pressed to it. He would give his best horse for the chance to nibble on one silken earlobe. Even her hands garnered his attention. Young ladies were not supposed to gesture with their hands, but Juliette seemed unable to prevent herself from gesticulating when she was excited about a topic. When her hands were ungloved as they had been in the library at Beverly Castle, Jacob found erotic images of her using those expressive hands flitting through his mind.

He turned from the window with a hiss. This was getting him nowhere but painfully hard. He sat purposefully at his desk and attended to the day's business with almost his complete attention. He then took himself for a grueling ride and finished the day at his club where he ran into Hugh Stalwood.

"Worthing! Join me. I haven't seen you in a fortnight it seems." As Jacob sat down and accepted a glass of whiskey from a footman, Lord Hugh continued. "What has been keeping you from these hallowed halls?"

Jacob glanced around but everyone was clearly well into his second (or third) glass of the evening and no one was near enough to hear their conversation. "The earl suffered another attack. We thought for a time this would be...it."

Hugh stopped with his glass halfway to his lips. "Good God, man. I had no idea!"

Jacob took a bracing swallow. "We've not put it about much. You know how my father is."

Hugh nodded. "How is he now?"

"Much recovered. Still weak, of course."

"Do the doctors—"

"They don't know really. He could live another month or another year."

"And what do you think?"

"Honestly, I'm not sure this time. He's...he's just so damned determined that I marry and soon that it feels a bit like a dying wish."

"Still fixed on Lady Eleanor?"

"I don't know. Yes," he corrected. "Yes he is. I mean I am. Fixed on Lady Eleanor, I mean."

Hugh raised his eyebrows and assumed his indolent lounging position, his elbows on the arms of his chair, his glass held between two hands. He even casually crossed his foot over the other knee. Jacob would have laughed at the affectation were he not trying so hard to convince his friend of his feelings for Eleanor.

"And how is that going? The courtship, I mean."

Jacob sighed heavily and sank deeper into the comfortably worn leather of his chair. "Truth be told, Stalwood, I'm not convinced Lady Eleanor is interested in me."

Hugh's foot dropped to the floor and he leaned forward. "How can that be possible? You're the Beautiful Beverly."

"What?!"

"That's what my sisters call you. I told them it's not at all accurate as you're only the heir to Beverly and as for your looks..." Hugh's look was eloquent in its lack of enthusiasm for Jacob's visage.

"Good God, I wish you hadn't shared that epithet with me. I'll never be able to greet your sisters again without wincing."

"Oh don't worry. I wince every time I look at them too," Hugh assured him. "The point is, I would think that Lady Eleanor's mother would sneak her daughter into your bed just to see her daughter as the future Countess of Beverly, not to mention the young lady herself. What makes you think her affections lie elsewhere?"

"That's just the thing," Jacob explained. "It's not that I think she is taken with another. She just doesn't seem overly... thrilled to see me when we do meet."

"Have you got her off alone?" Hugh asked.

"When would I have done that?"

Hugh rolled his eyes. "You're not going to try to convince me that you've never managed to sneak a young lady off into the garden for a bit of private conversation, are you?"

Jacob remembered being alone in the garden with Juliette—twice. He shoved the memories aside. "I have not had the occasion to do so, no."

"Perhaps you should exert yourself a bit more, then. Call

upon her when her mother is out. Five minutes in your company without the tiresome presence of a chaperone will work wonders for your courtship, I should say."

Jacob took a long drink. "I suppose you're right," he mused. The thought of being alone with the gorgeous Lady Eleanor should have had him at least mildly intrigued. Instead, he felt…nothing.

"Of course I'm right. Haven't you always said so?"

Jacob gave his friend a speaking glance. "I believe you were the one who always said you were right."

"Well in this case, it's true. Now are you joining me in the card room or not?"

Chapter Thirty

The next afternoon, Jacob took a chance and arrived unannounced at the Chalcroft home. The courting gods must have favored him for when the drawing room door opened, only Lady Eleanor entered, a maid bearing a tea service on her heels.

"My mother is not feeling herself today," Lady Eleanor said. "But I hated to think that you came all this way for naught so I've instructed my maid to sit chaperone while we have tea."

"Delightful," Jacob proclaimed sincerely. "Er...where is your maid?" he asked when the girl with the tea service left.

"She's dreadfully lazy," Lady Eleanor said matter-of-factly. "If we're lucky, she'll make her way downstairs by the time you leave.

"Ah."

"It's quite handy, usually, to have such a lazy maid. Except when I need a gown pressed or my hair fixed."

"I should think that would be a majority of the time."

"You're right," Eleanor said thoughtfully. "Perhaps what I meant was that the instances she is lazy—for example when it comes to her chaperoning duties or telling my mother how much I spent on new shoes—make up for her lacking in other areas."

Jacob laughed. "Lady Eleanor, I believe you are a mischief-maker."

"Oh most assuredly, Lord Worthing. Most assuredly."

"Would such a tendency allow me the liberty of referring to you as Eleanor?"

The strangest expression crossed her face. If forced to describe it, Jacob would have said it was one of…annoyance?

"Of course, Lord Worth—Jacob."

They resorted to small chat while Eleanor poured tea and filled delicate plates with a variety of small sandwiches and biscuits.

"This is quite a sumptuous spread," he remarked. "Especially considering my visit was unexpected."

"I have elder brothers who visit frequently and are always hungry. Cook is accustomed to providing vast quantities of food on a moment's notice."

"She would have served us well in the army."

This began a desultory conversation on his brief time in the war. Jacob counted himself fortunate that the war had ended within a year of his being old enough to serve, but he'd seen enough during that year that casual conversation about it was still uncomfortable.

"Eleanor," he finally said, determining that he would guide the conversation to a more fruitful direction. "We have known each other for a few years."

"Have we? It seems we've only just talked this Season."

"I suppose what I mean is that our families have a long standing relationship and as a result I feel we are…closer…as a result." He was babbling, he realized.

"I suppose," she said, her attention on stirring her tea carefully.

Jacob had the oddest feeling that Eleanor knew the direction he was headed and was trying to waylay him. Surely not.

"Did you know my dear friend Juliette is a marvelous artist?"

"It seems to me—I beg your pardon?"

"Juliette. She does lovely sketches, though she claims her watercolors leave much to be desired. Her father calls on her services regularly to assist him. He is an exemologist, you know."

Jacob suppressed a smile. "An entomologist. Yes, I know. Though Miss Aston had led me to believe her father sketched his subjects while she was compelled to hold the skewers."

Eleanor's perfectly arched eyebrows rose. "She told you that? Hmm." She seemed quite pleased with something and Jacob found himself worrying at the speculative gleam in her eye.

"Well, be that as it may," Eleanor continued with a casual wave of her hand. "She is extremely accomplished. She drew a detailed picture of a butterfly that was so lifelike, you'd have thought it was about to fly off the page."

"Indeed?" Jacob asked, disconcerted to find himself inordinately interested in seeing the sketch.

"Yes. It was perfect. Except for the body."

"The body? Of the butterfly?" At Lady Eleanor's nod, he asked, "Did she not draw it well?"

"Oh, she did. I just find butterfly bodies to be..." She shuddered delicately. "How can something with such beautiful wings have such an ugly torso? All those legs and those," she mimicked antennae over her head.

"I quite understand," he said gallantly, thoroughly amused.

"Juliette has promised me a sketch of butterfly wings with a fairy's body. She's going to let me choose the gown the fairy shall wear as my artistic input."

"I hope you shall allow me to view your collaboration."

Lady Eleanor laughed her delightful laugh. "A collaboration. I do enjoy that. In all honestly, Lord Wo—Jacob, I have no talent with a pencil. But I shall torment Juliette with the notion that I deserve as much credit as she for our collaboration."

"More mischief, Eleanor?"

"Assuredly, Jacob."

Jacob felt a moment of hopefulness. Eleanor was more animated with him than she'd ever been. He wasn't sure it could be termed a "spark," to quote Hugh Stalwood, but perhaps with luck and some more such tinder as they'd just shared, a spark could be coaxed.

Eleanor, decidedly more at ease with him than she had been when she'd first entered the room, refilled his plate with sandwiches and handed it to him absently while she relayed a story about the play she had seen the night before. "By the same man who wrote our dear Juliette's name, you know."

He paused, but only for a moment. "You mean...Shakespeare?"

"Indeed." She then proceeded to tell him her favorite parts.

Jacob nodded his head in all the appropriate spots and forbore from mentioning that Dogman was actually Dogberry and that Beatrice was not referring to actual clothing when she told Don Pedro, "Your grace is too costly to wear every day."

"Which is so strange," Eleanor finished. "Because I think that is exactly what Juliette said to me just last month when I pointed you out to her."

Jacob smiled, easily imagining Juliette tossing out Shakespearean quotes.

"Wait," Jacob said, realizing which quote Eleanor had just mentioned. "Why would Ju—Miss Aston use that particular quote?"

"I'm sure I don't know. Perhaps her father had restricted her clothing allowance. Although he doesn't seem to pay much attention to what she does. Still, my father has been known to ring a peal over my head when I've—"

"Perhaps if you recounted what you and Miss Aston were doing at the time she used the quote, we could discern the context."

Eleanor looked askance at him. "Goodness, you sound very like Sir Lewis when he's studying some new insect. 'discern the context,' indeed. Oh very well," she said with a huff. "Let me think." She tapped one elegantly manicured finger against her rosy pink lips and Jacob was sure that he should be having all sorts of lascivious thoughts about the action. But for some damned reason, all he could think about was Juliette

Aston and her damned Shakespearean quotes.

"Ah! Of course!" Eleanor exclaimed. "It was the very night I ran into you. At—oh dear, I can't remember whose ball it was. It was a lovely party. That much I do remember."

"Yes, yes, the night we met. Again."

"Precisely. Since, as you just pointed out, we've known each other for years."

Jacob gripped the arm of his chair to keep himself from twirling his hands in a "move it along" gesture.

"At any rate," Eleanor said with a shake of her golden ringlets. "I believe I asked Juliette's opinion on you, my lord."

"Me?"

"Indeed," she said with an inscrutable smile.

When she seemed disinclined to say more, he said, "And?!"

"And she used that quote. About you being too costly to wear every day. I was certain she must have meant something other than that she wished to dress like you for though you are a fine dresser, Lord Worthing, I assure you, Juliette looks best in her gowns."

Or out of them, was the errant thought that shot through his head.

"Do you have any idea what she—or I should say, Shakespeare—meant?"

While there was a possibility Juliette had used the quote to imply he was pretentious or above her station, there was also the distinct possibility she found him, well, rather handsome.

He opened his mouth to ask Eleanor more about the conversation in question when Rivers, the butler, arrived, cast a suspicious glance around the chaperone-free room, and announced that Miss Aston was here.

The lady in question swept into the room in a decidedly unladylike fashion, her hat askew, her cheeks pink from exertion, a laugh curving her lips.

"Oh Eleanor, I must tell you—oh! Forgive me! I did not

realize you had…company."

"Come join us, Juliette. Lord Worthing and I were just discussing Shakespeare, were we not, my lord?"

"Jacob," he mumbled, but nodded dutifully.

"Oh," Juliette said, looking surprised. "Ah, because you saw *Much Ado About Nothing* last night? How was it?"

"Well I quite liked Hero and Claudio, but I think she should have made him suffer more for treating her so ill."

Juliette smiled at her friend and nodded.

"But actually, we were discussing that quote you used. It had me so perplexed."

"To which quote do you refer?"

"The one about the duke being too costly to wear every day. Remember? You said it that night I introduced you to Lord Worthing."

Jacob hadn't taken his eyes off Juliette since she entered the room so he saw exactly when the pink flush deepened with embarrassment and she cast a furtive glance in his direction.

"I—I don't really recall what we were discussing when I said that."

"I'm sure you do! I believe I asked your opinion of Lord Worthing. You are quite handsome, my lord."

Jacob started, realizing Eleanor had addressed this last to him. "Er…I…thank you."

"Well it's a widespread belief so I don't think I'm telling you anything new," Eleanor continued matter-of-factly. "In any case, I pointed you out to Juliette that night—oh whose ball was it? It shall drive me to distraction until I think of it." She paused for a moment and then shook her golden ringlets again. "It will come to me eventually. I pointed you out to Juliette and when I asked her opinion of you, she gave that funny quote. I do so wish I could quote Shakespeare whenever I wished."

"Perhaps if you read the plays, you would be able to." This from Miss Aston.

Eleanor wrinkled her nose. "I think not. I—" she paused

as her maid finally entered the room and bent to whisper a question in her mistress's ear.

Jacob leaned forward and said in a low voice, "'Too costly to wear every day?' I am flattered."

Juliette's lips compressed into a thin line before she finally turned to him. "I shouldn't be if I were you. It's not necessarily a compliment."

"Lady Eleanor seemed to think it was."

"Eleanor—" she paused, clearly unwilling to say anything that might be construed as disparaging about her friend. "Was mistaken," she finished lamely.

"Perhaps you will clarify for me."

Juliette cast a glance at her friend who was directing her maid in sibilant whispers. "I assume you've been to court, my lord."

"Many times. Please, call me Jacob." It only seemed right, Jacob thought, considering he'd asked her best friend to do the same. He ignored the fact that he was trying to woo Eleanor.

She frowned slightly but continued. "I'm sure you would agree that, while beautiful, court costumes are—"

"Horribly uncomfortable, stiff, tight, restrictive," Jacob interjected.

"Well…yes, I suppose you could say that. I was going to say that while many courtiers are accustomed to wearing the formal dress everyday, for most people, they would prefer a simpler life for most days."

"So I'm the horribly uncomfortable, stiff one in this scenario?" Jacob was stung. And he was annoyed that he was stung.

Juliette cast a desperate look to Eleanor, but her friend had risen to discuss something with yet another servant at the door. Some household calamity that could not wait until Lady Chalcroft arose, he supposed.

Turning back to him, Juliette's expression turned resigned. "I simply meant that you, my lord—"

"Jacob," he interjected.

She ignored him. "Are of that class of gentleman who may rightly expect the very best..." she trailed off as if embarrassed.

"The very best of what?"

"Of everything. Not just clothing and horses and the like. But...well, friends. And ladies."

He paused a moment, beginning to understand her meaning. "And what do you mean by 'best' when referring to friends. And ladies."

She met his eyes, briefly, and he could read embarrassment in her gaze. "The wittiest, the most popular, certainly the most beautiful."

He frowned. "And that precludes...you? Is that your meaning?"

She straightened her shoulders and her expression hardened. "Naturally."

"But you are all those things," he protested. At her raised brows, he said, "Perhaps not the popularity bit, but really, that is a bunch of rot anyway. You're quite the wittiest young lady I've met and you are lo—"

She held up a hand to stop him. "I pray you do not continue. I was not seeking hollow compliments." He took a breath to defend himself but she rushed on. "I know my worth and am content with myself. You simply asked for clarification on a quote I recited before having met you and I have done so. I hope, Lord Worthing—" did she put an emphasis on his title? "That you will allow the subject to drop now."

Jacob saw Eleanor turn away from the door and rushed to say, "And what is your opinion of me now?"

"Oh you are still too costly for me, my lord. But a good fit for Eleanor, don't you agree?"

"Agree with what?" Eleanor said as she took her seat.

"That you and Lord Worthing make such a handsome couple on the dance floor. Everyone says so. I suppose it is because he is dark and you are fair."

Eleanor looked taken aback. "Oh but couples are ever so

much more complimentary when their coloring is the same, I think."

Jacob glanced at Juliette's hair. It was nearly as dark as his own. Was Eleanor implying—

"Nonsense, Eleanor," Juliette said. "Artistic perfection requires a balance of color and temperament, which is why—"

"Rivers has just informed me that Lord Worthing is here." Eleanor's father, Lord Chalcroft entered the room like a whirlwind. "Why did you not send for me, gel?" he asked his daughter.

"Because I gathered you would rather sit with him in your study indulging in spirits rather than drinking tea and eating biscuits with us in here," Eleanor retorted, knowing full well she was the apple of her father's eye and could get away with all manner of impertinence.

"Quite, quite!" her father chortled. "Well, Worthing? What say you? Shall we adjourn to more manly quarters?"

"Of course, Lord Chalcroft," Jacob said, standing immediately. He knew better than to disagree to anything the father of his future wife might offer.

"Lady Eleanor," he said with a bow. "Miss Aston." He tried to make eye contact with Juliette but she smiled politely at the floor and murmured her farewell.

Once inside Lord Chalcroft's study, Jacob took a seat and a glass of whiskey from his host. He pretended to drink, but thought it best to keep his wits about him with Eleanor's father.

"It is good to see you, Worthing. Enjoying Eleanor's company, were you?"

Direct, Jacob thought. "Indeed, my lord. She is a lovely young woman."

"Well dowered too," Chalcroft said with a good-natured chortle.

"I assure you, Lady Eleanor has no need of a dowry to be considered a worthy lady."

"Ah, having that conversation, are we?" Lord Chalcroft

took a hearty gulp of his drink. He appeared completely at ease and Jacob wondered how many men had asked to court Lady Eleanor since her come-out.

"Lady Eleanor and I seem in accord on a great many things," Jacob prevaricated.

Lord Chalcroft nodded agreeably. "Yes, yes. So what's it to be? Courtship or are you asking for her hand right away?"

Jacob frowned and immediately forced his expression to smooth. The weight he had first felt settle on him when his father had pleaded with him to marry grew heavier by a stone. He knew that he should ask directly for Lady Eleanor's hand. His father would certainly urge such a course of action; it was his last wish, as it were. And that Chalcroft would even mention marriage led him to believe he was in favor of the match.

"I should not wish to rush Lady Eleanor's affections. I should like to court her with your permission." Jacob refused to feel guilty. It simply felt wrong to rush the process. He and Eleanor did get along, but there was the strange feeling he got from time to time that she was trying to push him away. Or at least, in another direction. It would be grossly humbling to have her father's permission to wed her and have her refuse. He was not in the mood for humble pie today. He would wait and make sure of her answer before progressing. If that pushed back a potential wedding day, so much the better.

"Wise idea. Always best to let the ladies set the pace in matters of the heart." Chalcroft waved the decanter at Jacob, but spying the still-full glass, refilled his own instead.

"Now tell me the latest on your father? I gather I am one of the few to whom he has confided his condition."

Jacob was surprised Lord Chalcroft was one of the "few," but realized it made sense. His father would not seek an alliance with a family he couldn't trust with such personal information. Still, it seemed a bit...well, a bit like his father was playing Chalcroft as much as he was pressuring his son.

"He is not in pain, but shows few signs of recovery," Jacob admitted.

Chalcroft nodded somberly. "I trust he is seeing Williamson?" Jacob nodded. Williamson was a young doctor who was reputed to have had excellent success with patients suffering heart ailments.

He asked a few more questions about Lord Wilding before adroitly turning the conversation to matters of Parliament and specifically the bill Jacob's father was sponsoring. Jacob shared what he knew of the subject and tried to suppress the awful notion that he and Eleanor were simply pawns in their fathers' political machinations. He knew the political alliance was secondary to his father's wish to see him settled, but it was proving challenging to keep that in perspective.

When he finally felt he had visited long enough, he thanked Lord Chalcroft for the whiskey and offered to see himself out.

He was putting on his hat and coat in the front entry when Juliette ran lightly down the stairs, obviously headed for the front door. She clearly did not see him for she was humming to herself and seemed preoccupied with the button on her glove.

"Leaving as well?" he asked, startling a gasp out of her.

She glanced up and Jacob felt a jolt course through his body. He was acutely aware of everything about her. Though he had no artistic talent to speak of, he felt he could have drawn her visage down to the most minute detail in that moment.

Her bonnet had a pale blue lining that caused her eyes to appear lighter than normal—almost silver, he would say. Her lashes were startlingly dark in comparison and a faint rose wash crested each cheekbone, not quite disguising the pale scattering of freckles, perhaps a dozen in all. A few silken tendrils of hair had escaped their confines and lay against her cheek like a lover's caress, tickling at her jaw line, catching at the corner of her mouth. A mouth that was caught in mid-smile, one corner curved upward a little more than the other. Jacob was nearly overwhelmed by the desire to cross the few feet separating them, take her head in his hands and plunder that smiling mouth with his own.

"Damn," he said under his breath.

"I beg your pardon?" Juliette asked.

He shook his head and jammed his hat down on his head. "Nothing. I've…forgotten an appointment."

"Don't let me keep you," she said ungraciously, focusing on the recalcitrant button at her wrist.

"Here," he said, crossing the distance, and taking her hand. Juliette went completely still; she even stopped breathing. He was, perhaps, standing a little too closely for propriety's sake if he could tell when she exhaled. Or didn't, as the case may be. He deliberately took his time coaxing the small pearl button through its loop, brushing his bare fingers against the tiny patch of her wrist that was exposed.

"Thank you," she said shakily when he finally released her hand.

"Certainly," he murmured back. He seemed unable to look anywhere but at her. He noticed that she blinked three times in rapid succession and nibbled her lower lip nervously before taking a deep breath.

"Hadn't you ought to hurry?"

He raised his brows in question.

"To your missed appointment."

He scrambled to understand her meaning and then nearly laughed aloud as he remembered what he'd said not two minutes earlier. "Ah, no, I'm too late. It was not important. May I walk you home?"

Juliette caught her breath sharply, then said all in a rush, "That's not necessary. I…I walk it all the time. It's not terribly far. Surely you have more important things—"

"Come," he said, drawing her hand through the crook of his arm.

Once outside, he realized he had no idea where she lived. "Which direction?" he asked.

She pointed to the right and he set off at a leisurely pace.

"How was your conversation with Lord Chalcroft?" she asked.

"Dull." Jacob refused to focus on the fact that he had just asked Chalcroft for permission to court his daughter and that such a topic should be considered anything other than dull. He wanted to enjoy Miss Aston's company for however long he could stretch out their walk to her home.

"So tell me, Juliette. Do any other Shakespearean quotes come to mind when you see me?"

She looked at him sharply and he found her—dare he say it?—utterly adorable as she glared at him around the edge of her bonnet.

"I have not given you leave to call me by my first name, Lord Worthing," she began.

"Jacob," he interjected.

"But now that you mention it, yes."

"Do share, I beg of you," he urged when she was not immediately forthcoming.

She cast another sideways glance at him and in it he read pure mischief. "Very well. She cleared her throat and recited, "'In our last conflict four of his five wits went halting off, and now is the whole man governed with one.'"

Jacob thought a moment to place the quote. "Beatrice again?"

Juliette lifted one shoulder delicately. "She is a particular favorite of mine."

"What, and not your namesake?" he teased.

She rolled her eyes at that and Jacob almost laughed aloud. While his sister had rolled her eyes at him innumerable times, he knew of no proper young lady worth her salt who exhibited such behavior in public.

"So you think I should seek to emulate a love-lorn fourteen-year-old girl who throws her life away over a handsome face instead of a witty young woman who refuses to simper to the men in her life?"

"Threw her life away? *Romeo and Juliette* is considered a

tragedy of epic proportions. True love that will unite in death if life should thwart it."

"I just can't get over the happenstance that the friar's message to Romeo of Juliet's plan goes awry but the news of Juliet's death reaches him no problem. You'd think Friar John would do whatever it took to deliver such momentous news."

"Perhaps that was the real tragedy. After all, doesn't real life change because of some ridiculous turn of fate?"

"I suppose," Juliette admitted, but Jacob scarcely heard her for his own words suddenly hit too close to home. Was his own life not subject to the whim of fate that made the Chalcroft family desirable to his father as a marriage alliance? Suppose his father had instead had a fascination with the naturalists' world. Suppose he was interested in the bugs of Britain. A long shot, to be sure, but would he then have decided that Juliette would be the perfect bride for his son? Would an alliance with the Astons then be what was in the best interest of the Beverly earldom?

He laughed bitterly.

"What is funny?" Juliette was looking at him suspiciously.

He shook his head and slowed his pace. He was going to make this walk last as long as possible.

"Tell me Juliette," he began and when she started to protest, he stopped altogether and turned her to face him. "May I call you that? It's such a lovely name and it suits you even if your temperament is more of a Beatrice." He made his voice as low and seductive as possible, and gazed hotly into her eyes. He had no idea why it was suddenly so important to be on such familiar terms with Miss Aston, but it was and he would use every seductive weapon at his disposal.

She frowned slightly but seemed mesmerized by his gaze. "It isn't proper," she whispered.

"Very well, then I shall call you Beatrice. The name does not roll off my tongue as smoothly," at that her gaze dropped to his mouth and he felt it like a kiss. "But if you prefer it..."

"Yes," she whispered, appearing a bit dazed. "No."

"Yes to what? No to what?"

She shook her head slightly and returned her gaze to his own. "Yes, alright, you may call me Juliette. But not in public."

"Eleanor has allowed—"

"I'm not Eleanor. You're not…you're not courting me. Everyone expects you and she will marry so the *ton* sees nothing wrong with such liberties."

That reminder broke the sensual spell Jacob had been wrapping around the two of them. Or if not broke it, at least lifted it a bit, allowing some chill, sobering air to remind him of where he was and who he was with.

"And will you do me the honor of using my Christian name?"

"I—yes, Jacob."

It was ridiculous, really, that his name on her lips should please him so. He'd had the occasional mistress who'd called out his name in the throes of passion and it hadn't stirred him as it did now, when Juliette Aston, recently reformed wallflower, had murmured it.

They stared at one another for a long moment before Juliette glanced around. "We should continue. Someone is bound to wonder what we're doing standing here."

Jacob looked at the row of houses. The street was fairly quiet, but who knew who was peeking out of a parlor window looking for gossip. He wondered what his father would say if someone told him his son was caught gazing at the wallflower daughter of a bug scientist. For a moment, he rather wished he could find out, but then the sobering notion hit him that it might send the earl into a decline.

Reluctantly, he allowed Juliette to tug him along and they walked the rest of the way to her house in silence. As she opened the wrought iron gate, he blurted out, "What of Mr. Pickering?"

She froze, her hand on the gate, her face hidden by her bonnet. "What of him?" she asked.

"I have not seen him about town since my mother's house party."

"He has had business that keeps him from London. He writes that he shall return within the fortnight. Shall I write him that you wish to speak with him?" At this, she finally glanced over her shoulder at him and though her brim shadowed her eyes, there was a determined look about her lips, pressed into a flat line as they were.

"No! I...that is, I wondered if he was still courting you."

She laughed then, a harsh sound so unlike her hearty, genuine laugh. Jacob realized he liked knowing what her real laugh sounded like. "Yes, Lord Worthing. Mr. Pickering is still 'courting' me."

"It's just that I noticed you dancing and, er, talking with other men."

"Is that a crime?"

"Certainly not. I just wondered if perhaps you had..."

"What?" she whispered, her mouth softening.

"Decided to...consider other options."

He could see her eyes now, for he'd again stepped closer to her than was seemly, especially on a public street, but he could not read her expression. It was wiped clean of anger, interest, or embarrassment.

"Good day, Lord Worthing." She turned and walked quickly up the path to her door.

"Jacob," he called after her. She ignored him.

Chapter Thirty-one

Jacob stopped by Beverly House that afternoon to check on his father and take care of any estate business that may have arisen. He met his mother coming out of his father's room.

"How is he?" he asked when he saw the drawn look on her face.

She smiled wearily. "He's sleeping now. Or I should say again. Join me for some refreshments? I confess to not having eaten yet today."

Jacob took her arm and escorted her to the family parlor. "You'll make yourself ill doing that. Then father will have a fit because I allowed you to waste away."

His mother smiled, more fully this time. "He is rather over-protective of me."

"Rather?" Jacob rang for a maid and asked a meal as well as a bottle of wine.

"A lady never takes wine when it's daylight," Eudora said primly.

"You're not a lady right now," he replied, and at her gasp, added. "You're my mother and you've been pushing yourself too hard taking care of father. You're entitled to drink whatever you like."

"Apparently your father is not the only over-protective one," she said with a smile.

In short order a light repast was laid before them consisting of soup, bread, meats, cheese, and a plate of warm biscuits, not to mention a full decanter of sweet red wine. Jacob filled a goblet and handed it to his mother. After she drank several sips, he asked again, "How is he today?"

She set the glass down carefully and wiped her mouth delicately with a serviette before looking up. "I fear he hasn't much longer, Jacob."

"Why do you say that?"

She smoothed the serviette on her lap before answering. "He's always been so strong. He rarely catches colds. Even when injured, he always seemed to heal so quickly. Remember when that wicked horse threw him and he dislocated his shoulder?"

Jacob nodded.

"He was riding the next day, with his arm in a sling."

Jacob forbore from telling her that his father had only worn the sling when in her presence because she set such a store about it.

"But now...he seems so frail. The doctor finally admitted that your father's heart is not pumping enough blood to his body and that is why he's so tired. He said," she paused and took a rather large gulp of wine. "He said it would only grow worse."

Jacob nodded, remembering his last talk with his father.

"You knew," Eudora said.

Jacob looked at her guiltily. "Yes, but only recently."

He expected tears or at least a lecture. Instead his mother refilled their wine glasses and said, "It's a wonder I ever learn anything with you two."

He smiled and leaned over to squeeze her hand.

She took a delicate sip of soup before saying, "Tell me how you are. I feel like we haven't really talked in months. Or at least since the house party. How is the Season going for you?"

"Much the same as it does every year."

Eudora raised an eyebrow delicately. "Oh really? And do you court young ladies with intention of marrying them every year?"

"Well, the same except for that," he allowed.

"And how is your courtship going? Are you still focused on Lady Eleanor?"

Jacob glanced at her in surprise. "Well, yes. Why wouldn't I be?"

His mother refused to meet his gaze, and instead focused on sipping her soup carefully. "No reason. I just thought when you decided to marry, love would take you suddenly and completely. I actually imagined you would elope to Gretna Green just to save yourself the waiting for the banns to be read."

Jacob took a moment to consider his mother's words. He would have never considered such an impetuous course of action and was rather surprised at her.

"If you will recall, it was not my choice to find a fiancée this Season."

His mother smiled. "That is true."

As they finished their meal, his mother reached to pour more wine but stopped. "Perhaps I'd better exercise some discretion."

Jacob laughed and then taking advantage of their relaxed camaraderie, he asked, "What do you think of father's choice of Lady Eleanor for me?"

"Your father's choice? I thought Lady Eleanor was the most beautiful girl of the Season."

"She is."

"And that wasn't why you chose her?"

"Well, initially, perhaps. But father made clear that he considers her to be a worthy addition to the Wilding family. And then there's her father's support in Parliament to be gained."

"Her father's—surely you jest!" his mother said, aghast.

"Not at all. Although I don't think that was father's only reason in choosing her for me."

"Jacob," his mother began. She stopped and stared off into the distance until he said, "Yes?"

Turning back to him, she continued more hesitantly. "I must confess I'm at a bit of a loss when it comes to your willingness to marry a girl of your father's choosing."

"Why do you say that? Haven't I always been a good son?"

"The best," she rushed to say. "The very best. But that doesn't always mean the most obedient, especially when it comes to something so personal. Remember the...quarrel over your desire to go to Eton instead of Harrow?"

Jacob laughed. "A 'quarrel,' mother? I thought father was going to banish me to the West Indies."

"Well, heirs to the Earl of Beverly have always attended Harrow. I'm still not sure why you felt the need to break with tradition."

Jacob shifted in his seat, feeling a bit like a recalcitrant young boy. At the time, he remembered believing that he had to separate himself from his father, distinguish himself on his own merit, blaze his own trail. His father, of course, had not understood. He had eventually relented (Jacob suspected his mother had intervened), but it had left a breach in their relationship that had lasted for several years.

"I remember wondering if you two would ever reconcile after that. Thank goodness you decided to attend Oxford, else you very well might be considering marriage to a colonial in the West Indies instead the most popular girl in London.

"Still I wonder," she continued after a moment. "Do you...care for Lady Eleanor?"

"She is quite beautiful, and of a sweet disposition. Who would not be enamored of her?" he replied evasively. His mother was too perceptive by half and he did not want to have this conversation with her. And yet..."Why do you ask?"

"Caring for someone extends far beyond physical beauty which will only fade."

"She's quite the most popular young lady. Sure to be a good hostess."

His mother shot him an acidic glare. "Really, Jacob. Have I raised you so poorly? Surely your father and I have not set such an example that that is all you would expect from a wife."

"My unfortunate attendance at Eton aside, I have always

strived to live up to father's expectations of me. I have attended half a dozen Seasons, met hundreds of young women and none has moved me to marriage."

The image of Juliette Aston glaring at him around the edge of her bonnet rose in his mind and he ruthlessly ignored it.

"And now, in his last days...If my marriage to a young woman father approves of will make him happy, will allow him to rest in peace, then it is a small sacrifice indeed."

"But your marriage will last much longer than your father's passing," Eudora said, her voice choked. "Surely you misunderstand your father's true wish which is for you to be happy."

"I shan't be unhappy with Lady Eleanor," he said tightly.

"You are sure no other woman has caught your interest? You are not one of these impecunious young lords who must trade a fat dowry for his title. You have the luxury of marrying for love, and in our world, that is very rare indeed, my son."

Jacob stood abruptly and turned away so she would not see the conflict in his face.

"What would you have me do?" he asked.

She was silent for a long moment before she finally spoke: "Follow your heart."

He stared at her a moment, unsure of what she wanted him to say and so he only nodded shortly and left.

Chapter Thirty-two

Juliette came down to breakfast the next morning to find two letters awaiting her at the breakfast table.

"That's rather masculine writing," Aunt Constance said, peering over her toast and looking at the top missive.

A ridiculous hope bubbled up in her chest and she forced herself to calmly pour a cup of tea, adding milk and sugar, before she finally picked the letter up and opened it.

"It is from Mr. Pickering," she said, trying to quell the bitter disappointment.

"What does the cretin have to say?" Aunt Constance barked.

Juliette jumped and looked up. By the canny gleam in her aunt's eye, she knew she'd been staring unseeing at the letter. She wondered who exactly Constance thought she'd been thinking of; she was frighteningly certain Constance knew exactly who.

"Ah...let me see." She quickly scanned the letter. As usual, it was full of Mr. Pickering's accomplishments as a social climber and brilliant investor. It made frequent mention of his mother and asked not one question about her health, happiness, or who she'd been seeing while he'd been away these weeks.

"He says he will return by week's end and hopes my father will be in residence." She heard the flatness in her voice but told herself it was better than allowing active dislike to color her speech.

Aunt Constance made a disdainful harrumph and fiercely buttered another piece of toast.

Juliette picked up the second letter, instantly recognizing her father's handwriting. The letter was considerably shorter and typically straight to the point.

"Well?" Constance demanded when Juliette set the paper down in favor of her rapidly cooling tea.

She forced herself to take a slow sip and carefully returned the delicate cup to its saucer before saying, "It is from Father. He also plans to return by the end of the week. He says he needs my assistance with some drawings for a paper he is submitting to the Bristol Naturalists' Society."

"Ugh," Constance said with a grimace. "Please do not describe his work to me at breakfast. Or during any other meal, for that matter. What else does he say?"

Juliette stared at the letter, willing the words to change before her eyes but the wavering lines of script remained immovable.

"He says that unless I have found a fiancée by the time his paper is finished, we will both return to Hertford so that I may continue to assist him in his research."

"That is ridiculous!" her aunt expostulated. "The point of your being here was to find a husband. He can't simply take you away from London at the peak of the Season! Does he know that you've started attracting more notice?"

Juliette remained silent. Her father would not care if she'd suddenly become this Season's Original. It wasn't from lack of caring; he simply didn't understand how courtship worked. Hadn't Aunt Constance said Sir Lewis had been oblivious to Juliette's mother for years before she finally tricked him into asking her to dance.

"We shall simply have to redouble our efforts," Aunt Constance said. "With all the men you've been dancing with, surely one or two has expressed more than a passing interest in you. Think, gel. Who seems inclined to offer?"

Juliette suppressed a morbid laugh. While she had indeed started to become more sought after, none of the conversations she'd had with the men with whom she'd danced, talked, and visited had delved deeper than their mutual acquaintances. No one had asked about her family, or if she preferred prose to poetry. Certainly none had asked for the liberty of using her first name. None that is, except...

"Mr. Haddington, perhaps."

"Haddington? Decent enough, I suppose. What about the Pocock boy? You and he spent quite a bit of time talking at that musicale his parents hosted."

And hadn't spoken since, Juliette thought. "Perhaps...oh Aunt, I really don't think I—"

"Hush, hush!" Her aunt held up a hand and glared imperiously. "That is a defeatist attitude. Thank heavens Lord Wellington didn't subscribe to such silliness or we'd all be speaking French now. We shall simply consider this week to be our own battle of Waterloo. Now finish up," she said, gesturing to Juliette's half-eaten breakfast. "We've calls to make."

Aunt Constance formed her own version of Wellington's Seventh Coalition, calling into service her own maid, a new modiste, several of her well-placed society friends, and Eleanor and Lady Chalcroft in her quest to betroth Juliette quickly.

"Well it took your aunt nearly three years, but she certainly seems to be making up for lost time," Eleanor commented that night as she and Juliette fixed their hair in the ladies' withdrawing room at Lady Hadley's dinner party.

Juliette had not told Eleanor of her father's deadline, but she could not deny that Aunt Constance was clearly a woman on a mission. She had turned herself into the life of the party at dinner, appearing to shed ten years, perhaps twenty, as she engaged the entire table in a lively conversations about a long ago scandalous meeting with Prinny, as the Prince Regent was known.

From there, she relayed stories of her travels with Mr. Smithsonly, and even issued her opinion on current men's fashions. She had the table in stitches as she relayed an unfortunate run in with the playwright Sheridan when he mistook her for an actress at Drury Lane. It was the height of impropriety to even discuss actresses in mixed company, and yet Aunt Constance made it all so amusing and pithy that even Lady Hadley laughed aloud. But the sheer brilliance of Constance Smithsonly was that she was able to mention Juliette at nearly every turn, relaying real or imagined witticisms that her niece had uttered, so that by the time the ladies left the men to their port, everyone at the table was convinced she was quite the cleverest girl to grace London, though she'd scarce spoken a word.

Once the men joined the ladies in the drawing room where charades were due to start, Juliette and Eleanor found their traditional roles swapped, with Juliette surrounded by young men and Eleanor rather shunted to the side.

"Do not apologize," Eleanor said once they reached the retiring room. Lady Hadley's charades had involved props and costuming bits which had left everyone rather rumpled and ladies' coiffures in shambles. "I am positively thrilled for you!" she finished.

Juliette paused in the middle of trying to salvage her hairdo to give Eleanor a quick hug. "You are truly the best friend!"

"Of course I am. Did you ever doubt it?"

Juliette laughed.

Thinking again on Aunt Constance's spectacular performance at dinner, Juliette sobered. Even Eleanor would be hard pressed to wring an offer out of a man in less than a week. Wouldn't she?

"What is the soonest you've received an offer after meeting a gentleman?" she asked her friend. Perhaps because Eleanor was sensitive to Juliette's lack of success on the marriage market, she had never confided precisely how many offers she had received since her debut, though Juliette suspected it was dozens.

"Two days," was the immediate reply.

"Two days after meeting a gentleman, he asked you to

marry him?"

"Hmmm?" Eleanor scrutinized her hairstyling efforts in the mirror and adroitly re-pinned a curl. "Well, in actuality it was on the second day. I had been introduced to the gentleman in question at a ball one evening, he called on me the next afternoon and that night called on my father at his club to ask permission to marry me."

"Surely your father turned him down!" Juliette said, amazed.

"Oh no, my father always has me do it. He says he has no idea what kind of man will make me happy so he only sends them away if they are financially ruined or cannot hold their liquor. He has tried to persuade me to accept a few he was particularly fond of, however."

"How did you turn him down?"

"I told him I could not trust affections which had sprung up so quickly as they would surely wither as soon."

Juliette thought this was wise advice and wondered how she could reconcile herself to any proposal she might be able to eke out in the next days.

"Are there any men you feel have become good…friends who we might prompt to think of you in a, well, less *friendly* way?" Eleanor asked.

Unbidden, the image of Jacob Wilding rose in her mind. She pushed it firmly aside. "Well, no," She forced herself to say. "By which I mean to say that, whether they consider themselves a friend or not, the men of London I am being introduced to must know it is for the express purpose of marriage."

Eleanor sighed. "Yes, I suppose that's true of all of us. Pity we couldn't first just get to know the gentlemen on a strictly—what's that word, Juliette?"

"Platonic."

"Exactly. On a platonic level before we even consider them for husbands."

As presentable as they could manage without a lady's maid, they left the retiring room and made their way back downstairs. While they descended, Juliette asked as casually as possible, "Haven't you known Lord Worthing for years? Surely growing up so near one another must have allowed you to get to know him."

Eleanor glanced sharply at Juliette before returning her gaze to the stairs before them.

"I suppose, but really, when we were children, he was so much older than me, we scarcely spent any time together."

"But surely now that you're more of an age..."

Eleanor sighed. "I suppose. My father is pushing for the match, of course, despite his claims last Season that I must make my own choice of husband."

Juliette couldn't imagine a father not wanting Jacob Wilding as a son-in-law.

"Oh let's not talk about having to get married anymore!" Eleanor declared as they reached the first floor. "Let's just have fun tonight."

With only days remaining until her father returned to London, Juliette could not afford to dismiss the looming prospect, but she nodded dutifully and pasted a bright smile to her face. As they returned to the party, she wiped all thought from her mind except appearing wildly interested in what the gentlemen had to say and coyly getting them to say more of it.

By the time she left hours later, her cheeks were sore from smiling encouragingly but she had garnered three requests to be called upon.

Chapter Thirty-three

The next day's social activities were no less frenetic. It began with a luncheon at which Juliette was seated next to Mr. Pocock. On the ride over, Aunt Constance drilled instructions on lively topics of discussion to interest the men. Before Juliette climbed out of the car, her aunt pinched her cheeks hard.

"Ouch!" Juliette said, and as she raised her hands to her reddening cheeks, Aunt Constance snatched the lace fichu that made her low cut gown presentable for daytime.

Juliette gasped and looked at Constance as if she were mad.

"Oh don't look at me like that." Her aunt snapped as she took the footman's hand and climbed out of the carriage. As they made their way up the steps to the door, she continued, "It wasn't uncommon in my day for ladies to wear gowns so low, a bit of pink showed."

Juliette choked from equal parts horror and hilarity. "Surely not at a luncheon!"

The door swung open and Constance cast a shrewd eye at her niece. "Only the ones who wished to catch a husband quickly."

Trying to ignore the feeling that she was undressed, Juliette lifted her head and pasted a bright, vacuous smile on her face as they were ushered onto the back verandah where elegant tables were scattered for luncheon.

Mr. Pocock seemed to find Juliette even more fascinating than he had at his parent's musicale. Of course, she considered, it was probably not her sterling conversation, although she was prudent to keep to topics he would find fascinating. Mr. Pocock spent at least as much time addressing his comments to her bosom as her face. She would have sighed in frustration but each time she took a deep breath preparatory to it, his gaze dropped twelve inches.

That being said, there must have been something to Aunt Constance's strategy, for at the conclusion of the luncheon, Mr. Pocock asked for permission to call upon her.

When they returned to her house, Aunt Constance announced she was off to take a nap and advised Juliette to do the same as they would be making an appearance at not one but two balls that evening.

Juliette's maid was arranging her hair that evening when Aunt Constance swept into the room, her arms full of a shimmering, dark red fabric.

"Our victory gown!" She shook out the dress and Juliette gasped.

The gown was a lustrous garnet silk edged in matching velvet ribbons. The high-waisted bodice was covered with garnet mesh and the short, puffed sleeves were only mesh, to allow tantalizing glimpses of shoulders. It was the most beautiful dress Juliette had ever seen. It was also more daring than anything she had ever worn.

"Oh Aunt, I simply can't!" Juliette didn't feel worthy of such a magnificent gown. It was the type of garment only a bold and confident woman could wear.

"Nonsense. You must stand out tonight and catch the attention of all those men from the dinner party last night. Plus," she said, handing the gown to Juliette's maid and rifling through the jewel box on the dressing table. "If Pocock is there, we have to make him realize that there is much more to you than the bosom he was slavering over at luncheon."

Juliette closed her eyes in mortification but her Aunt was completely matter-of-fact.

"Don't suffer the vapors," she said tersely. "We have five days until your papa arrives. If he holds true to character, he won't spend more than a week in town. It is my plan to have you betrothed by the time he leaves so we may be free of him to spend a fortune on a trousseau."

Juliette laughed and surrendered herself to her aunt and maid.

The first ball tested Juliette's mettle as she found herself the object of much scrutiny and behind-fan conjecture. Heeding her aunt's carriage-ride instructions, she kept her head high, a slight, inscrutable smile on her face, and allowed the occasional oh-so-tiny yawn as if she found the proceedings eminently lacking in entertainment.

Well, she reflected, she had yet to muster the daring to actually yawn (though just thinking of it made her jaw itch to stretch open), but she felt she had mastered the smile. She simply pictured the painting of the Mona Lisa, whose likeness she had seen in an engraving at Beverly Castle.

Aunt Constance remained firmly at her side so that all would know she approved of her niece's rather daring ensemble and Eleanor, after a wide-eyed grin of delight, acted as if nothing were out of the ordinary. The small furor soon died down and the only ripples from her fashion splash were a rather increased number of gentlemen asking her to dance.

As she waltzed around the room in her final dance before departing for the Countess de Wynter's ball, Juliette knew she should be thrilled. She knew that several of the gentlemen with whom she'd danced would call upon her tomorrow. The heretofore incredible realization occurred to her that one of them—Mr. Pocock, as it turned out--seemed enamored enough that if she hinted her father was taking her back to Hertford within a fortnight, he might be emboldened to offer for her.

Yet she couldn't shake the feeling that she was acting a terrible fraud. Not a single one of the men she'd danced and talked with this evening even knew she was from Hertford or that her mother had died when she was young, or that she loved to read penny horrids. None of them could have known that green was her favorite color, or that she loved to sing but was always just slightly off key. Not one of them knew these things because they had only talked of their own hobbies and interests. They had spoken variously of their favorite bootmaker, a recently purchased horse, and a father's unfair tightening of the allowance drawstrings. And she had encouraged them to do so, with an approving nod from Aunt Eleanor. Worst of all, Jacob Wilding had not been in attendance. She'd had some half-formed fantasy that he would see her in this red gown and suddenly realize...exactly what, she wasn't sure.

Now, at the second ball, the feeling that she was playing a part that had nothing to do with who she really was continued. The Countess de Wynter ran with a faster set and Juliette's crimson dress only elicited admiring glances rather than gossip.

Though she pretended she was just casually glancing around the crowded ballroom to see who was in attendance, Juliette was scrutinizing every dark-haired man for a glimpse of Jacob Wilding. It was ridiculous. She knew it was. And yet, beyond the...desire to see his handsome face and perhaps touch his arm, she suddenly craved his presence. She wished to ask if he'd begun that new book, ring a peal over his head if he hadn't, inquire about his father, and, strangely, share her thoughts regarding the men she'd danced with tonight. Of course, she would never do the latter, but such were her feelings for him, she rather felt she could, were she daring enough.

It was on the second scan of the crowd that she saw him. It was ridiculous, really, for he wasn't even facing her. His back was turned and his head slightly bowed as if he were listening to someone much shorter than himself. And yet she knew the jut of his shoulder, the curl of the hair at his collar. Ridiculous, she chided herself, and yet, she just knew.

After a moment, almost as if he felt her stare boring into his back, he turned abruptly. Their gazes collided for a split second before she jerked her head sideways and pretended to be paying attention to Eleanor who was telling Lord Elphinstone a humorous anecdote about her old dance master.

Juliette frowned. Why was Eleanor allowed to speak her mind when Aunt Constance had warned Juliette time and again not to prattle on about herself. Lord Elphinstone laughed, not unlike the bray of a donkey, and Juliette reasoned that perhaps Eleanor wished for him to abandon her. Then again, with Eleanor's exquisite looks and lineage, she could probably spout arithmetic and men would hang on her every word. Juliette's looks were merely—she turned her head abruptly as if a siren's call had shouted her name. There, exactly where he had been a moment before, stood Jacob Wilding, but this time he was the one staring at her. His eyes burned hotly and she felt her body warm in response. She remembered her outrageous gown and elegant hairstyle and as she levelly returned his stare, she felt she had suddenly become the most beautiful woman in the room.

Eleanor's tug on her arm finally drew her attention from Lord Worthing. When she turned her gaze, it was to see the oddest expression on her friend's face: half humorous, half sheer cunning.

"Dear Juliette, Lord Kirkpatrick has come to claim me for a waltz. Perhaps you would be so kind as to share one of your waltzes with Elphinstone, here?"

Juliette glanced at the lovesick lordling who was staring at Eleanor morosely and shook her head. "I am feeling a bit parched. I believe I will visit the refreshment table."

Eleanor tossed an apologetic glance at Elphinstone and allowed the Scottish earl to guide her to the parquet dance floor.

Not wishing to remain in Elphinstone's presence—he was, after all, the same gentleman who had mistaken Shakespeare's line all those weeks ago—Juliette curtseyed briefly to him and turned to make her way through the press of people in search of the punchbowl. She was wondering where Aunt Constance had got to and whether she ought to seek her out, when a gentle grip on her elbow turned her around. Perhaps she should have been surprised, but tonight it seemed quite natural that Lord Worthing should be standing right there, asking her to dance.

She merely smiled her assent—something slightly more pleased than the Mona Lisa smile, but still quite reserved. How should she act? The last time they'd talked, he had apologized for kissing her. Yet now he looked like he would gobble her up given the chance. As Jacob's hand slipped naturally to the middle of her back and their gloved hands met, the only thing in Juliette's mind was the notion that she should remember every moment of this waltz so she could cherish it in years to come. As he spun her effortlessly around the room, she felt him pull her closer than was decorous and yet she would not have drawn away had her life depended upon it. She glanced up at him and found him staring down at her. It was not seemly to stare into a gentleman's eyes, at least one who wasn't your betrothed. But she was singularly unable to either look away or speak.

In the back of her mind she recognized and gave thanks for the fact that the song they were dancing to was one of the longer waltzes popular now. She inhaled deeply, pulling the clean, distinctive scent of him into her lungs. Of course, she suspected that she would find his scent equally attractive were he sweaty from a day of riding or hunting.

"You're blushing," he commented, his voice low and deliciously rumbly.

She laughed, embarrassed by her thoughts. "I'm not."

"You are."

"It's warm in here," she prevaricated.

"It's a chilly evening," he countered. And he was right, drat the man. The outdoor drizzle had been accompanied by unseasonably cold temperatures and even with the press of bodies in the ballroom, the air was cool.

Feeling suddenly bold, though not brave enough to hold his gaze, she said, "Perhaps my thoughts are improper."

She felt his fingers tighten on her back and thought she

detected a deepening of his breath.

"Then I must insist you share them with me."

She licked her lips nervously—really, who knew it was so difficult to be daring?—and glanced up in time to see his gaze drop to her tongue. At the sight, her own breath caught. Good Lord, she thought, he could kiss her right here in the middle of the ballroom and she would not bat an eyelash at the impropriety. In fact, if he so much as dipped his head an inch, she would hasten to meet him halfway. She felt the tips of her breasts lightly brush his lapels and realized they had moved even closer together. This was simply not done, she reminded herself and quickly cast a glance to either side of them. The dance floor was an absolute crush. Perhaps it was simple logistics that had compelled them to dance so scandalously close.

"I—" she stammered.

Obviously taking pity on her, he changed the subject. "You will be happy to know I have not only started *A Lady's Notorious Defense*, but stayed up all night to finish it."

"What is—oh! The sequel to *The Ironclad Case Against Miss Nelson*?"

"The very one."

"And? How was it? It must have been wonderful if you stayed up all night to read it!"

He smiled. "In truth, it was not a worthy sequel. I fear the author simply wrote it to cash in on the success of the first book."

Juliette frowned. "Then why on earth would you stay up all night?"

"I knew I would disappoint you greatly if I did not at least once in my life cast sanity and reason aside and indulge my love of truly rotten literature. Let me think, what was it you told me? Ah yes, that 'a true book lover would not have let mere fatigue stop him from finishing a novel.'"

And that's when she was absolutely sure she loved him. The awareness had been building for weeks, making its presence felt from time to time, ever since the house party at Beverly Castle. But when she realized this man not only listened to what she said, but *knew* her...well it was no wonder she fell. Head over heels, even.

"What is it?" he said, looking at her quizzically. "Do you feel ill?"

It took Juliette a moment to comprehend he must be interpreting her love-struck expression for ailment. The absurdity of the realization struck her and she began to giggle.

The look on his face grew still more perplexed. She wondered what he would say if she told him the truth. And *that* notion caused her to giggle even harder. He began to chuckle in return and it was a wonder that neither of them stumbled as they waltzed around and around the crowded dance floor. Their shared laughter gradually faded and in its wake left a contented mutual happiness. They continued to gaze at one another and Juliette memorized every perfect moment: his strong hand splayed against her spine; the other one holding her hand firmly but with great care; his delicious scent that was even more pronounced as she was practically pressed up against him; the sensuous feel of her skirts belling about her feet, wrapping around his leg as he guided her in a tight spin; even the hard press of his hips against her own as a clumsy couple behind her stumbled into her. She gasped as she felt the man's elbow knock her in the ribs and Jacob immediately drew her flush up against him to keep her from falling. He glared at the gentleman who offered up profuse apologies. After a moment her returned his attention to Juliette and, as if realizing he now held her indecently close, drew away, but slowly. So slowly in fact, that Juliette felt the separation as a minute series of disrobings, the cool air of the ballroom rushing in to cool the warmth generated by their two bodies. She took a shaky breath and glanced up at Jacob. He was staring down at her with a look she could only describe as desire. Could it be possible he felt something between them as well? Juliette knew it was a ridiculous notion. And yet...

Round and round they spun as the waltz drew to its impassioned conclusion. When they could drag it out no longer, she curtseyed deeply to his bow. She took his arm and they silently left the dance floor. She wished desperately that he would offer to escort her to refreshments or, even better, suggest a walk outside. But not far away, she spotted Eleanor talking to Aunt Constance and reality returned. Lord Worthing was not for her.

She stopped and gently removed her hand from the crook of his arm. She willed her smile to be carefree, but she was terribly afraid it wobbled tremulously. "Thank you for the dance, my lord."

Jacob chuckled and said, "I believe that is my line."

She wanted to grin at his jest, but suddenly felt as if she might cry instead. "You'd best dance with Lady Eleanor," she said in a strained voice.

At mention of Eleanor, Jacob's grin faded. He glanced up and Juliette knew he saw the woman he should have waltzed with. She could see the conflicted emotions on his face and longed to ease his suffering. Grasping her skirts in one hand, she whirled about and quickly threaded her way through the crowd. She didn't stop until she found herself in a small drawing room at the other end of the wing from Lady de Wynter's ballroom.

There she allowed herself to cry—great heaving sobs that stole her breath and constricted around the broken pieces of her heart.

When she calmed, she dabbed her eyes with her gloved fingers and tried to calm her breathing.

One thing was certain: she could never dance with Jacob Wilding again.

In fact, it would be best if she never saw him again. It was freeing, actually, to remove the notion of Jacob Wilding from her mind. It would allow her to focus fully on her goal of finding a suitable husband, and quickly. She inhaled sharply, as if preparatory to another sob. The thought of marrying simply to avoid a life of spinsterhood as her father's assistant suddenly felt so much bleaker than it had at the start of the Season.

How could she marry a complete stranger now that she knew what it was like to love someone? She thought of the men waiting to dance with her, those who'd asked to call on her. They knew nothing of her other than she was suddenly one of the fashionable young misses. They'd looked right past her last month but now she was suddenly worthy in their eyes.

The thought occurred to her that if she could not wed the man she loved, perhaps she should at least settle for the man who had offered for her when she was simply Juliette Aston, rather than the popular, yet empty-headed girl she had portrayed for the last weeks.

She was surprised at where her line of thought was taking her, but suddenly self-absorbed, tied-to-his-mother's-apron-strings Mr. Pickering had the appeal of having chosen her based on who she had been—publicly, at least—for the last three years. A frantic part of her mind shouted that he knew her no better than Mr. Pocock or any of the other young gentlemen who had found her so fascinating of late. All of her conversations with Mr. Pickering, as well as all of his correspondence, centered strictly around himself.

Juliette felt despair clawing at her peace of mind. "It doesn't really matter, does it?" she whispered aloud. If she was not married to the man she loved, it did not matter who she married. And Mr. Pickering deserved some merit for having valued her as a wife before she was the new "popular Miss."

"Very well," she said to the empty room. "Mr. Pickering it is." That small part of her that had protested was silent—stunned, no doubt by her decision.

She felt an odd calm sweep over her. It might not be the ideal path she had chosen, but there was some comfort in knowing exactly where that path would lead her and that it had been her decision to take it.

She realized that her fingers were ice-cold. She pressed them to her eyes, willing them not to appear a puffy, tear-reddened mess so that she might return to the ball shortly without eliciting undue concern from her aunt or Eleanor.

A few minutes longer, she reasoned, just to makes sure I'm perfectly composed.

Finally she stood, smoothed her skirts, and made her way back to the noisy ballroom. She looked for Aunt Constance rather than Eleanor on the off chance Jac—Lord Worthing was still in attendance on her friend.

Aunt Constance was nowhere to be found, but thankfully neither was Eleanor. Juliette realized she'd never made it to the refreshment table. She resolutely set out for it and was grimly pleased to discover the platter containing strawberry tarts was still quite full. She fetched a small plate and helped herself to two. And then, deciding that she really didn't need to appear dainty since she was already settled on a fiancée who was not even here, she dropped a third on top of the others in a neat little pyramid of pastry and fruit and set off to find a quiet corner to eat.

Her aunt found her as she was biting into the third tart —and realizing her eyes were much bigger than her stomach.

"What are you doing here in the foliage, Juliette? Breaks behind the palms are not in our itinerary."

Juliette set her plate down and rose guiltily. It crossed her mind to tell her aunt why it didn't matter if she continued to hide, but something stopped her; perhaps guilt that her aunt's considerable efforts were ultimately for naught, perhaps fear that she would read grave disappointment in Constance's eyes. There was plenty of time to reveal her decision when Mr. Pickering arrived in conjunction with her father.

She allowed her aunt to drag her back into the crowded mix of people, and murmured politely to Lord Someone-or-other when she was introduced. She refused to reconsider her decision and so promptly turned her brain off, allowing the mindless platitudes she'd been uttering for the last fortnight to trip lightly off her tongue.

It proved difficult a few times to maintain such bland

equanimity, such as when she was dancing the evening's final waltz with Mr. Pocock and they swept within inches of Eleanor and Lord Worthing. As luck would have it, the two couple's rotations were perfectly in sync so that when they swung around at the far end of the ballroom, Juliette was practically face to face with Lord Worthing whose gaze caught and held hers. Thankfully Mr. Pocock was not the most fluid dancer and he spun her again just before the proper time in the music so that when next they met up, Juliette was facing Eleanor who smiled broadly. Though she hated herself for it, Juliette found it difficult to return the smile.

This was her best friend, she chided herself, but that small little voice she'd heard earlier must have grown peevish for it now shouted out that Eleanor was her best friend who could have any man she wanted, and in fact, had shown no marked preference for Lord Worthing. What was wrong with Eleanor that she did not see that Jacob Wilding was possessed of a wonderful sense of humor, a keen intelligence, and a compassionate heart? Were their positions reversed and Juliette's father was as eager for her to wed Lord Worthing, she would have hired a carriage herself to take them to Scotland so that they might marry immediately and avoid the time it took to read the banns!

Mr. Pocock whirled her into a little flourish at the end of their dance that left her wobbling precariously. A warm hand at her elbow steadied her and she knew even before she glanced over her shoulder that Jacob had come to her aid.

"Thank you, my lord," she whispered.

He frowned at the miserable expression on her face but she pulled out of his clasp and fled without so much as a nod to Mr. Pocock.

Chapter Thirty-four

Jacob had arrived at the de Wynter ball feeling irritable and confused. He'd visited his father again this evening and was disheartened to find his sire even weaker than he was the day before. His condition had not, however, prevented the earl from harping on about the length of time Jacob was taking with his courtship.

"I trust you are not simply hedging, hoping I will die before you offer for the young lady?"

Jacob clamped his teeth tightly to prevent making a hasty and disrespectful response. He reminded himself his father was in pain. He unclenched his jaw and said, "It has scarcely been a decent length of courtship to rush an offer of marriage."

"Eh!" his father had grimaced, waving his hand dismissively. "Chalcroft and I have discussed the possibility for years. It's not like it will be a surprise to him."

The stone on Jacob's shoulders grew still heavier.

"You and Lady Eleanor's father may have talked for years, but she and I scarcely know each other. Even as children we did not play together." Jacob had the haziest memory of a much younger Eleanor not wanting to play with his sister outside because she was wearing a frilly new dress. Other than that, he could not recall one interaction they'd enjoyed until he was re-introduced to her this Season. "I will make my offer when I am ready."

His father pouted, paradoxically looking like a decrepit old man and a petulant child all at the same time.

His mother had arrived at that moment and Jacob was

saved further lecture on the subject by her insistence that his father take his medicine and get some rest.

He stopped briefly at his club for a fortifying drink and hopefully diverting conversation with Hugh Stalwood. The former requirement was easily filled, the latter not at all. He hadn't seen Stalwood in days and he realized he sorely missed his friend's lighthearted teasing.

Realizing he could not put off his social commitments any longer, he finally pried himself out of his comfortable leather chair and took himself off to the de Wynter ball where he was sure to see Lady Eleanor. On the drive to the countess's home, he called Eleanor's face to mind, desperately trying to rally his interest in her. He even closed his eyes to bring her features more clearly into focus. He frowned. Lady Eleanor had golden, springy curls, not lush dark waves. And her eyes were China-blue, not that dark slate blue that reminded him of the waters of the Channel on a brisk, bright day.

Good God, he'd been fixating on Juliette. Again. It was growing unnerving. At random times throughout his day, he found himself smiling at some teasing remark she'd made. All too often at night, he dreamed of her and his dreams were not of teasing remarks. They usually began with that one kiss they had shared in the gardens at Beverly Castle and invariably progressed far beyond where they had stopped. He woke in the mornings hard and frustrated.

His father's happiness and approbation was paramount to him, even more so now that the earl was facing his last days, but Jacob was loath to spend the rest of his life with a woman whose primary appeal was in fulfillment of his father's final wish.

His coach drew up to the de Wynter house and he leapt out of it before the footman had even reached for the door. He was full of frustrated energy and needed to dispel it in order to remain civil tonight. He took the stairs into the house two at a time and those up to the ballroom three at a time.

His heart was pounding lightly and he was a little out

of breath, but he felt calmer than he had in the carriage. He paused a moment before entering the ballroom to compose himself and entered the room. It wasn't five minutes before he saw her. Even had he not been attuned to her presence, his eye would have been drawn to her tonight for she wore a gown of garnet, elegantly simple and yet lushly alluring. It suited perfectly. He caught a tantalizing glimpse of the curve of her shoulder through the translucent puffed sleeves of her gown and longed to tug that sleeve down, to drag his lips over that creamy curve...

Tearing his gaze from Juliette, he purposely sought out Lady Eleanor and found her across the room, in the company of her father and a tall, dark-haired man he'd never met before. He made his slow way through the crowd, allowing himself to be stopped along the way. By the time he finally reached Lord Chalcroft, Eleanor and the dark-haired man were on the dance floor.

"Ah, Worthing!" Chalcroft said jovially. "Good to see you, good to see you! Eleanor's just gone to dance. Nothing to worry about with her partner, however, just a young fellow I'm talking to about some land in the Indies."

Jacob glanced to the dance floor where he caught sight of Eleanor beaming up at the man in question. He felt not the slightest niggle of jealousy and wondered if that was a good or bad thing.

Chalcroft's tone sobered. "I had word from your father. He is not improving, I take it."

Jacob shook his head slightly.

"Well, perhaps we should move things along, if you know what I mean. My daughter will certainly not hinder the proceedings."

Jacob thought Lord Chalcroft made it sound like they were engaging in a mundane legal settlement of perhaps a transfer of property or the settling of a lien.

"Has Lady Eleanor said anything that leads you to believe this?"

Chalcroft laughed again. Really, either the man had had much more to drink this evening than Jacob had, or he was just one of those annoyingly jolly people who laughed at everything.

"Goodness, no. Eleanor would flit about society for the next decade, obsessed only with her newest gowns and the latest hairstyles if I let her. But she's a good gel, nonetheless and for all I said about ladies setting the pace in affairs of the heart, sometimes we men need to take the reins. Here, let me call her over—"

"Sir!" Jacob said, when it appeared Lord Chalcroft would pull his daughter off the dance floor and betroth them right then. "I assure you, there is no need for a precipitous rush. My father is a strong man and sure to make a full recovery. I should rather he be...up and about...to enjoy the announcement and, ah, festivities."

Lord Chalcroft shrugged amiably. "Suit yourself, lad, suit yourself. Now if you'll excuse me, I've done my duty to Lady Chalcroft in making sure the crowd here is none too fast. I'm off to the card room. Good evening."

Jacob closed his eyes, reminding himself of his promise to his father—the only real demand his sire had ever made of him. He knew seeing Jacob wed to Eleanor Chalcroft would ease the earl's last days on earth. He opened his eyes, intending to seek the young woman out and make his intentions clear.

As if drawn by a siren's call, his gaze immediately settled on Juliette. She was making her way through the crowd, perhaps looking for her next dance partner. All thoughts of Eleanor or his father fled his mind. He intercepted her, caught her arm and when she turned, he murmured, "Dance with me."

They'd danced together before, but never the waltz. Never had he held her close in his arms as they traveled the length of the dance floor, her skirts billowing around his legs, her eyes bright as he confessed he'd stayed up all night finishing that damn book just to impress her. As their laughter ebbed, he gazed into her radiant expression. And he knew. He knew that he loved this woman, that she was the only one who could make him laugh like that, and who understood his absurd enjoyment of terrible novels, his love for his family, and all the other quirks that made him who he was.

He had to find a way to tell her. But as the dance drew to a close, the light went out of her expression.

At her mention of Eleanor, Jacob's grin faded. He followed her gaze and saw Eleanor Chalcroft. When he turned back to tell Juliette he did not care to dance with her friend, she was gone.

Chapter Thirty-five

Jacob spent the next several days avoiding his father, Eleanor, and Juliette. Of those, Juliette was the only one he truly did not wish to avoid, but he knew that she was often in the company of Eleanor, and truth be told, every time he saw her, he only wanted her more. It would be best if he didn't see her again, or at least until they were each good and married. To other people, of course. Dropping his pen, he pressed his fingers into his scalp. He'd been coming to work in the earl's study when he knew his father was napping, but unfortunately, even the densest Parliamentary reports was unequal to the task of shoving Juliette Aston out of his mind.

He flopped back in the desk chair and stared out the window. What would be so terrible, he asked himself, if he simply told his father he'd fallen in love with another woman and wished to marry her? His father's primary request had been that Jacob marry before the earl died, so he could go on to his eternal reward knowing the Wilding line would continue and the earldom secure. It had only been later that his father had fixated on Lady Eleanor as his choice for his son.

The idea, once sprouted, grew quickly in his mind. Had his mother not told him to follow his heart? Surely she would support his wishes and help his father understand.

With renewed purpose, Jacob re-inked his pen and returned his attention to the reports he was summarizing for his father in order to finish his work. If he was lucky, he could finish in time to speak to his father *and* call upon Juliette.

Finally, he set his pen down again. He'd perhaps not done the best job with today's work, but it was done and he was eager to put his plan into action. A quick check with the butler let him know his father was awake and enjoying a late luncheon. Jacob took the stairs two at a time—truly, this was becoming a habit, he thought with a grin—and knocked lightly on his father's door.

An hour later he emerged from Beverly House to a beautiful summer's afternoon. The day could not grow more perfect, he decided. His father had been disappointed that Lady Eleanor would not be joining the family, but when Jacob's mother had asked her husband if he wished a loveless marriage on his only son when they themselves had shared a loving union, the earl had relented.

Lady Beverly had practically glowed when Jacob told her the identity of the woman he wished to marry. "I had a feeling about you two," was all she would say, however.

Once at Constance Smithsonly's house, he was informed, Miss Aston was not at home.

"Unfortunately, my lord, neither is her father," the butler said upon receiving his calling card.

Jacob lifted his brows. Sir Lewis was back in town? he thought. That is fortuitous. The butler had no idea when either party would return and asked if he should relay a message.

Jacob smiled at the thought of having Juliette's butler deliver his courtship request, but merely thanked the man and left, feeling quite adrift now that his determination had no outlet.

A ride through Hyde Park (and back again just in case) showed no sign of Miss Aston. He decided it was beyond gauche to inquire of Lady Eleanor which social function her friend might be attending tonight and so spent his first night as a would-be fiancée in his small bachelor's house, wandering from room to room.

Chapter Thirty-six

A housemaid knocked on Juliette's door and informed her that a gentleman caller was awaiting her downstairs.

"Did he give his name?"

The housemaid froze. "No, miss. Should I have asked it?"

"That's alright. It's Abbott's afternoon off, I take it?"

"Yes, miss."

Juliette descended the stairs wondering if Mr. Pocock had come to visit again. He'd come two days ago bearing a posy and not much conversation. They'd sat under the watchful eye of Aunt Constance and engaged in desultory chitchat for the requisite twenty minutes and when Juliette saw him to the door, he bowed over her hand and thanked her heartily for the sparkling conversation. If he was back today, she had no idea what they would say to one another. Perhaps discuss Sir Lewis's return to London? But no, Juliette didn't want to say anything that might hint she wished him to speak to her father, for though Mr. Pocock was very nice, it had turned out they had even less in common than she and Mr. Pickering. He at least could talk for an hour. It was largely about himself, of course, but there was never that uncomfortable silence she and Mr. Pocock often suffered.

Juliette was wondering why on earth it was so difficult to find a gentleman with whom she could simply talk about life when she entered the parlor.

"Oh!" she exclaimed, completely caught off guard. "Mr. Pickering, I did not realize you were due back in town as of yet."

Mr. Pickering laughed as if she had told the most humorous anecdote. "Such a sly wit you have, my dear," he said, rising to take her hand and bow low over it, placing a rather wet kiss on the back. "As if I didn't specifically say I would be back in town yesterday and call on you today!"

Juliette waited until he turned to surreptitiously wipe the back of her hand against her skirts. She was sure he had written such direction in his last letter. It was probably just buried amidst the tedious details of the particularly good breakfast he'd had at his host's house and the explicit account of his mother's rheumatoid. Juliette gestured for him to resume his seat. "I trust your journey was...successful?"

Mr. Pickering smiled—preened, really—and smoothed his waistcoat over his rounded belly. "I shouldn't like to boast, you know."

Juliette admirably refrained from lifting her eyebrows.

"But I have secured two more investors for the venture I told you about."

She racked her brain trying to think of what he might have written. She could recall nothing save vague postulations of a brilliant undertaking whose success would assuredly gain him the notice of very important people.

Mr. Pickering continued. "Once we are wed, I shall have the final stake required to launch my plans."

"I--I beg your pardon," she stammered. "Did you say 'once we are wed'?"

Mr. Pickering laughed delightedly again. "There's my sly puss again. Teasing me, are you?"

Juliette's lips felt numb and her cheeks cold. It was a foregone conclusion, of course, what with him formally asking to court her months ago and his veiled comments at the Countess of Beverly's house party. And yet...Juliette rather expected a bit more...courtship from him. They hadn't seen each other in nearly a month and—

"Have you already spoken to my father?"

"I've requested an appointment with him when he returns home. And another with my solicitor in the next day or two. I expect it will be a bit too rushed to have the banns called this Sunday. Wouldn't be seemly, and mother does set a store by being decorous in all things. That's one reason she likes you so well, you know. You're very decorous."

Momentarily distracted, Juliette said, "I am?"

"Indeed. Mother quite likes that you don't put yourself out there like those young misses who are dancing every dance and collecting hordes of gentlemen admirers. You are quiet and reserved and in all manners docile," he finished approvingly.

Juliette was stunned into silence. Good heavens, did the man not realize she'd been miserable being "quiet, reserved, and docile?" And he clearly had not heard of her recent adventures as a scarlet-gown clad young miss who danced every dance.

Mr. Pickering was talking about which of her acquaintances he should like her to invite to the wedding breakfast when she finally snapped out of her daze.

"One moment, sir," she said, holding up a hand to halt his suddenly mind-numbing chatter. "Do you not think you should, well, ask me for the...the honor of my hand? In marriage?"

Mr. Pickering's peal of laughter was as unnerving as it was genuine and Juliette felt the world begin to crumble beneath her feet. When he'd first begun calling upon her, she'd made no demands of his time or affection. When he'd announced his intention to court her, she'd responded most submissively. Even during his few days at Beverly Castle, she'd not given him one reason to doubt his confidence in their arrangement.

"Good heavens, Lettie! You do enjoy bringing a man to mirth."

Lettie?! she thought, appalled at the moniker.

"I declare your wit will bring no end of entertainment to mother and I."

Juliette stood abruptly. "Sir, I must insist that you—"

she'd been about to inform him she would not answer to such a ridiculous nickname as Lettie. Mr. Pickering clearly thought she was about to say something else.

He stood and grabbed both her hands. He'd removed his gloves and his palms were clammy, though it did not appear the condition was on account of nerves. He looked most pleased with himself.

"Now, now, I know a girl's got her pride. Mother did always say even the plainest miss feels herself deserving of fripperies."

"Fripperies?" Juliette sputtered, unable to voice her affront at being considered the plainest miss, especially from a man who professed to want to marry her.

"Let's marry, Lettie." Mr. Pickering snorted with laughter. "Oh my, that's rich! 'Let's Lettie!' I believe your levity is wearing off on me." This sent him on another spurt of laughter. "Levity Lettie!"

She could only stare at him in shock as the lovely daydream that had been the past several weeks crumbled about her ears. She was no sought-after debutante. Not really. Her modest success had been due to the fact that she'd provided some mid-Season novelty by remaking her public persona. She recalled the decision she'd made the night she and Jacob had waltzed. Did it really matter if Mr. Pickering forbore from mouthing quixotic platitudes? Now that she considered it, she did not wish to pretend theirs was any sort of love match.

Still, a girl—even the plainest girl—had her limits.

"Please do not call me Lettie, Mr. Pickering. My name is Juliette."

"Oh ho! Juliette is it? A bit particular are you?" At her solemn nod, he chuckled. "Thought so! I can read you like a book. Not that I hold with reading books, mind you."

She debated correcting his assumption. In fact, some rather sharp words were on the tip of her tongue, ready to tell him exactly what she thought of his high-handed assumptions, when she paused. What good would such a declaration do? In the worst case, she might offend him to the point he cancelled his meeting with her father and departed, never to be heard from again.

She latched on to his last statement. "Did you say you don't care for books?"

"Indeed not. Either they're full of preposterous stories, ridiculous poems, or utterly amoral plays. I simply have no use for them."

It was one thing to be considered a plain, docile, meek miss, to be assigned ridiculous nicknames, and whose every utterance was considered ridiculously amusing. It was quite another to be denied her books.

"I quite enjoy novels, Mr. Pickering. I often find poetry inspiring and have been known to read Shakespeare's complete works in a summer. I will admit to an aversion to philosophy but I'm sure you can guess my feelings toward works of a scientific nature, given my father's passion for the natural world."

"Er...yes?"

"I should like it understood that I will continue to read —a wide variety of genres—*should* we wed." She could not stop herself from putting an emphasis on "should."

"Well, ah..." Mr. Pickering blustered, clearly unsure of how to proceed in the face of such grim determination.

"If you or your mother will have a problem with that, it is best we part amicably now before any meetings or agreements have been set."

"No, no, no. It's certainly not necessary to take such drastic steps. Surely a little reading now and again can be tolerated. Why mother even reads the paper once a month to see what those depraved politicians are up to."

"Everyday," she said firmly.

"Well, to each his own, what what?" he finally said, after moving his rather florid jaw soundlessly for several seconds.

Juliette felt an inordinate amount of pleasure at her small victory. She graciously nodded her head, but decided against ordering a tea tray as a peace offering. Were he meeting with her father this afternoon, Sir Lewis could be the one to offer refreshments, and then spend the time it took to consume them with Mr. Pickering.

She glanced outside and, seeing that it was a sunny day, decided to exert her will a bit more.

"If you will excuse me, Mr. Pickering—" really, did the man not even realize he'd not invited her to use his given name. Not that she would, of course, but he'd jumped right to a ridiculous diminutive of her name, the least he could do would be to make the offer. "If you will excuse me," she resumed. "It is time for my daily walk. I find the fresh air helps clear my mind."

"Shall I accompany you, then?" he asked.

"Not necessary!" she practically shouted. Then, regaining her composure, continued more sedately, "I prefer to go alone. Well, aside from my maid, of course."

"Very well. I suspect your father will invite me to dinner after our meeting so I shall see you this evening."

Juliette forced a smile to her face. "Until tonight, then," she said with a brief bow of her head.

Once outside, she practically ran to the park. Her maid's labored breathing was the only thing that kept her to a pace resembling a walk. Since she could not allow speed to exorcise her dissatisfaction, she resorted to pounding her feet against the ground as she walked, quite enjoying the dull angry clack of her heels against the walk. Her half-boots would probably need to be reshod after today's excursion, but it was well worth it. At the park, the lush green grass and leafy trees calmed her, reminding her of the wide-open spaces of Hertfordshire. A particularly stunning display of flowers reminded her of her time at Beverly Castle, but she quickly suppressed the memory, instead forcing her focus to study the shape of the petals, the buzz of a bee, the heat of the sun on her face when she tilted her head back.

"Juliette!" she heard her name called and turning, saw Eleanor walking along the graveled path on the arm of a tall gentleman Juliette had never before met. He looked vaguely familiar and Juliette realized she'd seen her friend dancing with him at the Countess de Wynter's ball.

Juliette took a deep breath. She had hoped to avoid her friend for at least a few more days. She knew Eleanor would be bitterly disappointed at her decision to marry Pickering and Juliette couldn't blame her.

She pasted a welcoming smile on her face and crossed the green to meet her friend.

"Juliette, do let me introduce you to Mr. Alexander Fitzhugh. Mr. Fitzhugh, my dear friend, Miss Juliette Aston."

Juliette made an appropriate curtsy and surreptitiously studied Eleanor's escort. He stood a full head and a half over Eleanor with broad shoulders and arms that looked to be putting the seams of his coat to the test. His hair when he removed his hat to bow was dark brown—no, dark red. Juliette couldn't decide as it seemed to change in the light as he moved his head. He wore it unfashionably short and it seemed to stick out all over his head instead of being neatly combed and pomaded forward. For all that he was dressed in obviously finely tailored clothes, he did not seem the type of man who usually attended Eleanor. There was a sensation, a force of tightly suppressed energy that seemed to emanate from him.

Juliette glanced at Eleanor and was rather shocked to find her friend gazing quite...well, adoringly was all Juliette could think of. Eleanor never gazed with any affection at her suitors—and what was she doing gazing at this man at all when she was practically betrothed to Lord Worthing?

Forcing her attention back to the conversation, she heard the tail end of Eleanor describing how Mr. Fitzhugh was a recent addition to the London social scene. Lords Elphinstone and Cambers soon joined them and as the men talked, Eleanor drew Juliette aside.

"I've not seen you since the de Wynter ball. Did you not receive my notes to come call?"

"I'm sorry," Juliette said. "I...was ill."

"Oh goodness. Nothing serious, I hope."

"No, no, of course not."

"What do you think of Mr. Fitzhugh?" Eleanor said, sneaking an admiring glance at the man in question.

"I've only just met him. I'm sure I can't possibly think anything of him."

Eleanor surreptitiously poked her friend in the ribs, eliciting a small yelp from Juliette. The three men paused mid-conversation to cast inquiring glances at the women but Eleanor just smiled and waved them off.

"I know your father is in town," Eleanor said.

"You do? How?"

"The footman said so when he returned from delivering my last note."

"Oh. Of course." The servant grapevine was by far the best source for accurate, immediate news.

"So I have a plan," her friend continued in an excited whisper.

"A plan? Whatever for?"

"To give you a little more time. In London. You said he was threatening to take you back to Hertfordshire if you were not betrothed soon."

"Yes, well...about that."

Eleanor ignored her. "The Duke and Duchess of Andover are retiring to the country early this year because of her condition. They are having their traditional end of Season ball in four days as a result."

"Yes? And?" There was no way Juliette would rank an invitation to such an exclusive event.

"Her Grace and I are second cousins. We played together as girls. I shall ensure you receive an invitation. You must wear your best gown—perhaps that crimson one that caused such a stir last week. When your father sees how popular and sought-after you are, he will surely realize that to take you from London early would be detrimental in the least."

"But—"

"I'm sure Mrs. Smithsonly will start to work on him as well. Your aunt really has turned into a gem."

"Yes but—"

"Has Mr. Pocock called recently?"

"What? Yes, but I really must tell you—"

Eleanor held up a hand, stopping her mid-sentence. "Mr. Fitzhugh looks like he wishes to leave. Isn't he divinely handsome?" she whispered.

Diverted, Juliette looked to her friend's escort. "Well, yes but what about Lord Wo—"

"Ah, we are off, it would appear," Eleanor said. Juliette was quite sure her friend hadn't heard a single word she'd spoken during their entire encounter.

Eleanor rushed over to Mr. Fitzhugh and gently chided the other gentlemen, "Now my lords, you are imposing on my morning stroll. I really must reclaim Mr. Fitzhugh for he has promised to show me a nest full of robin's eggs he recently discovered."

Eleanor and the mysterious Mr. Fitzhugh ambled off and Lords Camber and Elphinstone went the opposite direction, completely oblivious to Juliette who was glad for once to be an invisible wallflower.

She turned off the path again, leaving her maid to trail desultorily as she made her way across the closely trimmed grass, allowing herself to take long, unladylike strides as she made her way to a grove of trees where she was certain she wouldn't run into anyone else.

What was Eleanor about, walking with this Fitzhugh gentleman when she was practically betrothed to Jacob Wilding? Well, there was technically nothing wrong with a morning walk in the park—Eleanor's well-trained maid had followed at a discreet but proper distance. She and Lord Worthing were not yet formally betrothed. It was more that Eleanor seemed to be so interested in this Alexander Fitzhugh. Juliette had never seen her friend so taken with a man. Never had she seen Eleanor stare with fascination at a gentleman, much less exclaim that he was divinely handsome. She'd had a suspicious rosiness to her cheeks and…yes, a definite sparkle in her eyes.

A brief spurt of hope flared in Juliette's breast. If Eleanor and Lord Worthing were not engaged…but no, she reprimanded herself sharply. Eleanor's father would prevail on her and Eleanor would fall in love with Jacob, for who could not? Even if Eleanor and Jacob did not marry, he would surely marry a woman of his social rank. There was nothing between them. Not really. A rather remarkable waltz, several good conversations, and a single, extraordinary kiss.

"Stop it!" she hissed at herself when the ridiculous organ in her breast continued to pound in hopeful expectation. "Besides," she reminded herself. "It's already been settled."

The thought of Mr. Pickering, who was probably already returning to her house to meet with her father, slowed her steps.

She did not want to be in the house when her fate was sealed and so she wandered for over an hour until her maid was sighing loudly and meaningfully.

"Would you like an ice, Molly? We can walk over to Gunter's" she asked, feeling guilty for making the tired young woman trudge aimlessly about for so long.

"No, miss. Unless you'd like one," Molly dutifully replied. Juliette knew better than to push the issue. It would be well over an hour's walk and truth be told, her own feet were growing rather sore.

"Let's return home. Perhaps Cook will have made some lemon bars."

Molly seemed to perk up at the prospect of lemon bars and they set off for home.

Chapter Thirty-Seven

Fate, that fickle trickster, had conspired to arrange it so that her father had never returned to receive Mr. Pickering's request for an audience. As was Sir Lewis's wont, he had been caught up in conversation at one of his scientific society meetings and completely lost track of the time, only thinking to return home when his stomach began to rumble. Aunt Constance had left that morning to visit a friend in Guildford and so it was just she and her father for supper. Aunt Constance was not expected to return for at least a day or two, a schedule for which Juliette was immensely grateful. She did not know how she was going to break it to her aunt that she was going to marry Mr. Pickering.

Sir Lewis tucked industriously into his supper, pausing only now and again to ask for the salt or to wipe sauce from his mustache. Juliette knew when his immediate hunger was slaked when he began to tell her about his meeting, though she quickly lost track of who had argued which beetle arrived on English soil first.

The pudding had arrived before her father thought to inquire about his daughter. "How goes the marriage mart? About done with this nonsense, are we?"

Juliette took a fortifying breath. She didn't believe that the entire rest of her life constituted "nonsense," but she also knew that her father was incapable of thinking beyond his next insect study or scientific society meeting. Realizing there was no escaping it now, she said,

"Very nearly, father."

"Well then, how much longer? I should like to return

home as soon as possible. I've been working on a new manuscript—you'll want to read it, I'm certain. You see, I noticed this one particular specimen—"

Juliette knew that if she did not cut her father off now, she would be stuck at the table all evening. "I have all but secured Mr. Pickering's…attentions. I expect him to…formalize the proceedings very soon."

Her father looked surprised. "Decided upon Pickering after all, eh? Bit of a dullard if you ask me, but I won't be looking at him over breakfast, will I?"

Taken aback, Juliette asked, "Well of course. Who else has expressed any interest in me?"

Sir Lewis scooped the last of his trifle out of the bowl and licked his spoon clean, clearly uncomfortable. He finally shrugged. "Thought there was another one you were sweet on. Either way, he'll have to wait for the conclusion of the Naturalist Society meeting. I can't be distracted with contracts and wedding plans and such until that is over." He mumbled something about preparing for tomorrow's proceedings as he hastily excused himself from the table.

Left alone in the dining room, Juliette shook her head at her contrary father. "First he wants me to hurry this nonsense on, but only so far as it doesn't interrupt his meetings!" she told the potted palm in the corner. Her thoughts turning to her father's previous statement, she huffed, "A dullard, indeed!" That would be a compliment to his wit on a good day.

Though she cursed herself for being a coward, Juliette spent the next three days at home. Her aunt had returned the following afternoon and Constance had not been happy to discover what had transpired in her absence.

Juliette heard her screech, "What?!" from the entrance hall and knew her father had told her of Juliette's anticipated news. Opening her bedroom door just a crack, she could hear her father's confused murmurings. Having no idea that Aunt Constance had set her sights higher than Mr. Pickering for his daughter, he no doubt could not understand that lady's reaction.

"Where is she?" Juliette heard her aunt bite out and as the sound of stomping feet came up the staircase—truly, was it healthy for Aunt Constance to stomp?—she quickly closed the door and caught up a periodical, pretending to thumb through it when the door burst open.

"What is the meaning of this balderdash?" her aunt practically bellowed.

Even though she'd been awaiting her aunt's entry, Juliette could not stifle a jolt that caused her to drop the periodical. Stalling for time, she bent to pick it up and set it carefully on a small, doily-covered table.

"Welcome home, Aunt."

"Don't you 'welcome home' me, miss. I want to know why, when we nearly had London at your feet, you agreed to marry that nincompoop?"

Juliette felt tears sting the back of her eyes. They had become quite close these past days and the urge to confess everything to the older woman was nearly overwhelming. But if her aunt thought she was an idiot for marrying Mr. Pickering, what would she think if Juliette confessed she'd fallen in love with Jacob Wilding, whose betrothal to Eleanor would surely be announced by Season's end.

"I—" she stammered, one hand held up in supplication. Concern replaced the outrage in Constance's gaze and she took her great-niece's hand. Stalling for time, Juliette drew Aunt Constance to sit.

"Now tell me what has led to this rather startling decision," Constance urged.

Juliette took a deep breath and began to relate how she'd come to her decision—leaving out the part about not really caring who she married since it wouldn't be the man she loved. When she was done, her aunt simply frowned.

"Let me get this straight: you wish to marry Mr. Pickering because he saw fit to court you before the men of London started to appreciate your attraction? For that alone, you would consign yourself to a marriage of...of...convenience?"

"Well—" Juliette began. Her aunt was having none of it.

"But not the marriage of convenience where he's fabulously wealthy and you are from a powerful family. The sort of convenience where you settle for what's in front of you instead of reaching for that which is just beyond your grasp. You were gaining such popularity, Juliette!

"But with men who only noticed me because I'd suddenly begun acting like a silly peahen!"

Her aunt leveled a gimlet eye on her. "Are you telling me that showing interest in other people is silly? Are you implying that someone like your best friend Eleanor is a peahen?"

"Of course not but—"

"Because it seems to me you rather enjoyed having a full dance card, and only a complete dullard would wish to sit mutely at a dinner party while people conversed around her. Do you mean to tell me you were only acting these past weeks when you seemed to be enjoying yourself?"

"No. Of course I enjoyed myself. But none of the men who danced with me or even called upon me really knew me. They only saw my fashionable dresses and only heard me admire their wit or laugh at their jokes. Not one of them was interested in what I had to say on any subject."

"Not a one?" Aunt Constance asked, a wealth of meaning in her steely gaze.

She knows, thought Juliette. *She knows about Lord Worthing*. She felt her mouth open and close like a beached fish.

After a painfully long moment of silence, Juliette forced herself to speak. "It seems more honest to marry someone who saw worth in me before I was fashionable."

"Men are slow, child! How many times have I told you that? Of course they're going to like you when you're fashionable. The key was to use that temporary momentum to help you find a man who would see beyond that and appreciate you for the gem you are."

Juliette's eyes blurred and she felt a tear streak down her

cheek.

"Can I not talk you out of this idiocy?" her aunt asked softly.

Staring at her hands clasped in her lap, Juliette mutely shook her head. Constance sighed heavily and pushed herself to her feet. "Then there is nothing left for me to do, it would appear. I am going to return to my friend in Guilford. She begged me to visit longer but I told her I had a debutante to see properly betrothed. Failing that, I shall at least endeavor to be a good friend."

With the quiet click of the door behind her aunt, Juliette sobbed as she'd not done since her mother had died.

Chapter Thirty-eight

Sir Lewis was unsettled at the news that Aunt Constance was leaving London before Juliette's betrothal was settled.

"But who will chaperone Juliette at this ball? It's being hosted by an Earl—"

"Duke," Juliette interrupted flatly. In all honesty, she didn't even wish to attend, but the acceptance had been sent, Eleanor would be there, and it would be her last ball as an unmarried miss. Perhaps ever, she reflected glumly, as Mr. Pickering's status excluded him from many ton events that her father's humble title and Eleanor's friendship afforded her.

"Even worse!" her father proclaimed. "Aunt Constance, you mustn't leave yet. Surely a few days will not make much difference to your friend."

"I've already sent word that I'm on my way. If I don't arrive tonight, she will worry. Besides, you've yet to escort your daughter to a single event. Surely a father is an even better chaperone than a great aunt."

"I took her to be presented to the Queen *and* her first ball," he grumbled.

Despite her own despondency at Aunt Constance's departure, Juliette could not stifle a smile. If one did not know Sir Lewis, one might assume he had no wish to be bothered with his daughter's welfare, when in fact she knew he was worse at making conversation with people he didn't know than she had been. He could talk to or about his insects for hours, but humans were another matter entirely.

"We shall get on well enough, father. Allow Aunt Constance to leave in peace."

"Oh very well," her father said grudgingly.

Her aunt cast an ironic glance her way. "Last time I checked, I needed no one's permission to come or go. This *is* my house, you will remember."

"Of course—" Juliette began, but her aunt held up a hand to stop her.

"But seeing as how my wishes have been denied thus far, it is comforting to prevail in *something*, at least."

Juliette felt her face warm. Her aunt had been stoic since learning of Juliette's decision, largely keeping to her rooms for the last two days. Juliette had missed her company more than she would have ever guessed, but was too embarrassed to approach her aunt for commiseration. It did not escape her notice that embarrassment was not a promising emotion to feel about one's future husband.

Aunt Constance stood and pulled on her gloves. Juliette rose to see her off and Sir Lewis obligingly bussed his aunt's cheek before retreating to the library.

At the carriage, Juliette waited, unsure of her aunt's mood. When Constance opened her arms for an embrace, Juliette flung herself at her aunt, her throat choked with a myriad of emotions.

"Don't hesitate to send word should you need...anything," Aunt Constance said, her own voice slightly raspy.

Juliette only nodded and waved goodbye as the coach pulled away.

With a sense of dread, she turned to go inside and begin preparations for the ducal ball.

Against her maid's advice, Juliette decided to again wear the crimson gown Aunt Constance had picked for her. It was her last ball and though her betrothal had yet to be decided officially, she was going to avail herself of a married woman's freedom to wear what she liked.

"Wouldn't you rather the white lace dress for your last

London ball, miss?" Molly asked, holding up the frothy gown hopefully.

"Definitely not," Juliette said, searching through her small jewel box for a dangling pair of earrings.

Once dressed, she gathered up her shawl and reticule and swept downstairs.

Her father entered the front hall just as she stepped off the last step and visibly started.

"Is that what young girls are wearing nowadays? I thought white was de rigueur for debutantes."

"I'm hardly a debutante, father, and I am most certainly not a young girl."

"Still..."

"It's perfectly acceptable. Aunt Constance chose it specifically for me. Besides, I've already worn it about town and caused not a murmur of gossip."

"Well, if Aunt Constance approved," her father mumbled, already distracted by the butler who was holding his overcoat out.

Sir Lewis filled the time it took to drive to the Andover residence with a detailed recitation of all he'd been working on while Juliette had been in London.

"I do hope you'll have time to proofread it for me before your wedding. I've been working non-stop since you've been away and you know how I tend to make more mistakes in my grammar when I'm so focused on my research. At least this time I've kept all the papers in the same room, but I could use some help organizing them into chapters. I fear one of my specimens was not quite dead when I began inspecting it and I'm afraid it scurried away when I poked it with a needle. I spent a good hour tracking it down in my study and by that time, my papers were scattered all over the floor. Please, Juliette," he finished plaintively. "You are always so good at catching my errors and helping me stay organized and surely you won't need all three weeks to prepare for your wedding."

It was not the thought of the not-quite-dead specimen

that had her staring at her father in horror, nor was it dread at the notion of assembling a hundred pages of tightly packed scrawling notes into a manuscript. Rather, it was the reference to a set wedding date that had her feeling a bit like casting up her crumpets.

"Mr. Pickering and I are not even betrothed. Surely it is a bit premature to set a date."

"Hmmm?" her father asked. "Well, there will be no need to wait, will there? Pickering has sent word that he intends to call on me tomorrow morning. I'm sure we know what that means. We'll call the banns starting this Sunday and settle you, just as I promised your mother I would."

Juliette smiled tightly at her father. She was torn between frustration at him for pushing her into this loveless marriage, and understanding that he was driven by his pledge to her mother. Sir Lewis had always relied on his wife for all parental decisions and he and Juliette had only managed so well since Lady Aston's death because Juliette had simply assumed her mother's role of handling all things domestic.

She debated confiding in her father. Would he give her a reprieve if she told him about Mr. Pocock, about everything she'd done to find a husband. She opened her mouth to speak, but at that moment, their carriage came to a stop and she realized they'd arrived.

As they waited for the footman to open the door and hand them out, Juliette made the rash decision to pretend for one last night that she was a carefree debutante intent on merely having fun. She would parlay her meager success of the past few weeks into a night of dancing and merriment, collecting memories of her one and only ducal ball to pull out and cherish in the coming years. She stepped down from the carriage and accompanied her father up the stairs into the huge entry hall of Andover House.

Mr. Pickering had not been invited to the ducal ball, she reflected, and so for one last night, she would pretend he did not exist. It was, perhaps, not the kindest thing to do, but something inside her, some desperate, wild emotion, needed this one last time to pretend that the world was her oyster, that love and passion were waiting just around the corner for her.

They rounded a literal corner and Juliette felt the breath leave her body as they all but ran into Jacob Wilding.

"Lord Worthing!" she gasped as he apologized profusely. She felt her color heighten as she recalled her fanciful musings.

Realizing her father was awaiting an introduction, she presented him to Lord Worthing and as the two men exchanged pleasantries, she studied him closely, committing every detail of his face and form to memory. He was stunning in the gentleman's typical black and white evening garb, with shoulders that clearly needed no padding to appear broad and long legs encased in close fitting trousers. His thick brown hair had been ruthlessly combed into submission and while she preferred it slightly mussed as he'd worn it in the more casual environs of his mother's house party, the severe style only served to emphasize his strong brow, dark eyes, and full mouth. As she stared at the well-defined curves of his mouth, she felt her tongue dart out, as if of its own accord, to moisten her suddenly dry lips. Watching him as closely as she was, she saw his own gaze flick from her father's face straight to her own mouth where he appeared to watch as her tongue withdrew. Her breath seemed to seize in her chest and she felt a flush over her entire body.

"I hope you will save me a dance later, Miss Aston."

"Certainly, my lord," she replied breathlessly, completely ignoring her earlier resolution never to dance with him again. Why had she made such a silly edict, she wondered. Surely one dance could not—

"Intelligent fellow, that," her father said. "Pity you didn't set your cap for him. I dare say he's a few more brains than that Pickering fellow."

Juliette stared at her father in disbelief. "I thought you approved of Mr. Pickering."

"Well, yes, he's fine, if that's who you fancy. Still, he does seem to go on and on about his silly investments, doesn't he?"

Juliette stared at her father. This was the second disparaging comment he'd made about Mr. Pickering. And yet, he'd seemed to settle immediately on Mr. Pickering as a suitable match for her from the first day they'd met.

"Ah well," her father continued. "I'm sure one man is just as good as another at the end of the day, what what?"

Juliette was torn between laughing hysterically and sobbing uncontrollably. As a happy medium, she remained silent as they made their way the final steps into the ballroom.

She spent the next two hours in the crush of people accepting invitations to dance and allowing Mr. Pocock to fetch her cups of lemonade. She caught several glimpses of Eleanor throughout the night on the dance floor and across the huge room, smiling and talking with the gentleman she'd walked with in the park. As she had that day at the park, Eleanor seemed more animated than Juliette could ever remember her being with a gentleman. Eleanor always held her many admirers at a careful distance, winning them over with her beauty and her famous laugh, but never engaging fully with them. Tonight she seemed to hang on every word this Fitzhugh man said.

Finally deciding she would have to track her friend down and nag her for an explanation, she told her father she would return shortly and made her way through the press of people. She lost sight of Eleanor several times and by the time she reached the other side of the ballroom where Eleanor and Mr. Fitzhugh had been standing, they were gone.

"Drat!" Juliette said under her breath. She stood on tiptoe, trying to spy her friend's tall escort, but he was indistinguishable from the hundreds of other men in black eveningwear. At that moment Lord Elphinstone who, it turned out, had no memory of having spoken to her at the park a few days past claimed her for the next dance. She smiled politely as he led her through the steps of the cotillion, but all the while she was scanning the crowd for Eleanor. At last she spied her friend standing beside the door. Eleanor glanced surreptitiously about to see if anyone noticed her and then slipped unobtrusively out of the ballroom. Juliette frowned, wondering at her friend's actions. Her frown deepened when she saw Mr. Fitzhugh stride purposefully through the very same door not a minute later.

"Is something amiss, Miss Aston?" Lord Elphinstone asked. He looked as if he suspected her of preparing to soil the polished tips of his shoes.

"Not at all," she quickly replied. "It is quite a crush in here, isn't it?" she asked as she was jostled by another lady on the crowded dance floor."

"Not if one stays light on one's feet and views the other dancers as mere obstacles around which to gracefully glide." Juliette wondered that the man didn't choke on his own pompousness.

"Indeed," she replied sardonically. She counted out the minutes until the dance was done and, making a hasty curtsy, worked her way through the crowd toward the doors Eleanor had snuck out.

By the time she reached the glass paned doors, it was easily a quarter of an hour since she'd last seen her friend. Surely if Eleanor had visited the ladies' retiring room, she would have long since returned. Juliette stepped through the door and looked up and down the dim hallway. At the end of the passage to the right, she though she saw movement in the shadows. She took a hesitant step forward and part of the shadow moved away from the wall and toward her. Juliette recognized Eleanor as she drew closer, into the candlelight.

"Eleanor?" she asked. "Where have you been?"

"It was so warm in the ballroom—I've not seen a crush like this in years. It went straight to my head. I simply found a quiet room in which to rest. I'm feeling much better now. Shall we return?"

Juliette allowed herself to be tugged back toward the

door into the ballroom. Eleanor was talking quickly and...nervously? Juliette had never known her friend to be anything other than completely confident. As they stepped into the brightly lit room, Juliette gasped.

"Eleanor! What have you done to your hair?"

"What?" her friend asked, her hand going to her hair.

"Well...nothing terrible. It just looks a bit mussed." Juliette could not recall a single time during her friendship with Eleanor in which her friend's golden tresses were not perfectly coiffed.

"Oh, well, I laid down. On a sofa. I told you I wasn't feeling well."

It was plausible, Juliette reflected. There was still a hectic color in Eleanor's creamy cheeks. And yet, something didn't ring true...

At that moment, the door behind them opened and Mr. Fitzhugh stepped into the ballroom. He bowed correctly, but glanced from beneath dark brows at Eleanor with quite the most devilish gleam in his eye, completely ignoring Juliette. Accustomed to this as she was in Eleanor's presence, she instead focused her attention on her friend who, if possible, grew even more flushed. Realization dawned at what Eleanor and this Mr. Fitzhugh must have been about and Juliette felt her eyes grow wide in surprise. The gentleman in question straightened and departed briskly and Juliette turned to her friend whose attention was suddenly riveted on one of the pearl buttons on her glove. When Eleanor finally met her gaze, it was with a look of hesitation and...defiance?

Strangely, it was not this sudden revelation into her best friend's character that was at the forefront of her mind. All she could think about, really, all she could ever think about, was Jacob Wilding and how he didn't deserve a fiancée who would sneak off into dark hallways with another man.

"Eleanor, how could you?" she asked, her voice tight.

The shock in her friend's eyes was evident. Clearly Eleanor had expected her to be as supportive as she ever was.

But if she was expecting a denial or explanation, she was to be disappointed, for Eleanor came to the attack in a completely unexpected way.

"How could *I*? How could you?"

"What are you—"

"How *could* you agree to marry that Pickering oaf? My mother ran into your Aunt Constance yesterday while shopping. After everything we did to give you an opportunity to find someone—"

It was Juliette's turn to interrupt. "Someone who would what?" she asked bitterly. "Fall in love with me? Yes, Eleanor, I had several men finally show an interest in me. But just in this," she gestured to her crimson dress and elegant hairstyle. "This beautiful façade. None of them cared a fig about me. If I married one of them, I'd end up in the same position I am now. But at least this way, it is my choice and I know what I'm getting into. Besides, at least Mr. Pickering showed an interest in me before I was fashionable."

"But you hadn't given them a chance to fall in love with the real you," Eleanor protested.

"My father gave me a deadline," Juliette said flatly. "There was no way—" she broke off, her throat suddenly tight, tears burning the back of her eyes. She turned to leave, then stopped and said over her shoulder. "Lord Worthing doesn't deserve such treatment. He is..." She couldn't think of a single word to sum up Jacob Wilding and so tried to flee, only finding herself behind a crush of people who formed an impenetrable wall.

"Lord Worthing and I have no agreement, Juliette," Eleanor hissed into her ear. "Good heavens! I've been trying to push *you* into his arms for weeks! I don't know why you've resisted me. You're clearly infatuated with him."

Juliette stared at her friend in shock, "But he is quite set on you! Why wouldn't you...You said your father would push you to accept Lord Worthing when he offered. You never discouraged him."

Eleanor pursed her lips mutinously but said nothing.

Feeling tears prick the back of her eyes, Juliette turned and pushed through the throngs of people, ignoring Eleanor who called after her to stop.

She made her way to the other side of the ballroom, near the large wall of glass doors that opened, presumably, onto a terrace. She paused, one hand pressed to the cool glass, the other on the handle. Why would Eleanor say those things? Why hadn't she said them sooner? And did it really matter when the man in question was so set on marrying her friend and not her?

As if she'd conjured him with her thoughts, she heard him call, "Miss Aston."

Taking a deep breath, she turned slightly to see Jacob Wilding smiling politely, one gloved hand held out expectantly. "I believe this is our dance."

Chapter Thirty-nine

She frowned. Their dance?

"Miss Aston? Are you alright?"

She shook her head and said, "I need some fresh air."

"Of course. Allow me." He reached around and turned the knob, pushing the door open and escorting her out onto a wide tiled veranda. Sconces burned at intervals around the house and throughout the gardens behind the house, casting a soft, wavering light that, Juliette surmised, would hide any number of indiscretions taking place outside. Presumably, her own flushed cheeks and distraught expression as well.

She walked slowly around the corner of the house, then moved to the stone balustrade marking the edge of the terrace and rested her hands on it, willing her breath to slow. She was torn between anger at Eleanor for having so little care for this wonderful man, and dismay over...she wasn't sure what. A missed opportunity? If only Eleanor had told her earlier. She shook her head. That was a ridiculous notion. Even without his attachment to Eleanor, Lord Worthing would never view her as a potential bride. He esteemed his father who wanted him to marry a well-born bride. Lord Worthing would never be hers.

She started when she felt his hands settle on the bare skin of her shoulders. Even through his gloves, she could feel their warmth. He turned her slightly and asked, "Are you alright? Tell me what is wrong."

She looked up at him, his handsome face thrown into a contrast of light and dark by the torches. His dark eyes appeared black and fathomless and Juliette wanted nothing more than to abandon reason and throw herself at him. Instead, she tried to form a coherent thought. "I—" she began, her voice a mere whisper.

His gaze dropped to her parted lips and she could have sworn the temperature of the air between them rose. Like a lodestone pulled north, she felt herself drawn closer to him, felt his hands slide from her shoulders to her back. Looking up, she saw the intensity in his expression as he slowly lowered his head to hers.

The kiss began slowly, a soft brushing of lips. He pulled back slightly and she nearly cried out to think that was all he intended to give her. But after a quick glance at her heavy-lidded eyes, he returned to her mouth with greater pressure, molding and shaping her lips, teasing them open with the tip of his tongue. When she obliged, he swept in to taste and explore, the pressure of his hands pulling her closer still, urging her to respond.

Though still unsure of what to do, Juliette gave herself over to his kiss, moving her lips against his, drawing his lower lip into her mouth. When she nibbled gently on it, he moaned, a low, throaty growl that seemed to pierce her to her very core. He deepened the kiss still further, tilting her head back to allow him complete access to her mouth as he feasted upon it like a man starved. She slid her hands up the hard planes of his chest, over fine broadcloth, silk brocade, and skin-warmed linen to entwine around his neck. And still the kiss continued. It surpassed every splendid memory of the kiss they'd shared in the garden at Beverly Castle.

She'd always laughed at the expression "weak in the knees," secretly thinking the young women who used it when describing a suitor's stolen embraces were exaggerating. Now, however, she knew. She knew what it felt like to have her breath stolen by a kiss, her mind dizzy with passion. She felt her own knees buckle and clung to him for support. His response was to wrap his arms more tightly around her, drawing her in so that her body was flush against his, warm and supported.

He finally dragged his mouth from hers and she would have protested, but he turned his attention from her lips to the edge of her jaw, pressing open-mouthed kisses and gentle nibbles along the tender skin.

She dropped her head back, baring her neck to him and he obliged, trailing his tongue along the soft skin until he reached the hollow at the base of her neck. "So sweet," he murmured. "So beautiful."

She was panting and yet still felt as though she were not getting enough air. She ran her hands through the thick folds of his hair, then frantically tugged one glove off to better feel the silken strands. She gripped his head and dragged his mouth back to her own. A restlessness overtook her. Suddenly, her entire life seemed to have contracted, focused onto this one moment, here, with Jacob.

He caressed her back, one hand pressing her closer to his body, the other cupping her bottom, squeezing and lifting her up against him. She felt a ridge of hardness press against her and instinctively shifted so that it nestled between her legs. Jacob growled again and she felt the vibration of the sound beneath the hand she had pressed over his heart. He did not end the kiss, but held his open mouth against hers, panting heavily. She began pressing small kisses along his jaw and the skin of his neck above his collar. She slid her hands around his waist, beneath his jacket, and up over the broad muscles of his back. She dug her fingers into his shoulders, as if her grip were the only thing keeping her upright.

"Juliette." His voice was a low whisper, but she felt it resonate through her body. He slid the hand that had been cupping her backside up, over the light boning of her stays, to the cup her left breast, squeezing gently.

She inhaled sharply and when he moved to pull his hand away, she pressed forward, arching her back to press her breast into his palm. He squeezed again, the tips of his fingers brushing the soft skin above the low neckline of her dress. She lifted her head and met his mouth as it descended. This time she met the intimate forays of his tongue with bold swipes of her own. Juliette felt him tug at the tiny puffed sleeve of her gown, felt the evening air caress her now bare shoulder.

"I must—let me—please." His words made no sense, but she knew what he asked. She drew back slightly so that he could tug at the front her gown until one breast popped free, held high and prominent over the folded cup of her stays.

"You are so perfect." His words froze her. Nothing had ever been perfect about her. Eleanor had always been more beautiful. Other girls had been better at the pianoforte or watercolors. Other girls had always seemed more interesting to the men of London.

But as she watched the reverence in Jacob's eyes as he delicately traced her hardening nipple, she felt like a siren, beautiful, magical, and yes, perfect. When he gently tugged on her nipple, she felt a burst of sensation low in her belly, between her legs. She pressed her pelvis harder against him, delighting in the ripples that radiated throughout her body.

Jacob groaned again, louder this time, then dropped his head to her breast and drew her nipple into his mouth. Juliette closed her eyes and dropped her head back, reveling in his attentions.

It took a moment to hear the other voices over the pounding of her own heart.

"My lord, I fear you bring me out here to compromise me." A feminine giggle followed. Juliette inhaled sharply and tried to push Jacob back. He was still lost in the sensual haze and responded by flicking his tongue over the sensitive crest.

"My lord," she whispered.

At the same moment, a man said, "What else are moonlit verandas for?"

Jacob straightened immediately, whirling her around so she was shielded from view should the flirtatious couple come around the side of the house. Juliette hastily tugged her bodice back in place. Her skin felt flushed and sensitive, as if she had been sunburned. But as the air cooled her cheeks, sanity returned.

What had she done? This man was meant for Eleanor —her best friend. It didn't matter if Eleanor said she didn't want him. Juliette knew her friend's parents well enough to know that their tolerance in allowing Eleanor to refuse suitors would not survive an offer of marriage from an earl's son.

Juliette's skin flushed again, but this time with shame. She turned and fled, making her way around the house to a side door, then back into the main areas of the house where the ball progressed as if her world had not been tilted off its axis.

She scanned the edges of the room, looking for her father. There he was. Sitting in a chair half-hidden by a large potted palm. It must be a family trait, she thought, seeking refuge behind shrubbery and napping at events. He dozed with his chin resting on his chest, his beard spread out like a fan beneath it.

"Papa," she said, gently shaking his arm.

"Whassat? Oh, Juliette. Are we done, then?"

"Yes," she said, hearing the choke of tears in her voice. "I am done. Let us go home. Quickly, please."

Sir Lewis pulled himself to his feet. "You needn't chastise me. I was ready to leave an hour ago."

Juliette cast a quick glance around the huge ballroom but didn't spot Jacob. Not sure if she was relieved or disappointed, she pulled her father from the room and hurried him out to the front of the house to wait for their carriage.

Chapter Forty

Jacob listened to the man and woman around the corner as they exchanged innuendos and then turned to look over his shoulder to tell Juliette they were safe for the moment. She was gone.

"Damnit," he said, louder than he'd intended.

"I say, is someone there?" Jacob closed his eyes as he took a deep breath, then forced himself to round the corner, pretending to be startled by the couple who quickly stepped away from each other.

"Oh, it's you, Worthing," his friend, Hugh Stalwood said. The man turned to the young woman at his side. "Nothing to worry about, my dear."

Jacob nodded at the woman and strode past Stalwood, muttering, "You've the worst timing, Hugh."

Once inside, it took him a moment to adjust to the noise and brightness of a ball in full swing. His heart was still pounding from kissing Juliette. His fingers still tingled as if they could feel the satin smoothness of her skin. He searched the huge room but didn't see her. Pushing his way through the crowd, he ignored friends and acquaintances who called out to him. He would apologize later. He needed to find Juliette. He needed to tell her—He needed to tell her many things. He had intended the scorching kisses to occur *after* he proposed to her. He grinned to himself as he continued his search of the ballroom. He would not trade those moments on the verandah for any carefully laid plan.

He had nearly completed his circuit of the room when he saw her, waking her father from his hiding spot behind a potted plant. Jacob pushed his way through the crowd, but his progress was hampered by the crush of people leaving the dance floor. Keeping his gaze on Juliette, he saw her drag her father out of the ballroom. By the time he made it out of the packed room and to the front steps, Juliette's carriage was pulling away. Jacob scanned the line of carriages and knew it would take too long to wait for his. Juliette's house was not that far a walk.

He crossed the street and started running.

Several minutes later, he rounded the last corner and made for her aunt's house. Juliette's carriage was just arriving. He poured every ounce of energy he had into sprinting down the street, noting as the carriage pulled away that Juliette and her father were nearly to the door. He saw her turn and glance around as the man fumbled with his keys. Jacob skidded to a halt in front of the house next door as she caught sight of him. By the light of the gas streetlights he saw her eyes widen, saw her shake her head in a furtive movement. The older man opened the door and Juliette rushed inside, shutting the door firmly behind her.

Jacob stood there for several minutes, unsure of, well, anything really. Had she not wanted to talk to him? Had she not wanted her father to talk to him? Shaking his head, he came to his senses. Well of course he could not approach her father in the middle of the night on the man's stoop, looking a sweaty, rumpled mess. He had to do this properly. He'd been a fool for too long regarding Juliette but he would rectify that first thing in the morning. He would appear on her doorstep, properly groomed, and respectfully ask her father for her hand. He would come up with some grand romantic gesture to sweep her off her feet. She deserved that. He would tell her in no uncertain terms just how much she meant to him. Heart pounding in anticipation, he headed home

Jacob awoke the next morning with the feeling that it was the first day of a wonderful new life. By mid-morning, he should have settled his marriage suit with Sir Lewis; by luncheon he would be gazing at his betrothed. In less than a month, he would make her his in the eyes of God and England. Stretching languorously, Jacob rather imagined this must be what the cat-in-the-cream-pot felt like.

Ringing for his valet, Jacob strode into his dressing room, intending to pick out his suit of clothes himself. It wasn't every day a chap got engaged to the woman he loved, after all.

Within the hour he was suitable shaved and dressed, the merest speck of lint brushed off the superfine wool of his jacket. His boots were polished to a mirror-like finish and he'd even allowed his valet to tie his stock in a rather more intricate pattern than he normally wore.

"Shall I do, do you think, Branson? I must win a lady's hand today, you know."

"May I be the first to offer you congratulations then, sir. For no lady worth her salt would reject such a suitor as you," was Branson's effusive response.

Jacob chuckled. "You do know your job is not in danger, don't you? You needn't lather it on quite so heavily."

Branson bowed stiffly and Jacob bit back a smile. He'd been trying to joke with his valet since the man began working for him over a year ago. He was about to give it another go when a pounding at the front door caught his attention. His stomach clenched as he instantly thought of his father. No, he thought. Not today. Not so soon.

Leaving his valet behind, he bolted down the stairs and flung the door open. A young man in Beverly livery stood panting on the stoop, a horse behind him on the street.

"My father," Jacob rasped hoarsely.

"Alive, my lord," the young man gasped. "But he's suffered a terrible attack. Your mother sent me to bring you right away in case—" he bit off his words and bowed his head.

Brushing past the servant, Jacob threw himself on the saddled horse and swung it around. He dug his heels into its sides and crouched low over the pommel. Within minutes he was at Beverly House, bolting up the stairs, ready to pound on the door for admittance. He was expected, of course, and the door swung open as his foot hit the last step. He didn't stop to see who had opened it, instead sprinting up the stairs, running down the carpeted hallway, and only slowing when he reached his parent's door. He paused a moment, willing his breath to slow. He reached with shaking hand for the knob and opened the door. His mother glanced up as he entered and smiled wanly.

"How is he?" he asked, avoiding looking directly at his father. Somehow he felt if he could delay looking at his sire, he could delay accepting how bad he must be.

His mother had already returned her attention to her husband and answered with a shrug. "It was a terrible attack. We were preparing to go down for breakfast when it hit him. He just...crumpled to the floor like a rag doll."

Jacob finally forced himself to look at his father. The earl looked like a shadow of himself. Jacob remembered being startled a few weeks ago to realize that his hale, hearty father had weakened so much, but now he scarcely recognized the man he had looked up to and admired his entire life. Miles Wilding's cheeks were sunken, his eyes rimmed by purplish shadows, and his hair lay limply against his skull. Jacob took his father's fragile hand in his own, willing strength into his sire.

"What does the doctor say?" he asked, looking back to his mother.

Her lips thinned in displeasure. "He could live, he could die. Honestly, why do they call themselves experts? I could gain more assurances from a gypsy fortune teller."

In spite of himself, Jacob smiled at his mother's scorn. They sat together for much of the day, watching Miles Wilding sleeping, feeding him careful sips of water when he stirred, and rearranging pillows to make him more comfortable when he groaned. They'd spoken off and on as the hours passed, but had fallen into silence the last half hour or so. When his mother spoke again, it startled him.

"You look especially well turned-out today. Is there a special occasion?"

Jacob glanced down at his suit. It felt like days ago he'd dressed with such care to go and woo a wife. He looked back up and shrugged. "I was going to go propose to Miss Aston this morning."

"What? Jacob, how wonderful! Oh but—" she glanced at her husband before continuing. "You must go at once. Win over that wonderful young woman and make the both of you happy."

"I can't leave fath—" His mother cut him off.

"Yes you can, Jacob. Your father wants nothing more than for you to be happy, despite his little trek into madness about you marrying the Chalcroft girl. Go to her, convince her you love her more than any man ever could, and bring back the happy news to your father. Go," she said more forcefully, when Jacob remained seated, his jaw hanging slack.

He stood slowly, and as his earlier eagerness to see Juliette returned, he smiled at his mother. "You're going to love her," he promised.

"Silly boy," she replied. "I already do."

"What do you mean he's not here?" Jacob asked the butler at Juliette's house. It had not even occurred to Jacob that Sir Lewis might be out. "Is he expected back soon?" He hated the thought of waiting another day to approach Juliette's father.

"I do not believe so, my lord," was the butler's deferential reply.

Very well, he would see Juliette first. The thought had more appeal anyway as he was anxious to confess his feelings for her and eager to hear her return them.

"Miss Aston, then. Will you inform her I have come to call?"

"I'm terribly sorry, my lord. Miss Aston is not in either."

"Has she gone to the park?" He knew she took many

walks there—had he not run into her there himself?

"Er..." the butler seemed unsure of how to respond. "My lord, Sir Lewis and his daughter have left London. They departed not two hours ago."

"Left?" Jacob felt a bit slow at the news. Surely they'd not gone to a house party, had they? It was late in the season for such festivities, although not unheard of. Perhaps someone he didn't know? Scrambling to gather his wits—could nothing this day go right?—he asked, "Do you expect them to return by week's end?"

"My lord, I don't expect them to return at all."

"They've left for the Season?"

"That is my understanding," said the butler uncomfortably. Clearly the man wasn't sure that he should be sharing such information with a man who'd never visited before. Jacob was quite certain had he not presented his card with his title, the man would have long since shut the door in his face.

Jacob felt completely deflated. Juliette hadn't mentioned they were leaving town early. He stood on the stoop for a long moment, finally realizing the butler was looking at him expectantly.

"Have you their direction?"

The butler, clearly even more uncomfortable, said, "I do not. This house is owned by Mrs. Constance Smithsonly. Sir Lewis and his daughter are her relations."

"Yes, of course," Jacob murmured.

Finally deciding he'd divulged enough information, the butler moved to close the door.

"One more thing," Jacob said, his hand on the door. "Is Mrs. Smithsonly at home?"

"She is not. Now if you don't mind, my lord..." he trailed off.

Jacob removed his hand from the door and allowed the butler to shut it. He turned away and walked slowly to his horse. What was he to do now? he wondered. This was certainly not how he'd anticipated his morning turning out, he thought with a heavy sigh. From their conversations at his mother's house party, he knew Juliette lived in Hertfordshire, knew that her home was a rambling structure built in the Tudor style. He even remembered her telling him that a cherry tree grew outside her window. But he had no idea *where* in Hertfordshire she lived. How had they never discussed that? He rode unseeing back to Beverly House to check on his father and inquire of his mother if she perhaps knew where Juliette lived. His mother, it turned out, was resting. Thwarted on all fronts, Jacob settled in at his father's bedside to sit vigil until one of his parents awoke.

A thoroughly frustrating three days passed during which Jacob felt like a caged animal, pacing the floors of his townhouse and Beverly House. His mother didn't know where Juliette's home was either, though she had offered to send a letter to Constance Smithsonly and inquire. Knowing such correspondence could take another week, Jacob agreed for it was the only lead he could think of.

Staring out the window of his father's sick room, it suddenly came to him. He slapped his forehead in exasperation with himself. "Eleanor!" he said.

"What was that, dear?" his mother asked.

"Lady Eleanor Chalcroft. She surely knows where Juliette lives. They've been friends for years."

"Do you think she will wish to share such information with you? You were courting her just a week ago, were you not?"

Jacob paused halfway to the door. There was that. Still, he'd never felt any return of interest from Eleanor. In fact, she had seemed at times to be frustrated by his attentions. And hadn't she always brought up Juliette in their conversations? It was almost as if she'd been trying to push the two of them together.

"I think she will, mother," he said with a detour to kiss her cheek before bolting out the door.

It came as no surprise to Jacob to find that Lady Eleanor was not at home, even though it was ridiculously early for a lady to be out and about. Perhaps the fates were punishing him for being so slow to recognize his feelings for Juliette. Perhaps he had to suffer now in order to be worthy of her. He smiled ruefully at his melodramatic thoughts. The tutor who had tried to teach him Greek literature would no doubt be thrilled at the analogies.

Deciding to burn off his frustrations, Jacob turned his horse to Hyde Park and allowed the horse his head once he saw Rotten Row was empty of pedestrians. He zigzagged back and forth on the bridle trails before drawing his horse to a walk. He was sweaty and windblown, but still frustrated as he dismounted and stared out across the Serpentine. Unattended by its distracted master, his horse ambled to a stop and began cropping clumps of grass. Jacob was lost in thought, trying to come up with a plan to reach Juliette when his attention was drawn to the right where movement under a shady tree drew his gaze. The couple beneath the tree must have become aware of his presence at the same time, for they pulled apart quickly and seemed to be trying to avoid eye contact with him. Something about the woman was familiar...She moved and a stray beam of sunlight struck her golden curls.

"Lady Eleanor?" he said without thinking. Had he been thinking, he would have pretended not to notice the embrace, of course, would have pretended he hadn't even seen them, and tactfully moved on. But his only thoughts today were for Juliette and social nicety was forgotten.

Realizing she'd been caught, Eleanor emerged from beneath the tree, a tall man Jacob had never seen before right behind her.

"Lord Worthing," she said coolly, clearly determined to brazen it out.

Jacob's eyes widened in surprise. Despite—or perhaps because of—her popularity, Lady Eleanor had never strayed from rigid propriety with her suitors. It was most out of character for her, and yet, Jacob could barely suppress a smile at her carefully inscrutable face as she faced her former suitor.

"How fortuitous I should find you here," he began.

"We had no arrangement, my lord," she rushed to say.

"No, no. Of course not," he said placatingly. "Actually, I wished to see you because...well, because." He paused and wondered which of the two of them felt more uncomfortable. "I need to reach Miss Aston." He heard Eleanor inhale sharply but pressed on. "She has left London. I know she lives in Hertfordshire but I do not have her address. I thought you might be able to give it to me."

"Why?" she asked sharply.

"I beg your pardon?"

"Why do you want to reach her?"

"That's not something I'm prepared to discuss with you," he answered awkwardly.

"Well you will discuss it with me if you want my help," she practically shouted. Behind her, the tall man stepped forward and touched her elbow possessively. She glanced over her shoulder and nodded reassurance to him. Turning back to Jacob, she said, "Juliette is engaged to be married."

"What? To whom?" Jacob felt his stomach drop. His hands felt cold, his face wooden.

"Mr. Pickering, if you must know. He approached her father the morning after the Andover ball. It was quickly arranged and they packed up and left before luncheon." Her voice had risen in volume again.

"But..." Jacob began.

"You're too late, Worthing. You were a fool not to win her sooner. Now you've lost her." This last said with more venom than Jacob could have imagined the beatific Eleanor capable of.

"Are they married?" he hissed.

"I beg your pardon?"

"I said are they married yet or simply betrothed?"

"Of course they're not married yet. The banns have yet to be called. You don't think Pickering would go to the expense or trouble to obtain a dispensation, do you?"

"If they're not yet married, then I am not too late," he said fiercely, though with more certainty than he actually felt.

Eleanor's expression said she considered him the worst sort of fool. "And do you really think Juliette will appreciate your sweeping in at the last moment and 'rescuing' her?"

Jacob frowned. "What do you mean?"

"You've had weeks to appreciate her, to fall in love with her, to beg her to marry you! Do you know why she agreed to marry him? Do you?"

Jacob shook his head, at a loss.

"She accepted him because he was the only man to woo her *before* she became popular. Her aunt Constance and I assured her that if she were more vivacious and talkative in public, the men would flock to her. But she didn't want someone who only saw her as a pretty prize. Even though Pickering hasn't the first idea who she really is, at least he didn't choose her based on her ability to act like a social butterfly. You, however, had scads of time to get to know the real her. You had plenty of time to see that you were perfect for each other. Yet for some asinine reason, you kept trying to court *me*, even when I all but pushed you away!"

"My father is dying."

That brought her up short. Her mouth dropped open unbecomingly for a moment before she recovered enough to say, "What do you mean?"

"I mean my father's heart is failing. He's had several attacks over the last year, but several serious ones more recently. Since he found out he may not have long to live, he's been pressing me to marry. Once I agreed I would actively seek a wife, he decided that you were the best choice because...well, for a variety of valid reasons."

Eleanor frowned and brought her fingertips to her lips. "I'm so very sorry" She lowered her hand. "So why are you here trying to track down Juliette instead of challenging Mr. Fitzhugh," this with a gesture to the tall man behind her, "to a duel or some such nonsense?"

At that, Jacob finally smiled. "Duels are not at all the thing anymore." Sobering, he continued, "I could not bear the thought of *not* spending the rest of my life with Juliette. I told my father as much. I'm sure I should be chagrined to admit that my mother assisted in my cause, but I'm just glad my father came around and agreed that I should marry who I choose. Er...I mean no offense to you, Lady Eleanor."

She shooed the apology aside. "Really, we would not suit at all. I could have told you that weeks ago." She took a deep breath and gazed out across the Serpentine. Clearly coming to a decision, she turned back to Jacob.

"Berkhamsted. It's a ways past St. Alban's. I don't know further direction than that. John Coachman always takes me right there."

"I will find it," Jacob vowed.

"You'll not have an easy job of it," Eleanor warned.

"What do you mean? Finding Berkhamsted?"

Eleanor shook her head slightly. "Convincing Juliette to accept you."

"Why? Does she not—" he paused to swallow, his mouth suddenly dry. "Does she not care for me, do you think?"

"Oh I'm sure she loves you. But she will have some idiotic notion that she's not good enough for you or that I'll be heartbroken or that she shouldn't go back on her word to Pickering, or some such nonsense. Our girl can be stubborn at the most inopportune times."

Jacob had scarcely heard Eleanor's words past "sure she loves you." Elation coursed through his veins and he longed to be on his horse, racing for Berkhamsted. "I'll convince her," he assured her.

Eleanor sniffed. "Yes, well, make sure you do."

Jacob grinned, then grabbing Eleanor by the shoulders, planted a kiss on her forehead. The man behind her—Fitzhugh did she say?—stepped forward with a growl, but Jacob waved him off as he sprinted to his horse and spurred the beast homeward.

Chapter Forty-one

Juliette stared out the rippled window of her family's home in Berkhamsted, watching yellow flowers nod in the breeze. She and her father had arrived home several days earlier and, clearly believing there was little to organizing a wedding, Sir Lewis had implored Juliette to help him straighten his research papers. She smiled to herself. Straighten was an understatement if ever there was one. Sir Lewis's notes on the latest genus of bug he had discovered had been scattered across nearly every public room of their sprawling home. It had taken Juliette two full days just to collect them all. She'd spent another day rifling through the papers, trying to get an idea of what information her father wished to share with the scientific community, for very often in her father's research notes he went off on tangents that had nothing to do with his main topic. Such had been the case this time as well and Juliette now had one large stack of notes and illustrations on a brown beetle that could apparently dive underwater for food, as well as a smaller pile on the stages of a tadpole's life and the consistency of pond algae—clearly Sir Lewis's interests had expanded over the summer.

She couldn't find it in herself to be frustrated with her father's chaotic notetaking. This would no doubt be the last project she could assist him with and she had found herself strangely melancholy at the thought.

Neither was she upset with her father for requiring so much of a newly-engaged woman's time. She and Mr. Pickering had agreed to have a small ceremony and a wedding luncheon for immediate family only. In truth, Juliette expected to have only her father in attendance. Though she believed Aunt Constance would come if called upon, she still felt as if she had disappointed her aunt and because that disappointment so closely mirrored her own, Juliette had decided not to ask her to come. She simply had to invite Eleanor, though she knew her friend's disappointment was at least as great as Constance's. Then, too, there had been that mysterious man Eleanor had been...involved with in the hallway of the Andover ball. Juliette sorely wished she could have talked to her friend and discovered what all that was about. Perhaps Eleanor had finally lost her heart and her head to a gentleman.

Juliette also regretted that she had not been able to say goodbye to her friend before she and her father hastily left London. She had suffered alternating bouts of guilt at what she had done with perfectly rational arguments with herself that Eleanor had clearly cared not one whit for Lord Worthing. Nonetheless, the two women had been through too much together not to invite her. Besides, there was every chance her friend would be otherwise engaged. The Chalcrofts were no doubt preparing to return to their country estate.

Juliette turned from the window. She would need to select one of her gowns to serve as a wedding dress. She had no interest in having one made for the occasion, but perhaps she could trim one of her existing dresses. She felt she needed to make *some* effort regarding her wedding, else it might set a bad precedent for the marriage. She paused with her hand on the cabinet knob. The weight in her heart was like a lump of lead, cold and immovable. The thought of spending her life with a man she did not love—who she knew did not love her in return—was suddenly unbearable. She wondered if she would have felt the same sense of loss had she never met Jacob Wilding.

Juliette dropped her forehead against the slick wood of the armoire. Just the thought of Lord Worthing made her simultaneously ecstatic and morose. She wondered what he must think of her for leaping off the cliff of propriety into hedonistic abandon. She smiled wryly at that. *Hedonistic abandon.* She would have to remember that phrase. Perhaps in the years to come when she was quite out of her mind with ennui, she could pull that phrase out and remind herself that for one magical night, she had been anything but insipid and uninteresting. Her cheeks grew warm as Juliette allowed memories of those short moments in Jacob's arms to flood her mind and body. Her breasts suddenly felt heavy within the confines of her corset and her heart seemed to have increased its pace even though she remained standing perfectly still.

She wondered what he thought of their encounter; if he was used to women throwing themselves at him, if he had enjoyed it as much as she had, if he thought of her still. He had called her perfect and, in that moment, she had believed him.

Turning her head, she rested one flushed cheek on the cool finish of the cabinet. She really had to stop this, she scolded herself. She would not get anything done before the wedding if she spent hours mooning over a man who would never be hers.

Straightening, she tugged open the armoire and scrutinized the gowns within. She adamantly refused to look at the puff of crimson silk that had edged out from between two pale pastel gowns. She would never be able to wear that gown again, though it would forever remain her favorite gown. She'd forbidden her maid from brushing it or ironing it for it retained a faint scent of Jacob in its precious folds. She would not indulge in a whiff now, however, as she had to focus on a gown in which to marry Mr....Juliette shook her head to clear it. Mister who? she though frantically. Pickering. Mr. Pickering. Theodore Pickering. Slightly panicked with a vision of herself forgetting her fiancée's name during the ceremony, she thrust her hand into the wardrobe and pulled out the first gown her hand encountered. She slammed the doors shut before looking to see what she'd chosen for her wedding gown. At least it was lovely, she thought. Surely that must be a good sign. It was a pale blue striped poplin with the overskirt gathered up just below the knee to show an underskirt of ivory satin. The high-waisted bodice had puffed sleeves, a straight neckline, and an intricate pattern of silk ribbon.

Juliette rang for a maid to assist her into the gown. She'd yet to wear it as it was one of the last gowns she'd purchased at Aunt Constance's insistence and she wanted to make sure it needed no alterations.

Molly, her maid, arrived in answer to her summons and as she helped Juliette out of her current gown, announced that a visitor was making his way to the house.

Juliette's heart sank. She hoped it was not Mr. Pickering. He had escorted her and her father to Hertfordshire but had left the next morning saying his mother would need his assistance with the wedding plans. It had been on the tip of her tongue to ask if his mother was getting married, but decided she hadn't the energy to explain her joke and she'd had quite enough of being called a "silly dear" every time she'd made a comment on the trip to Berkhamstead. It was her understanding he and his mother would be arrive just a few days before the wedding, right after the final banns had been called.

"Could you tell who it was?" Juliette asked.

Molly shook her head and lifted the blue striped gown over her mistress's head. "I just saw a gentleman on horseback turn into the drive as I was coming upstairs.

That didn't sound like Mr. Pickering. He was very fussy with getting road dust on his suit and preferred to travel by coach.

"Most likely it's just a neighbor coming to call. Or perhaps one of father's naturalist friends out to investigate his insects."

Molly shuddered at the though of Sir Lewis's bugs and Juliette smiled in commiseration. The maid smoothed Juliette's skirts and said, "Now, miss, what for your hair? I saw a lady at that park in London with fancy twists to her hair I could try on you."

Juliette sat at her dressing table and removed the pins from her simple chignon. "Whatever you like."

"Come now, miss," Molly protested as she brushed out her mistress's hair. "We must do something special for your wedding. I could twist this up like so and then on the day of your wedding, we could tuck little flowers here and here."

Juliette watched the maid poking at her hair and forced a smile to her face. It was certainly not Molly's fault that she felt no anticipation for her nuptials, and the maid seemed very excited by the prospect of showing off her skills.

Molly paused to answer a soft knock at the door. She held the door open and turned back. "Jenkins says as how there's a gentleman come to call on your father but Sir Lewis is nowhere to be found."

Juliette glanced at Molly in the mirror. "Have him leave his card and tell him father will contact him directly."

"That's the thing, miss. He did give his card and this isn't a regular gentleman." Molly crossed the room and handed Juliette a heavy cream-colored card with crisp black letters engraved on it.

When Juliette saw the name on the card, she nearly dropped it. Jacob Wilding, Baron Worthing. "Why—" she began, but her mouth was suddenly so dry, the word stuck in her throat. Clearing it, she tried again. "What did he say he wanted?"

Molly shrugged her shoulders and both women turned to look at Jenkins, the young footman who was standing in the doorway.

"He didn't say, miss," he began with a slight bow. "But he did say he would like to speak with you seeing as how Sir Lewis is not to be found."

Juliette imagined she looked rather fishlike as she sat there, mouth agape, trying to decide ten things at once. Why did he wish to speak with her father? How did he discover where they lived? How on earth could she possibly face him after what they'd done? Did she look presentable?

This last question was most easily decided. She turned back to the mirror. Her cheeks were vivid with color and the blue of her gown did seem to brighten her eyes…

"Molly, can you finish my hair? Quickly?"

"Yes, miss," Molly said, snatching up a comb and tucking a few hairpins in her mouth.

"Jenkins," Juliette said, looking at the footman in her mirror so as not to disrupt Molly's efforts. "Would you inform Lord Worthing that I shall be down directly and then ask Cook to send in refreshments?"

"Yes miss," the footman said with another bow.

Her heart pounding at a ridiculously fast pace, Juliette took a deep breath and slowly let it out. Her stomach was a whirl of butterflies and she pressed her hands against it in a vain attempt to calm them. Molly was taking forever to finish her hair. "It needn't be perfect, Molly," she said by means of hurrying the maid along, although of course, it very well did need to be perfect. She had no idea why Jacob was here but she needed whatever boost to her courage looking her best could provide.

At long last, Molly tucked the last strand in place. Juliette leapt to her feet and all but dashed out of her room and down the stairs. She forced herself to slow as she made her way down the hall to the sitting room. She did not want to enter out of breath. She had to appear calm and unconcerned, as if this were simply a social call with a friend, and not the fearful unknown of seeing the man she loved for the first time since making love to him when she thought she'd never see him again. She paused with her hand on the cool brass of the doorknob and took a final deep breath.

She entered the sunlit room with an equally bright smile on her face that she hoped would pass for carefree and confident. Jacob was standing at a window looking out at the grounds. Clearly he hadn't heard the door open, a fact for which Juliette was grateful as it gave her a chance to drink her fill of him while composing her features. A moment later, he must have sensed her presence for he started and turned toward her.

She desperately tried to read his facial expression but backlit as he was by the window, all she could make out of his features were that they were all present. She tried to speak, found her voice refused to work, and cleared her throat as discreetly as a completely silent room would allow. She opened her mouth once again, but Lord Worthing spoke first.

"Miss Aston. You are well, I hope?" Though the words were pleasant, Juliette thought she detected a tightness in his tone. Her heart rate accelerated on its own and she frantically groped for something witty and casual to say.

"I am...fine," was her clever rejoinder.

Rousing herself to her manners, she gestured to a settee. "Won't you make yourself comfortable, my lord?"

He came forward toward the proffered seat and she felt her heart stutter in her chest. Dear Lord, he's handsome, she thought. Truly, there was nothing about the man that did not appeal to her on a deep, visceral level. And it wasn't that she was oblivious to any imperfections of face or form, but somehow those flaws, superficial as they were, made him even more attractive to her. She remembered when he had called every bit of her perfect. At the time, she thought he'd been trying to make her feel good or flatter her in some way. Now she wondered if he found her own flaws as appealing as she found his. The thought made her stuttering heart suddenly race.

The entrance of a maid bearing a tray with lemonade and biscuits broke her from her fevered reverie. She took a fortifying breath, directed the maid to set the tray on the table between Lord Worthing's settee and an armchair, and promptly sat herself in said armchair. Once the maid departed, Juliette latched on to the first conversational gambit she could think of.

"How is your mother?"

"Very well, thank you," he replied.

"Lovely, lovely. And, er, your father? I do hope he has recovered from his ailment."

"Unfortunately, he suffered another attack—quite a

severe one—the day after the Andover ball."

At the mention of the ball, Juliette felt her cheeks flame scarlet.

"I am devastated to hear so, my lord. Do you think he will mend quickly?"

Lord Worthing looked to the window and was silent for a moment. "It is my sincere hope that he will." Turning back to Juliette she could see him take a deep breath of his own. "But that is not why I am here today."

"Of course, my lord. I'm sorry my father is not here for you. He's searching for more specimens," she said, with a flourish of her hand to indicate the great outdoors.

"It's just as well," Jacob responded amicably. "I should like to speak with you anyway."

"Oh?" she said, with only a slight waver in her voice.

He slid down the settee and turned so that their knees were practically touching. "Miss Aston—Juliette," he began, then reached for her hands. As if in a dream, she watched his strong, tanned hands envelop both of hers. His hands were warm to her suddenly chilled fingers and he rubbed the backs of her hands with his thumbs.

"Would you do me the very great honor of consenting to be my wife?"

So mesmerized by the touch of his hands on hers, it took her a moment for his words to sink in. When they did, she felt her eyes widen as she looked up at him. She couldn't read the expression on his face; it could be one of hopeful nervousness or resigned dread.

"I—" she began and then realized why he was asking. A lump in the back of her throat warned her of threatening tears and she resolutely swallowed it down.

"I thank you my lord, but there is no need."

Apparently it was not the answer he was expecting for she could clearly read dumfounded surprise on his face.

"I promise I have not told anyone about…er…that night. And I won't. You have my word on it."

"But—" he began.

"I have agreed to marry Mr. Pickering, you see, and would not dream of imposing myself on you. I appreciate your noble gesture. It wasn't my intent to…trick you into marriage. I simply…"

"Impose yourself? Trick me? I never thought any such thing," he said indignantly.

"Oh. Of…of course not."

"Is that what you think?" he demanded. "That I've proposed marriage out of a sense of guilt?"

"Well, n—you mean you didn't?"

He scowled and stared intently at her, clearly studying the frown on her brow, the confusion in her gaze. Then his gaze dropped to her lips and she could scarcely remember to breathe.

"No," he said, his voice much softer now, low and husky. "I asked you to marry me because," at this he looked back up, into her own eyes. "Because quite frankly, I love you."

She gasped aloud at this statement. Never in her wildest dreams had she imagined she would ever hear those words from Jacob Wilding. Perhaps her very wildest dreams, the ones she kept hidden in the furthest recesses of her heart, but certainly never with any expectation that her dream would come to life!

She remained silent, continuing to stare in amazement at the perfect man before her.

He clearly was beginning to grow uncomfortable at her continued silence. "Well," he said, so low she could scarce hear him. "Will you?"

Another moment of amazed silence on her part passed before she roused herself to respond. "Yes!" she practically shouted.

The spell of uncertainty she'd unwittingly cast upon him broke and he grinned. He hauled her to her feet and into his embrace. With one arm tightly wrapped around her waist and the other cradling her head, he lowered his lips to hers and kissed her. She curled her own arms around his shoulders and returned his kiss with every ounce of love, longing, and joy she had been ruthlessly suppressing for months.

Long moments later he finally lifted his head. "Well?" he asked.

"Well what?" she mumbled, still in a passion-daze. "I said yes, I will marry you."

He lifted his eyebrows and stared at her meaningfully.

"Oh!" she exclaimed. "Yes! Yes! I love you too!" And with that, she initiated a kiss that was just at potent, just as eloquent as the one he had given her.

Some time later, they found themselves on the abandoned settee. Jacob's arm was around her shoulders and she was quite scandalously draped against him, her head on his shoulder.

She cleared her throat nervously.

"Yes?" he said, tipping her chin up so that he could see her face.

"How did you know I was going to say something?"

"Aren't you?"

"Well, yes, but I might have just been clearing my throat."

He smiled and kissed the tip of her nose. "I just knew. Now what were you going to say?"

Suddenly uncomfortable, she sat up. "What about…well what about Eleanor?"

Jacob took a deep breath and blew it out slowly. "Well, that is a long story."

Juliette glanced pointedly around at the empty room. "We seem to have time on our hands."

With a nod, he told her, about his ailing father's "last wish," how his father had latched on to Eleanor's name because of her family, how he himself had hoped that some feeling would develop if they spent enough time together.

"It didn't?" she whispered.

"It couldn't."

"Why do you think that is?"

He smiled gently. "She wasn't you. She didn't love penny horrids. She couldn't quote Shakespeare, she wouldn't induce me to eat something terrible by describing it as pungent. She didn't make me feel like I could share my deepest fears and greatest hopes. And she didn't make my fingers itch to touch her."

"Eleanor is lovely," Juliette defended her friend weakly.

"I agree completely. But she wasn't perfect for me. You are."

She smiled tremulously at that, torn between giggling happily and crying pathetically. It was silly, really. She'd always been completely happy with herself, but three painfully unsuccessful years on the marriage market had taken their toll on her confidence. It was a relief to have someone tell her she was perfect just the way she was.

She frowned and nibbled her lower lip.

"What is it?" Jacob asked, rubbing the back of his fingers over her brow to smooth out the frown.

"I still can't help feeling bad about Eleanor. She was the only one—until now—who, well, I suppose who saw my worth."

Jacob chuckled. "I sought out Eleanor to learn the direction to your house."

"You did?"

He nodded. "Do you know where I found her?"

She shook her head.

"Under a tree in Hyde Park, in, shall we say, close embrace with a gentleman."

Juliette raised her eyebrows. "Tall fellow? Reddish brown hair?"

"I didn't heed him enough to notice his hair color, but he was very tall. Why? Had you seen him with her before."

"Once at the park—though not embracing beneath a tree. Another time..." she paused as she remembered the night at the Andover ball. The night she and Jacob...

"Does he seem worthy of her?"

Jacob seemed to be trying to suppress a grin. "It was very hard to tell based on a quick glance in his direction. But I can tell you this: I don't think Eleanor will settle for anyone who isn't worthy of her. Besides she's stronger than she makes out. Smarter too. I believe Eleanor will be just fine." He paused and then seemed to remember something. "She said something else," he said, frowning in concentration.

"What?" Juliette, taking her turn to smooth his brow.

He captured her hand and pressed a kiss into her palm.

"She said that I should have known weeks ago that I cared for you. She said she knew from the start that she and I would never suit."

At his words, Juliette felt a weight slip off her shoulders and she felt her smile widen. Unable to restrain herself, she threw herself at him and kissed him full on the mouth. He chuckled through their kiss, but pulled her even closer against him, squeezing her as if he never meant to let her go.

Unbidden, the image of Mr. Pickering rose up in her mind's eye. She sat back, covering her mouth in horror.

"What is it?" Jacob asked.

"It's...well, it's Mr. Pickering. I...I accepted his suit, you see."

"But you're marrying me," Jacob said.

Juliette nodded. "Yes! Of course I am. But I shall have to tell him before we can...make any further plans."

"I will talk to him if you like."

Juliette saw the steely determination in his eyes and her heart fluttered ridiculously at the primal maleness of his expression. Really, she should find it amusing, but she couldn't help being secretly thrilled at his possessive tone. She quite liked feeling absolutely cherished.

Returning to the matter at hand, she shook her head slowly. It was a tempting offer but she knew this was something she needed to handle. "Thank you, Jacob. But I feel I should be the one to tell him I have changed my mind. I am certain his heart is not engaged and so it will only be uncomfortable, not painful."

"When will you be able to tell him?"

"I believe he is due to come visit tomorrow."

"Very well. I will stay at the inn until it is settled. There is a local inn, isn't there?"

Juliette nodded, her head floating lightly as if she'd drunk too much champagne.

"Should I speak to your father before then?"

"That, I will let you do!"

Chapter Forty-two

The wedding itself would certainly have been classified as painfully small by London standards. Fortunately, it was quite respectable by Berkhamstead standards. Aunt Constance had practically crowed her approval when she'd arrived two days before. "I knew it!" she exclaimed. "I knew you wouldn't simply roll over and settle for anything less than what dear Mr. Smithsonly and I had enjoyed!

"You did give me a bit of a scare, however," she admonished her great-niece. "That was unkind to say the least. My nerves might not have stood the strain."

Juliette laughed aloud, completely impervious to her aunt's attempts at making her feel guilty. "I'm glad your nerves have come through the ordeal intact."

Eleanor had come as well, accompanying Aunt Constance. Juliette had had only a moment to speak in private with her friend and had tried to coax her to speak of Mr. Fitzhugh, but Eleanor was remarkably close-mouthed about the man, which made Juliette suspect there was more to her friend's fascination with the man than there had been with any of her other suitors.

"Fine, keep me in the dark," Juliette pretend-pouted. "So long as you make sure I am invited to your wedding celebration."

Eleanor's smile did not reach her eyes and she looked away quickly, though not before Juliette caught a sheen of tears. She would have pressed her friend about it had she not been pulled away to greet Jacob's parents.

Fortunately, the earl had recovered enough to attend his

son's wedding and while he had retired before the wedding luncheon, he had made sure to tell Juliette how pleased he was with his son's choice of bride.

Lady Wilding had embraced her new daughter-in-law tightly. "I knew it would be you!" she'd whispered in Juliette's ear. "I am ever so happy for the both of you!"

Lord Hugh Stalwood had attended as had Lady Avis Lidgate, Jacob's sister. She had travelled without her children or husband and was to return to them the next day, but she said nothing would have kept her from her younger brother's wedding.

A dozen more faces, distant cousins, childhood friends from Berkhamstead…all in all, the morning was a blur of good wishes, stolen glances with her new husband, and a delicious feeling that all was right with the world.

That feeling continued long after the last guest had departed. Those staying at the Aston's home were sent off to play parlor games and at last Juliette and Jacob were alone in the large guest room the housekeeper had made up as a bridal suite for them.

"Finally," Jacob said as he drew Juliette to him and took her lips in a kiss that left her feeling a bit light-headed.

"It was a lovely day," Juliette said. "But I did wish it would end so that I might have you to myself."

Jacob nibbled along the underside of her jaw. "I knew I should have pressed harder for Gretna Green."

Her giggle was smothered by his lips. He cupped her face in his hands and kissed her softly at first, but with increasing ardor. Juliette gripped the sides of his jacket and returned the kiss with all the love in her heart. She felt tears prick her eyes at the sweet intensity of the embrace. After seemingly endless moments, Jacob drew back and stared down into her face, an expression of awe on his face.

"You are so beautiful," he murmured.

She smiled and started to shake her head but he kissed her silent. "You are. Your eyes, this satin skin," this accompanied by a caress along her cheek. "These lips." His thumb brushed along the damp fullness of her lower lip. "And this glorious dark hair." At that, he began plucking out hairpins, gently freeing her hair of its intricate styling of twists and curls. He slid the handful of pins into his jacket pocket and then combed his fingers through her tresses. The delicate tugging brought goosebumps to Juliette's skin. He gathered a handful of silky strands and brought them to his face where he inhaled deeply. "God you smell good," he said and Juliette could no longer contain herself.

She tore off her other glove and ran her fingers through his own dark locks, tugging his head down to kiss him with inexpert, but heartfelt kisses. Her breaths grew short and rapid. She could feel her heart pounding and its frenetic pace made her suddenly impatient. She began to tug at his jacket, gasping in frustration when she couldn't budge the tightly fitted garment.

"Shhh," he whispered against her temple, slowly stroking her back as he held her pressed against him. "We have plenty of time. Let me make this right for you."

"It is right for me," she said, but took a deep breath and willed herself to calm down. He paused in his gentle caresses to peel the jacket from his shoulders, then tugged his cravat off, dropping both items to the floor. He returned to her, cupping her face in his hands as if cradling the most precious thing on earth. He stared into her eyes for what felt like an eternity, and Juliette felt the rest of her impatience fade away, replaced by a languor that seemed to melt her very bones. He kissed her deeply and instead of trying to match his movements, she passively accepted his mouth, then slowly began to respond in kind, tickling his upper lip with the point of her tongue, before sucking gently on his full lower lip.

A low, raspy groan escaped him, and she smiled against his mouth, thrilled to have affected him as much as he affected her. She slid her hands up his chest and looped them around his neck as she felt him deftly freeing the row of tiny buttons down her back. Though the room was warm, her skin was so hot that the rush of air as he parted her dress made her shiver. He quickly smoothed his hands along the bare skin of her upper back, warming her and causing her to nuzzle into the crease of his neck. She inhaled deeply, relishing the pure male scent of him. She flicked her tongue out, drawing it along his skin and was delighted by the taste of him, salty and warm.

He tugged at the shoulders of her gown and she paused, her hands clasped to her breast preventing the dress from slipping off her entirely. He stared solemnly into her eyes, waiting. Taking a tiny step back, she dropped her hands and shrugged slightly, sending her bodice down. It caught on her hips and she watched him watch her hands as she slowly pushed the silk over the curve of her hips. It pooled around her feet and she stepped out of its folds. He seemed entranced by her beaded slippers as she lifted first one foot and then the other to remove them, allowing them to fall heedlessly to the floor.

Jacob seemed to come out of his reverie at the clunk of heels hitting the floor. He stepped forward, catching one finger in the neckline of her chemise and tugging gently. She took tiny steps in response to the tugs until she was mere inches from being pressed up against him. Beneath her stays, her nipples contracted, her breasts feeling as if they were swollen. He deftly unlaced her stays and peeled them from her body. Her head suddenly felt too heavy for her neck and she let it fall back, shivering at the sensual feel of her undone hair sliding along her back. Jacob immediately accepted her invitation, closing the remaining distance between them, catching one arm around her waist, the other supporting her head as he lifted it up and caught her lips in a hot, open-mouthed kiss.

Juliette clung to his shoulders, her stomach muscles clenching nervously as she felt him bend and scoop her up into his arms, carrying her the short distance to the massive bed. An awkward moment when he tried to hold her one-handed while turning down the covers with the other made them both laugh and dissipated her nervousness.

He laid her gently on the soft linen sheets and stood to tug off his shirt. He unbuttoned the fall of his trousers, but did not strip them off, instead, divesting himself of shoes and stockings before joining her. His weight bowed the mattress and caused her to roll toward him. He turned sideways at the same time and they were suddenly pressed together: chest to chest, hips to hips, legs to legs. He caressed the indentation of her waist through the thin fabric of her chemise.

"This right here," he whispered, indicating the curve from her ribs to waist to hips. "This is perfect." His hand settled in the space as if it had been made to fit her, or she him.

Juliette felt her face flame from pleasure and a bit of disbelief. "I'm not—"

He cut off her words with a brief kiss. When he lifted his head, his caress resumed. "Perfect," he said definitively, and Juliette decided she would yield to his clearly superior judgment on this issue.

His hand ran further over her hip to her thigh, drawing up her chemise on the return trip to her waist as he delivered another slow, soft kiss. Juliette felt like she was floating, completely awash with a feeling of being exactly right. His touch and kisses were reverent, his soft words of praise acting like balm on a soul that had too long doubted its worth. She lifted her hips and he slowly slid her chemise up to her waist, then lifted her to a seated position so he could pull it over her head. He paused to cup her face in his hands, kissing her lips with a tenderness that was her undoing. She couldn't believe he was hers. Tears sprung to her eyes and her breath caught as she stared at his handsome face bathed in the wan light of the candles.

His brows drew together, and she could read the concern in his eyes. "What's wrong?" he whispered.

She offered a tremulous smile. "Nothing. It's perfect."

He stared another long moment before capturing her lips for a deep soul-searing kiss. She pulled him down on top of her, reveling in the feel of his weight pressing her into the mattress, as if she were completely protected by his strength. She traced her fingers down his back, marking the ripple of muscles, the knots of his spine. When she reached the gaping waistband of his trousers, she hesitated, and then tentatively began easing them down. Jacob paused in his intense plunder of her mouth to assist her, kicking the offending garment off.

He returned to her and drew her up against him. She gasped as the evidence of his desire pressed against her thigh. Her heart pounded, partly from excitement but partly from nervousness. She felt like such a novice. Some irreverent part of her brain found this thought amusing. A young lady's entire worth seemed to center around her innocence and yet here she was, wishing she knew what to do.

"Tell me," she whispered.

"Tell you what?" he murmured in between slow kisses down her neck.

"Tell me what to do. To...please you." Her cheeks burned with embarrassment—if he couldn't see her blush in the dim light, he could no doubt feel the heat radiating off her face.

He lifted his head to stare into her eyes, then cupped her warm face in one hand. "Sweetheart, just touching you is almost more pleasure than I can stand."

She frowned slightly, not sure if she believed him. He chuckled, a low rumble that she felt more than heard.

"Put your hands on me," he finally said.

She slowly raised both hands and lightly brushed them over his collarbones, delighting when she heard his breath catch. Emboldened, she slid them over the hard roundness of his shoulders, back across his chest, along the sides of his waist. His breathing deepened and when she glanced back at his face, she froze at the look of intense yearning on his face.

"Don't stop," he said hoarsely, pushing up slightly so she had more room to maneuver.

She licked her lips and saw that his gaze was intently focused on her mouth. Lifting up, she kissed him, initiating the delicate flick of tongue as she allowed her hands to encircle his trim waist, her fingers exploring the ripple of muscles along his back. He deepened the kiss, plundering her mouth with an intensity that nearly stole her breath. She responded by dragging her hands down, lightly tracing the firm globes of his buttocks, trailing her nails through the coarse hair on his thighs.

Jacob tore his lips from hers. "Enough," he gasped.

She glanced sharply at him, sure she'd made a mistake, her hands frozen at her sides.

"I—" he paused. "I need to make this good for you and if you keep touching me like that, I'm likely to lose control."

Juliette smiled, delighted that she apparently had so much effect on him.

"Find that amusing, do you?" he growled, before swooping down to attack her neck with a series of kisses and nibbles.

She giggled—who knew passion and humor went together—and then gasped, clutching his shoulders as his lips trailed down the smooth expanse of her chest. He paused as he reached one delicately ruched nipple, reverently kissing it before moving to the other to pay it equal homage. She had no idea that part of her body was so sensitive

Juliette ran her fingers through his hair, tugging at it in response to the tug of his mouth. His lips slid lower, tracing the line of her ribcage, eliciting yet another shiver of delight. Her stomach sucked in of its own accord as his tongue painted delicate whorls on the sensitive flesh. Jacob scooched lower on the bed and she inhaled sharply, irrepressible shudders wracking her body when he pressed a kiss to her intimate center, his tongue delicately flicking along a tender ridge. She felt sensation build into a knot of tension, a knot that felt like it must break into a thousand pieces. It continued to build but suddenly he levered himself back up over her, his arms braced on either side of her head.

"I can't wait," he said, his voice a harsh whisper.

She could only nod, wrapping her arms around his ribcage. She felt the press of his sex as he settled between her legs. He kissed her again, softly, and for all his claims of impatience, he moved with incredible slowness, drawing her lower lip into his mouth, stroking the hair back from her face, gently parting her below. She felt the hard press of him and braced herself for pain, but instead felt only a heavy fullness that was strange and yet delightful. He continued to move, slowly, so slowly in fact that she pressed her heels into the mattress and lifted her hips. She was rewarded with the settling of his body fully against hers as well as a sharp gasp from Jacob. He waited a long moment, allowing her to grow accustomed to him before slowly drawing back and sliding forward, each time slightly increasing his tempo.

Juliette felt a renewal of the tension low in her abdomen. Her fingers dug into Jacob's back and she tossed her head from side to side. She stared up into Jacob's eyes, mesmerized by the intensity there as his gaze burned into her own. Beads of sweat gathered along his brow and a slight frown drew his eyebrows in.

"Juliette," he rasped and the sound of her name on his lips made the tension increase deliciously. He reached between them to part her further and adjusted his angle slightly. She gasped at the resulting sensation and her hips bucked involuntarily. He gripped them in his hands and increased his tempo yet again.

Suddenly, a wave of heat rolled over her body, consuming her with its intensity. She shuddered, gasped for air, shuddered again. Above her, Jacob's breath grew labored and as the last ripples of her pleasure eased, he moaned low and deep and thrust again, once more, and a final time before collapsing forward over her, his weight propped on his elbows, his head resting in the curve of her shoulder.

Minutes passed. Juliette had no idea how long, so lost was she in the delightful afterglow of their lovemaking. Finally, Jacob lifted his head, smiling down at her with a look that made tears burn the back of her eyes. She bit her lower lip to prevent them from pooling. He watched as her teeth slowly released the abused lip and then dipped his head to gently kiss it.

"I love you," he whispered.

She felt a smile bloom on her mouth, unfurling until she was quite sure she was grinning idiotically. He drew her down to lay against him, her head cradled on his chest.

One candle had already sputtered out and they were dozing lightly when Jacob sat up abruptly.

"What is it?" Juliette asked worriedly.

"I nearly forgot! I've a present for you."

She smiled in bemusement. "Surely it can wait until morning, Jacob. Come back to bed," she purred. It was the first time she had ever used such a tone—indeed, she didn't know she had the ability. It must have been effective for it stopped Jacob in his tracks. He nearly climbed back in bed, but shook his head.

"No, I have to give it to you tonight. You'll understand." He rummaged through his leather valise that sat open on a table by the window. "Aha!" he said, pulling out a slim rectangular object wrapped in tissue paper and tied with a red satin bow.

As soon as he handed it to her, Juliette knew it was a book. Glancing at the expectant look on his face, she grinned.

"Open it," he prodded when she continued to gaze adoringly at him.

"Alright, alright!" She laughed and pulled the ribbon and tissue off in a hurried rush. Turning the book over, she opened the cover and laughed with delight.

"*A Lady's Notorious Defense*," she read aloud.

"You have not read it yet?"

She shook her head as she smoothed the cloth of the cover. "You were going to lend it to me when you finished, remember?"

He dropped a kiss on her nose. "Now it's yours."

She handed it back to him. "Read it to me."

"What, tonight?"

"Just a chapter," she implored.

"It's not really that good," he protested.

"Of course it's not. That's not the point."

He laughed. "Very well." He arranged the pillows so that he could lean back against the headboard while Juliette lit another candle on the side table. She turned back and curled up along his side, her head on his chest, her arm about his waist, her leg wrapped around his.

"I rather like this," he said as he opened the book and thumbed through to the first page. "I believe I could get used to this."

"Good," she said imperiously. "Because I want you to read to me every night."

"Every night?"

"Well, I suppose I could read to you as well."

"I would like that."

"Of course you would. I do voices."

"Voices?" He asked with some confusion.

"Yes. Different voices for all the characters. And my own for the narrator, of course."

"Perhaps you should read this then. I only have one voice."

She shook her head, her silken hair rubbing along the skin of his chest. He tightened his arm around her shoulders and pressed a kiss to the top of her head.

"You read tonight. I'll read tomorrow night."

With a smile of pure contentment, he began to read, "Miss Nelson batted the bridal veil away from her face as she rode her mount into the night." Jacob choked on his laughter.

"What's so funny?" Juliette lifted her head to look at him.

"A bit apropos, that." He laughed even harder at the confused look on his bride's face. "I'll show you later," he said.

Clearing his throat, he continued, "The night was dark and stormy and Miss Nelson knew that the day would be no lighter, for her life was consumed with misery and strife."

"Poor Miss Nelson," Juliette commented. "I feel so sorry

for her."

"Why is that?" Jacob asked, grinning at the look of pure contentment on her face. "Because my life is so full of happiness and peace."

Jacob took her lips in a deep searing kiss and while they did return to Miss Nelson's misadventures, it was a good bit later...

I hope you enjoyed Juliette and Jacob's love story. If you did, it would mean so much if you would leave a review—they really help independent authors! Thank you so much and please come visit me at www.michellemorrisonwrites.com

About The Author

Michelle Morrison

Graduating magna cum laude with a degree in technical writing did not guarantee Michelle Morrison an exciting career writing about NASA's latest discoveries. Writing historical fiction proved much more entertaining and she hasn't looked back since.

"Relationships intrigue me. Whether they're between lovers, parents and children, or friends, the dynamics of human interaction and how we help each other grow are the cornerstone of all my stories."

Books In This Series

The Unconventionals

Sometimes, what's expected is not what your heart demands.

The Lady's Secret

Lady Eleanor Chalcroft was the Season's reigning beauty and had her choice of eligible suitors. And if they treated her like a coveted, empty-headed prize to be won, that was to be expected in noble marriages...until she met a man who was all wrong for London's high society, but completely right for her.

Lady Disdain

Sarah Draper runs a charity kitchen in the London's slums as penance for her disastrous fall from grace. She has built a protective cocoon around her heart and has become a master of self-sufficiency even as she secretly craves more from her life. Only a brash American with no cares for propriety would be foolish enough to woo her.

Made in the USA
Las Vegas, NV
12 March 2025

19456149R00215